A *New York Times*, *USA Tod[...]* [...]
author, Elle Kennedy grew u[...] [...]
and holds a BA in English from York University. From an early age,
she knew she wanted to be a writer and actively began pursuing
that dream when she was a teenager. She loves strong heroines and
sexy alpha heroes, and just enough heat and danger to keep things
interesting!

Elle loves to hear from her readers. Visit her website ellekennedy
.com or sign up for her newsletter to receive updates about upcom-
ing books and exclusive excerpts. You can also find her on Facebook
at facebook.com/AuthorElleKennedy, on Twitter @ElleKennedy, on
Instagram @ElleKennedy33, or on TikTok @ElleKennedyAuthor.

ALSO BY ELLE KENNEDY

ROGUE

ELLE KENNEDY

PIATKUS

PIATKUS

First published in the US in 2023 by Bloom Books, an imprint of Sourcebooks
Published in Great Britain in 2023 by Piatkus

1 3 5 7 9 10 8 6 4 2

A CIP catalogue record for this book
is available from the British Library.

ISBN 978-0-349-43595-4

Printed and bound in Great Britain by Clays Ltd, Elcograf S.p.A.

Papers used by Piatkus are from well-managed forests
and other responsible sources.

Piatkus
An imprint of
Little, Brown Book Group
Carmelite House
50 Victoria Embankment
London EC4Y 0DZ

An Hachette UK Company
www.hachette.co.uk

www.littlebrown.co.uk

CHAPTER 1
CASEY

Fenn: How's your day going, cutie?

MY ENTIRE FACE NEARLY CRACKS IN HALF THANKS TO THE GIDDY smile that overtakes it. It's almost disgusting what one little text from Fenn Bishop does to my heart rate. I felt my phone buzzing in my pocket during French class, half a dozen texts in quick succession, but I couldn't check it, otherwise it would've been confiscated. So I sat there dying for the bell to ring. Now, between classes, I stand at my locker and read the messages that remind me this place isn't real life. Nobody knows me here at St. Vincent's. All the rumors and whispers constantly buzzing around me whenever I walk down the hall—they don't matter. *I* know the truth. And so does Fenn.

That's all that matters.

The giddiness intensifies as I scan the rest of his texts. He's been doing this every day since we became friends. Texting me good morning. Checking up on me. Sending me dumb memes because he knows I haven't smiled in a while.

It still feels so surreal. Fenn was a stranger to me for so long, just another upperclassman my sister occasionally hung around with. And then my car accident threw my entire world into chaos, and there he was with an easy grin and a strong shoulder for me to lean on. He befriended me, for no good reason other than he saw I needed someone and decided it would be him.

And for no good reason, I let him in.

As I head toward my media class, I type out a quick response.

Me: Oh, you know. The usual BS.
Fenn: Wanna ditch last period? I'll come pick you up.
Me: Sloane would kill you.

We aren't exactly public, Fenn and me. At least not where my family's concerned. My dad and sister barely tolerate a friendship— I can't imagine how they'd react to finding out Fenn and I are officially dating. I honestly don't know who would lose their shit more. Last time she caught him hanging around, Sloane basically told Fenn she would put a hit out on him if he touched me. And Dad, well, if he didn't have to clear it with the board of trustees, he'd have built a moat around our house by now. I'm not sure he really thought it through before accepting a headmaster position at an all boys' boarding school in the middle of nowhere and brought his two teenage daughters along. Sloane and I were bound to fall for a couple of Dad's delinquents.

Fenn: Worth it.
Me: You say that now.
Fenn: Nah. I'd risk Sloane's wrath any day of the week. You're just that cute.

My stomach does a happy flip. He's too good at that. Or maybe I'm too easily impressed. Fenn throws the slightest compliment my way and I become a puddle of mush. It's nauseating. Lately, he's the best part of my day.

Me: Meet after school?

Fenn: Can't wait. Usual place?

Me: Yep. I'll text you when I get home.

I'm still smiling as I enter the classroom and take my seat in the second to last row. Not even Sister Patricia's stern glare can hinder my mood. Although of course, she frowns upon smiling. Everything is frowned upon in this stupid school. St. Vincent's is run by a group of super strict, terrifying nuns who view the girls more like wards than students. Every morning begins with fifteen minutes of chapel. Every class has assigned seating. My pre-calc teacher, Sister Mary Alice, even walks around slapping a wooden ruler against her thigh, ready to smack your wrist if you don't finish your equations fast enough.

I hate this place.

"Hey, Casey." Ainsley bumps my desk as she walks up. "Remember to take your meds today? I assume you do that at lunch so you can take them with food?"

Just like that, my spirits sink.

I clench my teeth, pretending not to notice the way she smirks at the prospect of spending another full hour picking at the bones of my carcass. I imagine she's one of those girls who was dismembering her dolls and cutting off all their hair when she was little. Throwing rocks at squirrels to hear them scream.

Lucky me, I'm her new favorite toy.

People say that when faced with a seemingly insurmountable challenge, we tend to either rise to meet our potential, or regress to escape the problem. For me, I'm still stuck at the point of indecision. Neither fight nor flight, but grin and bear it. Close my eyes and bite down. If I'm being honest, though, I don't think I've ever been Team Fight. Before I transferred to St Vincent's from Ballard Academy, I probably would've been part of the flight camp, so I guess my current state is a step up from that.

Ainsley slides into her seat behind me, then taps my shoulder.

"What?" I hiss, turning in my seat.

She stares blankly. "What? I didn't do anything."

"Ladies." Sister Patricia scolds us from the front of the class, where she's setting up today's video. It's already October, and I don't think she's taught us a single thing since school started. All we do is watch movies, usually musicals, that I'm starting to suspect come from her home collection.

"You're imagining things," Ainsley tells me. "Better up your dosage."

Beside Ainsley, her best friend, Bree, is giggling. "Yeah, for real." The brunette chews loudly on her gum, then coughs when she nearly chokes on it. I don't usually judge people with low IQ, but Bree Atwood is the kind of stupid you genuinely feel sorry for.

A few minutes later, class commences. And by class, I mean we proceed to sit in the dark watching a bad VHS-to-DVD transfer of a West End production of *Les Misérables* while Sister Patricia sits at her desk mouthing every line.

"Sister Patricia?" Ainsley calls out.

"What is it?" The irritated nun casts a glance in our direction.

"Shouldn't we leave the lights on?"

Sister Patricia sighs, one eye on the TV. "Quiet, Ms. Fisck."

"I just don't think it's a good idea to keep us trapped in the dark with an unstable student."

I swallow a tired sigh. Within days of me transferring to St. Vincent's, Ainsley had the whole school believing I'm a mental case. One bad hair day shy of a straitjacket.

Not like it hasn't crossed my mind. I don't remember what happened the night of the accident, so in a sort of quantum sense, I guess anything could have. I'm basically Schrödinger's cat in a box of poison. But what's more plausible? That I was the target of some phantom driver, or that I got high off my ass at prom, looking for attention, and plunged my car into the lake? You can only rant about the one-armed man for so long before you're forced to consider the possibility it's all in your head. Maybe I *am* nuts. Maybe I *did* have a breakdown that night and simply can't remember.

Sister Patricia's response is an annoyed frown, but her focus remains on the film. Even the nuns know the rumors, and I'm sure more than a few believe them. I'm almost surprised I haven't yet been snatched coming out of the bathroom and hauled into the chapel for an impromptu exorcism.

"I'm not being mean," Ainsley says with feigned innocence. "Darkness and loud noises can be triggering. Right, Casey?"

I continue to ignore her and stare at the floor, concentrating intensely on the black shoe scuffs and dotted patterns in the tiles. Ainsley's been at it since first period this morning. In AP history, she remarked on my shoelaces. You know, is it a good idea for someone *in my condition* to be walking around with those. In physics, she suggested to our teacher that perhaps I should complete my assignments in crayon, lest I fashion a pencil into a weapon.

"How does it work?" she continues. "Like do you hear voices? Are they talking to you now?"

I glimpse several smirks in the darkness. Hear a few soft snickers. Girls can be vicious. I always knew this in theory, but once you become a target, it's hard not to grow disillusioned. Not to become disappointed in your peers. Maybe it makes me an anomaly in this world, but I've always tried to treat people the way I want to be treated.

Sister Patricia shushes the class, though she doesn't peel her eyes from the screen. Her mouth is still moving silently.

"I saw this biopic on Netflix once," interjects Bree, the feckless sidekick who couldn't find a personality of her own if she tripped over one. "It was about a woman who heard voices through her microwave."

"Oh, I know that one," Ainsley says. "She drove her car into a city bus because she believed it was a government surveillance unit tracking her."

I'm crazy, is the gist. Delusional, dangerous, and on a hair trigger.

I wish. If I were all those things, maybe I'd have the courage to retaliate against these jerks. As is it, I've done the only sensible thing: ignore them. Every day, I brace myself against the snide comments and perpetual rumors. At first, Sloane said it wouldn't last more than a few days. Ainsley's just a bully and soon enough she'd get bored and move on. But her fascination hasn't dissipated, and my resolve has withered. With each relentless assault, I've grown more self-conscious. Sorry for myself. Sulking in the misery of becoming the main character at a new school where only the worst parts of my reputation precede me.

"Casey. Hey, I forgot." Honestly, you almost have to admire her persistence. That Ainsley's yet to reach boredom is remarkable. "I'm having a party next week."

She's not especially clever, but what she lacks in material, she makes up for in purity of malice. Ainsley doesn't have some long-simmering grudge against me. I didn't steal her boyfriend in third grade. There's no history here. She's simply a rotten person who enjoys being a bitch.

Her tone turns saccharine. "You can come if you promise not to park in the pool."

I focus on the musical number on the screen, pretending not to hear the giggles. Fuck these girls. I don't need their approval. Don't need their friendship. Even if they'd all welcomed me to St. Vincent's with open arms and tried to make friends with me back in September, I still wouldn't trust them. I had a big friend group at Ballard Academy and look how that turned out. Every single one of them betrayed me after the accident. Smiled to my face and laughed behind my back. They spread rumors about the worst night of my life, turning me into a laughingstock.

I had to learn the hard way that loyalty is rare in high school. Which is why I'm not interested in buddying up to any of these girls, not when they showed me their true character right out of the gate. There are only two people I trust these days.

My sister.

And the one guy who never fails to put a smile on my face.

So I keep staring straight ahead and mentally count the minutes until I can see Fenn.

CHAPTER 2
CASEY

AFTER SCHOOL I THROW ON MY RUNNING SHOES AND WHISTLE FOR Bo and Penny, who hardly wait for me to open the front door before they bolt down the driveway toward the sun sitting low above the tree line. For a couple of big golden retrievers, they've got engines like racehorses and the patience of caffeinated toddlers. They sprint most of the way to the forest path between the dorms and my house on the edge of the Sandover campus, where Fenn is waiting for me.

I'm still not tired of the way he always looks deep in thought before his head lifts and his blue eyes light up. That embarrassed grin he smothers as he wraps his arms over my shoulders and kisses the top of my head.

"Hi," he says. Never more than that. But it's the inflection that makes it our own secret language. Everything we need to say in one tiny sound.

"Hi."

I lock my arms behind his back and stay there awhile. Because even on days I remember my armor, school is exhausting.

"You okay?" Fenn says against my hair.

He's almost a foot taller than me, letting me nestle against his chest. He must've ditched his blazer in his dorm because he's wearing only his Sandover-issued button-down, the sleeves rolled up. He smells so delicious. That boarding school tuition doesn't skimp on the good fabric softener.

"Uh-huh," I answer. "You give good hug."

I feel his laugh fan over my cheek. "Oh, yeah?"

"Mm-hmm."

"'Kay. Knock yourself out."

I give him one last squeeze before I let go, shielding my eyes from the sun to spot Bo and Penny harassing some creature up a tree.

"Guys," I shout in reprimand, and they quickly dash away from the tree.

"How long can you stay?" Fenn quickly unbuttons his shirt and lays it down on the grass for me to sit on.

I can't help but snort.

"What? It's called manners, Casey."

"Any excuse to take your clothes off." Not that I hate it. Playing soccer has given him ridiculous abs. Which he's not shy about.

"Eyes are up here, sweetheart." He winks at me and sprawls out beside me.

Something weird happens when the guy you like says he likes you back. Everything becomes hyperreal. Vivid. Those dimples I hadn't paid significant attention to before? They now occupy an inordinate share of my thoughts. I can't stop staring at his lips, the bottom one fuller than the top. Or noticing how he always seems to miss one tiny patch of dark-blond stubble on the corner of his jaw whenever he shaves.

It's impossible not to let my gaze drift to his bare chest again. His sculpted muscles and tanned flesh make my fingers itch to touch him. I swallow through my dry throat and force myself not to ogle him. Sloane mockingly refers to Fenn as the golden boy, and it's hard to disagree with that assessment, only not in a scornful way. With his blond hair, golden skin, and tall, muscular frame, he's hotness personified.

I still can't believe he's actually mine.

"I can't stay long," I tell him. "Homework. And Dad's making dinner. So…"

"So I better not waste my time then."

With a naughty grin, he reaches for my hand and pulls me to sit across his lap. My resulting squeak is a cross between surprise and delight. Then my pulse quickens, as Fenn catches me around the waist to hold me tight and presses his warm lips to mine.

It begins innocent enough at first. A sweet kiss. The soft brush of his lips. My fingers find their way down his bare shoulders to travel the firm ridges of his abs, and I feel his muscles contract under my touch. My tongue seeks his while he tangles his hands in my hair, gently cupping the side of my face.

I know he wants me. I hear it in the soft groans muffled in his chest. Feel it when he skims the skin at the small of my back. I sit up and comb my fingers through his hair, deepening the kiss and breathing heavy.

Fenn's always the first one to pull away.

"You're killing me," he whispers with heavy-lidded eyes.

"I don't know who you're trying to impress by trapping us on first base all the time."

"Trapping? Damn." He flashes an indignant smirk. "I get no credit for good behavior with you."

"Not really, no."

"Ah, come on, Case. Just let me be the good guy." Now he offers an adorable pout. "That's all I'm asking. We don't have to rush things."

"Bet you say that to all the girls."

"Don't do that," he says, pushing a few strands of hair behind my ear and letting his fingertips gently travel down the side of my neck. "I'm here with you. That's all I care about now."

He's endearing, but also a little infuriating. Fenn's exploits are infamous in the prep school circles. It's not like I'm ignorant of how he used to get around, and pretending otherwise is pointless.

And it's frustrating, because between the two of us, he's the more seasoned traveler, yet he digs his heels in if I tempt him to venture much further than the front yard.

"I know, and I'm not trying to rush things…" I slide off Fenn's lap and cradle Bo's head when he comes pushing his way under my arm. "But you're starting to give me a complex."

He frowns. "How so?"

"Every time you stop, I wonder if it's because I'm…" I feel my cheeks heat up. "I don't know…bad at this or something. I mean, my resume isn't extensive."

Even before the accident, my dad was a zero-dating tyrant. And Sloane had every guy at Ballard and Sandover scared to come anywhere near me.

"Your resume?" Fenn sounds completely befuddled.

"Yeah. There was Corey Spaulding who asked me to Lisa Lesko's birthday party freshman year and then ended up making out with her cousin in the guest house. Sophomore year I made out with Corey's best friend, Brad, but mostly to get back at Corey for the Lisa Lesko party betrayal. And then there was A.J. Koppel last year, but I think he only kissed me to get back at Lisa Lesko for cheating on him." I pause in thought. "Oh my God. I just realized Lisa Lesko is the common denominator in my entire kissing history. What do you think that means?"

Fenn stares at me for a second before bursting into laughter. "What the fuck's happening right now? What are you getting at?"

"You'd tell me if I wasn't a good kisser, right?"

He blinks, still chuckling. "Seriously?"

"Seriously."

Fenn composes his face when he realizes I'm not laughing. "Are you kidding me? You're a good kisser. Exceptional, in fact. Fucking phenomenal." He sighs. "Don't take my hesitation to mean there's anything wrong with you. This is me trying to do the right thing. For once."

He does that a lot, and it makes me a little sad for him. Yeah, he's had more one-night stands than a highway motel, but he isn't a bad guy. Somewhere along the way, he got it in his head he's undeserving.

"Okay."

"I mean it." He takes my hand to kiss the inside of my wrist. Which basically melts my insides to molten goo and makes me want to tackle him all at once. I don't know where they teach guys this stuff, but he was paying attention. "There isn't a single thing about you I'd change."

Inside I'm bursting, but I only nod and find a stick to toss for Penny. I don't know if I'll ever get used to him.

"Have you really only kissed three dudes?" He looks intrigued by that. "Weren't you a cheerleader at Ballard?"

I snicker. "Is kissing a gazillion guys required of being a cheer-leader?"

"Well, no, but…" He glares at me. "Fine. I'm stereotyping."

I grin at his grumbled concession. "Yes, I was a cheerleader," I confirm. "And yes, I've only kissed three guys."

I was a lot of things at Ballard Academy. A cheerleader. Head of yearbook committee, which is a huge honor for a junior. I had a best friend—Gillian Coates, who I haven't spoken to since the spring.

I was popular at Ballard. A different kind of popular than my sister, who all the boys coveted and all the girls feared. Sloane used to tease that I was one of those annoying girls who every boy wants and no girl can hate because I'm too genuine. Whatever that means. I've never been anything but myself. And I think Sloane gave me a lot more credit in the "every boy wants me" department, seeing as how I captured the interest of a mere three.

She wasn't wrong about one thing—almost everyone at Ballard *did* like me. Until the rumor mill turned me into a nutcase, and suddenly I was cast aside. And I know for a fact that Gillian and my former friend group *still* whisper about me. I see it on social media sometimes, the dumb comments about me on people's posts. It's embarrassing.

"Not to change the subject," Fenn says then, "but have you noticed Sloane being weird? Because RJ's starting to worry me."

I think it over. On the drive home after school, she was definitely less than chatty. But I didn't dwell on it because it meant I got to skip the daily debrief when she drills down into everyone who was mean to me that day. Whose ass she needs to kick. Which tires to slash. My older sister is my ultimate protector, even when I don't need protecting. Honestly, I'd let her leave bags of flaming dog turds in every locker on campus if I thought it'd make a difference, but as intimidating as Sloane is, there isn't a machine conceived by woman or man that can halt the gears of high school gossip.

In general, though, I don't know if I'd classify her behavior as weird so much as lovesick. Ever since she got back together with RJ, she's been sort of obsessed, walking around inside the opaque aura of a love haze. I'm happy for her, but it's sort of creepy. Sloane used to shun the notion of romance. Now she's peddling love to everyone like she's running a multilevel marketing scheme door-to-door.

"She's been pretty distracted this week," I answer. "All she does is text RJ. If I didn't know better, I'd think those two were getting ready to run away together."

Fenn shrugs. "If they did, I'd have our room to myself, so…"

"I'd say it's normal for a new relationship, but nothing about Sloane is normal lately, so what do I know. They're in their own bubble, I guess."

"Yeah, well, good for them, but RJ needs to get over it."

Fenn's consternation is sort of endearing. He only just patched things up with his stepbrother, and I get the sense he's feeling a little jealous. Starved for attention, maybe.

"I don't know how to describe it," he adds. "Every time I look at him, it's like he's trying to figure out how to tell me my grandma died or something."

Huh. "Okay, that's a little strange. Maybe that's just how his face looks?"

RJ's a nice guy, but he does have strong antisocial tendencies. Sort of like a resting bitch face. For an extroverted guy like Fenn, it must be downright alien.

"Like a couple days ago, I came into our room after practice and caught him on the phone. With Sloane, I assume. But he looks up at me like a deer in the headlights, and his eyes shift away. It's stupid, but I swear I saw that same look every time someone talked about my mom being sick. When they were all afraid to tell me how bad it was getting."

"I'm sorry." I reach for Fenn's hand and entwine it with mine, holding it in my lap.

I know what it's like to lose your mother, although mine didn't die from a drawn-out illness. She died suddenly, no warning at all. A freak drowning that nobody saw coming. And I was only five years old, young enough that I don't remember much from those days. Only brief moments. Glimpses of the funeral, all the people constantly in our house for days afterward, while my sister and I tried coming to terms with the concept of death and the scary notion that Mommy was never coming back.

"My dad was already checking out at that point," Fenn says absently, rubbing circles into my skin with his thumb. "Obviously he was at her side every second, but I was invisible to him. He knew she wasn't going to be around much longer, so he totally shut down."

Silence falls between us. I feel the sadness emanating from him and wish I could make it better. I think about my own loss, that huge hole left in my life after Mom died. I barely remember her, which makes it worse. I don't even have some cache of warm, wonderful memories to crack open whenever I find myself missing her.

I do have one cope, which is kind of embarrassing, but I bite my lip and decide to voice it, because I hate to see Fenn hurting.

"I talk to her sometimes," I admit shyly. "My mom."

"You do?"

"It's dumb, I know."

"No, it's not."

I shrug, because silly as it is, I couldn't stop if I tried. "When I get overwhelmed or scared, or even if I'm really happy about something. I imagine she can hear me, that she's in the room somewhere, and I just talk to her."

"What do you say?"

"Anything. Everything. Like when it suddenly hit me that I want to be a veterinarian, I told my mom before I said anything to Dad or Sloane." A bittersweet smile tugs on my lips. "I know I was probably imagining it, but I swear I felt her presence that day. That she was proud of me for figuring out my path."

Fenn throws his arm over my shoulder and pulls me closer. "Wish I could do that. I haven't felt my mom in a long time. It was empty after she was gone. That was it."

My throat tightens, heart squeezing in acknowledgment of his pain. I rest my head against his bare shoulder and once again wish I could offer something more than platitudes and silly tips to soothe him. Fenn's still so haunted by the loss of her. It's always there. In the moments when he doesn't think anyone's looking. In the way he knows without words how I'm feeling when I think about my own mother. In the dozen ways he sort of hates himself, even if he doesn't think I notice.

At least he lets me see him. I'm one of the few who do, and I'm grateful for that. It takes courage to be a little broken.

"Hi," he says. Gives me a little shake.

"Hi." I feel the smile in his voice. Sure enough, when I tip my head, his lips are curved in a playful grin.

"What do you think about me taking you on a real date?" he asks quietly.

My heart skips a beat. "And what does a real date look like?"

"How do you feel about picnics? Saturday afternoon we can take the dogs for a walk and find a nice spot to set up."

It's hard to picture Fenn Bishop skipping through the forest with a picnic basket, but I'd pay money to see what he comes up with.

"Sounds perfect."

CHAPTER 3
FENN

My stepbrother is caught in a perpetual trance lately. Used to be you couldn't pry his eyes away from his computer screen, but at least he'd occasionally mumble a response to conversation. Now I can't seem to get so much as a grunt out of him while we get ready for class in the morning. His head has been buried in his phone since the second he woke up.

"Dude." I throw a tennis ball across the room that flies past his head to thump the wall.

RJ whips around in his desk chair. "Fuck's sake. What?"

"Have you heard anything I've said for the last ten minutes?"

"No? I don't know. Christ. What do you want from me before eight a.m.?"

"I get you're pussy-whipped these days, but how about sparing a little time for your friends now and then?"

Fuck. That sounded clingy. Was it clingy? I don't know how to do this whole brother thing. I was an only child my entire life. And now I've got this stepbrother who ended up being cooler than I anticipated.

When we met five seconds before our parents' wedding and were standing there in our tuxes sizing each other up, I honestly didn't expect to ever like the dude. Hell, it took me a couple of weeks to even remember his name. But then my dad got RJ into Sandover, and we were thrown together as roommates, and now…well, I guess we've bonded. Sounds cheesy as hell, but it's true. We might come from vastly different backgrounds and are polar opposites in terms of our attitudes toward socializing, but somehow this weird new familial relationship works.

Or at least it did before he went and fell for Sloane frickin' Tresscott. Of *all* the chicks he could've gone after, he picks the headmaster's daughter. The ice princess. The girl who'd rip my balls off if she knew I've had my tongue in her little sister's mouth every day this week.

"Did you have a point, or are you just being needy?" RJ finally puts his phone down and hauls himself out of his chair to start getting dressed. As it is, we'll only have time to grab a quick pastry at the dining hall before first bell.

"You have to do me a solid this weekend. I'm taking Casey out for a picnic on Saturday."

He glances at me over his shoulder. I think I catch something of a grimace before he turns back to his closet.

"What's that got to do with me?"

"Keep Sloane busy for me." I sit on the couch in the middle of our spacious dorm room and put my shoes on. "I know she's not Team Fenn on this, and I don't want every date with Casey turning into a standoff."

"So, this is happening?" RJ furrows his brow as he throws his bag over his shoulder. His tie is undone around his neck like it's a statement against The Man. In reality, he's been at Sandover for two months and still can't tie the thing without my help most days. "You and Casey?"

The question catches me as odd. And he takes on a strange demeanor full of mysterious subtext that makes me uneasy. "Yeah, and…?"

"What are your intentions there?" he asks.

"Intentions?"

What the hell? Granted, we aren't great at the heart-to-hearts, but I thought RJ understood how I feel about Casey. She's not some conquest to me. This girl is special.

"Did Sloane put you up to this?" I ask warily.

"Just asking the question," he says with a shrug that's a bit more pointed than his words suggest.

He's not entirely wrong to be suspicious. Not even a little. Under the surface of what he knows about me, there's a ship-killer of guilt lurking in the darkness. Because I'm an asshole for wanting her, and an even bigger asshole for letting this happen against my better judgment. With every day, every kiss, I'm a little closer to ruining her.

RJ stands between me and the door, a not-so-subtle signal of the sincerity of his interest. I asked for his attention, and now I'm not getting out of here until I've satisfied it.

"I'd never hurt her," I tell him, my voice coming out gruff. I want it to be true. And that's the best kind of honesty I can give him.

Appraising me, RJ clearly wants to say something else, but my phone buzzes in my pocket. I release a breath, surprised at the relief to be let off the hook. Then I see my dad's number on the screen and curse under my breath.

"It's my dad," I mutter, then put the call on speakerphone with a curt, "Yeah?"

I'd have let it go to voicemail if I wasn't somewhat thankful for the rescue. This stare down with RJ was getting intense. I can't imagine where his interest is coming from except that Sloane is far more put out over our relationship than I had assumed. Part of me wonders if she might be on a campaign to turn RJ against me, so long as Casey and I are together. I know it comes from a good place—she wants to protect her little sister—but Sloane is ruthless when she wants to be.

"Good morning," my dad answers with a pathetically cheerful

voice I assume he's doing for the benefit of RJ's mom on the other end. "Did I catch you before breakfast?"

"Yeah, what do you want?"

These days he's on my phone more times than in the last several years of my life combined. It's all part of his sudden character turn toward some network TV dad impersonation that's both disturbing and insulting. Ever since Michelle came along, it's like he's discovered his paternal roots and is trying to make up for a decade of benign neglect. Or at least he wants RJ and his mom to believe he's trying to be a better father.

I'm not buying it. People don't change overnight. Hell, I'm not convinced people change at all. They just get better at hiding their malfunctions. So, no, I don't believe my father suddenly stopped being a selfish prick and now cares about pesky matters like "family."

Where was Mr. Family Man after Mom died? Nowhere near me, that's for sure. Before her death, he and I were close. We laughed together, went sailing. I even got him to play video games with me sometimes. We used to have fun.

Then she was gone, and Dad completely iced me out. He buried himself in work and relegated me to afterthought territory. When he did remember my existence, he'd feel guilty and throw money at me, then disappear again.

And eventually, I liked being left alone. I mean, what teenager wouldn't want to run wild with zero consequences? No matter what I did, what crazy shit I got into, Dad didn't even bat an eye. The summer before sophomore year—back when I was still at Ballard like seventy-five percent of the rejects who now attend Sandover—I threw a party at our house in Greenwich that resulted in the entire place being trashed and the cops showing up after a dozen noise complaints—and Dad couldn't care less. He just hired a cleaning service and then went into his study to finalize some deal he was negotiating with a tech company in Japan. When I was expelled from Ballard and that snooty Swiss prep school? He didn't even blink. Merely wrote another check and shipped me off to Sandover.

So whatever *this* is, this unwelcome olive branch he keeps trying to wave in my face, I'm not interested. I lost interest years ago.

"I hoped we could talk again about Christmas break," Dad tells me. "Taking a little family vacation with all of us."

"Uh, yeah. I think it's a little late for that trip to Disney World, Dad."

"Michelle suggested we go somewhere with mountains. Maybe some skiing?"

"What do I care? Do whatever you want. I've got other plans."

"Think about it," he urges, apparently choosing to ignore my blatant rudeness as some sort of psychological warfare. "In the meantime, Michelle and I wanted to come out for a visit sometime soon. We could take you boys out for a nice dinner. How does that sound?"

"Hard pass."

I end the call without the slightest trace of remorse. Not even the flicker of disapproval in RJ's dark eyes triggers any sort of repentance. I get we're stepbrothers now and this affects him too, but RJ would do better to butt out. He can't possibly appreciate eighteen years of history based on knowing David for a few months. Most of which we've spent in this dorm.

"That was messed up," my stepbrother says. "You could try a little."

"I could, but I don't want to. Trust me, don't fall for this act. He doesn't deserve you caping for him. And these conversations go much quicker when I don't pretend to participate."

"Maybe it's not an act," RJ points out.

I roll my eyes at him. For some obnoxious reason, he's been on my case this past week about how I should be open to reconciliation. But he doesn't know my dad or what it was like waking up one morning and realizing my father had chosen to stop noticing I existed. At least RJ's dad had the decency to get sent to prison.

"I told you, this nice guy bullshit is just that—bullshit. Showering you and your mom with gifts and vacation suggestions. Trying to be your buddy. It's fake. He's trying to impress your mother. Make himself look good so that when they eventually divorce, she doesn't take half his money."

Hesitation creases RJ's features.

"What?" I demand.

"I don't know…" He fidgets with the bottom of his tie.

"What?" I repeat.

"Part of me thinks maybe the marriage will actually work out," he finally admits.

My jaw drops. "Dude."

"I know."

"Since when?"

He offers a shrug. "They seem happy."

"They're newlyweds. Of course they're happy right now. He probably ate her out on the kitchen counter this morning."

RJ blanches. "Gross. That's my mom. Anyway, I'm not saying it'll last. Only that I might not be totally shocked if it does."

I shake my head at him in reprimand. "What happened to your cynicism? It was my favorite thing about you. I fucking blame Sloane for this."

"I don't mind seeing my mother happy," he grumbles as we head for the door. "So sue me."

When we reach the doorway, though, he stops and looks at me. He hesitates again, blocking my way.

I lift a brow. "Was there something else you wanted to say?"

After a beat, he breaks eye contact and steps out of the room. "Nothing," he says without glancing back. "Forget it."

CHAPTER 4
RJ

Sloane is livid. I thought I'd seen her mad before, but this is something else. That eerie kind of quiet stillness that conceals the inferno of rage inside. I'm not even sure she's breathing.

"What are you thinking?" I ask but receive no response.

An hour ago, she called me out to our spot off the overgrown forest trail where an old bench sits among the shrubs. I came straight from swim practice, getting Lawson to cover for me with Coach and make some excuse for why I had to dip out early. She didn't clue me in as to what prompted the sudden SOS, but it's safe to assume it comes back to the decision that's been looming over our heads for a week now.

And with Fenn making the bonehead move on Casey, he's forced our hand.

We knew we'd need to confront him about his role in Casey's accident, but Sloane's been going back and forth about whether to speak with Casey first. Her reasoning is that Casey deserves to know and Fenn doesn't deserve a heads-up to prepare what he'll say, but I suspect she's afraid of the repercussions that might arise when her sister finds out. She's terrified Casey will spiral into depression again, and maybe this time won't be able to crawl out of that dark place.

And I think she's worried Casey's feelings for Fenn will cloud her judgment about what to do next. I *know* Sloane wants to give the tape to the cops. That idea, however, makes me sick to my stomach. I can't snitch on my stepbrother.

But I also can't go against my girlfriend.

I hate being stuck in the middle.

"Can you give me a hint at least?" I press.

Above us a bird or something jostles the canopy, and my girlfriend flinches, blinking out of her spell.

"She could have died," Sloane insists, like she's mid-sentence of an intense argument in her head that I haven't been privy to. "Fenn left her there alone with a head wound. Casey could have been bleeding out." She recoils from the overwhelming image it conjures and starts to pace. "He could have killed her, RJ."

"Okay, maybe," I say gently. Disagreeing with her now is taking my life in my own hands, and I'm not trying to die tonight. "But she also would have drowned if Fenn hadn't been there to rescue her from the sinking car."

Sharply, she rounds on me. "So you're taking his side."

"No. I'm giving you some perspective to consider the context."

"Fuck your context."

"Sloane." I let out a breath. "We still don't know who the other person was in the video. The first person we saw running past the camera. We have no idea who they are and if they were driving the car. And in the absence of that information, it's easy to want to put all the blame on the one person we can identify."

Sloane scoffs, throwing her hands in the air. "I don't have to be fair. My baby sister almost died, and Fenn has been lying about it for months! That's shady, RJ. It's shady!"

She's not wrong. It doesn't look good for my stepbrother. And it's rotten luck that only Fenn was dumb enough to flash his face at the boathouse security camera. If we knew who drove out there with Casey in the first place, Fenn's decision to flee after saving her would be a minor footnote to this entire ordeal. Something for the epilogue of the closed case. Instead, his actions that night, and every day since, appear more suspicious than heroic.

"I think you need to figure out where your loyalties lie." She advances on me, dark gray eyes burning like hot ash. Indignant, she points a finger in my chest that would get my back up if she were anyone else.

"You know I can't do that."

I take her hand, which she quickly yanks back. These days, I give her an infinite amount of slack, considering the circumstances. But I'm not taking ultimatums either.

"Sloane, I love you, but there's no way I'm taking sides between my girlfriend and my stepbrother. What he did is fucked up, yeah. But I'm sorry, I don't think we should crucify the guy until we know the whole story." I shrug. "At this point, I think you tell Casey and let *her* decide what to do."

"No," she says, clearly unsatisfied that I'm not on board to feed her revenge fantasies. She flicks up one eyebrow in challenge. "I'll just tell my dad and we can go to the cops. They can figure it out."

My shoulders tense. She wields the idea like a knife to my throat, and my patience is now waning. I want a way forward as much as she does, but throwing Fenn under the bus because we don't have the real culprit is not an outcome I'm keen to entertain.

"I'm not standing in your way." I sit on the bench and implore her to lower her weapons. "If that's what you believe you have to do, that's your right. But if you go that route, you need to understand that you could be blowing up Fenn's entire life, maybe even taking away his freedom, without having all the details. If you're not ready to fill Casey in yet, then at least let me talk to Fenn before you do anything else. Get him to admit the truth. Explain his side of things."

Her lips tighten. "You know he'll just lie to you."

"No, I don't know that. I think he'll tell me the truth."

Sloane meets my eyes for a moment. Long enough that the desire to swing on me fades. For now.

Reluctant, she sits beside me. "Let me see the footage again," she orders.

On my phone, we rewatch the boathouse security footage from prom night. No matter how we zoom in or slow it down, Sloane can't identify any clue to who it is we see fleeing the scene soon after the car careens off screen and into the lake. And she watches Fenn. How he races out of frame to pull Casey from the car, then returns to lay her gently on the ground. How he texts Sloane from her sister's phone, proving those damn things actually are waterproof because it had been fully submerged.

"If he hadn't texted, there's no way we would have thought to look there," she mutters.

The lake is a good distance from the Ballard Academy gym where Casey disappeared from the dance. Definitely not a trek anyone was taking on foot at night unless they knew the way. As Sloane described it, the boathouse was a place people went to drink, smoke, make out, or engage in whatever other illicit behaviors. AKA the last place anyone would think to look for a girl like Casey.

"We might not have found her for hours," Sloane says, still clutching my phone in her hands. But I feel her icy fury thawing.

"Look, I can't imagine what possessed Fenn to leave her there," I say roughly, "or why he hasn't come forward this whole time. But I think it's obvious that when he went in the water, he was trying to do the right thing."

Sloane chews on it for a while, her brow furrowed. She isn't the forgiving type. My girlfriend is the kind of person who carries her grudges around in her pocket. Nurturing them. I'm not sure if she knows who she'd be without them. I get it. It was a monumental bit of character growth for her to find a way to forgive me for every mistake I made on my way to being with her now.

I just need her to stretch a little further.

"I hate you," she says with a huff.

"I know."

I wrap my hand around her thigh and squeeze softly, because I can sense her resolve weakening, and she'll punish me less if I remind her why she stays with me.

"Fine." She sighs resentfully. "Yes, if he hadn't been there, she would have died in the car."

She's offering a small amount of grace for a guy she'd still very much like to dismember with her bare hands. It's enough, though.

"Thank you for acknowledging that."

"All right. Talk to him first. Try to get his side of things." Sloane rises to her feet, done with me for the moment. No one likes hearing *don't kill anyone yet* less than Sloane Tresscott. She's a fighter to her core. "But if he won't come clean…"

I nod grimly. "I know."

She's giving him one chance here, and one chance only. For his sake, Fenn better grab this lifeline before it becomes a noose.

CHAPTER 5
FENN

"Mr. Swinney?" Casey says with her jaw jutting open. "That guy who looks like an old moth-eaten wool coat that's fallen off its hanger in the back of the closet?"

It's an apt description, and I almost choke myself laughing as we find a nice shady spot to throw down our picnic blanket Saturday afternoon.

"It's the perfect cover," I answer. "Who'd suspect, right?"

The Sandover Prep campus is deceptively large, extending for hundreds of acres beyond the main facilities. Much of it is untouched woodland that most of us have barely explored. Today we wandered off one of the walking trails to discover a hollow among the evergreens. Autumn is in full swing. Everywhere else on campus, the leaves are starting to turn in an array of reds and oranges, the ground becoming crunchy and brown. Here, there's still a lot of green to be seen.

We sit, and I begin setting out some snacks I brought. I found a small gourmet grocery about a half hour away that I paid to put something together. Had it delivered to the dorm this morning. Best of all, I got them to procure two raw marrow bones from the butcher shop in Calden, the small town closest to the Sandover campus.

I waste no time tossing the bones at Casey's two salivating golden retrievers, who snatch up their respective bones and race off to find a quiet place to gorge. Good. That'll keep them busy for a while.

"So, you followed him?" Casey says with a laugh.

"Yup. And this place was not easy to get to. Which, you know, makes sense. RJ and I spent the night traipsing through the woods in the pitch-black. Getting cut up and tripping over rocks every other step."

"I would have been terrified," she says nervously. "You could have found his murder shack or something."

"The thought did occur to me."

I'm having the hardest time concentrating on the conversation, not entirely sure the words are coming out in the right order. Casey is beautiful against the backdrop of sunlight filtering through the trees. I get distracted by her strawberry-blond hair catching in the breeze and the way she licks her fingers after biting into an orange slice. The simplest things about her get me all weird in the head. I'd consider it a sickness if I didn't prefer to spend time with her than do just about anything else.

"The real fun was hauling ass out of there thinking we were about to get caught by a bunch of heavily armed drug traffickers who were going to cut off our fingers and send them to our parents."

"All that so RJ could keep seeing Sloane." Casey smiles to herself. "He's a piece of work."

I pull a bottle of prosecco out of my backpack along with two glasses I stole from the dining hall. For some dumb reason, I struggle to pour because my fingers are shaky.

"Are you okay?" She watches me with amused concern. "You're kind of shaking a lot."

"You make me a little nervous," I confess.

Casey cocks her head. "I find that hard to believe."

"It's true."

Lately I've made it a point not to lie to her. Any more than

I already have and no more than necessary. I'm trying this new path of absolute uncomfortable honesty. Sort of. It's complicated. I don't know. I guess it feels like I'm trying to compensate for all the other ways I'm about to screw her up.

"That's ridiculous."

I hand her the glass I've somehow managed not to spill all over the blanket. "Trust me, you're well out of my league."

"You're cute when you're full of crap."

She laughs off my comment as an attempt at being charming. For some reason, this girl's got it in her head I'm a catch. I don't know whatever gave her that idea. Sometimes I wish I could tell her all the rotten secrets that would send her running.

"Here, try this one." Casey pops a cheese cube in my mouth and watches me for a reaction.

I chew slowly. "Oh, that's kind of weird."

"Right? Like red wine."

"How would you know?"

She snickers. "What, you think you're the first person to offer me alcohol?"

I don't know why I like it so much when she laughs at me.

Being with her, here, I've never been more content. Casey has a way of blotting out everything else around us, and I'm lighter. Free. Happy. It's never continuous, though, because between those pure moments, a current of dread runs through my head and reminds me that it's only a matter of time. Before I disappoint her. Become such a toxic influence on her that I corrupt the goodness that makes her special.

Casey doesn't suffer from the malignant apathy and disenchantment to which the rest of us have succumbed. She isn't another jaded trust-fund baby whose soul is cold and empty. She's hopeful and sweet. Kind and generous. All the things that get wrung out of us, she's somehow managed to retain through terrible ordeals that would have understandably crippled others.

She's sort of my hero.

And if I weren't such a selfish bastard, I'd leave her alone before I break her.

"What are you up to tonight?" she asks as she plucks a mini powdered donut out of a little container. "Getting into trouble?"

"The fights are tonight." I roll my eyes. "RJ wants me to go with him, since he technically has to make an appearance after dethroning Duke."

"I can't picture RJ running things. Being the new Duke."

"That makes two of you."

My stepbrother never wanted the responsibility or power of being Sandover's top dog. When he challenged Duke for leadership, he was fighting for his own autonomy against a corrupt system. In other words, he wanted to run his own criminal rackets without handing over a cut to Duke fuckin' Jessup. What he didn't realize is the machine keeps turning no matter who's in the driver's seat. Whether they like it or not.

Casey leans back on her elbows, giving me a curious look. "Have you ever participated?"

"Fought? Sure. Couple times."

I can't read her reaction, but I expect her to be disappointed. It's one of those things that takes the shine off the penny. Participating in Sandover's tradition of guys beating the crap out of one another every Saturday night probably isn't the most attractive trait in a potential boyfriend.

"Was it recreational, or…?"

"You mean was I doing it for fun? No."

Plenty of guys do it for shits and giggles. Some do it to prove something. Others because they like it. That's not me.

"Maybe it's a failure of character, but both times I've gone in there, it's because I had something to solve. A score to settle or whatever. Squash a beef."

I don't take any kind of pleasure out of violence. Just on some occasions, physical conflict is efficient. Everyone knows the rules and they work. Mostly.

"I'm not judging. But I definitely can't imagine you in a fight," she says, chewing on her lip as if she's trying hard to conjure the vision in her head. "Not with that angel face." She wipes a teasing finger of powdered sugar on my cheek.

I've heard it my whole life. Fennelly Bishop, the pretty boy. But when I do step toe-to-toe with another guy who has no qualms about beating my face in, I don't hold anything back. Something is unleashed in me when I taste blood. I get vicious. It's a bit like blacking out, some deeply repressed part of me taking over. But then that's also sort of a cop-out, like I'm passing the blame. Maybe I do enjoy beating the shit out of someone every now and then. Maybe we all do.

"Who did you fight?" she asks. "Anyone I know?"

"Only one you'd know is Gabe."

Her jaw drops. "Isn't he your best friend?"

I grin. "Not for those ten minutes in the ring."

Man, that was a brutal fight. Gabe and I have known each other since kindergarten, so obviously we'd gotten into a scuffle or two over the years, but that night was a bloody, bare-knuckle brawl that left both of us beaten to a pulp. I can't even say who won. Can't remember why we were even fighting that night.

Ah, right. I fucked a chick he had his eye on. Broke the bro code. I had it coming when he called me out at the fights.

"Have you still not spoken to him at all since he got sent away?" Casey asks quietly.

"Nope." Unhappiness ripples through me, along with a clench of guilt. "I still don't even know where they sent him. Gabe's parents are ridiculously strict, so I guess it makes sense they chose the one military school that's impossible to get any information on."

"Yeah, Lucas is always saying how impossible his parents are. It drives him crazy."

I inwardly bristle at the mention of Lucas, which is a stupid reaction because Casey is allowed to have friends. Hell, these days, with everyone at Ballard still whispering about her, and now the girls at St. Vincent's, I want her to have as many friends as possible.

But I can't deny I feel a spark of jealousy knowing how close she and Lucas Ciprian are.

Not that there's anything wrong with Lucas. He's a good kid. Gabe had a soft spot for his younger brother, especially since their father constantly compared the two. Lucas definitely has a younger-brother-in-his-older-brother's-shadow syndrome happening, and I know Gabe sensed the jealousy because he was always trying to boost the kid's confidence.

"Apparently it's gotten worse since Gabe got caught dealing," Casey tells me. "Mr. Ciprian's been extra hard on Lucas. He calls him pretty much every day to lecture him about 'honest work' and not following in his brother's footsteps."

"Maybe Lucas needs to fight, then," I say lightly. "Release some of that frustration."

"Hey, what if I came with you tonight?" she suggests, tipping the wine glass to her lips. "See what all the fuss is about."

I wince at the thought. "Bad idea. Girls don't go to the fights. Trust me, it's not the sort of place you want to be."

"Why?" She raises a combative eyebrow. "Because we're too precious and frail?"

"Yeah, exactly."

"Rude."

I have to laugh at the little glimpse of her defiant streak. I'd pay to see what she thinks rebelling looks like.

"If you want to roll around in the mud a little, you can wrestle me." I narrow my eyes in challenge.

Hers flash wide. "You wouldn't dare."

I take her glass and set it aside. "I totally would."

Then I pounce. Before she can wiggle away, I grab her around the waist to lay her down. She squirms while I tickle her ribs and kiss her neck, beating my back and shoulders with soft jabs.

"You're dead, Fennelly," she threatens between hysterical laughter.

"Keep trying all you want, I'm not ticklish."

I am a good sport, though, so I let Casey get some leverage to pin me down. She rolls on top of me with a triumphant smirk.

"Now you're at my mercy," she declares, quite proud of herself.

Holding her hips, I have to concentrate with significant effort to keep from poking her with an erection.

"All right, I surrender," I say huskily. "Do your worst."

She leans down to press her lips to mine. I'm at half wood and silently begging she doesn't feel it. Not that I don't want her riding my dick, but I'm not trying to force things with us. I wasn't kidding when I told her I want to take it slow.

Fuck, though, she can kiss.

I don't know what special magic she's conjured, but tasting her makes me practically feral. Like *throw her down beneath me and rip her clothes off* kind of mental. So when she grabs my hands and pushes them up her ribs, I can't help skimming my thumbs across her stiff nipples over her thin sweater. She makes the softest moan in my mouth, and I lose all but the last strands of my self-control. Palming her tits, I squeeze them until she starts moving her hips back and forth.

Groaning, I roll Casey over on our sides and pull away. Just far enough that our lower bodies aren't touching while I kiss her neck. Because if she let me, I'd fuck her right here and it'd be amazing. It'd also be the quickest way to blow up everything we could have been.

"Don't be in such a rush," I say when her face falls. "We have time."

It's not what she wants to hear. I know even as she tilts her head to kiss me back, her soft hands combing through my hair, that she's wondering if she's done something wrong. She hasn't, of course, and I wish I could explain it in a way she'd understand.

That the only person who's bound to mess this up is me.

CHAPTER 6
CASEY

FAMILY DINNERS IN MY HOUSE ARE NONNEGOTIABLE. WEEKENDS included, no exceptions. If Sloane or I need to skip a dinner, it requires a written essay and a PowerPoint presentation highlighting all the reasons we must be excused. Okay, not quite, but pretty much. Dad takes this one tradition very seriously.

I'm still on a high from my date with Fenn as I help Sloane set the table. Dad's puttering around in the kitchen, making the finishing touches on whatever dish he plans to force upon us tonight. The truth is, our father is a terrible cook. We all know it. But he insists on doing it. Sloane thinks he's trying to play both roles, the stern breadwinner and the nurturing houseparent, but keeping house has never been his strong suit.

"Why are you smiling like that?"

I look up to find my sister's suspicious gaze on me. "Oh. I didn't even realize I was."

She relaxes. "Apology accepted."

A burst of laughter flies out. "I'm not apologizing for smiling! People smile, Sloane. Deal with it."

I finish laying out the napkins and then dart into the kitchen for drinking glasses. A few minutes later, the three of us are seated at the dining room table. Bo and Penny sit near Dad's chair, begging with forlorn faces while he serves a huge portion of lasagna on Sloane's plate.

She balks at the portion size. "Dad," she protests, "I've got a track meet on Monday. You trying to kill me with carbs?"

"I thought carbo loading was a legitimate strategy runners use before a race." He gives her a blank look. "Isn't that what you said the other day?"

"Yes, but I didn't mean I wanted you to serve me *half* a lasagna." She cuts the massive piece in half, sticks a fork in the middle, and plops the second piece onto my plate.

I snicker. "Thanks."

As we eat, Dad peppers us with questions, most of which are directed at Sloane. And from the way she keeps wincing and groaning, I know she's regretting the big talk she had with him last week, when she asked if it would kill him to ask her about her life instead of always assuming she was doing okay. Looks like it totally backfired on her—Sloane is notoriously private, so I know all the prying is killing her. I don't feel that bad for her, though. Welcome to my life. Dad is always grilling me about something.

I bite back a laugh when he starts asking her about RJ. "Mr. Shaw treating you well?"

"Oh my God. No. We're not talking about my love life." Sloane shoves a bite of lasagna into her mouth and chews extra slowly to avoid speaking more words.

Dad gives up and turns his attention to me, asking how my day was. "Mr. Bishop came by to walk the dogs?" he prompts.

He sounds as thrilled about me spending time with Fenn as he does about Sloane and RJ. But Dad doesn't vocally object to my friendship with Fenn anymore. He keeps his disapproval to himself because he knows how much my time with Fenn means to me.

If it weren't for Fenn's friendship, I might still be locked in my room, obsessing over the night my car wound up in the lake.

Wallowing in self-pity. Waking up multiple times a night from bone-chilling nightmares. Yes, the nightmares still come, but not as often as before. And these days, when they do wake me, I call Fenn and he comforts me. He told me it doesn't matter what time of day or night it is. If I need him, call him.

Still, I know Dad isn't in love with the idea. Even before the accident, he always viewed me as fragile. I was the baby, the one who needed extra protecting. Sloane, meanwhile, was the rock. The resilient one. I'm not jealous of my sister, never have been, but I can't deny I feel resentful sometimes. Not necessarily toward her, but because I get tired of Dad acting like I'm not as strong as she is. Not as tough.

I can be tough when I need to be. I survived that night, didn't I?

"Case?" he prompts.

"Oh, yeah. He did. We walked to the lake. It was nice."

More than nice. I can still taste him on my lips.

I feel my cheeks warm up and change the subject before the blush can take hold. "I forgot to ask you—can Lucas come over and watch a movie tonight? He texted right before we sat down."

Dad picks up his water glass and takes a sip. Then he nods. "Yes. That's fine. Lucas is always welcome." He glances at Sloane. "I haven't seen Silas around this week."

"He's busy with swimming. I'm busy with track. We haven't connected."

I know my sister well, and there's something rippling under the surface of that noncommittal answer. I'm just not sure what it is. I think back to recent conversations with Fenn and try to recall if he'd mentioned anything about a possible beef between my sister and Silas Hazelton, her BFF at Sandover. But nothing comes to mind.

"Anyway, enough about us," Sloane chirps, turning the tables on our father. "How was *your* week, Headmaster Tresscott?"

"Chaotic," he answers, wrapping his fingers around his wineglass. Dad drinks one glass of red wine every night and no more than that.

He's honestly the most predictable person I've ever met in my life. "I need to fill two open teaching positions. I was only able to find a suitable candidate for one, so the boys will have a sub in modern lit until the position is filled. Subs are a pain in the butt."

"Two open positions?" Sloane says, raising a brow. "How'd you lose *two* teachers in one week? What are you doing over there? Hazing them?"

Dad looks amused. "No. There was a family emergency, and they both had to resign. They happened to be married."

"See?" she says. "This is why the institution of marriage should be abolished."

After dinner, as Sloane and I load the dishwasher, I conduct my own interrogation. "Are you and Silas fighting?"

She turns toward me, her dark ponytail falling over one shoulder. "No. Should we be?"

"No. But Dad's right—I haven't seen him around."

She shrugs and shifts her attention back to rinsing the empty lasagna pan under the sink. "I've been chilling with RJ. All that make-up sex, you know?"

"Nope, I wouldn't know," I answer sheepishly, because I've never even had sex, let alone the make-up kind.

"Yeah, well, let's keep it that way for a while," my sister says, snapping into maternal mode.

"I'll see what I can do" is my light response.

That instantly gets her back up. "What does that mean?"

I turn to find her gaze boring into my face. Flickering with suspicion and something else I can't quite decipher. "What?"

"I mean, who might you be having make-up sex with, Case?"

"Oh my God. Nobody. I was making a joke." She remains unconvinced, and I roll my eyes. "I'm not sleeping with Fenn, if that's what you're thinking."

Yet.

I'm not sleeping with Fenn *yet*. But I keep that thought to myself.

I'm not looking for a fight with Sloane tonight. Besides, if Fenn has anything to say about it, sex won't be on the table for another decade. He's determined to go excruciatingly slow.

She bristles at the sound of his name. Her mouth opens, eyes darkening again. She looks as if she's about to say something I'm not going to like, but then the doorbell rings.

"Lucas is here," I say, oddly relieved by the interruption. "You mind finishing up?"

After a beat, she nods. "Yeah. Sure."

In the front hall, I open the door to let Lucas Ciprian in. As usual, Dad is hovering in the doorway leading to his study. He does this every time anyone with a penis enters our home, needing to scope out the situation to determine whether he believes said penis will remain in its owner's pants. If Dad gets even a whiff of suspicion otherwise, he usually wanders over with a blithe smile and suggests, *Hey, why don't we all watch a movie together? Doesn't that sound like fun?*

I still remember the look on Duke Jessup's face the first time Dad pulled that trick. I'm sure Duke came over thinking he was going to get laid—instead, he spent the night watching *Indiana Jones and the Temple of Doom* with Dad sandwiched between him and Sloane. I don't even like Indiana Jones, but I came downstairs to watch with them solely for the comedy appeal. And I'm not talking about Harrison Ford's cheesy one-liners.

Dad doesn't interfere with Lucas, though. He's the one who introduced me to Lucas in the first place when he arranged for him to tutor me in chemistry first semester of sophomore year. For four months, Lucas came over twice a week with his textbooks and an easy smile, and it didn't take long for the two of us to become good friends. Next to Fenn, Lucas is one of my favorite people.

"Hey." I greet him with a big hug, ignoring Dad's laser focus boring a hole into us. "Come in."

"Hey." He gives me a quick squeeze before stepping back to seek out Dad's gaze. Lucas knows the drill. "Hi, Dr. Tresscott. Thanks for having me."

I grab Lucas's arm and practically drag him to the stairs. "Let's go upstairs and pick something to watch. I vote for a rom-com."

"Does my vote ever count?" he asks wryly.

I beam at him. "No."

"Door open, Case." Dad's warning tickles our backs as we head up to my room.

As instructed, I leave the door open, but only a crack. Then I throw myself on the bed and hug one of my fluffy, white throw pillows. Lucas kicks off his shoes and joins me, making himself comfortable as he leans against the headboard.

"You look happy," he tells me, eyes narrowed.

I giggle. "Is that a problem?"

"No. Of course not. Just want to make sure you're aware."

"I'm aware."

He grabs the remote from the nightstand and clicks on one of the streaming sites. Rows of movie poster thumbnails fill the screen, and he begins scrolling through them.

"Rom-com, you say?"

"Yes, please."

I rest my head on the throw pillow and watch Lucas's profile as he peruses the selections. He's got a great profile, I realize. We're such good friends that sometimes I forget Lucas is actually kind of hot. He has dark hair that always looks a bit rumpled, in that cute, just-rolled-out-of-bed way. Dark eyes. Dimples. A little cleft in his chin. He's not as tall or muscular as his older brother, Gabe, but he's just as good-looking. Better looking, in my opinion. I didn't know Gabe Ciprian well, but he always came off as very cocky. I'm okay with some cockiness in a guy, but too much of it and they veer too close to douche territory. Like Sloane's ex, Duke. Duke is cocky to the max and therefore douchey to the max.

The chime of an incoming text jolts me out of my thoughts.

I reach for the other nightstand to grab my phone, smiling when I see Fenn's name.

Fenn: Miss you already.

My heart instantly beats faster. I'm such a goner for this guy. Like, dead.

"Who's that?" Lucas peers toward my screen.

"Oh. Just Fenn." I clear the notification before he can read the message.

"Yeah? What's he saying?"

"Nothing. He's going to the fights tonight to keep RJ company." I grin. "I hear RJ wants nothing to do with his new leadership role."

Lucas responds with a snort. "He doesn't. But like it or not, he's the new king of Sandover. Too bad my brother's not here to enjoy the free pass."

"What do you mean?"

"Duke took a cut of every sale Gabe made," he explains. "Gabe was always livid about it. He was like, *I'm the only drug dealer who can't even enjoy all the fruits of his labor.*"

"Drug dealer problems, amirite?"

Lucas laughs. "I mean, Duke was taking his cash for no reason other than Duke's a greedy asshole, so yeah, I'd say that's annoying. RJ, though—he wants nothing to do with any of the rackets. Ever since he knocked Duke out in that fight, guys keep trying to pay RJ, and he's like, *Leave me the fuck alone.*"

I laugh too. "I swear, you Sandover boys are messed up."

"Not all of us," he protests. Then there's a pause. "Are you and Fenn still hanging out a lot?"

He doesn't know the half of it. In fact, no one knows that Fenn and I have been practically sucking each other's faces off this past week. I can't tell Sloane yet, not unless I want to be responsible for Fenn's murder, and possibly my own. I don't have a single girlfriend

I can share the secret with either, since everyone at Ballard is dead to me and everyone at St. Vincent's thinks I'm insane.

I don't usually talk to Lucas about romance stuff, but I'm nearly bursting from the need to tell someone, and I can't stop the confession from slipping out.

"We're kind of dating now."

His expression turns to shock. "Seriously?"

"Yeah," I say shyly.

"Since when?" he demands.

I sit up, holding the pillow in my lap. "About a week. It just sort of happened. We were friends, but then we kissed and…" I bite my lip to stop another smile from splitting my face open. "Well, it's a thing now."

Lucas sets the remote on the mattress and shifts around so we're facing each other. I can tell from his expression that he's not thrilled by this development.

"Be happy for me," I plead before he can voice his disapproval. "I know you don't like this—"

"I don't," he agrees.

"But I'm asking you to support me on this." I reach for his hand, wrapping my fingers around his. "I've had such a shitty year, Lucas. You know how bad it's been."

"I know." His voice softens.

"There aren't many rays of sunshine in my life these days." I squeeze his hand, and after a moment, he laces our fingers together. "Your friendship is one of them. Sloane is one of them. And now Fenn. I really like him."

"I get it. He's Fenn Bishop. Every girl likes him, Case. That's the problem."

"If you're implying he's still sleeping around, I promise you he's not. He's been a player in the past, I know that. I'm not stupid or blind."

"He has his own fuckin' hashtag," Lucas grumbles. "Player is an understatement."

My eyebrows shoot up. "He has a hashtag?"

"Yeah. It's ridiculous. Look." Lucas fishes his phone out of his pocket and opens Instagram. He types something, then flips the screen over so I can see it.

My curiosity gets the best of me. Sure enough, #FennBishop is an actual hashtag. Fenn's been tagged in what seems like hundreds of posts. Not all of them are from girls. There's a lot of party pictures. Shots of him with Gabe or Lawson or Silas at some party or another. Shots of him on the soccer field, his golden hair shining in the sunlight, his features taut with concentration.

But…yeah…there are definitely photos of him with girls. Very pretty girls with their hands all over him. His arm slung over their shoulders. Lips locked in drunken kisses. It's not the most flattering portrait of Fenn's escapades before we got together, but it's nothing he didn't tell me about either.

"I know all this," I say quietly, handing the phone back. "And I don't care."

"You don't care." Lucas sounds dubious.

"No. Fenn's been honest about his past." I scoot closer and rest my head on Lucas's shoulder. "Give him a chance, okay? You don't have to worry about me."

"Fine," Lucas says in a grudging tone. "I'll try not to worry. But if he does anything to hurt you…"

"Then I give you permission to beat him up," I say graciously.

"Thank you."

I smile against my friend's shoulder. "He's been good for me. He really has. And he's always upfront and honest, no matter how uncomfortable it makes him. I promise you, Fenn doesn't keep secrets from me."

CHAPTER 7
SILAS

MONDAY AFTER SWIM PRACTICE, I DROP BY SLOANE'S HOUSE, SINCE lately she doesn't respond to texts. For the last week she's made herself a ghost, and I had to hear it from Lawson that she once again patched things up with the antisocial asshole RJ.

I've never known Sloane to be exceptionally reasonable. Her wheelhouse tends to be a cozy corner at the nexus of stubborn and spiteful. Take the roller derby death match that was her relationship with Duke—none of us on the outside looking in understood what we were watching, but the objective seemed to be inflicting as much damage as possible. With all the on-again-off-agains, they stuck it out longer than they had any right to; Sloane, apparently motivated by attrition, willing to die starving him out. At least that makes more sense than those two having any genuine affection for each other.

And now we get to experience the lackluster sequel with RJ Shaw. It's like she's addicted to dirtbags. Of course, I have to keep my mouth shut because Sloane doesn't take well to criticism.

Honestly, though, I don't fucking get it. A part of me wouldn't be surprised if this whole thing is some long con on her part. If she's pulling Duke's strings, finding a new way to get under his skin because she'd grown bored of the endless laps around the roller rink.

That would explain why RJ went on that kamikaze mission to unseat Duke from his throne.

When Sloane answers the door and finds me standing there, she lets out a weary sigh.

"Nice to see you too," I say. The rewards for being Sloane's friend are few and far between.

"What's up? I'm in the middle of homework."

"Haven't heard from you in a while." I squeeze past her to let myself in when she pretends she's too busy to catch up with her best friend. "Came to make sure you were still alive."

"I've been busy." Despite that, she lets me follow her upstairs.

My gaze rests on her ass, hugged by a pair of black yoga pants. Can't deny I'm disappointed that she'd changed out of her Catholic school uniform. I might have a girlfriend, but that doesn't mean I can't appreciate how good Sloane Tresscott looks in a short, pleated skirt.

We enter her bedroom, where I sit on the end of her bed while she leans against her desk. Sloane's room is the least girly place you'll ever see. She's not the sentimental type, so there's no bulletin board covered with photographs and concert ticket stubs. The only piece of art on the wall is a poster of her favorite band Sleater-Kinney, and the brightest color in the room is the yellow throw pillow I rest my elbows on as I lean back.

"So. What's keeping you busy?" I ask.

"You know. Life and whatever."

I raise my eyebrows. "'Whatever,' as in RJ again?"

"And other stuff. What's this about, Silas? I can't right now." She fidgets, impatient but also distinctly distracted.

I've known Sloane for years, so I can always tell when the gears in her brain are turning. Her focus is continually drifting from me to some mysterious thought snapping its fingers inside her head.

"I told you, I wanted to check in on you. It's not like you to ghost out."

The gentle poke penetrates something beneath her hard candy shell, and her demeanor softens. She runs a hand through her dark hair before tucking it behind her ear. "Yeah. Sorry. I wasn't trying to ghost. Don't take it personal, okay?"

"Okay."

She sinks into her desk chair and flashes a little smirk. "How's Amy?"

"She's good. How's RJ?"

"He's great."

Something about the way her face goes a little dreamy at the sound of RJ's name makes me bristle.

"What?" She narrows her eyes at me.

"Nothing," I lie, then remember it's practically impossible to deceive this girl.

"Just say it," she orders.

Fuck it. Normally I'd keep my mouth shut, but I suppose I've gotten a little impatient of waiting for Sloane to get her head on straight and stop wasting time with losers.

"Look, I know you're into the guy, but…if I'm being honest, I think it's a bad idea. You two as a couple." I straighten up, shrugging one shoulder. "I think you dodged a bullet breaking up with him after you guys had that huge fight. You should've trusted that instinct instead of taking him back."

"Well, I didn't ask for your approval, so thanks anyway."

Her response is precisely what I expected. Sloane hates dissent. She's got an opinion about everything, but God forbid anyone offer the slightest criticism of her choices. Even when they have her best interest at heart.

"What are friends for?" I crack.

Her forehead suddenly creases. "Speaking of that huge fight," she starts. Then pauses, her expression growing more and more shrewd. "How'd that happen, anyway?"

"Well, you fucked Fenn. What else did you expect?"

My attempt at keeping my tone to light sarcasm doesn't quite succeed. It comes out as an accusation instead, and her features instantly harden. Which only annoys me, because, seriously, what *did* she expect? For RJ to jump for joy and thank her for hooking up with his stepbrother?

And don't even get me started on that. Her and Fenn. Sloane's always been secretive, but usually not with me. I thought we told each other everything, and then I have to find out from Lawson that she slept with Fenn?

"That's not what I'm talking about." She peels herself away from the desk and squares up to me, hovering. "How did RJ manage to find me and Fenn talking in the woods that day? Weren't you supposed to be running interference, *friend*?"

Her accusation hangs in the air between us, thickening it with tension.

"You said you wanted me to tell RJ to meet you at the bench," I say irritably. "That's how I remember it."

"Bullshit. I told you to cover for me. Instead, he just happens to show up in the one place I needed him *not* to be at the exact wrong moment. Almost like it was intentional." Her sarcastic smile lacks all traces of humor. "Weird, huh?"

"Or it was a simple misunderstanding."

"Come on, Silas. I'm insulted if you think I'm that dumb."

She's so dramatic.

Denial is generally the best policy, but it's obvious she's not buying my bullshit. And a part of me has been itching for this fight for a while. Since the second RJ entered our lives, he's caused nothing but friction in all my goddamn relationships. Might as well clear the air so that Sloane and I can put this behind us and move on.

"All right. You got me." I stand up, because I'm not enjoying the way she's looming over me like she's the adult and I'm the little kid getting reamed out for stealing cookies. "I thought you were going to meet Duke, so I did my teammate a solid. I figured RJ deserved to know if he was another pawn in the endless dysfunctional chess match between you two."

"I fucking knew it." She throws her hands up and turns away.

"You should take pity on the guy and cut him loose. Using him against Duke—"

"That's got nothing to do with any of it!" she interrupts, anger coloring her cheeks. "Why are you so obsessed with this?"

"I did it for your own good," I shoot back. "Are you seriously not seeing there's a pattern emerging? You constantly picking douchebags to go out with? I was trying to save you from yourself."

"Oh, fuck off, Silas." When she spins to face me again, her eyes are tiny pyres waiting for a corpse. "At least have the balls to admit you did it on purpose to sabotage RJ and me for your own benefit."

"What does that mean?"

"It means I know when a guy's trying to fuck me."

This accusation is a grenade. Tossed into my hand with mere seconds before it explodes.

Sloane stares at me, waiting for a denial—for me to put that pin back in the grenade. To defuse this bomb that's threatening to blow up our friendship.

My hesitation costs me.

"Goddamn typical," she growls.

The grenade goes off. Boom.

I try to backpedal. "Sloane—"

"You're so fucking pathetic, Silas. No. I'm not falling into your arms. Go home."

"Oh, come on." I shake my head at her, my irritation reaching new limits. "That's not what I said. Take it down a notch. You're blowing the whole thing out of proportion."

"Am I? Because I don't think I am. I see you now, dude. And all your sketchy moves. You tried to sabotage my relationship. You tried to lie to me about it under the guise that you're looking out for me. That you're *such* a good, caring friend. Yeah, right. We're not friends, Silas. You just burned that bridge." Sloane stares daggers at me. "So please get the hell out of my house before I set the dogs on you."

CHAPTER 8
FENN

COACH HAD A BUG UP HIS ASS AT PRACTICE THIS AFTERNOON. HAD us doing drills and shuttle sprints until we collapsed. The soccer field is now fully fertilized with vomit. I'm still queasy and can barely feel my legs when I get back to the dorm. As usual, RJ is at his computer with headphones on when I walk in our room and throw my bag down.

"Hey," he says, spinning around in his chair. He takes off his headphones.

"Hey."

The acknowledgment takes me by surprise. I'm almost startled to hear him speak. Lately, it's been easy to forget he's in the room. For almost a week now, he's been quieter and more withdrawn than when he was the reclusive new arrival with a loner complex and chip on his shoulder.

"We need to talk," he tells me.

"Yeah, okay. Let me hit the shower first."

I'm already peeling off my shirt and grabbing my kit to go clean up. I'm drenched in sweat and covered in grass and whatever else I fell in. I smell rancid.

"No. We need to talk now," RJ says grimly. He hits a key on his keyboard, then gestures to one of his monitors. "Watch."

"Watch what?" I ask irritably, as a monochrome video begins to play on the screen.

"Just fucking watch."

For a few seconds, I don't understand what I'm looking at. Only RJ's intense attention on me suggests I keep watching.

Then I see it.

The car blurring across the screen. Those taillights still haunt my nightmares, their glow painting the forest and turning the lake's surface a shiny crimson.

I stand there and watch in real time, my breath a revving engine between my ears, as a couple of minutes later a figure runs from the scene in a hooded sweatshirt, sopping wet, face concealed and turned away from the camera.

The image damn near knocks me over. A gut-punch that reverberates through my limbs and settles into my bones. The shaking sets in and it doesn't relent.

Without a word, RJ fast-forwards the video until we see me dash through the frame, running toward the lake.

My lungs seize, no oxygen reaching them as the memories of that night crash into me.

Casey wasn't screaming. There were no pleas for help. If she wasn't knocked unconscious by the initial impact, she was already succumbing to shock. Or the drugs, maybe. Whatever it was, I didn't know when I ran into the lake and swam out to the car. I saw her eyes fighting to stay open. How they locked with mine before her head lolled and her body went limp. Blood dripping down her face from a head wound. I remember how fast my heart was beating as I wrestled, with every shred of strength I could muster, against the bitter cold water to pry the passenger's door open.

It was when I reached across Casey's half-submerged body to release her seat belt that I saw it. And my mind went blank. Until that moment, I was only concerned with getting her out.

But then I spotted Gabe's jacket snagged on the parking brake, the pocket seam ripped, as if he'd torn out of it to escape.

Suddenly, a collision of thoughts sent shrapnel flying through my head. And in the noise, a silent moment of clarity struck me like getting smacked across the face.

I took the jacket. Clutched it under my arm while I pulled Casey from the car.

Even soaking wet, she was so light. Frail. Or maybe it was adrenaline. I barely felt the muddy bottom swallowing my shoes as I trudged to shore with her in my arms. Her face was pale in the ruddy darkness when I laid her down.

Everything came quickly to me after that. I searched for pockets in Casey's dress and found her phone, which was miraculously still working despite getting wet. I texted Sloane where to find her. Casey was unconscious, but breathing and stable. She was out of danger, and it would only be minutes before help arrived.

Before I left, I whispered to her. Told her I was sorry but that she was safe now. Her sister was on her way, and everything would be all right. Because of course I couldn't stay. I didn't have any answers to what had transpired there, only that my best friend since kindergarten had apparently left Casey to drown. I had to find Gabe and talk to him. Figure out what the hell had gone wrong and why he'd done it. There had to be an explanation.

But I never got one.

Gabe vanished that night. By morning he'd already been shipped off to military school, and no one would answer my calls. To this day, we haven't spoken. And he has no idea I'm the one who covered for him.

Or, hell, maybe he has a hunch. After all, nobody's gone out there to interrogate him, right? Gabe's smart enough to know that means the cops don't have him in their sights, and if he knows that much, then he must suspect I'm the one who had his back. Same way he had mine in sophomore year when I needed it. From the moment we met, Gabe has been my ride or die.

And I'm his.

RJ abruptly stops the video. I snap out of my own head to see him staring at me in betrayal and accusation. Nothing less than I deserve, I guess. And even though I've known for a long time this day was coming, I thought by now I'd have some answers.

Instead, I'm as clueless as the rest of them and well over my head in guilt and lies.

"You get now why I'm having kind of a problem lately," RJ says with a tone so flat yet severe, I'm more than a little concerned what he might do next. "What were you even doing there?"

My brain kicks into overdrive. Gabe had texted me to meet him. The prom was lame, and I already had a good buzz on. I thought we were going out to the boathouse to smoke and chill. I had no idea by that point that Casey was missing or that we'd realize later she'd been drugged.

"All right, look. I know it's not great."

"Why?" RJ interjects. "Make me understand it."

I avoid his harsh, questioning gaze. "It's complicated, okay?"

"No. Complicated is leaving the scene, Fenn. Even if I could wrap my head around that part, you had to go and buddy up to Casey afterward?"

"It wasn't like some plan I had."

"Yeah, I bet." He huffs a sarcastic laugh. "You just accidentally became her best friend."

"If you'd seen her back then—"

"You're dating her!" he shouts, throwing himself back in his chair until it bumps against his desk. "For fuck's sake, dude. That is so beyond messed up."

"I know. Shit." I sink onto the couch and drop my head in my hands, tugging at my hair.

It's not like these thoughts haven't occurred to me before. All I do is beat myself up over how far out of hand this had gotten over the last several months. How many times I should have stopped myself but was too scared to admit the truth. Too weak to stay away from her.

I'm well aware that I've made a lot of bad decisions since prom night, that I had other options available to me, if only I'd been thinking more clearly. At the very least, I could've given Casey the partial truth. Admitted I was the one who saved her, and just left Gabe's name out of it altogether. I could've kept the part about finding his jacket to myself while I discreetly tried to piece together his role in all this.

"I wanted to tell her," I confess. "Maybe not right away, but the moment she and I got closer, it was always on the tip of my tongue. Every time I saw her, I almost blurted it out, but I could never get the words out because I was buried under a mountain of guilt for leaving her there, and I didn't want her to hate me. And then days went by, and months, and now…" I groan under my breath. "I waited too long. Now if I say something, so much time has passed that it looks like I *did* have some shady plan."

Dread squeezes my chest tighter. The moment I tell Casey I've been lying by omission, she'll be gone. I have no doubt about that. And the notion sends me into an agony spiral.

"I wish I didn't feel this way about her," I mumble. "It'd be easier if I could leave her alone, but—"

"Stop, man. Listen to yourself for a minute. This isn't a choice anymore. You've had time to figure your shit out and tell her the truth, but it's not in your hands anymore. Sloane's seen the video."

Fuck. There are few things in this world I'm truly afraid of. Sloane is high on that list.

I slowly raise my eyes to his. "What'd she say?"

"Seriously?" RJ is incredulous as he shakes his head. "She's on the warpath. I've kept her at bay so far, but she's had it with sitting around. She's talking about telling her dad and turning you in to the cops. Letting them figure it out."

Another spike of anxiety screams through my chest. A sharp, stabbing sensation that nearly chokes me. Without being able to talk to Gabe, I can't face an interrogation. I wouldn't know where to begin, but I can't throw my oldest friend under the bus.

At the same time, Casey deserves my loyalty too. She's waited all this time to find out what happened to her. After I kept chickening out each time I felt the urge to come clean, I sort of convinced myself it would eventually soften the blow if I knew the whole story before I told her. Only that hasn't happened, and it's looking less likely that it ever will.

Unless I give up Gabe's name.

And I can't do that. I owe him, damn it.

"I convinced her to let me talk to you first," RJ says. "You have to give me something here, Fenn. Otherwise, she'll run right over me to get to you."

He's watching me. Waiting. RJ and I only just got back on good terms, and already I can sense that trust shattering. I hate this. Keeping secrets and lying. I've wanted us to have a real relationship as stepbrothers, but here I am again, my loyalties tugged in all directions and feeling like I'm failing all of them.

But I can't give him what he wants, and it's making my stomach churn. It doesn't feel right pointing the finger at Gabe when all I have is a dirty jacket. Because as much as I do trust RJ, I don't believe for a second he wouldn't run to Sloane with that information. And Sloane, without a doubt, would give Gabe's name to the cops in a heartbeat.

"You have to give me more time," I beg him. "I know it doesn't make sense, but trust me on this."

RJ glowers at me. "That's not good enough. Do you get what I'm saying? She's ready to pin the whole thing on you. At the very least, you're getting expelled. At most, the cops charge you with I don't know how many counts. Leaving the scene, withholding evidence…"

He's right. What I did was technically a crime, no matter how well-intentioned. Not like I haven't considered it.

"That's if Sloane doesn't kill you herself and ask me to help her dump the body," he finishes, sounding defeated. "So please, help me out here."

I gulp down the lump of sheer misery in my throat. "There's more to this than you understand. I'm still piecing it together, but I need—"

"What does that mean?" he asks, exasperated. His patience is well exhausted at this point.

"It's comp—"

"Right, complicated." He sighs, rubbing his forehead. "Listen, I've kept Sloane from telling her dad or the cops for now, but she's going to tell Casey. That's a given. I'm here as your brother asking you to tell me the truth. You can't keep it to yourself anymore."

My gut clenches harder, frustration and panic warring inside me. I'm nowhere near close enough to a good explanation. I've spent months badgering Gabe's family for a way to contact him, and to no avail, because his parents hate me. I spent hours online compiling a list of every military school in the goddamn country, then proceeded to call each one asking if a Gabe Ciprian was enrolled and was either hung up on, laughed at, or politely told to fuck off. Turns out, schools don't offer students' names and information to random callers. Who would've thought.

If I had more time, maybe I could figure out a way to get to Gabe and ask him what happened that night. I'm sure it would all make sense if I had the missing pieces. There's no way he would just abandon Casey to die. He's not a bad person. Something went wrong, and I simply need to find out what it is.

"Let me talk to her," I insist, grasping at any sense of charity RJ has left. "Casey should hear it from me."

His expression is wary. He's understandably reluctant to put himself out on a ledge for me again.

"Please," I say hoarsely. "I promise. I'll tell Casey myself. Let me have this."

He goes silent for what feels like forever. Then he curses under his breath and says, "I'll try, but I can't make any promises on Sloane's behalf. My advice: beat her to it."

CHAPTER 9
SLOANE

MY KNIFE SCRAPES VIOLENTLY ACROSS THE PLATE AND ITS ANGRY screech makes the whole room flinch. Dad briefly pauses midsentence to pull a face like I did it on purpose. What does he want? It's a tough piece of meat. Maybe if he hadn't left it on the grill like he was trying to torture nuclear launch codes out of it, I wouldn't be trying to coat a piece of charcoal in mashed potatoes to trick my throat into swallowing it. I doubt even the dogs would find tonight's protein portion palatable. As if to prove that point, only Bo bothers begging tonight. Penny is asleep under the table, her head resting on my foot.

"Why didn't Silas stay for dinner?" Dad asks from the head of the dining table.

Because he's a lying, backstabbing prick, and he's never coming for dinner again.

I swallow my fury along with the bone-dry bite of steak. "He had homework," I say instead, because as much as I appreciate my dad is making an effort to stay involved in my life, I'm not about to start confiding in him about personal stuff.

My ex-friendship with Silas falls under "personal stuff."

So does my relationship with RJ.

And my newly formed, intense hatred for Fenn. That absolutely needs to remain a secret right now. If Dad found out what Fenn did, he might actually kill him.

Speaking of killing Fenn, apparently RJ did no such thing tonight, judging by the texts that keep making my phone buzz in my lap. We're not allowed to have phones at the table, but I knew RJ was talking to Fenn after soccer practice, and there was no way I was missing this update.

RJ: He says it's complicated.

My gaze flicks to my lap.

Complicated?

It's *complicated*?

That's his reason for leaving my unconscious sister in the dirt and not telling a single soul all these months that he was the one who'd pulled her from the sinking car?

No.

No, I refuse to allow that to be his explanation. I *refuse*.

I draw a calming breath, but it does nothing to soothe the eddy of anger swirling in my gut along with Dad's charred steak.

"What do you think about sitting down with Mrs. Dermer sometime next week?" Dad is saying. "She'd be more than happy to offer her advice."

I glance over at Casey for some clue as to what I've missed. Then I realize Dad was talking to me.

"Me?" I ask, tonguing burnt bits of meat from between my teeth.

"Yes, Sloane." He takes a long sip of red wine to emphasize his annoyance. "College application deadlines are coming up. Wanda could look at your essays, perhaps."

"I haven't even started yet."

"Therein lies the trouble."

I smother a sigh. The misfortune of being the headmaster's

daughter—he wants to recruit his entire faculty to manage my college admissions.

"I've still got, like, two months. Relax."

I haven't even thought about college lately. I simply can't handle another hassle right now. If it's not bad enough I've got Silas creeping around behind my back like I'm going to wake up one day and realize my prince has been waiting in the shadows all along, I'm getting tugged in all directions between RJ, Fenn, and what's best for Casey.

"Tone, young lady."

"What? Why are you suddenly hassling me about college? Pester Casey for a while, will ya?"

She snorts a laugh at me. "Hey. What'd I do?"

"It's clear you've been distracted recently," Dad says, fixing a frown in my direction. "I don't want you forgetting where your priorities should be."

"I'll get to it. Jesus."

If he had any idea the Everest-sized mountain of shit I've been dealing with lately, maybe he'd cut me some slack. But of course, I can't tell him. RJ begged for a chance to turn Fenn into a decent person overnight. And telling Dad means telling Casey, and maybe that's what I'm most afraid of.

"College essays aren't something you can put off to the last minute, Sloane…"

Another message from RJ pops up and I surreptitiously lower my gaze. Essentially, he couldn't get much of anything out of Fenn. Some vague assurances and not much substance. No explanation whatsoever for why he didn't stay with Casey, much less what made him keep it a secret all this time.

RJ: He wants to be the one to tell her.

I type a response under the table, while Dad continues lecturing me about my lack of focus.

Me: I don't trust him.

RJ: Not like he has much choice now. He has to tell her.

"Are you listening, Sloane?" my father demands.

Casey kicks me under the table. I shoot her a glare because that hurt.

"Yes, I hear you," I say to him, continuing to text. "Get my butt in gear or whatever. Anything else?"

Me: And who knows what he'll say. He's lied to all of us this whole time. What's one more?

RJ: It seemed like he was genuinely sorry.

Me: Then he would have told you the truth. He's still hiding something.

"Sloane," Dad barks. "No phones during dinner."

"Actually," I say, pushing back from the table. "I'm done."

With this meal and this conversation. I'm a pot that boiled over hours ago and is sitting empty on the stove, flames licking at the backsplash.

"Sit down. We eat as a family."

"I said I'm done. I'm going for a run."

I hear utensils hit the plate in frustration behind me as I go to my room to change clothes and tie my hair up in a bun. I grab my shoes from the mudroom and head out the back door.

It's after dark, and while I mostly know these trails blindfolded, I stick to the lighted path that is the main trail toward the center of campus. I'm not in the mood to twist my ankle on a protruding tree root tonight.

I don't get far before I hear quick footsteps behind me. I glance over my shoulder to find Casey huffing and puffing, running double-time to catch me.

"Go home," I call behind me, pushing my pace to convince her she can't keep up.

"Come on, Sloane. Ease up."

"I can do this all night. You don't want to be around me right now, Case."

"Stop already. I've got a brick of burnt steak and a pound of mashed potatoes in my stomach," she whines. "Don't make me chase you."

She comes up beside me, breathing hard and already dripping sweat. I tease her, speeding up when she thinks she's caught me. Then suddenly I hear a thud and a startled yelp. I pull up to see her in the dirt behind me.

"You okay?" I hurry toward her, offering my hand to help her up.

"Yep." She pops to her feet, still smiling, if a little embarrassed. "Tripped."

"You should have stayed home."

"Or you could be a big girl and explain why you're in such a foul mood today. Is this about Silas? He looked upset when he left the house earlier."

"He should be upset. Fucking asshole."

Casey's eyebrows fly up. "Oh. Okay. I thought you said you two weren't fighting."

"We weren't. Now we are." I start walking because it feels like if I stand still a second longer, I might combust. "Don't worry about it."

"Of course I'm going to worry about it! He's your best friend." She matches my stride. "What happened?"

"It doesn't matter."

"Clearly it does," she argues.

"Oh my God. Fine. He set me up, okay?"

I feel Casey's baffled gaze on me. "Set you up how?"

"When Fenn asked me to meet him to talk about what happened between us junior year, I told Silas to cover for me with RJ." Lingering anger continues to ripple through my limbs. "Instead, he sent RJ into the woods to catch us."

She gasps. "Why would he do that?"

"Why do you think? He wants to fuck me. So he tried to sabotage my relationship."

She goes silent, and when I look over, I see her expression is still awash with confusion.

"I don't believe it," she finally says. "Silas wouldn't do that."

"He would and he did." Bitterness coats my throat.

"Are you sure there isn't another explanation? Silas is a good guy."

I can't help the burst of annoyance that goes off inside me. "Jesus, Case. Stop being so naïve. Not everyone is good or bad. Sometimes good guys end up being total assholes." I shake my head at her. "Stop putting these guys on a goddamn pedestal."

"Ah, okay. I get it. This is about Fenn." Her voice is tight. Displeased.

"It's not about Fenn."

But it is.

I've wanted to strangle the guy ever since I saw his face on the security camera. Not only that, but it's painful keeping things from my sister. I hate doing it. At the same time, I know the moment she finds out what really happened, her blissful ignorance will be shattered, and she'll spiral back into the darkness that's always waiting right on the periphery to consume her again. It seems like no matter how much she tries to put on a brave face, something comes along to snatch her back.

"I know it's awkward, okay?" she says with a sigh. "Like, in theory, it's weird that I'm dating a guy you hooked up with—"

I come up short. "Dating? What do you mean you're dating him?"

She blinks. Shamefaced.

"What the hell, Case? Last time I asked you about it, you insisted you were just friends." I knew she had a crush on him, obviously, but they'd both assured me it was platonic.

"We were friends," she replies. "And now we're more. I didn't want to say anything yet because I knew you wouldn't approve."

The gust of anger nearly knocks me off my feet. They're together now? The absolute nerve of this guy. He leaves her to die, then buddies up to her for months, and now he's goddamn *dating* her?

"No," I growl.

"Sloane, come on. I know you think I'm too naïve and inexperienced for him, but—"

"Naive?" I cut in, laughing without an ounce of humor. "We are so far beyond naive right now."

"What's that supposed to mean?"

"It means you have no idea what you've gotten yourself into."

CHAPTER 10
FENN

Despite the fact I haven't moved a muscle in bed, my watch keeps asking me if I'm working out and would I like to take a moment to breathe. Here, let me guide you through a moment of mindfulness to reflect on your mistakes before you're put against a wall for the firing squad. My heart rate hasn't slowed for hours since RJ ambushed me, as I've scrambled in my head to figure out how the hell I'm going to come clean to Casey. How to explain myself while completely incapable of offering her any satisfying answers.

Fuck.

I might be having a panic attack.

Or I'm going into cardiac arrest. Maybe the movie of my life will do me a favor and finally kill me off.

Loss has been on my mind a lot lately. I keep thinking about how small my world got after my mom died. Death does that, peels away everything right down to the core. My mother was gone. And then my dad was too. Grief tends to create a pocket of emptiness in your life that no amount of sex or illegal substances can fill.

Then I saw those taillights. A car half-submerged in the lake.

Casey filled that pocket with light. A billion stars breathed into existence. It's corny as shit and twice as depressing, but entirely true.

She's more than special. She's the kind of person they don't make enough of, who inspires everyone else with her compassion and goodness. Completely unselfish or self-impressed.

So of course, I came along and poisoned her. A slow, nearly imperceptible death.

The air in here has gotten thick and it lodges in my throat. RJ and I each went to bed about an hour ago after lights out, and I'm now lying silent in the darkness with only my thoughts to taunt me. I've been staring up at the ceiling waiting for an epiphany to point me toward a strategy. So far, one hasn't presented itself.

I swallow a groan and roll onto my side, phone in hand. I dim the screen to not disturb RJ and find myself scrolling through old chat threads with Gabe.

His very last message to me was to meet him at the boathouse because he was sick of prom.

That's it.

Everything else is my frantic messages after he was gone.

So I scroll further and further back, my chest clenched as I read years' worth of chats with my best friend. Stupid jokes. Dirty jokes. Dumb memes. Dirty memes. Making plans. Confirming plans. And here and there, deeper shit.

> Hey. I know it's the anniversary of your mom's death. Lemme know if you want to do anything to get your mind off it today. Here for you, Bishop.

> Jesus, G. I can't believe your dad reamed you out in front of everyone like that. I hope you know everything he said was total BS. You're not a dead end.

My gaze snags on one exchange in particular. It's cryptic on purpose, but we both knew what I was referring to when I sent him the message.

Me: Thanks for looking out, G. Appreciate you doing that for
me. Who tf knows where I'd be if you didn't.
Gabe: Ride or die, Bishop. You'd do the same for me.
Me: 100%

Fuck. I miss him. I like RJ a hell of a lot, I really do, but Gabe
and I have history. We've been raising hell since we were little kids.
We lost our virginities on the same night at a freshman party, for
fuck's sake, then gossiped about it afterward like a pair of schoolgirls.
He's one of the few people I can truly be myself around.

Gabe, and now Casey.

I feel totally and completely stuck between the two. No wiggle
room whatsoever.

When the tightness in my chest becomes unbearable, I text
Casey to get this over with.

Me: You awake?

It's nearly twenty agonizing minutes before she responds. The typing dots blink on the screen then disappear. Twice. Three and four times.

Casey: Yeah.
Me: Sorry if I woke you.
Casey: You didn't. What is it?

Her abrupt tone catches me off guard. Yes, it's past midnight,
but she said she wasn't asleep.

Me: Can we meet up?
Casey: It's late.

Again, that gives me pause. She's never had a problem sneaking
out in the middle of the night before.

Me: Please. It's important.

The dots blink with indecision. Something's up with her and it gets all the hairs on my arms standing up.

Casey: Fine. See you in 20.

"You sneaking out?" RJ rolls over in bed as I stand in front of my closet getting dressed.

"Yeah. Going to talk to Casey. Get it over with. I can't stand thinking about it anymore."

His bedsheets rustle as he sits up. I glance over, see him running a hand through his rumpled brown hair. Even in the darkness, I can make out his unhappy expression.

"What is it?" I ask.

"Before you go. You should know," he says. "Sloane told her."

My heart stops.

Because of course she did. Fucking Sloane.

"You couldn't have warned me earlier?" I demand.

"I didn't see her text until now. She sent it when I was already in bed."

"Awesome. Fucking great. Your girlfriend just made an impossible conversation that much more difficult," I tell him, pulling on a hoodie. "So thanks for that."

"Sorry, man, but this one's on you."

Sure, I dug this grave. I've known for months I was up against the clock and that every day I spent with Casey I was braiding the rope from which I would eventually hang. Still, feeling the empty air under my dangling feet is a little different. The floor's dropped out, but the fall didn't snap my neck. Now I'm writhing with hands tied behind my back and watching the faces of everyone gathered stare in horrific anticipation of my last breath.

I have no idea what I'm walking into as I trudge across campus and take the trail into the woods toward Casey's house. Sloane has snatched away any chance I had of getting Casey to understand I was only trying to help and got in over my head. It's not like I had some dastardly plan to pose as her beta male best pal to trick my way into her pants. But I'm sure that's exactly what Sloane's been putting in her head all night. Brilliant.

For nearly twenty minutes I'm left to stew on it until Casey finds me in the beam of her flashlight. Struck by the moment's sudden arrival and her eerily silent approach, I'm left speechless. All the preamble I'd hastily written in my head goes blank.

"Casey—"

"Stop." The sharpness in her voice is a sound I've never heard before, and it cuts me off at the knees. "There isn't anything I want to hear from you."

"Casey, please—"

"You're a liar, Fenn. And an asshole. And probably the worst person I've ever met in real life."

She doesn't let me see her, remaining hidden behind the light that forces me to shield my eyes. But her voice contains the gravelly strain that comes with tears, and it rips me apart knowing I'm the reason she's crying.

"That's fair," I say weakly. "But—"

"How can you even show your face after you left me there passed out on the ground? Who does that?" Her voice pitches up another notch, and I don't think I've ever felt so small. "You let me cry on your shoulder all this time. Pretending to understand. And what, laughing at me? Congratulating yourself for how well you pulled it all off?"

"No, fuck. Of course not." I make a move toward her and think I feel a rock breeze past my arm. "That's what I'm trying—"

"Right now, Fenn. Tell me the truth. It's the only words I want to hear. Why did you do it? Why did you lie to me all this time and never tell anyone you were there?"

My chest clenches, hands trembling with agony. What am I supposed to say? That my best friend might have drugged her and left her for dead? And my first instinct was to cover for him? That I'm *still* covering for him, because I can't square it in my head how someone I've known practically my entire life could almost kill a girl and walk away from it.

And not just a girl. Not just Sloane's little sister. But basically the kindest, sweetest person any of us can claim to know. The one person who least deserves all the shit we've put her through.

If I could only tell her a fraction of that, maybe I wouldn't have this hollow feeling in my gut. But I can't make the words come out, and it's then I realize, when she drops the flashlight and my vision slowly adjusts to her red, swollen face shiny with tears, that I've always been a bastard. I thought I could bury the worst parts of myself. For her. Except in some sick twist, she's what makes me so terrible—I'd do anything for her, except be a decent person.

I finally find my voice. "I wanted to tell you. But I waited too long. So long that eventually I felt like it was too late to—"

"It's never too late to tell the truth," she cuts in. "And you haven't explained why you had to wait in the first place! Why not tell everyone the night it happened?"

Because he's my best friend.

Because I didn't know you.

Because I left you there instead of calling 911.

The words get stuck in my throat. When Casey and I were strangers, it would have been much easier to admit that my loyalties on prom night lay with Gabe and Gabe alone. And back then I still believed I'd have a chance to get the truth out of him. I didn't expect his parents to exile him into a black hole and that I'd never talk to him again.

But Casey and I are no longer strangers, which means that now, telling her my loyalties weren't with *her* first feels like a betrayal.

"Fenn," she says, softly begging me to end this suffering. Give her the one thing she wants most, that only I can offer. The truth. "Please."

"I…can't," I mumble, and I deserve every bit of what happens now.

Casey sniffs and wipes her face. "I guess you always knew this would happen, huh?"

My own eyes feel hot. Stinging hard. "In the worst possible way."

She takes a step back, her running shoes crunching the dry leaves beneath them. "Okay. Okay, well. I guess this is done now." The breath she lets out sounds unsteady, wheezy.

The lump in my throat almost chokes me. I blink wildly. I bite my bottom lip so hard, I taste copper on the tip of my tongue.

"Please," I find myself begging.

"Please what?" She takes another step away.

"Please don't leave me," I whisper.

A strangled sob flies out of her mouth. "Fuck you, Fenn. The next time you see me, run the other way. We're not friends. We're nothing." She's walking backwards now, her movements unsteady, jerky. "I mean it. Don't *ever* talk to me again."

CHAPTER 11
CASEY

A SUDDEN IMPACT JOLTS ME AWAKE. BUT I CAN'T MOVE. IT'S DARK, save for colored tiny lights that blur my vision. A sharp, throbbing sensation rips through my skull. And then I'm freezing. Water rises up my legs. I struggle against my restraints, screaming, thrashing, only succeeding in tightening the force holding me in place. The water gushes inside the car, climbing my torso, while I yank on the door latch.

Suddenly it gives way, pulled from my grasp.

Fenn finds me in the glow of the dashboard lights.

I'm relieved to see him as he reaches across my body to unhook my seat belt. But when I try to pry myself free of the car, I find the straps still firm across my body. I reach for him, desperate. But he shoves my hands away, gripping the belt across my chest and cinching it tighter.

His dead stare is impervious to my frightened pleas for help.

"Fenn!" I scream.

I claw at him. Fighting even as he again forces the door closed with me inside. The water rushes up my neck, overcoming my mouth and nose. I take one last gulp of air and watch Fenn rise to the surface, leaving me trapped inside the car descending deeper into pure darkness.

Then I'm floating free in the endless black void. Released from the car but inescapably pulled deeper, my limbs exhausted and too heavy to swim for the surface. The silver light of the moon is an unreachable point, growing smaller, far above my head. I stare up at it as I sink, aware of every second of my journey toward death.

I don't know what finally tears my eyes open. I wake screaming with the blankets tangled tight around my legs, encased and thrashing inside the cocoon of knotted sheets.

It's seconds before I notice the sun pouring into my room and take several gasping breaths. I feel my phone under my pillow and my first instinct is to text Fenn. The person I've turned to when the nightmares leave me shaken and licking the taste of blood from my mouth.

Only this time, he's the reason I'm drenched in sweat and my chest is on fire.

"Is that what it felt like when you knew you weren't coming back up?" I whisper to Mom.

I don't get an answer before Dad bursts into the room looking pale. He's tailed by the dogs, who jump onto the mattress to investigate the commotion.

"Are you all right?" He sits on the edge of my bed as I push up against my headboard. "What happened? Another nightmare?"

"I'm fine," I mutter, ducking away from his attempt to wipe my hair from my face. Then I shove Bo's snout away when he tries to lick my cheek. All this hovering is too much. "You know you don't have to come charging in here every time like I'm being eaten by the monster under my bed."

"If you'd heard you scream," he says, somewhat offended.

"I'm fine."

"Maybe it's time to talk to someone again, sweetheart."

Why do people always say "someone" like they can hide the pill in a rolled-up piece of bologna?

"You mean another shrink?" I scoff. "Pass."

"I'm not sure it was a good idea to stop seeing the therapist," he tells me.

"I tried it. It didn't help. I haven't remembered anything new about the accident at all."

"That wasn't the sole reason for going to therapy, Case. We can't just ignore your diagnosis and hope it goes away on its own."

My diagnosis can fuck right off. I have PTSD, I get it. But talking about it hasn't alleviated any of the symptoms. I still get the flashbacks. The nightmares. The sheer panic that grips me at random moments of the day. My psychiatrist, Dr. Anthony, prescribed medication to try to help me, but I didn't feel like myself when I was on the meds, so she took me off them. It's ironic—they pumped me full of pills to ease the post-trauma symptoms, those bouts of crippling, emotional numbness, and the pills just made me even more emotionally numb.

"I'm not going back on meds," I say flatly.

"That's not what I'm suggesting. I just think you need to keep talking about the trauma," he presses with the look he gets when he's trying to psychically change my mind. "Ignoring PTSD symptoms can lead to other issues. Depression. Substance abuse. Eating dis—"

"Disorders," I finish. "Yes, I remember." I throw the blanket off and climb out of bed. "I'm fine, Dad. I'm not depressed. And I'm not doing drugs or starving myself. So please, drop it. I need to get ready for school."

At breakfast, Sloane sneaks worried peeks my way as I force myself to eat the omelet Dad prepared. It tastes fine, but it's a struggle to finish it. Not because I'm succumbing to an eating disorder as he fears, but because my appetite is nonexistent. My stomach is too unsettled, twisted into knots after the shock I received last night.

Fenn has been lying to me for months.

Months.

He's held my hand and hugged me and let me cry in his arms.

He let me go on and on about how devastating the accident was. How it ruined my life. I lost my friends. My school. My reputation.

Yes, I get that Fenn wasn't responsible for the accident itself—Sloane said the security video made it clear he wasn't the driver. But that doesn't change the fact that he lied. And I could have died while I was lying there on the bank of the lake, unconscious, bleeding from a head wound.

I could have *died*.

I feel Sloane watching me again and shove the last bite of omelet into my mouth. I need this breakfast to be over. I can't deal with any of this right now. The vicious cycle of overprotection and aggressive mothering that engages every time Dad tells my sister I'm off my rocker again.

She waits until Dad leaves for work to finally bring up what's weighing on her mind. "So RJ talked to Fenn."

The legs of my chair scrape the hardwood floor as I abruptly push back from the table and walk over to dump my plate in the sink. The dogs follow me, hoping and praying that some breakfast scraps fall to the floor and into their eager mouths.

"I'll be in the car," I mutter before stalking out of the room.

For months, my life hasn't been my own. Everyone feels entitled to, or responsible for, some piece of it. All of them muscling their way toward the center. And none of them hear me. They assume anything I say is a riddle to decipher, when really, sometimes I simply want to be left alone.

But on the drive to school, Sloane can't help herself.

"I know you don't want to talk about it," she starts.

"So, you're going to anyway." I keep my gaze out the windshield.

"Have you spoken to Fenn?"

Please don't leave me.

My heart shrieks with agony as his tortured plea whispers through my mind.

God. I can't erase the torrent of pain in his blue eyes when he'd asked me not to leave him, and yet at the same time it sparks a jolt of fury. How dare he look at me like that? Like *I* was the one in the wrong. Like I was committing some atrocious act by walking away from his sorry ass.

"I know you mean well, but I have one request," I say, still staring straight ahead. "Never mention Fenn's name to me again." It stings in my teeth. Turns my tongue sour.

"Okay…" Sloane slides a brief glance at me.

I know she wants to ask for details, and I hope my demeanor is projecting that she does so at her own risk.

"But we have to figure out what to do about the security video," she reminds me. "It's probably evidence tampering or something if we don't give it to the cops. And there might be a chance they can use it to figure out who was driving—"

"I don't care," I mumble to myself. I'm restless and exhausted. Sorry I didn't feign sick and stay in bed.

This day hasn't even started yet, and I can't wait for it to end.

"What'd you say?"

"I said I don't care," I repeat, louder. "I don't care who was driving. I don't care about any of it anymore. Delete the video for all I care. I'm done with all of this. I want to move on and forget about it."

"Case."

In disbelief, Sloane watches the side of my face while I turn to look out the window at the parking lot and into another day of whispers and innuendo. The butt of every joke. A one-dimensional person reduced to a single event.

"I'm serious," I tell my sister. "I don't care about the accident or the tape. It's over."

I hop out of the car and slam the door behind me, not giving Sloane a chance to argue or dive into another long and involved conversation about my emotional state. My *state* is fed up. Thoroughly bored with myself. Tired of this rut and knowing every day when I walk into school, I'm the girl who got fished out of the lake at prom.

"God, Casey. You look terrible." Ainsley spots me walking to my locker. She catches up, flanking me with Bree. "Rough night?"

Sloane would have some witty comeback. A biting remark that would cut Ainsley off at the knees and devastate her so completely, her grandkids would have bruises.

But I hate confrontation. What's the point? As much as I like to imagine a different version of myself, I'm not the girl who likes to fill the hallway with her voice, to make everyone stop and look. Instead, I put my head down and keep walking, quick enough that they'd feel silly following, until finally I'm around the corner and out of sight.

As I grab my textbook for first period, I catch a glimpse of someone watching me a few lockers down. Jazmine something or other. She's in half my classes. I said hi to her on the first day of school, and she'd merely shrugged and muttered, "Yeah, okay."

As far as I can tell, she keeps to herself, same as me. Except in her case, it seems to be self-imposed. She's pretty enough that she could easily hang out with girls like Ainsley and Bree, yet she prefers to sit alone in the dining hall, focused on her phone. Me, I'd give anything to have someone to sit with at lunch. An ally who isn't my older sister.

Jazmine smirks when our eyes meet. I don't know what she finds so amusing, but I avert my gaze and walk away.

CHAPTER 12
RJ

FENN IS BARELY PRESENT ON THE WAY TO BREAKFAST BEFORE CLASS in the morning. Vacant, shuffling across the courtyard to the dining hall with his head down. I had to catch him on the way out of our room to put shoes on when he almost walked out barefoot. I don't know what to do with him like this. This isn't the Fenn Bishop I know. The guy with the easy grins and dirty jokes and weird comments. In the hot food line, he's an empty vessel. Caught in a trance. I pull a tray for him and stick food on it because I'm not sure he's aware of his surroundings. I suspect it's just automatic motor responses that get him as far as our usual table to sit and stare blankly at the distance.

Fenn's been utterly devastated since he came back from seeing Casey last night, which I took to mean things didn't go well. How could they? Casey's a forgiving girl, but everyone has their limits. Whatever she said to him, it snatched his soul from this meat suit and now all that's left is the eerie absence of his former self.

"Do you want to talk about it?" I say cautiously.

I don't get even an eye twitch in my direction.

"How much did you tell her?" I ask.

Sloane texted late last night after Casey came storming in, all revved up and fuming. But Casey wouldn't elaborate about how much information she managed to drag out of Fenn. If any. Sloane said she'd never seen her sister so enraged.

I try another tack, seeing if I can jostle his brain awake like pull-starting a lawnmower. "Sloane hasn't decided yet about going to the cops with the video. It would help things a lot if you could make me understand what happened that night. Why you didn't tell anyone."

Fenn blinks but doesn't seem capable of responding. Whatever it is that's kept him guarding this secret, its hold has only gotten tighter. He does relax a little, however, after he manages to pick his way through some breakfast. Gets a little color back in his cheeks. Enough that he nods to acknowledge Lucas when he drops into a seat at our table.

"You hungover?" Lucas says with a grin, unwrapping a muffin. "You look like you woke up next to the toilet."

Fenn shrugs and gulps a glass of juice. "Something like that."

Lucas picks off a piece of his chocolate muffin and chews around it while he turns to me. "So, listen. I need a favor."

The kid isn't shy. I'll give him that.

"Oh, yeah?"

"It has to do with my brother."

At that, Fenn becomes alert, showing signs of life with mention of his best friend. He and Lucas talk about almost nothing else when they get together. But Gabe was before my time.

"Okay," I say slowly. "What about him?"

"I finally know the name of the military school they sent him to." His gaze flicks briefly to Fenn, whose shoulders have gone stiff. "Got it out of my Uncle Diego on the phone yesterday. Apparently he's the one who helped Dad get Gabe a slot there. So I did some research and realized it's even worse than we thought. They literally have him under, like, twenty-four-hour lock and key at this place."

"All right. What's my part in this?"

"If you're up for the challenge," he says with a goading smirk, "you can find a way to contact him for me."

"Can't you just ask your parents?"

Lucas snorts. "They haven't spoken his name since he left. Mom starts muttering a prayer every time I mention it, and Dad loses his shit. They won't let me talk to him. According to them, he shamed our family."

Grinning, I shove some scrambled eggs into my mouth. "That's some old-school shit."

"Dude. You don't know the half of it. Finding out your son is dealing drugs is like the ultimate shame for my dad. I doubt Gabe will ever be welcome in our house again." The notion brings a cloud of sadness to Lucas's eyes. "Anyway, I want to talk to my brother. Can you help?"

I consider it for a moment, because it's a tough task and I know there isn't much in it for me. Unlike most of his trust-fund peers, Lucas's dad is a tightwad with cash. Which means Lucas is honestly kind of a mooch most of the time. So it's not like I can expect any monetary compensation for this gig. I guess this is what they mean by goodness of your heart.

"Yeah, all right," I tell him. Because it sounds like an interesting challenge, and I've gotten to know Lucas well enough that I understand how much it's bothered him not talking to his big brother. "Text me the name of the school and anything that might be helpful."

"Hey, uh…" Fenn concentrates on his scrambled eggs rather than look up. "If you do figure it out, I want to contact him too."

I'm startled by the twinge of jealousy that ripples through me. I have to remind myself that no matter how close Fenn and I have been getting lately, we've still only known each other a few months. It makes sense he wants to talk to his longtime friend. When faced with the existential crisis of a broken heart, Sloane on a rampage, and possible jail time, of course he might need the counsel of someone who's known him longer than the expiration on a carton of milk. And I imagine he's feeling a little light on friends lately. Silas has made himself scarce the past couple of weeks, which means Lawson isn't around much either. I see them at swim practice whether I like it or not, but Fenn's gotten iced out. A casualty of Silas's petty beef with me. Much as he can, Lawson has remained a neutral party. I think mostly because he's even less impressed with Silas's recent heel turn than I am.

In lit class thirty minutes later, I grab my usual seat beside Lawson just as a tired-looking man with thick-rimmed glasses walks in to set his coffee mug and stack of books on Mr. Goodwyn's desk at the front of the room.

"Hello," the man says with a three-pack-a-day grate in his voice. The stench of cigarettes travels quickly to the back row of desks. "I'm Mr. Matarese. I'll be your instructor this week. Maybe next week too. We'll see."

He's got an intense aura about him like he's seen some shit. The kind of guy who spends the weekend polishing his gun and watching *Full Metal Jacket*. Cuts lines of Sylvia Plath out of books and tapes them to his fridge.

"What, like a sub?" someone asks.

"Does this mean we don't have a quiz today?" Asa the kiss-ass interjects. "What happened to Mr. Goodwyn?"

Mr. Matarese opens a file folder full of stapled pages and hands stacks to the first people in each row to pass back.

"Mr. Goodwyn resigned his position for a family emergency. You've got twenty minutes for the quiz. Keep your eyes on your own paper."

Lawson chuckles to himself as we both grab our quizzes.

"You know something about this?" I ask suspiciously.

Gray eyes gleaming, he gives me a coy shrug while pulling a pencil from his bag. "Of course not. How could I?"

By Thursday, Fenn is still a walking coma patient and barely saying anything to anyone. And to add insult to injury, the subtext with Silas is getting unbearable. Lawson's set his sights on the new junior, which leaves Silas and me as stretching partners for cooldown after practice.

If you've ever looked into the face of someone while they've thought about holding your head underwater until your limbs stop thrashing, you can imagine the awkward.

Silas is scowling. Gritting his teeth. Seething and spiteful, but too chickenshit to say his piece, so he communicates in dirty looks and silent treatment, lest I confuse any of our interactions for friendly.

When we get out of the showers and he pretends not to notice he's blocking my locker, I've finally had it.

"Get it off your chest already," I snap. "Or get out of the way. I don't care which."

Lawson, who's standing fully naked a few feet away, smothers an excited grin because he's been dying for this confrontation for two weeks. Lawson Kent loves chaos. It didn't take more than a few hours at Sandover Prep for me to learn that. The guy craves destruction, both self and otherwise, on a level that's almost scary.

Silas turns, throwing his gym bag over his shoulder. "I take it Sloane told you."

"She did. And it's fucked up."

He shrugs in an attempt to look nonchalant, even when we both know he'd rather bust knuckles.

I'd take that fight, no hesitation. Except Silas is a coward and prefers being a passive-aggressive asshole. Trying to make Sloane feel small or insecure so she'll run into his arms is a beta fuck move, and it's finally shown me his true face. He was decent to me when I first got here but stopped being nice the second Sloane showed interest in me. Since I suspected almost instantly that he has a thing for her, it's sort of validating to finally have that confirmed.

"I'm not going to apologize for trying to protect my friend from some random new guy I barely know," Silas says.

"Fine. Don't apologize. Just know I'm on my girlfriend's side. Always."

"Meow," Lawson drawls. He claws at the air, enjoying himself.

"Whatever, Shaw. Have fun in the never-ending drama that is Sloane Tresscott."

Nothing gets resolved, and I don't try to stop him when he rolls his eyes at me and leaves. Because there's not much left to say to each other. He's not sorry and I'm not forgiving, so we're at an impasse.

Anyway, I've got other shit to deal with. After I finish getting dressed, I meet up with Fenn and Lucas in the computer lab. I texted them before swim practice to wait for me there. Took me a couple of days, but it wasn't as hard as I thought to figure a way through the communications blackout at Gabe's school. Although there is one small catch.

"Five grand," I tell Lucas.

"Fuck off, seriously?" He's aghast at the price tag, and I don't blame him.

"I tried to talk him down, but I wasn't in a great bargaining position." I'm almost positive I'm not the first person this dude's shaken down. "I found a security guard at the school who is willing to take a bribe to pass a message."

"That's it? I was thinking something like we get him to sneak Gabe a phone."

"No, nothing like that. Students are legit strip-searched and have room inspections every day."

Fenn throws a sideways look at Lucas. "The hell kind of place did your dad send him?"

"If they find a violation," I continue, "they don't just get kicked out. It's a whole corporal punishment situation over there."

"Jesus." Fenn spins away in his rolling chair then gets up to pace the rows of dark computers.

Lucas slumps, dragging his hands through his hair. "Dude, I don't have five grand. Not even close."

"That's the best I can do on short notice."

I feel bad for him, but this isn't my usual sort of gig. I can't hack my way through a firewall to Gabe. The human element tends to make these things much more complicated.

Fenn quits pacing. "I can cover it," he says. "I'll wire you the money tonight."

I nod. "Done. I'll let him know."

Lucas shoots up from his chair. "What, seriously?" He's gaping at Fenn.

My stepbrother shrugs, blue eyes going shuttered. "No sweat. Won't even make a dent in my account."

I don't doubt that.

"Fenn, thank you, man." Lucas is practically ecstatic with relief. "I wish I could say I'd pay you back, but—"

"It's cool."

"Anything you ever need, I've got your back."

"Text me what you want the message to say," I remind them. "Both of you. I'll pass it along."

"Hey, uh, one thing." On our way out of the lab, Fenn stops Lucas. "How's Casey? You talk to her lately?"

Lucas suddenly becomes a little cagey. Apparently all that gratitude didn't last long. "Yeah," he offers in a noncommittal tone. "We talk."

I want to be anywhere else, but I can't walk fast enough to get out of earshot. Watching Fenn pine is getting exhausting.

"Okay, and?" Fenn pushes.

That gets him a pained look. "I'm not getting in the middle of anything."

"Dude, come on."

"I'm sorry. She doesn't say much." Lucas seems as desperate as I am to be anywhere else than at the mercy of Fenn's brokenhearted grasping. Maybe that's why he goes for the jugular, hoping it'll be enough to get Fenn off his back. "Only thing she's sure of is that she wants nothing to do with you."

CHAPTER 13
CASEY

Lucas: Fenn asked about you earlier. Kind of cornered me on it, actually.

Me: He can rot in hell.

Lucas: Tell me how you really feel lol

LUCAS IS STILL TYPING, SO I PUT DOWN MY PHONE FOR A SECOND and finish brushing my hair as I get ready for school on Friday morning. When I check again, there's a long message waiting on the screen.

Lucas: If it helps, I never thought Fenn was good enough for you anyway. I watched him and Gabe get into all kinds of fucked-up stuff over the years. The dude drinks too much, like he thinks it makes up for his lack of substance.

I'm typing an objection before I can stop myself. A sudden instinct to defend Fenn.

Me: Just because he's a lying asshole doesn't mean he lacks substance.

I know how Fenn comes off to most people. And I suspect it's intentional. The party boy facade masks all the ways he's still struggling to hold himself together. Fenn feels everything so deeply in ways most people will never understand.

He's also entirely undeserving of my defense, so I push the thought aside. Whatever good qualities he has, he did something unforgivable. There's no coming back from that. I don't care how sad and lonely he is. I'm not about to get suckered into that trap again, and even the momentary urge to feel sorry for Fenn reignites the smoldering embers of my rage. He took my friendship for granted and made me a doormat. Because kindness is a quality people never fail to abuse. They assume it makes us weak and naive. I guess in my case they're right.

I *was* weak and naive. I was stupid to trust him. Stupid to love him. And the anger I feel toward both him and myself stays with me all morning.

During first period, I could snap pencils with my eyelids. It doesn't help that throughout class, Ainsley and Bree sit in front of me and can't shut the hell up, their voices like yappy, barking dogs in the middle of the night who won't let me sleep. I don't want to listen, but it's impossible to concentrate on anything else.

"Gray's taking me to Boston this weekend to see Taylor Swift from his dad's skybox," Bree gushes. "It's going to be, like, the most."

"Are you flying in?" Ainsley asks her.

"No, I'm pretty sure the skybox is inside the building."

Sister Katherine looks over from her desk as the two giggle to themselves. We're supposed to be working on our outlines for the major history paper due next month.

"Focus on your work, ladies," she chides.

"You could ask Lawson out and we could double," Bree says as if the teacher hadn't even spoken.

Lawson? As in Lawson Kent?

That gets my attention, mostly because I can't imagine that guy going on a *double date*. Have they even *met* him? From what I know of Lawson, his idea of a good time would be doing lines of cocaine off a girl's bare butt and then daring each other to jump in front of moving trains and try not to die.

"Right, sure." Ainsley gives a sarcastic laugh.

"Don't you still like him?"

"Duh. He's basically obsessed with me. He just doesn't know it yet."

Bree cocks her with confusion. "Didn't he call you Amy the one time he talked to you?"

"Shut up." Ainsley huffs her frustration. "He'll come to me. I just need to find a way to get close to him first."

"You know where he hangs out. That nasty bar in town. You should go there and make him notice."

Wow, that's sad. Imagine thinking it's that hard to get in Lawson's pants. Or that he'd even remember your name the next morning.

I'm tempted to text Lawson and let him know he's got a secret admirer. I think I still have his number in my phone from when he messaged me after the accident to see if I was okay. I thought that was really nice of him, but then Sloane and I bumped into him on campus one morning on our way to Dad's office, and he'd donned a blank look when I brought it up and admitted he must've texted when he was high or drunk.

I must let a snicker or two slip because suddenly Ainsley jerks up.

"Mind your business much?" She turns around with nostrils flared. "Are you spying on our conversations now?"

Bree gives me a snide look. "That's creepy, Casey."

"Oh my God, you're going to, like, stalk us, aren't you?" Ainsley raises her voice because she likes an audience. "Eavesdrop so you can show up everywhere we go. That is so disturbed."

Bree turns to Ainsley, suddenly serious. "No, but the concert's sold out. She won't get in."

"Fucking seriously?" I laugh in Ainsley's face. "I'd rather count the blood vessels on the inside of my eyelids than follow you two vapid imbeciles around all weekend."

I don't know where it comes from, but I snap. The entire class stops to watch me fully lose my shit. At a neighboring desk, that girl Jazmine is laughing into her hand.

"I have sweaters with more personality," I aim at a shocked Ainsley. "And I don't know what's wrong with this one," I say, nodding at Bree who turns to look behind her, "but she's obviously suffered some sort of traumatic brain injury from all the pills her mother was popping while she was pregnant."

The bell rings, and before Sister Katherine can break us up or throw me in detention, I grab my bag and slap my quiz on her desk. Then I walk out of there on a strange high that has me a little dizzy. My fingertips are cold and sensitive when I open my locker and stick my head in to take deep breaths. I don't know where that came from, but it was exhilarating. Like I'd been hijacked. Fully disembodied and not in control of my own voice.

And I loved it.

Because fuck those girls. Fuck this school.

I'm coming out of my shell armed.

When I pull my head out of my locker, I notice someone out of the corner of my eye. Jazmine leans against the wall of gray metal, once again sporting a smirk on her face.

"What's your problem now?" I demand, fixing her with a scowl.

"Not a thing." Her lips curve again, dark eyes dancing with humor. "That was fun."

It was. But I don't know this girl and I'm still wary of her intentions.

"So, what do you want?" I put my history textbook away and grab my homework for second period.

"Nothing. I'm just impressed," she says, watching me. "About time you show some backbone. I keep hearing about your sister cutting people down. I was starting to think she was the only Tresscott with some actual balls."

I slam my locker shut. "Whatever."

I'm almost surprised Ainsley and Bree haven't shown up with their crew for a rematch, but the hallway remains bitch-free. I start walking to second period while Jazmine matches my steps. Her skirt is about three inches shorter than regulation, the top two buttons of her white shirt unbuttoned. Mine are buttoned to the neck.

"Feel a little taller now, don't you?" Her voice holds a mocking note. "The colors are brighter, right?"

"If you say so."

"What's next for those two?" she asks with a laugh. "You've had weeks to think about what you'd do when you worked up the nerve."

She's not wrong. They've been on my case since I transferred to this school. Cruel. Relentless. Ainsley especially, with her insatiable appetite for tormenting me for little else than sick entertainment.

Yeah, I've thought about it.

"Not sure what's next," I answer. "All I know is I'm officially out of patience, so they better watch their step."

"Or what?"

I glance over, dead serious. "Or I'll ruin their fucking lives."

CHAPTER 14
LAWSON

THIS DESOLATE ISLAND OF MISFIT BOYS HAS BECOME AN UNBEARABLE prison of boredom. I'm almost sorry I was so efficient at causing the departure of the soon-to-be ex-Mr. and Mrs. Goodwyn. They did make a cute couple. And yes, I know it makes me a diabolical asshole, seducing two teachers and destroying their relationship, but I enjoyed playing with them. Besides, I'm not the one who said those marriage vows. Ergo, it's not my problem they cheated on each other with me. But it is my problem that they're gone. They were a nice distraction from the ever-so-dull normality of being that has become the life-sucking status quo at Sandover.

I hate monotony.

Fucking loathe it.

"Every hour you spend in here is accelerating your midlife crisis," I tell Silas, who is nested on the couch with his phone. Thumbs furiously engaged. "Unless that thing can suck your dick, put it away."

"Can't you find some way to entertain yourself for one night?" he mutters. "I don't feel like going out."

No, he'd rather spend his Friday night sulking in a dead-end relationship with Amy because he was punching way above his weight class when Sloane subjected him to the verbal equivalent of yanking his pants down and laughing at his penis. Poor baby. Instead of being an adult about it and finding some willing participant to bed down and get over it, he's decided to throw a moping party. Self-pity is so excruciatingly tedious.

"We could watch each other jerk off," I suggest instead.

"Lawson, seriously. Go bother someone else for a while."

Buzzkill.

Tumbler full of bourbon in hand, I wander out of our room and find a whole lot of nothingness. It's like a goddamn psych ward around here. Empty halls under flickering lights. Everyone locked up in their rooms watching TV. It's Friday night. What the fuck is wrong with these people?

I poke my head in RJ and Fenn's room, but that's a mistake.

"Come on," I announce to Fenn, who's lying in bed with his headphones on. "Get up. Let's go out."

"Dude, no. I'm not in the mood." He grumbles and tosses a notebook at me from across the room.

"Incredible." I lean in the doorway, shaking my head in disapproval. "Half this floor is pining over a Tresscott when there are plenty of quality candidates out there waiting for a guy to take a body shot off their tits."

"You haven't talked to Casey, have you?" he asks through the one-track lens that filters out everything else. "No shit, I'll give you five hundred dollars if you get her on the phone."

"All right, well, that sounds like a horrific misuse of my time. So no." I glance at RJ's side of the room, which looks like it's barely been touched in days. "Where's your better half?"

"RJ? I don't know. With Sloane, I assume."

Of course. Those two have become disgusting.

"Fine, then. I'm off." I pause, however, to glance back at Fenn. His sullen face is cause for concern. "I'm not going to come back here to find you swinging from the ceiling fan, correct?"

"Piss off, Lawson."

"Right. Buenos noches."

My absolute last resort is playing pool by himself in the lounge, which is basically an extra-large man cave full of leather couches, game tables, and a snack bar that the Sandover staff restocks daily.

Duke Jessup is a cringeworthy drinking buddy and a worse wingman, but he has protein powder where his gray matter should be, so his buttons are easily pushed, which is itself a sort of diversion. He's in a pair of plaid pants and his trademark muscle shirt, feet bare as he walks toward the end of the pool table to break. If he weren't such an insufferable jackass, maybe I'd try to fuck him. With his dark hair and piercing eyes, Duke is undeniably hot.

But alas…the whole insufferable jackass thing.

"How far the mighty have fallen," I drawl and grab a cue off the rack. "Traveling a bit light these days, I see."

There was a time when an entourage followed Duke wherever his feet touched the ground. Not so much anymore. The dethroned ruler of Sandover looks lonely in retirement.

"Laugh it up, chucklefuck." He walks around the table, lining up his next shot. "Your buddy is already losing control of this school. He can't hold that mountain forever."

"It's funny how much you care about this, because he cares so very little."

RJ fought Duke for supreme command of this obscene kingdom against his will. It was purely a mission of self-preservation that, admittedly with some convincing, got wildly out of hand. RJ accepted the job reluctantly and is still fighting a losing battle to dismantle the authoritarian systems to which we've all become so accustomed. Mostly, he wishes everyone would leave him the hell alone. Meanwhile, all Duke wants is his royal court back.

"You know, Lawson." Duke sinks his shot and then another, concentrating only on the table and the geometry of his next move. "I know you came here to pick a fight or whatever. Normally I'd oblige, but I'm not into it tonight. Stay and have next game if you want. Otherwise, get the fuck out of here."

Under other circumstances I might object, keep poking until I hit a nerve. But he's kind of dull this evening.

"You're no fun," I tell him. "None of you assholes are any fun tonight."

I hand him my cue, then pop back into my room long enough to grab my phone and jacket.

Somewhere in this town, there must be trouble lurking that's worthy of my considerable talents. As it goes most nights, I have the driver deliver me to the doorstep of the squalid little bar in Calden, where, thankfully, there are actual signs of life.

It's well known that this is one of the few places within a sixty-mile radius where minors can get suitably inebriated if they slip the right bartender a generous tip. Which means tonight the place is filthy with drunken prep school teenagers all hornily gawking at one another from across the room. The restroom stalls rattle with hurried hookups while I do a bump at the sink with a football jock from Ballard with exceptionally long eyelashes.

"Do I know you?" he asks, squinting like he might recognize me in the right light. "You look familiar."

I haven't the slightest clue, but that doesn't mean we aren't acquainted. Who can keep track?

"I can put my dick in your mouth if that might help jog your memory."

He forces a grim laugh and takes himself elsewhere because he can't take a joke. Children. So sensitive.

A few Don Julios later, I don't remember how I got here or why I came, only that even getting trashed seems more effort than it's worth. I find myself in a booth with a group of loud St. Vincent's chicks who smell of vodka-cranberries and hairspray. They talk about their boyfriends while angling to drink more than the girl next to them, so I know how eager they are to cheat on their unsuspecting beaus.

"New game," one of them announces, and I don't know if she's talking to us or her phone. Her mascara is a cloud around her eyes while she flaps her hand at the table to command our attention. "Taking turns, you have to answer every question we ask for sixty seconds. If you don't answer, you have to take a shot."

"Yes!" Another one pounds the table. Her ponytail has fallen, and her hair hangs like it's passed out over the toilet of her head. "We need shots!" she screams to the bar, and by some miracle they arrive moments later.

They smell like cheap well liquor, which I'm sure the bartender will charge as Grey Goose. Because why shouldn't he.

"You first." A blonde props her chin on her fist and gazes deeply into my blurry eyes.

"The answer's yes," I preempt, a grin tugging on my lips.

"You don't even know what I was going to ask."

"Don't need to."

"Ever had sex in public?"

"Yes."

"Ever had a threesome?"

"Yes."

"You're not doing it right," her friend chides. "What's better during sex, coke or weed?" She's so impressed with herself that I have to laugh.

"Everything's better on coke. Except camping."

We go around the table like that until it devolves to them daring each other to kiss because there's nothing more outrageous to straight girls than performative queerness.

"Courtney got eaten out by her cousin," one of them announces after gulping down my tequila, which she grabs right out of my hand like I'm not even here.

"Shut up, Beth!"

"What? You did."

"Cousin by marriage," she screeches, her face burning red. "And I didn't know he was Terry's nephew at the time."

"He was running the go-kart track on Cape Cod." Beth giggles, quite amused by manual labor. "Her mom basically married a carnie."

"God, you're such a cunt. He owns, like, amusement parks or whatever."

Things go sideways as the two of them bicker and their friends take sides. I take that as my cue to slip away, while the bar staff turn on the ugly lights at two a.m. and practically start pushing everyone out with brooms.

One of them hangs back a moment while I'm settling my tab. She saunters up to me at the end of the bar and gives me a half-tempting smirk.

"Lawson, right?"

I don't remember if I told them, though the circle of prep schools around here is a small one. No one is truly anonymous.

"I heard about an after-party, if you're down," she tells me, inching closer. "You can share our ride."

"You're a junior, aren't you?" I ask. Not that I discriminate, but I'm not about to be the only senior feeling old as death around a bunch of Catholic school girls trying to out-slut each other behind the rectory or whatever.

"Yeah, so?"

I've got to hand it to her. *Yeah, so* is a great answer. My motto, in fact. And her confidence is probably the reason I say, "Maybe another time."

"Good." She smiles enticingly, flashing a set of perfect white teeth. Then she grabs my phone from the bar top and holds it out for me to unlock.

I watch in amusement as she calls herself on it. Adding her name to my contacts. I like bold chicks. They're fun.

"Ainsley," she says, batting her lashes at me. "Don't forget. We can find a few things to try that you haven't answered yes to yet."

Now there's an idea.

CHAPTER 15
FENN

"Bishop, what the hell was that?" Coach growls from the touchline when I send a sitter sailing over the net during Monday's practice. "Pick your head up and place the damn shot."

Our keeper punts the ball back into play, and I get clobbered going up for a header. I take Kenny's elbow in the neck and stumble on my hands and knees trying to spin after him. From the corner of my eye, I see Coach launch his water bottle into the stands.

I don't blame him. I've been shit at practice today. Two steps behind during this five-on-five scrimmage and feeling like a JV first-year. I'm usually one of the sturdier guys on the field, but today I'm getting bodied off the ball left and right. Can't seem to find the energy.

"Bishop!"

Coach barks my name and jogs over to the touchline for my thrashing.

"Hey, get your head in the goddamn game," he snaps from behind reflective sunglasses. "I don't care whatever bullshit's going on up in that skull of yours, you need to focus. Now get out there and put the damn ball in the net, or you'll be taking penalties until sunrise tomorrow."

It's not for lack of trying. He doesn't know the considerable effort it's taking to be even this half-present. Truth is, since Casey stopped talking to me, I haven't been able to concentrate on much else. I spent the weekend sliding into a pit of despair, and I'm only about halfway up the slick, slippery wall, still trying to climb my way out. Each time my thoughts drift to her, my grip gives way and I'm back on my ass at the bottom of that pit. Staring up at a tiny dot of light so high above my head, reaching it feels impossible.

When we line up for a free kick and I take a point-blank shot straight to the face, I don't feel the ground come up to catch me. The pain is so hot and intense, I can't open my eyes. The whistle blows and that's practice. Coach calls it rather than risk peeling my corpse off the field.

"Dude," our team captain says in a low voice. "You okay?"

And that's when I know I've hit rock bottom. When Duke frickin' Jessup shows genuine concern for me. His uniform damp with sweat, he follows me toward the side doors of the sports building.

"I'm fine," I mumble, dragging my feet as we head for the locker rooms.

"This is all your brother's fault," Duke says darkly.

I look over, only half-interested. "What?"

"Shaw. The motherfucker shows up and everything's out of whack now. Don't tell me you haven't noticed."

I give a tired laugh. "Bro. RJ won that fight fair and square. You gotta get over it."

"Never," Duke vows and stalks past me through the door.

After a shower, I pull my phone from my locker to see no new notifications. I know I shouldn't, but there's nothing that can curb the compulsion to text Casey again.

Me: I know you hate me right now. Please, can we talk? I'm sorry.

I watch the screen, waking it when the brightness begins to dim.

Waiting for the blinking dots. They don't come, so I get dressed and toss my sweaty practice jersey in the laundry bin. When I check my phone again, her response slaps me in the face.

Casey: Fuck off forever.

Yeah, I know. It's about what I expected, only more explicit. Still, I can't help hoping the next message I send is the one that will catch her in the right mood.

My luck doesn't get any better when I get back to our dorm room to find RJ on the couch with Sloane.

Goddamn it. I'd rather take that ball to the face again, thanks.

"Stop texting my sister," she snaps right off the top.

"Please." I go to the fridge and grab two cold soda cans to press to my cheeks. "Can you just write it down and leave it on my bed? My head's killing me."

"I don't give a shit." She jumps to her feet, all revved up and spoiling for a fight. "Casey told you to leave her alone. If you can't do that, you're going to deal with me instead."

"I get it, Sloane. You'll rip off my dick and feed it to me." I lie on my bed and silently hope if I stay very still, she won't see me.

"You think it's a joke, but you have no idea the damage you've done to her."

With my eyes closed, I hear Sloane's angry footsteps rush closer.

"She's been a completely different person since she found out what you did. She's withdrawn, confrontational. Having angry outbursts at the slightest thing. You know she blew up at some girls who were bullying her last week?"

"Good," I answer, because it's about damn time Casey sticks up for herself. "What's the problem with that?"

"I wasn't there, but I heard that Casey said some nasty things to them, which, sure, for me might be normal. But for my sister, it's completely out of character."

"Ever think your expectations about who Casey is are what's holding her back? Sounds to me like she's finally sick of letting people walk all over her."

Sloane slaps one of the cans from my hand, and I open my eyes to find her hovering over me.

"Before you, she was the sweetest person I've ever known. She was better than all of us." Sloane's voice cracks slightly. "You stole that from her, Fenn. And I hope it kills you every day."

Without another word, she marches off, brushing past RJ when he attempts to catch her. She slams the door on her way out.

"Thanks for the backup," I tell him. I pick up my other can and replace it on my face.

"You deserved it."

"Still could've used the backup."

"I told you, I'm not getting in the middle of this." He sinks into his chair. "Off topic—what's the message you want me to get to Gabe? You never texted me, and my guy wants it tonight."

Fuck. I've been stewing over it for days, and I realized last night what an impossible task this is. What can I say that I'd want RJ to see? Anything I can think of is either an outright admission or would make RJ suspicious, and I know well enough now the consequences of piquing his curiosity.

"On second thought," I tell him. "I'm good."

"What, seriously?"

I sit up when the cans on my face have warmed to hand temperature and cease to provide me any relief. "Yeah, don't worry about it."

Bottom line is, I can't risk drawing any more attention. After this latest altercation with Sloane, her pin's been pulled. It's only a matter of time before she pops off and annihilates my whole world.

Now that I know the name of Gabe's military school, I simply need to find a way to get my own message to him. I might not have RJ's methods of contacting sketchy school guards, but I've got cash and that can go a long way.

It's obvious RJ wants to press the issue, but someone knocks on our door then. When he opens it, there's a box on the ground.

"Who's it for?" I ask warily.

RJ brings it inside and sets it on the coffee table while I come to sit on the couch.

"Me. From your dad." He furrows his brow.

"Oh. Never mind." I turn on the TV, which still has the video game paused where RJ and Sloane left off.

RJ tears into the cardboard box. "Whoa," he says a moment later. "Damn."

"What is it?"

"A memory expansion card. I'd mentioned something to Mom about needing to get one. But, uh, this is way more expensive than what I was looking at."

"Of course it is."

What David Bishop lacks in genuine emotion, he makes up for in monetary wealth. Since the wedding to RJ's mom, he's been on a hearts-and-minds mission to get on RJ's good side, as if doing so somehow proves he isn't a bad father. It's emotional warfare, and he's a manipulative asshole.

"I probably need to call him and say thanks, right?"

"For what? Trying to buy your approval? Fuck him."

RJ still looks hesitant, eyeing the memory card.

"Do we seriously need to have this talk again?" I grumble at my stepbrother. "You're new to this, so let me lay it out: My dad doesn't give a shit about you. Or me. Or anyone else. He equates spending money with actual human emotion, so he doesn't have to, you know, be a person. Don't fall for it."

Precisely on cue, my phone buzzes.

I throw it at RJ because I know David will just keep calling, and eventually RJ will wrestle the phone from me. I don't have the energy for it tonight.

"Fenn?" my dad says when RJ puts him on speaker.

"Yes, RJ got the thing. He's very impressed." I pick up a controller and start playing RJ's guy in the game. "Tell the person at Best Buy they did a good job."

"Oh, excellent. Hope it's what he needed."

"Yeah," RJ pipes up. "Thanks, David. It's perfect."

Christ, he's embarrassing.

"Fenn, can we talk a minute?" Dad says.

"Busy."

RJ rips the controller out of my hand and replaces it with the phone. He's such a pain in the ass.

"Yeah, what?" I ask, taking the phone off speaker and walking to my bed to sit down.

"How are you?" Dad's voice takes on a nervous note, as if he expects me to lash out at any second. "I wanted to check in and see how things are going."

"Sure." I chuckle. "What's this really about?"

"I'm interested," he insists defensively. "I want to know how you're doing."

"Why, is Michelle there? Yes, Dad, everything's swell. We're both having the best time ever."

He doesn't rise to my sarcasm, which is somehow worse, and instead proceeds right along. "Listen, I wanted to mention again about us coming up to see you boys at school soon. Is there a day of the week that's best for you? If you want to send me your schedule—"

"Uh-huh. Tap the phone twice if you're being held hostage. Should I alert the board to call the crisis negotiator?"

"Fennelly…"

"Yep, okay. Good talk, bye."

"You're a prick, you know." From the couch, RJ regards me with disappointment.

I'm used to it by now.

"Yeah, I know."

He goes back to playing his video game while I lie in bed failing to turn off my brain and find a moment's peace. Sloane thinks it's been my mission to corrupt Casey and turn her into another angry, jaded fuck like the rest of us. But that's the last thing I want. Yes, I'm glad she stood up to her bullies, but Sloane's right. It isn't like her to be loud and confrontational. It represents a worrying shift in her personality that's entirely my fault.

The idea that Casey is suffering is killing me. I'm certain I could fix this if I could just talk to her. Except she won't answer the phone, and I'm sure Sloane has threatened everyone we know with painful mutilation if they help me.

By lights out, my head's in knots. So tangled up, I'm not thinking straight. Later, after the halls have gone quiet and RJ starts snoring, I peel out of bed and get dressed.

If Casey won't take my calls, I have to make her see me.

CHAPTER 16
CASEY

I'M STRUCK WITH IRRATIONAL ANGER WHEN AN INTERMITTENT and indistinct tapping noise penetrates my subconscious, jolting me out of a dream that recedes from memory even before I've left it. I had an accent, I think. Something very posh and British. Makes sense I was exploring an interpretation of an Agatha Christie mystery after spending all night binging an old black-and-white miniseries.

So it's with thoughts of murder and betrayal I wake.

Blinking against the blurry darkness of my room, I glance toward the window and the sound of a single sharp tap against the glass. I already know I won't need it, but as I get out of bed, I reach underneath to grab Sloane's old softball bat because I like the idea of holding it.

Out on the lawn beyond the shrubs and the barrier of the motion-sensor flood lights, I spot a hooded Fenn standing with his phone in his hand.

On my nightstand, my phone lights up. I let it ring a while, considering what he could possibly say I'd want to hear. Or how he might manage to whittle away at my resolve. Because I'm still quite content being pissed at him. Forever, if I can help it.

The screen goes dark.

I could do it. Stand in the shadows until he's exhausted his fortitude and goes home convinced that I'm well outside his reach and always will be now.

Then it lights again, buzzing, rumbling on the bedside table. Until my curiosity compels me to pick it up.

"What?" I say coldly.

"I have to see you. Please, Casey."

The familiar sound of his voice, deep and husky, makes my heart squeeze with pain. I used to love hearing that voice slide into my ear. Now it just brings the sting of tears.

"If I wanted to talk to you, I wouldn't leave my phone off all day."

"You could have blocked me. But you didn't."

"I still can."

"I'm coming up," he says.

I go to the window to see him disappear into the shadows. By now, Fenn knows how to maneuver around the sightlines of Dad's motion sensors, finding the blind spots on the periphery.

"Don't," I warn softly. "I'm locking the window."

"No, you're not."

Asshole. I don't know which part is more annoying—that he's so sure of himself, or that he's right.

"If my dad catches you—"

"So don't let him."

Damn it.

I throw open the window just before Fenn hauls himself up and hops inside. He lands gently and pauses to listen for any indication he's woken the house. He's lucky the dogs are the least alert creatures on the planet. Fifteen cat burglars could crash through the ceiling on those SWAT team ropes, and Bo and Penny wouldn't bat an eye. Bo would go back to chewing on his bone while Penny rolled over in her plush dog bed.

"You're an idiot," I grumble.

Satisfied he's remained undetected, he stands and levels me with an intense stare that makes me take a step back. Sometimes I forget how intimidating he can be. Six feet tall, muscular. With his dark hood covering his blond hair, he gives off a dangerous vibe. But I'm not scared of him. I never have been. He might be bigger and stronger than I am, but I know without a doubt that I can bring him to his knees with one sharp word.

"What part of *go to hell and stay there* didn't you understand?"

"What's this I hear about you going off on those chicks at school?" he responds, ignoring me.

I frown. "What? How'd you hear about that?"

"Sloane."

Okay, wow. I guess I can't even count on my sister to keep her dumb mouth shut. I thought it was obvious the Fenn embargo applied to her as well.

"What happened?" he pushes.

"No. My life is none of your business anymore. You don't get to show up here and demand anything from me. So, if that's the only reason you came, you can go now."

"Of course it's not the only reason." He reaches for me, but I point the bat at him, using it to define the demilitarized zone between us. "I'm worried about you. Whether you think I'm allowed to or not isn't the point. I can't help that I care."

"Do you not hear yourself?" A bitter, sarcastic laugh bubbles out of me at his audacity. "Since you left me lying wet and unconscious on the ground in the pitch-black that night, you haven't once stopped to consider how I feel about anything. That's your problem."

"Casey." His face falls. Part of me likes it.

"The truth hurts, huh?"

"All I've done is think about you." His voice is rough. Shaky. "And I've made some huge mistakes. I accept that. I'm not asking you not to hate me. Be angry. But also, forgive me."

"Oh my God. It's like you live in a pretend world where consequences don't apply to you."

In what imaginary realm does he think we come back from this? That anyone would accept what he did and just offer a mulligan and move on?

"This isn't like cheating, Fenn. You didn't kiss another girl at my sweet sixteen. You left me to die and lied about it."

He opens his mouth to cut me off, but I stop him.

"No, wait. Worse than that. You did all that, and then schemed your way into my life, knowing what you'd done. That's some level of sociopathic I can't even get my head around."

He huffs a noise of exasperation at me and turns away to pace. "You make it sound like I had some dastardly plot the whole time. You think I could have planned it this way? I've been scared shitless since the second I saw that car sticking out of the water. I've been running on adrenaline and instinct ever since."

Fenn pauses in front of my dresser. In the mirror I watch him notice the dried leaves and wildflowers tucked into the frame. Mementos from our walks.

Now grim reminders of how gullible I was to trust him.

"What's the matter?" I ask, unable to stop from mocking him. "Awfully quiet over there."

"I came to check on you that first time," he says hoarsely, "when I showed up at your door, because I had to know you were okay. That you were recovering. But when I saw you, it ripped my chest open. You were pale and thin and looked like you hadn't slept in weeks. There was this darkness over you. It killed me knowing it was because of that night and I should have done more. I thought, maybe, it would make up for something if I could be there for you. I could do some kind of penance."

"So now I'm your charity case, is what you're saying. Well, I'm letting you off the hook. You've more than paid your debt. Please spare me from any more of your guilt."

"Fuck!" He roughly drags his hands over his face. "Why do you have to act like you don't know how I feel about you? I'm not here for my conscience, Casey."

"Then get to the point. I still have no idea why you came."

"Because I need you to forgive me. I miss you."

A piece of my heart splinters off. As much as I hate him, there's still a part of me that *doesn't* hate him. A part of me that misses our walks. Misses the way it feels to have his warm, hungry lips pressed against mine.

Fenn has always been able to see right through me, and he does so now. "You miss me too," he says softly.

"No," I lie.

"You miss me."

He takes a step closer. I take a step back.

My fingers tremble around the softball bat, and his blue eyes drop to it.

"Put the bat down, baby."

A sob catches in my throat. I think this might be the first time he's used that endearment, and it succeeds in breaking off another chunk of my brittle heart.

"Don't call me that," I order.

"Case. Put it down."

When I still refuse, he closes the distance between us and yanks the bat from my hand. He drops it on the floor, and then his hands capture my face. Gently but with intention.

"I'm sorry I hurt you," he says, expression swimming with regret. "Forgive me."

"No."

He lowers his head, his lips a mere inch from mine. "Please," he murmurs before brushing a kiss over my mouth.

My first instinct is to fight him. Kick him in the balls and toss him out my window. Instead, I capitulate to weakness. I wrap my arms around his back and grab fistfuls of his hoodie, opening my mouth to let his tongue taste mine.

I hate what he did. And yet, my body still misses him. Just the scent of his hair in my lungs is the happiest I've been in days.

Fenn only noticed me after prom, and I've been addicted to him ever since. Something happens when he touches me, a chemical reaction that overwhelms every other thought, and it's enough. For a moment, anyway. Just to kiss him and have this before the drug wears off.

The hardest part of holding a grudge is remaining dedicated to the cause, choosing principle over gratification. When we stumble toward my bed, I can't be bothered to consider how this undercuts everything I've said till now. He wants me, and I want him, and I think we both hate ourselves a little for it.

I push him onto the mattress, and then we're lying on our sides and he hitches my thigh over his hip. I whimper when I feel his hard-on, the proof of his need for me. Breathing hard, I undo the button of his pants. My hand slides beneath his waistband, seeking out what I've been wanting for so long. He's thick and hard beneath my fingers.

Neither of us speak. We're both afraid to break the spell. His mouth is locked on mine as I stroke him. He rocks into my hand, shuddering when I squeeze the hard shaft.

Fenn pushes his hand up under my T-shirt to run his fingertips down the bare skin of my back. Our tongues slowly slick over each other. He groans into my mouth. Runs one hand down to cup my ass, as his lips now wander their way along my neck to kiss my shoulder.

I can't resist the desire to let lust shut off my brain for a while. Hit pause on all other thoughts and just feel him. Pretend we're still good. Still happy.

"Tell me you don't still have feelings for me," he whispers.

But he has to go and ruin it.

It's like a shot of ice water through my veins. I put both hands against his chest and push. "Whatever feelings I had died when you betrayed me."

His brow creases as I disentangle our legs and climb off the bed.

He doesn't understand how both things can be true. That I still want him. And I want nothing to do with him.

Fenn scrambles to his feet, his pants still undone, hair tousled from my fingers running through it. "Casey, please."

"You should go."

"I know I did a terrible thing, but I'm begging. Give me another chance. I can make this up to you. I promise."

"There's only one thing you can do to even have a shot of forgiveness," I remind him. "Tell the truth. Why'd you do it?"

Again, his face contorts in pain, as if this secret he harbors grows more pernicious and physically destructive the longer he carries it. A parasite consuming him from the inside.

But still, he says nothing. He bites his lip and stares at me with that tormented expression, and it only cements that he made his choice a long time ago.

And it wasn't me.

"Go home, Fenn." I heave a bone-weary sigh. "And don't come back."

CHAPTER 17
FENN

I'VE BARELY SAT DOWN IN SECOND PERIOD ON WEDNESDAY BEFORE MY name is called and I'm summoned to the lobby of the administration building. In the hall, I catch up to RJ heading in the same direction. He's already loosening the green-and-blue striped tie I helped him with earlier. Damn near moaning with pleasure as he pulls it off. I swear, RJ removing a tie is akin to chicks kicking off their heels after a long day.

"What'd you do?" I demand.

"Me?" He pushes open the double doors leading to the courtyard. "I didn't do shit."

We emerge into the crisp morning air, where I falter a step.

"What?" RJ says.

"I just realized…" I hoist my messenger bag higher on my shoulder as a tingle down my spine warns I might have to make a run for it. "If this was a summons from the headmaster, he'd call us to his office, not the lobby."

"Unless the cops are waiting in the lobby. Seems like a cop thing to do."

Fuck.

"Could this be about Gabe? The money you wired to the guard at his school?"

"Highly doubt it." Confidence lines RJ's tone. "My work is untraceable."

I let out a breath. "Long way?" I ask.

RJ nods. "Long way."

We make a loop around the courtyard to the far side of the admin building, which allows us to get a look at the main parking lot. No police cars. None marked, anyway. Still, I'm not convinced this isn't a trap.

Clearly RJ agrees, because he mutters, "I've got a bad feeling."

We slip in the back door and take our time making our way toward the lobby. As our sneakers move soundlessly over the gleaming hardwood, we're both braced for something to jump out at us. This building is colder than just about anywhere on campus. The air smells better, too, which somehow makes it all the more ominous.

A thought occurs to me. "You don't think this is because I went to see Casey last night, right?"

"Wait, seriously?" RJ stops walking and shoves me in an alcove. "What'd you do?"

"Nothing. Snuck in her window—"

"Fenn."

"She let me in," I protest. "We got in an argument. But then we sort of made out. Anyway, it didn't go exactly to plan, and she kicked me out."

"Damn it." For a second, he looks like he might want to take a swing at me. Instead, he grits his teeth and pokes his head around the corner. "If she told Sloane, or her dad noticed you leaving…" He trails off uneasily. "They could be here to arrest you."

"Then why are you here?"

"Maybe they need to question me about the boathouse footage and how I got it."

Shit. For a moment, I do consider bolting. A brief and vivid montage of my life as a fugitive plays less cinematic in my head than it looks in the movies. Then I think about Gabe, completely unaware what's transpired since he left Sandover. How much I still don't know about that night.

Why hasn't he sent a message back to Lucas, damn it? I haven't been able to find my own way of reaching him yet, which means everything hinges on his response to his brother. I doubt he'd share anything overtly incriminating, but I know Gabe Ciprian like the back of my hand. If Lucas chooses to show me Gabe's message— and I can't see him being a dick and not doing that—then I need to pray Gabe included some sort of hint that only I can decipher.

"Come on," I tell RJ. "If they take me in, you can pawn my watch to bail me out."

In a strange way, the walk down the wide corridor toward the lobby feels a bit like getting wheeled into the operating room when I got my tonsils out. I was terrified and on the verge of tears, biting my tongue because Mom told me to be strong. I felt grown up that day, facing down my fate.

I think I could do time. Just keep my head down and pay the craziest fucker in the joint to watch my back. Being filthy rich has its perks.

Then we come around the corner and my stomach drops.

"I changed my mind," I tell RJ. "I'm making a break for it."

"Coward."

David and RJ's mom stand in front of a portrait on the wall, pretending to admire it and looking awkward. Michelle is clad in a ribbed ankle-length sweater dress that hugs her body like a glove. I can't deny that RJ's mom is hot. She has glossy dark hair she wears loose around her shoulders, big hazel eyes, and cupid's bow lips that I once read somewhere is supposedly the mark of, like, supreme beauty or something. I'm sure if Dad married her for a physical feature, though, it was her ass.

"Dude," RJ warns. "Stop checking out my mom."

"David, there they are," Michelle says, tapping him on the shoulder. She waves us over. "Boys, come give us a hug."

Yeah. Pass. I'm pretty sure the last time I hugged my father was at Mom's funeral.

RJ dutifully goes to embrace his mom, who she squeezes him tight and says, "Ah, buddy, it's so good to see you. I missed you so much."

Dad and I stand there in silence, watching the mother-son reunion. Dad, who had his hands inside the pockets of his wool trousers, pulls one hand out and extends it at me. I stare at it without shaking.

"What are you guys doing here?" I ask.

"We decided to surprise you," Michelle says with a beaming smile. She releases RJ and takes a step toward me as if she's going to hug me. Then she sees my expression and falters. "It's nice to see you again, Fenn."

"Yeah. You too." We both know I'm lying. But while I feel fine about being rude to my father, I can't be an outright dick to Michelle. She didn't do anything to me.

"Thanksgiving seemed too far away," she adds, linking her arm through RJ's. "So, we decided it would be fun to call the pilot and fly out here for the day. Take you boys to lunch. How does that sound?"

"Sure. Great," RJ says without much enthusiasm.

"Wonderful!" She releases him and claps her hands together. "This makes me happy."

"All right, then," Dad says gruffly. "The car's waiting outside."

The newlyweds start walking, but I hang back slightly. "Don't make me do this," I mumble to RJ beside me.

"If I have to, so do you. Suck it up."

He shoves me forward and now it's too late to dash, so I force my feet to carry me to the waiting Lincoln town car Dad hired for the day. I feel like I'm marching toward my execution.

They take us to what passes for a classy joint in the tiny redneck town outside Sandover's gates. Dad makes an embarrassing fuss about picking the perfect table and asking to see a wine list, like it isn't barely one in the afternoon.

"Seriously. What's the occasion?" I ask, pouring myself a glass of champagne because, well, can't let it go to waste. And I'm not sitting through forced family time sober. "Long trip just for lunch. Come to announce the divorce?"

"Hardly," Dad says cheerfully, reaching for Michelle's hand. "Like Michelle said, we were eager to see you boys."

"I missed you," she says, smiling at RJ. "I can't get over how different you look."

"Swimming." He shyly leans away when she tries to brush his hair back. "We're in the gym a lot."

"He's being modest," I pipe up. "Don't want the leader of an underground fighting ring and organized crime syndicate going soft."

He kicks me under the table, but I don't spill a drop of my champagne.

"You're not still getting into fights?" Michelle says, frowning at her son.

RJ shoots me a glare.

"I think he's pulling your chain," Dad interjects.

I wink at my stepmom. "Officially, the faculty stopped making the students fight in the pit after that freshman slipped into a coma. But then things happen, right?"

David and Michelle force a laugh because we're all having such a great time. The appetizers arrive, and I help myself to a crostino of prosciutto and fig. Then I drain my glass and help myself to more champagne.

The mood is shit, and half a bottle deep into the entrees, it hasn't improved. Michelle is now telling some inane story of her book club with the other well-kept women of the neighborhood. For a single mom who'd carted her son around from city to city for years, she seems to be fitting right in with the Greenwich crowd. Of course, the likelier option is that her new "friends" are smiling to her face during book club and calling her a gold digger behind her back. Rich ladies are nothing if not predictable.

"For weeks we've been discussing this novel that everyone absolutely hates," she says through a barely contained laugh. "Totally loaded on wine and ripping it to shreds."

My champagne glass has mysteriously gone empty. But when I reach for the bottle, David pushes it out of reach. Doesn't matter—RJ hasn't touched his, so I annex it for myself in a hostile takeover. My dad notices and frowns at me. I ignore him.

"Then, finally, someone notices Shelby hasn't said a word all afternoon. Well, Claire, because she's Claire, sloshing a glass of red wine everywhere and nearly spilling it all over the Turkish rug she never shuts up about, she actually throws—I don't know what it was, a hard candy maybe?—at Shelby and demands to know why she's being so quiet."

Yes, Shelby. Please. Speak your truth, sister.

"Shelby's face turns this bright strawberry red, and then with a look of abject horror that honestly frightened me, she slaps her hands over her mouth. Now I've been a flight attendant for a long time, so I know that look. I push my chair way back just as bright green liquid spews through her fingers is all directions. Shelby spent the week on some cleanse, drinking nothing but kale juice four times a day. Until she burst all over the room. So now, Claire is on her knees, drunk and sobbing, because her Turkish rug is completely ruined."

RJ snickers.

"Shelby texted me last night with a screenshot of the cleaning invoice Claire emailed her. Five thousand dollars." Michelle's eyes go wide. "Can you believe it's costing five grand to clean a damned rug?"

"You should have seen the cleaning bill Lawson's dad got after his last party in the Hamptons," I say helpfully. "Just getting all the semen out of the pool cost, like, two grand."

"Fenn," Dad growls.

RJ is now laughing into his napkin. "Dude," he sputters.

"What?" I blink innocently.

To my approval, Michelle looks like she's also fighting back laughter. Stepmommy has a sense of humor, at least.

Dad clears his throat. "Fenn, why don't you fill us in on how soccer's going?"

I nudge RJ. "Want to see something hilarious? Hey, Dad, what's the offside rule?"

"Fenn." My father levels me with a warning scowl.

"What? I've played soccer since I was six years old. Surely you've picked up something by now from all the games you've attended."

"Fenn," RJ murmurs, clearly tired of my shit. "Stop."

"Oh, wait." I reach the bottom of another glass and hold it out to Michelle. "Would you be so kind?"

"I think you've had enough," Dad says, touching her arm before she can top me up.

"Spoilsport." I look back at Michelle. "So, in twelve years, you know how many times he's seen me play? Guess. This'll be fun."

"Enough, Fennelly." Dad wipes his mouth and drops his napkin on the table hard enough to shake our empty glasses.

"Oh," Michelle says brightly, as if she's suddenly solved the issue of world hunger. "Why don't we take a walk, buddy?"

RJ is already pushing his chair back. "Awesome idea."

Mother and son practically sprint to the door, and I don't blame them for making an escape. If I'd been smarter, I would've done a tuck-and-roll out of the car on the way here.

"Happy now?" Dad grumbles at me across the table.

I give him a dismissive shrug. "I told you this was a bad idea."

"You're drunk and embarrassing yourself."

"I'm fine. And we both know you're more worried about your own reputation."

Dad shakes his head, unhappiness filling his eyes. "All right,

Fenn. You've made it abundantly clear you're not interested in giving this family a chance."

I had a family. She died. And he crawled into his shell and turned his back on me for seven years.

He pushes his plate aside and rests his elbows on the table. "Can we talk about what's actually bothering you? Michelle says you've told RJ that you don't think I care about you."

"No. I think what I said was, you didn't give a shit and couldn't care less if you were paid to."

He's briefly aghast I'd say such a thing out loud, much less to his face. This is on him, though. Should've thought twice before letting his teenage son down half a bottle of mediocre champagne and then cracking open the chest of family trauma.

"What on earth would make you think something like that?" His features grow more strained. "You're my son. I've cared about little else since the day you were born."

"Wow. Dude. It's impressive you can say that with a straight face."

"What am I supposed to do to convince you otherwise? I'm here, aren't I?"

"Yeah, now that you've got some new bimbo stewardess wife you want to impress because she's making you feel inadequate. Like, fuck, Dad. How do you not see that's worse?"

"Michelle's been nothing but nice to you. If your mother were—"

"Nope." I throw my napkin on the table, and before I'm aware of it, I'm pointing a butter knife at my father. "You keep her out of your fucking mouth."

"Fenn!"

Whatever. I drop the knife and reach across the table for the champagne bottle. Dad reaches it first and tries to hand it off to the waiter who appears beside me.

"I'll take that off your hands," I tell the server.

"No, Fenn. Sit down," David orders.

"Nah. I'm just gonna take my friend here and get loaded in the parking lot, if it's all the same to you."

The confused waiter looks at my dad, the three of us with our hands on the bottle. "I don't think I can—"

"It's cool, man."

I tug hard on the champagne bottle and carry it with me as I storm out of the restaurant.

CHAPTER 18
CASEY

It's midnight and I can't sleep. What else is new, though? Immediately after the accident, I could barely get ten continuous minutes of sleep, let alone the prescribed eight hours. Then, as I began to heal, I started sleeping more. Three hours. Five. Six. Until eventually I managed to make it through an entire night without being awakened by nightmares. These days, the bad dreams still come, but not as often as they did. Falling asleep is much easier too.

Until Fenn shredded my heart to pieces.

It's been a week since I discovered the truth, and in that week, I haven't slept more than a few hours a night. Which means I'm wide awake when Bo scuttles to the foot of the bed and starts whining.

I look up from the glowing screen of my phone, on which I'd been mindlessly scrolling a celebrity gossip website. "What's up, bud?"

Whining again, he gives me a pleading look.

"You need to go out?"

At the word "out" Bo scampers toward the bedroom door.

I get out of bed, my bare feet cold against the hardwood. I roll on a pair of socks and grab a long cardigan, shoving my phone into the front pocket.

I step into the dark hallway, where I squeak in surprise when I bump into Penny, who's lurking in the darkness. Bo has already lumbered downstairs.

"Sweetheart?" The noise draws my father out of his room. Rubbing his eyes, he gives me a worried look. "Is everything all right?"

"It's fine," I assure him. "I'm going to let the dogs out to pee. Bo woke me up whining." I include the lie about me sleeping because if Dad suspected I'm suffering from insomnia again, he'd send me back to the shrink.

"Don't forget to rearm the alarm when you come back inside."

"I won't," I promise and head downstairs to put on my shoes.

Outside, I shiver in the cool October air and trail after the dogs, who run toward the tree line. They both have shy bladders and refuse to go to the bathroom unless they're hidden in the bush. I appreciate their discretion.

I tip my head up to the clear night sky and focus on the moon. It isn't quite full, but almost. Ugh. I'm not a fan of full moons. For some reason they make me irritable. Right now, though, my irritability has more to do with the fact that my phone is buzzing, and there's only one person who would text me this late.

Sure enough, it's Fenn.

Fenn: Can't sleep. Miss you too much.

My throat goes tight, tears prickling behind my eyelids. Why can't he leave me alone? And why can't I block him? I've tried. I've clicked *BLOCK* a dozen times already. Yet I never last more than a few minutes before I hurriedly undo the action.

I'm not ready to let him go, but I also don't want anything to do with him. My tired heart can't keep up anymore.

With trembling fingers, I type a response.

Me: You need to leave me alone.
Fenn: My dad and RJ's mom showed up yesterday to take us
to lunch. I got wasted and caused a scene.
Me: I don't care.

I put the phone on silent and shove it back in my pocket. I whistle toward the trees, but neither Bo nor Penny come racing back to me. Damn it. They'd better not be chasing some poor squirrel that had the misfortune of being awake this late.

I whistle again. When the dogs still don't return, I curse under my breath and walk toward the woods, jumping when a motion-activated floodlight suddenly flashes on, nearly blinding me. I'm still seeing black dots as I move through the trees, my shoes crunching over dried leaves.

"Guys," I call in warning. "Come."

They don't come.

"Swear to God," I growl into the dark woods, "if you killed another squirrel, and I have to spend the next hour washing your bloody faces, you're going to lose your lake privileges for a whole week—"

I stop in my tracks and gasp when I see the cause for their disappearance.

"Bo! Penny!" I say sharply, feeling my face pale as I lunge toward the dogs, who are sniffing at the dead rabbit lying on the path.

For some reason, they'd decided not to eat the thing, and I suspect that's due to the rustling sound we hear in the bushes, the fast departure of a third creature in the forest. The culprit of the bunny murder, most likely.

"*Here*," I command the dogs.

They're obedient enough that they snap to my side. Still, their ears are perked up, hackles raised as they warily inspect our surroundings.

"Stay," I warn, then hurry toward the remains of the rabbit.

My stomach sinks once I have a better view because I discover there's more than one victim. A few feet from the adult rabbit are the bodies of two babies. They must have been only recently born—they're completely furless, eyes and ears sealed shut. My gaze moves and I notice two more dead babies, or kittens as they're called. I never understood why rabbit offspring would be called kittens. Dad tried explaining it to me once, but it wasn't a great explanation so much as a "that's just what they're called."

Bo and Penny must've interrupted whatever carnage had gone down here. A fox, I suspect. The foxes in this area sustain themselves mostly on wild rabbits. It was a real boon for this one to come across an entire nest, likely right when the doe was returning to feed her newborns.

My eyes feel hot. Man. She led the predators right to her doorstep. At least my dogs scared Mr. Fox off before he could feast.

In my peripheral, I see Bo creeping closer, and I turn with a severe, "Stay."

He stops in his tracks but doesn't look happy that I'm apparently the one to benefit from his impromptu midnight snack.

If it weren't so late, I would probably run back to the house, grab some rubber gloves and a box, and come back to collect these poor sweet dead bunnies. Give them a proper burial. My father and sister wouldn't even blink—they've participated in many an animal funeral over the years. Usually, though, it's because I brought home an injured bird or bunny or even squirrel that needed tending, and they ended up dying. The only successful animal rescue I've conducted in my life was the bluebird I nursed back to health. I named her Pudding.

But there's no hope for these bunnies. They're all—

Squeak.

I freeze. From behind me, Penny rumbles out a low growl from deep in her throat.

"Shh," I tell her, then look around, straining to hear the sound again. That was definitely a bunny.

A balloon of hope expands in my heart. Did any of the babies survive?

Oh God. Please let them have survived.

While my dogs miserably watch from the spot to which I've banished them, I scour the immediate area, reaching into bushes and peering at tree roots to try to locate the hutch. I finally find it in the ground cover at the base of a tree.

Pulse racing, I peek inside and gasp when I see movement. Survivors!

No. Only one, I realize a moment later. Of the four hairless little bodies I find in the nest, only one is alive.

It screams again, that horrible squeaky shriek that makes my heart hurt.

"It's okay, little one," I coo as I gently pick it up. "You're safe now."

Not quite, though. The chances of this baby surviving are slim to none. Under normal circumstances, I wouldn't even touch it. I'd move the nest to a more secure location and hope that its mother would return at some point. But the mother is dead—I'm staring at her bloody, broken body. Which means there's nobody coming back to feed this defenseless creature.

Which means I have to do it.

"It's okay. I've got you now." With delicate fingers, I place the tiny rabbit in my pocket, then straighten up and head back to the dogs.

Bo practically glares at me as I gesture for them to follow me. Penny longingly stares back at the abandoned feast.

Although the death of any creature, big or small, makes my entire body clench with pain, I'm also mindful of the circle of life. The age-old dance between predator and prey.

"Let Mr. Fox have them," I say sadly. "He earned it."

I reach the porch just as my father is stumbling out the front door, eyes wild with concern. "Casey! Why were you gone so long? Why didn't you answer your phone?"

"Sorry. I put it on silent." I meet him in the doorway. "Ran into a little snag in the forest."

"What happened?"

"A fox got into a rabbit hutch. The dogs scared him off."

The baby rabbit takes that moment to squeak loudly.

"Casey." Dad's tone is thick with suspicion.

"Yes?" I say innocently.

"Is there a rabbit in your pocket?"

"Maybe?" I press my lips together to stop a laugh.

Dad stares at me for one long moment. Then he sighs. "I'll go find a shoebox."

CHAPTER 19
SILAS

Sloane is being more stubborn that usual. I hoped space would give her some perspective on the situation, let her come to her senses. Yet it's been more than a week now, and she still won't respond to my texts.

I sent her a whole long message assuring her I'm not trying to get into her pants. I appealed to our friendship, the tight bond we've had since freshman year. Don't get me wrong—there's a part of me that would take her up on it if she floated the idea of hooking up. But I get it. It's not happening.

Anyway, I've got a girlfriend. And Sloane's back with RJ. So, whatever. Let's move on.

I'd always thought of her as a rational person. Prone to anger and poor taste in men, yes, but essentially logical. Well, it seems her self-destructive penchant for dating losers has corrupted her higher brain functions. She needs a detox, except I can't get close enough to help her see that, goddamn it.

"Like, back me up here," I tell Amy. "That's obviously a red flag. She's become a completely different person. Stopped hanging out with her old friends. All since this new guy basically took over her life."

"What do you think of this area?" Amy says, moving her laptop closer as we sit on her bed. Her bare legs are draped over mine while she scours the internet for the best neighborhoods to live in London. "I think I like Notting Hill. Remember I made you watch that old rom-com? It was set there."

"Sure." I honestly can't give less of a shit, nor can I remember a single rom-com she's ever made me watch.

She bookmarks a page and moves on with the dogged determination of a homicide detective.

"I know you think it's dumb because it's ages away, but I need to start thinking about this now if I'm going to get my parents on board with me spending my gap year in England. If I show them I've done the research, they might feel better about bankrolling the venture, know what I mean?"

"Yeah, sure." I'm barely listening. And I'm starting to regret sneaking into her dorm tonight.

Amy's been on my case for days to come visit her at Ballard. Then I get here, and she spends the first hour in the bathroom on some new skincare routine that just makes her face smell like glue. And now she wants to do *research* the whole time while I'm sitting here counting the seconds of my life slip through my fingers.

"If one of your friends suddenly stopped talking to you because she was seeing someone new, you'd be suspicious, right?"

"People change when they're in a relationship," Amy says absently, scrolling through photos. "They want to spend all their time together." She lifts her eyes from the screen. "That's normal."

"Right, but this is extreme. We never used to fight."

There was a time Sloane appreciated my opinion. But now, whatever brain worm RJ slipped in her ear has fundamentally altered her personality.

"You don't like the guy, right?"

"He's just such a step down for Sloane," I answer with a scowl. Personally, whatever. He's fine. For her? Please.

Amy frowns. "Sounds like she just wants you to be happy for her. If you won't do that, maybe it's better you two take a break for a while."

My scowl deepens. "I don't think you're getting a clear picture of things."

Finally, she takes the hint and closes her laptop. "Maybe if we spent more time together…"

"I'm here, aren't I?"

"It's just that you talk a lot about Sloane lately. Kind of all the time, actually."

"I'm sorry I can't pretend to be interested in London hot spots."

Amy rolls her eyes. "We don't have to talk about London. Or anything, in fact."

She leans in to kiss me, that cloying glue smell filling my nostrils. I force myself not to breathe through my nose and try to ignore the sticky-wet texture of her skin against my chin. I swear, most of the cosmetic stuff that girls do to themselves is a major turnoff.

Still, when she reaches down to stroke me through my jeans, I put the thought aside and let her take my shirt off. She tosses hers aside to show me she's wearing my favorite bra, which is a nice gesture. It's white with red trim and stacks her tits up nicely.

For all she can get on my nerves sometimes, Amy's a sweet girl. And she's got fantastic tits. The first time I got my hand up her shirt at her sister's dance recital, I almost bust a nut just palming one soft, heavy breast.

I dip my fingers inside one bra cup and pull it down to show me her tiny pink nipple. Tug on it a little while she travels down my body to unzip my jeans and stroke me. She looks up under those thick eyelashes and sweeps her light brown hair over one shoulder before she applies her tongue, licking the tip.

Pleasure skitters up my spine. I close my eyes, and then, for some awful reason, an image of Sloane sucking off RJ gets stuck in my head. Duke was bad enough, and we all know where he's been. The new kid, though, by his own admission has bounced all around the country. Probably hooking up with only the finest suburban meth addicts. I wonder if Sloane's even had him tested for STIs.

"Is this okay?" Amy pumps her hand. "Do you need me to do something else?"

It's only then I realize she's been at this a minute, and I'm only getting about half wood here.

"No, it's fine. Just use your tongue."

Amy typically gives good head. She enjoys it. So I try to concentrate, squeezing her tit and tugging the hard bud of her nipple. But she's at it for a while, and I still can't get up to full mast. Eventually she sits up, shaking out her hand cramp with a frustrated huff.

"I'm sorry," I say. "I guess I'm just tired. Swim practice took it out of me."

She cocks her head at me while I tuck myself back into my jeans. "Swim practice," she echoes, dubious. "Or…here's an idea…" She gives an angry snort. "This is about Sloane."

I tense up. "Why would you say that?"

"Because, Silas, she's all you talk about anymore." Amy makes a mocking face and affects a poor imitation of me. "*Sloane's mad at me. Sloane's being a bitch. Sloane has a new boyfriend.*"

"I think I take offense to that characterization."

She jumps off the bed and fishes her shirt from the floor. "Seriously, you're kind of obsessed with her, and I'm not okay with it."

"You're being ridiculous."

Amy's tone gets increasingly sharper. "Oh, really? So you don't have a thing for her?"

For the second time during a pivotal moment in a critical conversation, my idiot self hesitates a beat too long.

My girlfriend's face collapses. "Oh my God."

"Amy, come on. It's not like that."

She ignores my half-hearted defense, tears welling up in her eyes.

"I think I knew even when we first started dating." Her teeth dig into her bottom lip, which is trembling visibly. "But I wanted you so much, and I figured at some point, if you liked me enough, you'd get over it." She sucks in short, muted breaths and wipes her cheeks. "I have done everything to be what you wanted, but none of it mattered because you never liked me at all, did you? You were never capable of loving me." A strangled sob fills the room. "You were just killing time until Sloane was single."

"Amy—"

"I was nicer to you than you deserved," she says with tears streaming down her ashen cheeks. "You're not a good person, Silas."

"Come on. You're blowing it way out of proportion. I don't have a thing for Sloane," I mutter, finally managing to get the denial out.

"I don't believe you."

"It's the truth," I lie.

"Fuck you, Silas." She turns away, her shoulders stiff. "It's over. Just go."

My instinct is to stay. To spend the night reassuring her until she comes around again. This isn't the first time her insecurities have sent her over a cliff—I know with the right amount of sweet words and soft reassurances, we can move past this. But as I get off the bed and put my shirt on, I realize I don't give a shit anymore. This half-assed relationship has sapped enough energy out of me, and I can't find it in me to care.

Hell, she probably just did me a favor. Saved me from having to come up with an authentic-sounding breakup speech.

"I'm sorry," I tell her, only half meaning it.

Then I grab my shoes and duck out the door.

Leaving Amy's room, I let out a breath heavy with relief and head toward the stairwell. A door opens halfway down the hall and a familiar face greets me. A dusky complexion and big, amber-colored eyes.

Mila Whitlock.

Before Casey's accident, Mila was Sloane's best friend. Hot too. Tonight, she's in a pair of tiny boxer shorts and a black sports bra that shows off her high, perky tits and tight abs. She's got a great body.

A slow, amused grin spreads across her face when she notices me walking with my shoes in my hands.

"Have fun?" she says.

I shrug. "Think I just got dumped."

Mila laughs in my face. "Good for her. 'Bout time she showed a little backbone."

"Yeah, thanks for your support."

"Sorry not sorry." The curvy brunette waves at me over her shoulder as she saunters off. "Sweet dreams, Silas."

CHAPTER 20
CASEY

A FUNNY THING ABOUT CATHOLIC SCHOOL: MOST OF US AREN'T even Catholic. Our parents dump us here for the structure or arguably "superior" academics. For the sanctity of an all-girls institution. In my case, it was a matter of geography, the result of my dad's job landlocking us to Sandover and its immediate commutable radius. But then, there are the girls who genuinely hail from religious families. That's how you get a girl like Jazmine. Her devout parents living the immigrant American dream, sending their daughter to an exclusive private school in the hopes it strengthens her faith and good, moral character.

So far, it doesn't seem to be working.

Jazmine sits next to me in class now. After she witnessed me snipe at Ainsley in the hall last week, she decided we were fated to be friends, told me to call her "Jaz," and is now my constant companion at school. I still don't know what I think of her, but I can't deny she's fun to be around. She's fluent in sarcasm. Smart as a whip. Her main goal in life is to become a famous actress, much to her parents' dismay. They wanted an obedient Catholic girl who'd find a respectable job and husband, and instead, they got the total opposite. Jaz insists she's moving to New York or LA after graduation and never getting married.

"Hey," she greets me as she slides into her seat. "How's Silver?"

I look up from my physics notes. We have a unit test this morning and I'm ill-prepared. It's been an exhausting few days. "Still alive. Miraculously."

When I brought the baby rabbit home four nights ago, none of us expected she'd live through the night. Sloane, who knows how quickly I get attached, keeps reminding me that something like less than 10 percent of orphaned rabbits survive. But my little gal has defied the odds so far. Well, I don't know if she's actually a gal, since it's impossible to tell yet. I picked a gender-neutral name, but I like to think it's a female.

"Has she opened her eyes?"

I bite my lip in concern. "No," I admit.

Which tells me Silver couldn't have been older than a day or two when I rescued her. Baby rabbits usually open their eyes when they're about ten days old. Silver's are still squeezed shut.

She's fighting to stay alive, though. I feed her kitten milk replacer with a syringe twice a day. Keep her hydrated. Make sure she's warm and cozy in her shoebox. But I know the chances of her surviving without her mother are slim.

Sister Margaret stands from behind her desk and claps her hands sharply. "Quiet down, ladies. Georgia, please pass out the test papers. And keep them facedown, everyone!" She points at the clock over the door. "Pencils cannot touch the page until the clock strikes nine."

"Because God forbid someone gets a one-minute head start," Jaz says under her breath.

The test is easier than I expected, and I turn it in to the sister with ten minutes to spare. Afterward, we head off to pre-calc where Jazmine gets detention after she cheerfully informs Sister Mary Alice that the next time the nun hits Jaz's wrist with that ruler, Jaz is going to hit back. The sister is outraged, face redder than Jazmine's sore wrist as she screeches, "Detention, Ms. Reyes!" while the class laughs into their hands.

When it's time for lunch, we fall into step with each other on the way to the cafeteria, Jazmine's obscenely short skirt drawing frowns from several girls, all of whom are wearing their skirts at regulation length. She remains oblivious to the stares as she tells me about some movie she watched last night.

Best thing about her is she sincerely doesn't give a shit what people think about her, which is a valuable weapon when you're a teenager. We were walking down the hall last week when some girl coughed the word "slut" under her breath. Totally unperturbed, Jaz stopped in front of the lockers and pretended to look devastated.

"Oh no!" she'd cried. "You found out that I lost my virginity in a threesome to those two seniors from Ballard? You're right, Marissa, I *am* a slut, and I'm sooooo embarrassed and—oh wait." Jaz grinned. "That was you."

Then she took my arm and we left, leaving a stricken Marissa to backpedal with her wide-eyed friends. I asked Jaz if that story was true, and she'd nodded in confirmation, saying one of the boys in question was her older brother.

The girls at St. Vincent's fear her. Funny enough, I think they're also a little scared of me now. Ever since I snapped at Ainsley, I've heard the way their tone has changed in the cafeteria when they whisper about me. They're not laughing anymore. They avert their gazes when I pass, and I'm not going to lie—I kind of like it. I didn't know it could feel like this.

"Attention is a weapon," Jaz tells me when she sees me noticing the change in everyone's demeanor. "Girls like them…" She nods at Ainsley and Bree, who are walking up to the lunch line as we claim an empty table. "They always made fun of me too. There was this trio of witches at my old school who made my life miserable freshman year."

"Really?" I can't imagine someone as confident as Jazmine getting bullied.

"Oh yeah. They trashed my fashion sense. My makeup. Kept

telling me to get back on my raft and paddle back to Cuba." She rolls her eyes. "We're from Puerto Rico, assholes. Anyway, it got to me back then. I used to hide. I'd take my lunch to a bathroom stall or eat in the art room with my teacher because I was terrified of them."

"Is that why you changed schools?"

"Fuck no," she says adamantly. "I transferred here in sophomore year because my dad got a new job and had to relocate. But about halfway through that horrific freshman year, I had my come-to-Jesus moment. Which, ironically, didn't happen at a Catholic school."

Laughing, I set my tray down and take a seat.

"I realized I could keep hiding and let them make me ashamed for the rest of my life, or I could turn that attention against them. Become so conspicuous, they'd be afraid to look. The best defense is a good offense, Tresscott."

"I'd say it's working."

"Damn right it is. And you know what? The moment I legit stopped caring what they thought about me, the better I felt about myself. Matter of fact, I love me a whole lot more."

I'm starting to understand what she means. There's real power in controlling our own narrative. So when Ainsley turns from the lunch line with her tray to stare at me, I stare back.

Why choose to be the wilting flower when I can be the thorn?

"Look at the freak table." Ainsley wears a haughty smirk when she and Bree approach us. But there's a slight shake in her voice. She's unnerved by my eye contact. Good. "You two giving each other matching tattoos with sewing needles later?"

"Ew," Bree groans. "That's, like, how you get pink eye."

Ainsley gets a laugh from the girls at the neighboring table, but it's forced and hesitant and recedes as soon as Jazmine glances in their direction.

"We'd invite you," I say apologetically, "but I wouldn't want our plans to conflict with your dick-eating contest."

The answering gasps and laughter from the cafeteria startle me.

I notice the forks paused midair and phones raised. It's a sick sort of endorphin rush, and I know I like it more than I should.

"What?" Bree pouts at Ainsley. "You said we were on a diet."

"It's keto," Jazmine says, biting her lip to keep a straight face.

I almost snort.

"Speaking of dicks, Casey, how many of them did you suck when you were locked up in the mental institution?" Ainsley's comeback silences the room.

"Just one," I tell her. "It was the day your dad came to visit me."

"What the hell, you stupid bitch!"

Ainsley launches her tray at me. I dodge, and her salad flies off her plate and onto the floor. Jaz and I take our cue to bolt among an eruption of noise and camera clicks. We dash out of there, nearly dizzy with laughter.

"That was fun," Jaz says when we come to a skidding stop near our lockers. "Do it again tomorrow?"

I'm still giggling. "I think she wanted to hit me."

"Would you hate me if I said it would have been kind of funny?"

I shrug. I've never been in a fight before. Fenn used to talk about them at Sandover, and it always made me curious what it feels like to throw a punch.

As if he knows I'm thinking about him, my pocket buzzes. He's been texting all day, as per usual.

"What's that face?" Jaz asks.

"Nothing."

"Who keeps texting you? That guy still?"

"Yup."

"And you're still over it?"

"So over it."

When I get to sixth period, the sister sends me out with a pass to the headmistress's office before I've even sat down. A few minutes later,

I'm looking into the stern eyes of the Reverend Mother, who points a bony finger and says, "Sit down, Ms. Tresscott."

Her bleak, austere office offers two industrial metal chairs that look like they were pillaged from a prison dumpster. Her desk is an oppressive force in the room, like it was carved from a single massive trunk of an ancient redwood. In the dimly lit space, the deep wrinkles of her pale, hardened face play tricks with the shadows.

I take a seat in one of the uncomfortable visitors' chairs and watch as she settles behind her desk.

"I feel remiss I haven't spoken to you sooner," she begins with no pretense of friendliness. The Reverend Mother is an intimidating presence, and she likes it that way. "How do you feel you are settling into St. Vincent's?"

I should be terrified of her, so I don't know why that question strikes me as funny.

Yeah, good, Reverend Mother. After two months of dodging near-constant harassment, I finally made a friend. But I keep that to myself.

"Fine," I say instead.

"Are you certain? I thought that was the case too, as none of your teachers mentioned you were having any troubles. But there is some concern among the sisters that you're beginning to present a disruption in class."

"Weird. Because up until a week ago, I'm not sure I've said more than ten words at one time since the semester started."

It's rich of them to pin the problem on me when Ainsley and her copycats have been the instigators to every interaction. Short of throwing myself out a window, how was I supposed to avoid that?

"Sister Katherine informed me of an exchange between you and two other students in class last week. And I'm told there was an altercation in the cafeteria today. Evidently, in both instances there was some disturbing language involved."

For fuck's sake.

"Well, for the record," I say calmly, "Ainsley was the one shouting slurs."

I can't remember if I called her a cunt out loud, or if that was just in my head, so I keep it to myself.

"Perhaps you have an impression of devout women as delicate things, but I assure you, Ms. Tresscott, the women here are not fragile. And we do not tolerate disobedience. If your outbursts continue, you will find yourself in front of me again. That's not something you should look forward to."

I give a sarcastic laugh. "So Ainsley gets to keep being a heinous bully, and I'm supposed to shut up and take it, right? That's how this goes?"

"If you don't wish to have me call your father," the Reverend Mother says flatly, "I suggest you take our conversation to heart and return to class."

I go back to class, where I stew for the rest of the hour, wondering how it is that the bully walks away scot-free while her victim is chewed out for finally showing a backbone. After the bell rings, I head to my locker, where Sloane is on me before I've had a chance to switch out my books for sixth period. Pouncing like a cheetah and digging her teeth into my ankle.

"You got sent to the office?" she demands with that strained tone of frustration she inherited from Dad. "I just heard some chicks whispering about it at their lockers."

"So?"

"So? What the hell, Case?"

I slam my locker shut and walk away, only to have her chase me.

"Would it kill you to spend some time in your own life instead of hitching a ride on mine?" I ask with an irritated sigh.

Her eyes flash. "Okay, you know what? You've been a fucking brat lately, and I'm sick of it. What's your deal?"

"Oh my God, Sloane. You're not Mom, and I don't need a

keeper. I'm fine. Also, you don't need to wait for me after school today. Jazmine's driving me home."

Before she can stop me, I dip into my classroom and shut the door in her face.

I can't be responsible for Sloane's savior complex anymore. If she wants to martyr herself on the tombstone of our mother, that's her damage. She can leave me out of it from now on. Maybe at one time I needed to lean on her, but it's become suffocating. Not to mention exhausting, dragging her guilt around on my back. Everyone keeps telling me I have to get past what happened, but then they won't let me heal. It's become part of them, like they need me to stay sick so they can congratulate themselves for being so selfless and support-ive. If I refuse to be their burden, what will they have to complain about?

At the end of the day, I find Jaz waiting for me outside on the front steps, drawing in her sketchpad. I flop down beside her and fill her in on my lashes from Reverend Mother.

"Also, have you seen her office?" I ask, shivering.

Jaz grins. "Once or twice."

"It's terrifying. What's with that weird cabinet?"

"You know she's got like an altar to some ancient demigod in there."

"Right? I don't know why she gives me serious *American Horror Story* vibes. And I can't help thinking under those robes she's sport-ing some seriously fucked-up tattoos."

"The perfect cover," Jaz says solemnly.

"Hey, do you want to do something this weekend?" I ask, slightly hesitant. It's been a while since I had a friend to hang out with that wasn't Fenn, and I'm sort of nervous I might be jumping the gun. "My sister's being a pain in the ass, and I can't spend another weekend locked in the house with her hounding me."

"Yeah, okay. I'm down."

As we're talking, I notice a very conspicuous car pull up in the loop where parents and hired help wait for students. It's a silver Porsche, sleek and disgustingly expensive. Sunlight sparks off Lawson Kent's signature sunglasses when he steps out and comes around to lean against the passenger side.

Then I notice a smiling Ainsley jump up from the top step where she'd been waiting. Beaming, she starts to stride toward him.

It gives me a terrible idea.

"You know him?" Jaz asks, admiring Lawson's tall, muscular frame.

"Gotta go. I'll text you."

"What—"

I'm already gone. I have to take it at a jog to beat her there, but I succeed, running up to Lawson just as Ainsley gets within spitting distance. Without missing a beat, I reach up and throw my arms over his shoulders.

"Hey, handsome," I greet him.

Ignoring his bewildered expression, I lay a kiss on him.

With tongue.

"What are you doing?" he whispers when our lips part, those light gray eyes dancing with intrigue.

"You complaining?" I whisper back, then nip at his bottom lip.

Lawson chuckles. "Never."

"Good." I pull back with a mischievous smile. "Now how about you give me a ride?"

CHAPTER 21
LAWSON

CASEY TRESSCOTT IS A BIBLICAL BEAUTY. FORBIDDEN FRUIT. THE little sister. To taste is to commit one's soul to eternal torment and damnation.

I've witnessed the utter devastation she's wrought on poor dear Fenn, and I don't envy his anguish. Although I'm still not sure what he did to deserve being banished from the Tresscott sisters' good graces. Everyone is so hush-hush lately, which means they're leaving my mind to fill in the blanks.

And everything my mind comes up with leans toward the depraved.

"I think you're lost, little girl." I eye Casey in the passenger seat as she puts her window down, letting the cool autumn air sweep her golden hair around her face like a wild conflagration. "You know Sloane would kill me for this."

"Then don't tell her."

Uh-oh. I've seen that look before. She's a girl determined to pour kerosene on the town and set it ablaze. The schoolgirl uniform only adds to the rebellious aura she's emitting.

My gaze lowers to her bare legs, tanned and shapely. The hem of her skirt rides up a little, flashing a bit of thigh.

I shouldn't be checking her out, I know. But forbidden fruit is appetizing to look at. Bet she tastes great too.

But I'd never go there.

I think.

If I weren't sober, who knows. Luckily, I haven't indulged in any party favors today, so my head is clear and I'm pretty sure I can trust myself not to break the bro code and poach Fenn's girl, ex or not. I probably wouldn't have let her in the car otherwise.

Okay, that's a lie. Sober or intoxicated, I was curious the second she said *give me a ride*.

"And for whose benefit is this little excursion on the wild side?" I ask with a chuckle.

"So many questions…"

"Call me curious."

I've certainly been kissed with less explanation, but rarely by someone as emphatically off-limits as Casey. Which is in no way a complaint. I could do with a disruption in the status quo, and I'm dying to see where this goes, even if I have a feeling I know the motive for her sudden rebellious turn.

"We wouldn't be trying to inflict some existential damage on Fenn, would we?" I waggle my eyebrows. "You know you're going to get us in trouble."

Casey betrays a moment of hesitation before she steels herself again. "Would you care?" She glances at me with playful eyes. "You love trouble."

"Guilty."

I blow through the intersection rather than turn left toward the road that would take us back to Sandover. Casey notices but doesn't voice an objection. She got in this car, after all. And I plan to make the trip worthwhile for her. Plus, it's bound to stir up turmoil when her absence is noticed.

I can't wait to watch the fallout.

"Anyway, this isn't about Fenn." Her voice turns bitter with his name in her mouth.

"Enlighten me, then. Who are we making jealous?"

"Jealous? Nobody. The question you should be asking is—who are we pissing off?"

An approving grin spreads across my face. "I like this already. Who are we pissing off, Casey?"

"Ainsley Fisck." She shoots me a sidelong look. "I can't see you two traveling in the same circles. How do you even know her?"

"Can't say that I do. She gave me her number at the bar."

"And you actually made plans with her?"

There wasn't a plan, per se. Ainsley had been adamant over text that I make a show of picking her up from school today, and *surely* I could get my hands on a sexy car. Of course, I obliged, partly because I can't walk away from a challenge, but mostly because I've been bored ever since the Goodwyns fled Sandover. Besides, I've done worse things than steal a car to get laid.

"'Plans' is a generous way to phrase it," I answer. I shift gears and speed up a little, then glance at the passenger seat. "She a friend of yours?"

"I intend to destroy her."

No hint of hyperbole there. Her jaw is set as she turns her attention toward the road.

Interesting. In a pride of lions, Casey is a dove. Gentle as they come. But it looks like she's found her claws.

"Sounds fun," I inform her.

She responds with a laugh, which leads to a whole slew of giggles as she informs me, "Your phone is exploding. I bet it's Ainsley. Can I look?"

"Go for it."

She plucks my phone from the center console. I look over in time to see the glow of triumph light her blue eyes.

"Ainsley?" I confirm.

"Oh yeah. She's losing her shit. Here, listen." Casey adopts a high-pitched, outraged tone. "*What the fuck, Lawson! WHAT THE*

HELL WAS THAT!" She uses her regular voice to add, "That second one was all caps, by the way."

"Of course."

"*You better have a good explanation for this! Omg, Lawson. Answer me, you asshole!*"

I snicker.

"Can I answer her? Please?"

Even if I wanted to say no—which I'd never do, because that word doesn't exist in my vocab—Casey's hopeful face is impossible to resist.

"Have at it," I say graciously.

She's chuckling to herself as she types away. "Sent," she declares, and I turn to find her beaming at me.

"What'd you say?"

"Don't worry, I wasn't too mean. Here we go. Ahem." Casey clears her throat as if she's about to recite a speech in front of a packed auditorium. "'Yeah, sorry about that, babe. Casey and I go way back. Decided to catch up with her instead.'" She sets the phone down. "That's going to make her livid."

"Nice touch with the *babe*."

"I thought so."

Only about ten minutes out from St. Vincent's, civilization gives way to thick amber forests and the blunt ridges of the Appalachian range. Casey braces her feet and grabs the armrest when I accelerate into the turns of the winding mountain road that peers over the river below. Then, when the twisting curves become easy, meandering straightaways, she drags her fingers over the lavish leather seat, admiring the luxury interior.

"Whose car is this?" she asks. "I've never seen it before."

"It's a loaner."

I was walking out of the dining hall from lunch when Ainsley concocted this scheme and informed me of her vehicular preferences. Frankly, it sounded like a headache and more squeeze than the juice was worth, until I happened to walk by a Porsche Boxster in the senior dorm parking lot. What can I say? The tempting little number spoke to me.

Her gaze narrows. "Why do I think that means stolen?"

"You want out?" I tip my head in challenge.

If she's having second thoughts, better to run on home before it gets dark. Animals come out at night.

"No," she replies. "I like trouble too."

We'll see. While I'm happy to entertain her vengeful dalliances, I find myself under no obligation to shield Casey from her choices. I'm nobody's keeper. People are responsible for making their own decisions—and dealing with the consequences of them.

CHAPTER 22
RJ

IT'S TAX DAY, AND I'M THE GODDAMNED IRS. IT WAS BAD ENOUGH when I had morons stopping me in the hall to ask about scalping Celtics tickets or drag racing for pink slips. Now I can't have dinner without some kid I've never met nodding at me as he drops a plain white envelope in my partially open school bag sitting on the floor.

"You see this shit?" I say to Fenn, who is reluctantly picking at his chicken pot pie.

He gestures over my shoulder. "Here comes another one."

"It's been like this all day."

This time, a guy from our floor sidles up and slaps a wad of cash in my hand like we're doing a drug deal. For all I know, we just did.

"I mean, fuck, where's it all coming from?" I grumble.

Fenn puts his head down and resumes his contentious battle with his food. "Probably best not to ask those kinds of questions."

"But am I sanctioning hit jobs? Gun running? This feels like mafia shit."

"Probably not," he says with a less-than-convincing shrug. "Then again, I don't put anything past this place."

It's not just the envelopes being shoved under our door and stuffed in my gym locker. My phone's been blowing up all day with

Venmo and PayPal notifications. Vast sums of anonymous cash funneling its way into my accounts for who knows what sort of illicit activities.

"I'm seriously getting paranoid here," I tell him.

Silas rolls his eyes. He hasn't said much since he sat down beside Fenn and started eating his dinner, one hand scrolling his phone.

"I've seen *Goodfellas*," I say, watching as a former acolyte of Duke's gives me the eye from across the room. "This is what it looks like right before I get raided by the Feds."

Fenn sighs. He's made progress over the last few days, if glumly finishing a meal can be considered progress. But he's still depressed most of the time. Sulking over losing Casey and whatever inner turmoil has him protecting his secrets like nuclear launch codes. On occasion, though, he manages to hold a conversation about something that isn't one or both Tresscott sisters.

Duke's buddy strides toward us. Fenn knows him from soccer, but I've never talked to him. Weaving through tables, he reaches into his jacket's inner pocket. I've seen this part of the movie too. Riding high in May. Shot down in June.

"All I did was take a few punches from Duke," I remind Fenn. "People have killed for less."

"You're being dramatic."

Still, part of me flinches when the guy approaches and whips his hand out of his pocket. But he doesn't brandish a weapon—rather, he pulls out a roll of bills with a rubber band around it and quietly slides it across the table to me.

"Next Friday night," the guy says with a cagey squirm about him. "I've got a little poker game going. With your permission, of course. You're welcome to come."

"What the fuck do I care?" I push the money away. "Tell people to stop asking about shit. Do whatever you want."

Baffled, as if I'm the crazy one, he departs with a furrowed brow and leaves the wad behind.

"You see?" I scowl at the guy's retreating back. "It's like talking to a brick wall."

"They think it's a test," Fenn says. "They're confused."

"Tell me how the hell I explain a sock drawer full of stacks of hundred-dollar bills when the FBI breaks down our door." I quickly throw the cash in my messenger bag and zip it shut, kicking it under the table. "For that matter, how do I deprogram them? This shit isn't funny anymore."

"Wish I had your problems," Silas mutters to himself.

That's not all of mine he wishes for.

Fenn sets down his fork and takes a sip of water. "It was your bright idea to fight Duke. This is the consequence."

"How many ways do I have to tell them they're free now? I don't want their damn kickbacks."

"You showed up here a couple months ago and thought you'd change the whole world order of things," Fenn says, sounding frustrated. "But it's like US intervention in the Middle East, man. This is thousands of years of culture that won't be undone overnight. Not in our lifetime."

"Not on my watch."

I climb up on my chair.

"The fuck are you doing?" he groans. "Sit down, you idiot."

"Your attention, please," I announce to the dining hall, which hushes to a startling silence as if God himself had spoken. "It seems there's some misunderstanding. A few of you haven't gotten the memo."

"Seriously, dude," Fenn insists. "Shut the fuck up."

"The old regime is dead," I tell my classmates. "I declare this land a benevolent anarchy. There are no leaders here."

They stare at me in stillness for a moment. Expressions blank. Then the doors of the dining hall flap open.

"Mr. Shaw." Mr. Colson, a member of the science faculty, frowns and points one finger at the floor. "Down from there."

I take my seat, and normalcy immediately resumes as the room fills with conversations.

"You happy now?" Fenn says, shaking his head. "All that did was convince them you're crazy."

I'm getting there.

In the far corner, Duke sits with his lackey Carter. They're both watching me, Carter's expression murderous while Duke's is a mixture of annoyance and resignation. I know it drives him crazy he lost top dog status at Sandover, but the fact that I was able to drain his bank account so easily now keeps him resigned to accept that fate.

Me, I almost regret it now. Yes, beating him in the fight and using the threat of robbing him again succeeded in Duke no longer confronting me in the halls with vague threats and beating his chest. But I miss the days when every dude in school wasn't hassling me on a daily basis, asking for permission to jerk off.

I shift my gaze off Duke and try to focus on what Fenn is saying.

"They don't like change. They're out of sorts and need to be ruled. You think you want anarchy, but I'm not sure you understand what that looks like under these conditions."

"*Lord of the Flies* would be preferable to this," I mutter.

Silas looks up from his phone and scoffs at me. "Oh, fuck off with this act."

"What's that supposed to mean?" I ask warily.

Since the shit that went down with Sloane, Silas has mostly kept his distance. He's been giving me the cold shoulder at practice, content to mumble snide remarks under his breath. Guess he's feeling bold today.

"Your one complaint boils down to being pissed off about getting piles of cash you've done practically nothing to earn," Silas replies. "You don't like the arrangement, fine. But spare us the insincere bullshit."

"I'm insincere?" He's trying my last nerve. "Look, I've let some shit slide because I respect the game, but you took your shot with Sloane and fell on your face. I'm with her now and that's not changing, so you're welcome to get used to it or fuck off."

"RJ, come on," Fenn says. Always the diplomat.

Silas looks as though he might have a few parting remarks, but then thinks better of it. Instead, he picks up his tray and leaves.

Fenn cocks his head at me. "Was that necessary?"

"Yeah. It was." I pick up my fork again. "I'm not gonna pretend to be broken up about it. And neither should you."

"He's my friend," he says with a shrug.

"Your friend?" I echo, snorting. "Then you should probably know—your *friend* is the one who sent me out to the woods to find you and Sloane that day. He set you up."

I'd been reluctant to tell Fenn until now. Thanks to his moment of petty jealousy, Silas has already lost any chance of repairing a friendship with Sloane. I figured the punishment already fit the crime, which meant there was no need to bring his friendship with Fenn into it. But if he's not content to take the L and walk, I'm not about to protect his reputation.

CHAPTER 23
CASEY

I'VE NEVER BEEN OUT THIS WAY BEFORE. WELL NORTH OF THE LAKE, through the narrow mountain passes and winding county roads. Sloane's never liked road trips and, well, since the accident, I haven't done much driving.

"You're developing a taste for it."

Lawson sounds amused while he watches me stick a hand out the open window to feel the wind travel between my fingers. The Porsche races at ever-increasing speeds past country houses that catch a brief glimpse of us through the trees.

"Maybe a little," I admit.

He narrows his eyes. "Don't ever let anyone make you ashamed of living, Casey."

I have no good reason to trust Lawson Kent. His nefarious reputation precedes him through this life and the next. If even half of what people say is true, he's a drunk, a drug addict, a philanderer, and generally lacking in any discernable moral center. But he's free. Completely unfettered and unconcerned. No one tells Lawson what to do, and he regrets nothing, beholden to no one.

Right now, I just want to follow his example, because there's a sort of freedom in embracing our most primal selves. We can be scratched off this planet at any moment, so why not enjoy ourselves?

"Can I give it a try?"

He glances at me. "You want to drive?"

"No apologies, right?"

His answering grin is almost proud. "Exactly."

We pull off at a scenic overlook with the sun quickly falling toward the rolling horizon. We get out of the convertible and stand beside the wooden rail. In the back of my mind, I know Sloane is already wondering what happened to me. I should have been home over two hours ago.

"You ever think about how when no one knows where you are, it's like you've stepped outside of time?" I wonder aloud.

We could disappear. Keep driving in the wrong direction and get lost. Stay lost. Become someone else. Invent a new reality and write ourselves out of an existence that's always felt inevitable.

"Every day," he says, watching the sky turning to purples and pink. "It's kind of like, somewhere, every possible version of ourselves is making every conceivable decision." He chuckles. "Inflicting infinite new variations of us on the universe. Makes you think, fuck, what does it matter if I have another drink or fly to Thailand?"

"Or steal a car and go joyriding."

"Or that." He combs his fingers through his light-brown hair, which comes nearly to his shoulders, slicking it away from his forehead.

I never took Lawson seriously before, so I suppose I never noticed how handsome he is. Or how his usual sarcasm and crassness obscure the sincerity in his eyes when he isn't trying to convince you of his intense desire to be perpetually alone. I know that instinct.

"You know, all in all, I'm starting to think you might not be such a bad boy," I tease.

"Careful," he says and tosses me the keys to the ill-gotten Porsche. "I can't have you spreading such vicious lies."

As I'm getting acclimated to the driver's seat, Lawson buckles himself in. "I assume you're familiar with driving stick?"

"Huh?"

"You have done this before?"

"Oh, yeah. Well, once or twice."

He shakes his head with a genuine chuckle. "No better way to learn."

Surprising both of us, I get the car in gear and drive back out on the road. Thankfully the traffic is almost nonexistent.

"Like riding a bike," I say when the gears protest to my determined shifting.

He snorts.

It takes a few miles, but I get the hang of it, those lessons from my aunt over summer vacation coming back to me quickly. Her old Chevy pickup was a bit less precious about the clutch than this one, though.

"Hey, you hungry?" I see a sign for an old-fashioned creamery and convenience store up the road that makes ice cream from its own milk cows in the pasture out back. "They have soft serve."

"Fuck, that's adorable."

"What?"

"I was thinking a bar, but sure, ice cream sounds good."

We end up in the center of a cute little town. The kind with lights strung up over the road between lampposts, and sidewalk cafes opening for dinner. After we get our ice cream, we decide to take a stroll past the shop windows of mom-and-pop joints preserved like a time capsule of pre-internet society.

We come to a small park in the center of town with a picnic table. I climb up and take a seat, licking a glob of butterscotch before it slides off the side of the cone. It's starting to get a bit too cold out for ice cream, but mine is melting fast despite the cooling air temperature. I should have gotten it in a cup like Lawson did.

"Oh, I should have mentioned this before, but I can't stay out obscenely late," I warn Lawson, who hops up to sit beside me, lifting his spoon to his lips. "I have to get home and feed my bunny."

He pauses mid-lick, slowly looking over at me. "Oh. Okay. Well, you need to work on your dirty talk. But I can work with this." He's biting his lip now, seemingly to keep from laughing. "How do we feed the bunny? You got a vibrator? Or just your fingers?"

I almost drop my cone. "Oh my God. No. I mean that in the literal sense. I have an actual bunny to feed."

His forehead creases. "So we're not talking about your pussy?"

"*No.*" My cheeks are scorching.

After a beat, he starts to laugh. Deep and genuine. "Jesus Christ."

"What?"

"You're so fucking pure, I feel dirty just sitting here next to you. You have a pet rabbit?"

"Sort of?" I fill him in on the rabbit rescue of the other night.

Meanwhile, he's gazing at me in fascination, as if he walked into a remote village somewhere in the Amazon and discovered a new species. I get the feeling he genuinely can't relate to me.

He confirms this when he says, "Who the fuck are you, Casey?"

"What?" I say defensively.

He seems a bit unnerved, another groove digging into his forehead. "You fought off a bunch of foxes—"

"I didn't fight them off—"

"—to rescue an orphaned rabbit, and now you're literally handfeeding the damn thing like Snow fucking White. People like you exist in animated movies, not real life."

"You sound like Fenn." I hate even bringing him up, but it slips out before I can stop myself.

That makes Lawson snort. "Fenn and I are nothing alike. He's the Disney prince to your Disney princess. Dude thinks he's all dark and tortured, but it's the kind of surface torment you find on teen soaps. He wouldn't last a day in the same house as my father."

I don't miss the bitterness that colors his tone. Sloane told me once that Lawson's dad is some kind of supervillain, but she hadn't offered any details.

"And how does your father torment you?" I ask curiously.

Lawson becomes unusually close-lipped, and I regret asking, suddenly realizing I might be treading beyond TMI territory. For all I know, he's been dealing with domestic abuse or worse. And I, a virtual stranger to him, am the last person he probably wants to confide in.

"It's fine," I say, reaching over to touch his knee. "Don't answer that."

His gaze lowers to my hand. He gets a strange look but doesn't push my hand away.

"Yeah, we'll save that for another time," he says with a dismissive shrug. "Tell me more about your bunny." He winks. "How does the breastfeeding work? Do you burp it after?"

Unfazed, I bite into a piece of my waffle cone. "I use a syringe. And there's no burping required. But I do have to rub her button with a cotton ball after I feed her so that she goes to the bathroom."

"Her button?" he echoes blankly, and then, when he notices my reddening cheeks, he presses his lips together in silent laughter. "Ah. I see."

"Basically, I keep stroking it until she's done and—"

He howls, doubling over. "Fuck, you gotta stop. Please."

I'm laughing now too. It sounds insane and horrifyingly sexual the way I phrased it. But I'm glad I managed to lighten the mood again.

After we quiet down, he stares at me with a crooked smile. "I think I'm in love with you."

I roll my eyes. "Shut up."

"So pure," he says again, more to himself than me.

"I'm not pure," I argue.

"You are," he corrects. "Which means…you probably need to think about what you're going to do tomorrow."

"About what?"

"Damage control with your little friends. I should have warned you sooner, but being seen gallivanting the streets with someone of my ill-repute does have its social consequences."

"Like how? Everyone will think we did it?"

"'Did it,' she says, like we're on a family sitcom."

"Now there's something wrong with the way I talk?"

"No." He licks ice cream off his spoon like he's trying to flirt with it. "Not if you're on the Disney Channel."

"If this is your pathetic ploy to get me to not like you, it won't work."

"If I were trying, you'd already be running."

"Ha. Give it your best shot, then. Startle me with your depravity."

"All right. This semester I fucked a couple of married teachers. Jack and Gwen Goodwyn."

"Oh." I'm not sure what I expected him to say, but that wasn't it. "Like a threesome?"

"I wish. It was one at a time. But at the same time." He sighs glumly. "They both resigned, unfortunately. It's been quite boring since they left."

I smother a laugh. "Right, yeah. I could see how it would be."

He watches me almost sympathetically over his double scoop of black cherry ice cream. "Have I scandalized you beyond repair?"

"Nope." I'm surprised, sure. But hardly clutching my proverbial pearls. "I guess I didn't know for sure that you were, like, bi, I guess?"

He shrugs. "Labels are…limiting. I hate them. I don't think of myself in terms of bi or gay or straight. I enjoy sex and I'm attracted to people, sometimes in blurry amalgamations."

"You know, that sounds oddly reasonable when you put it that way."

"I think so."

There's no denying Lawson tends to invite the negative reactions he gets from people. He makes a point of putting them on edge.

Sloane's not so different, even if their methods are. Like my sister, though, I think Lawson ultimately wants to be understood. With RJ, she fought so hard to scare him off because she liked him that much. Knew when she decided to open her heart to him, he'd have earned it. It's manipulative, and a messed-up way to treat people, backfiring more often than not. Still, there's a broken sense of logic to it.

"Tell me something," he says. "You and Fenn are on the outs, right?"

My guard immediately shoots up. "True."

"Why?"

"What do you mean, why?"

He grins. "I mean *why*. What was the reason for the sudden split? Nobody's talking."

He's not wrong. Only four people in the world know what Fenn did that night. Four who have kept this secret between us. And while Sloane claims to be furious at Fenn, not once have I felt like she or RJ have my back on this. RJ's loyalty is to his stepbrother. Sloane says she's loyal to me, yet she's still talking to Fenn, giving him details about my school life and how many fucking detentions I get. How is that taking my side?

So when Lawson asks, I decide to be honest instead of dodging or lying. Because maybe I'm hoping he might be the one person selfish enough to not take their sides.

"What do you remember about prom?" I ask him.

He's understandably taken aback when he furrows his brow at the topic. "Honestly, not much. Think I blacked out."

"That makes two of us." I laugh darkly. "But I just found out that Fenn's the one who pulled me out of the car."

Lawson blinks at me. "Christ, are you serious?"

"And it's on video."

"Holy shit." Setting his cup of melted ice cream aside, he turns to face me fully. "Was he in the car?"

"No, and we don't know who was. There's someone else on the

video but not enough to recognize them. Meanwhile, Fenn refuses to explain why he didn't say a word about any of this. Why he rescued me and then just left me on the ground. Unconscious. With a head injury." Anger rises inside me. "Who does that?"

"That's fucked up," Lawson agrees, and coming from him, that says a lot.

"Right?" I shake my head. "So…yeah…you can imagine why that would strain a relationship."

"No shit." His silvery eyes focus on me, searching my expression. "If he gives you an explanation that makes any sense, will you forgive him?"

"I don't know," I admit. "Either way, I'll never forget."

It's getting dark, so we throw our trash out and make our way back toward the car. Lawson is quiet and pensive, obviously still reeling from the revelation.

"Sorry for dropping all that on you," I say sheepishly. "I kind of killed the fun."

"No, what?" He flinches. "God, no. I'm just over here contemplating what filthy, depraved debauchery I'll have to concoct on our next adventure to top this."

I lift a brow. "Next time?"

"I could arrange an elaborate art heist if that's more to your liking. In either case, there are options and costumes are encouraged."

"That sounds suspiciously like asking me out on a second date."

"A date?" He gives an innocent look. "I'm only proposing a tentative agreement for future friendly mischief."

"That does have a nice ring to it," I say shyly.

Despite the inevitable backlash that will come from me cavorting around with someone as prolifically notorious as Lawson, I had such a good time today. That's worth more to me than sanitizing myself against gossip at this point.

"Hey." I stop him a second when we get back to the Porsche. "I know you probably thought I was crazy the way I basically assaulted you back at school. And, um, sorry about that. But you could have blown me off or been a dick about, and yet you weren't. And I had a good time. So…yeah. Thank you."

I expect a clever if slightly crude retort. Instead, he leans against the car and crosses his arms.

"Of all the people I know, Casey Tresscott, you're the last one I'd want to be a dick to."

"Cool," I say, biting back a smile. Because that might be one of the nicest things anyone's ever said to me. Which is sort of sad if I want to dwell on it. So I don't. "But if anyone asks, I had no idea the car was stolen."

He flashes a grin. "Deal."

We should go. It's gotten dark and I'm afraid to see what time it is. I'm sure he's got better things to do.

Only he doesn't budge and neither do I. We're standing here in the middle of nowhere, nameless. We could be anyone. Lawson inches closer, or maybe it's me. I shiver at the chilly autumn breeze because for just a second, it looks like Lawson Kent is going to kiss me.

Until my feet fully leap off the ground at the startling buzzing in my pocket.

"Oh, shit," I hiss, watching dozens of notifications for texts, missed calls, and voicemails flash on the screen.

"What?"

"We must have lost reception at some point. I've got like a million messages coming in."

Each successive text from my dad and Sloane is more hysterical. And there's at least as many from Fenn. Sloane must have gotten desperate to rope him into the search. I'm snatched back to reality by the image of Dad pacing around the house, thinking the worst. Sloane trudging through the woods searching for me.

"We have to get back," I tell Lawson. "As quickly as possible."

CHAPTER 24
CASEY

"Much as I'd love to be a gentleman..." It's dark when Lawson pulls up alongside the brick entrance to Sandover's campus. "I'm letting you off here instead of your house."

"Don't even feel bad about it. If my dad didn't try to have you arrested for kidnapping, Sloane would douse you in gasoline and light a match," I reply, unbuckling my seat belt and throwing the door open before he's come to a full stop.

"Then this is where I leave you, fellow rebel."

"Hey, out of curiosity. What do you plan to do about the car?"

"Oh, this?" He glides his hands appreciatively over the leather steering wheel. "Probably leave it in a handicap parking space in town. Asshole who owns it had it coming."

I fight a laugh. "Well, good luck with that."

I grab my backpack from the floor of the passenger seat, then hop out of the Porsche and hurry off in a dead sprint across campus and back home.

I'm somewhat relieved to see the front yard isn't crowded with patrol cars, but every light in the house is on and the tension emanating from inside is palpable as I approach. I take the walk up the driveway slow, so I can catch my breath, but there's nothing I can do about how sweaty I am from that run.

Just before I go inside, I shut off my phone.

"Hey, I'm home," I call with what I hope sounds like nonchalance. "Sorry I'm late."

Before I even get the door shut behind me, Dad charges into the foyer. Sloane pounces from the kitchen. They're on me and shouting incoherently over each other, absolutely bombarded by panic and anger.

"Where have you been all night?"

"Why didn't you answer your phone?"

"I've been trying you for hours."

"Whoa. What's going on?" I feign surprise as I kick off my shoes. "I didn't realize my phone died."

Sloane snorts. "Bullshit. Let me see it."

"Why didn't you come home with Sloane after school?" Dad interjects. His face is red and practically throbbing, deep ridges carved into his brow.

"Jazmine asked if I wanted to hang out and do homework together. So we went to her dorm instead. Studied, watched a couple movies. Then she dropped me home and now here I am. Not sure what the big deal is—I told Sloane."

They both stay right on my heels when I go to the kitchen to chug a glass of water and pour another. From the looks of things, they started making dinner—veggies chopped and a pot of water on to boil—but must have aborted when I didn't show up.

"Bullshit," my sister says again. "You told me Jazmine was giving you a ride home, not that you were chilling at her dorm."

"Oh my God. The plans changed. I don't need your permission to make friends."

"That's enough attitude," Dad snaps.

"Since when am I getting interrogated for being late for dinner?" Anger heats my cheeks. Sloane gets to sneak around all over town while Dad barely notices. I come home late one time and it's like a jailbreak from Alcatraz.

"This is serious, Casey!" Dad shouts in a decibel I haven't heard in years. "I can't believe you'd be so thoughtless and irresponsible."

"I'm seventeen!"

"That doesn't mean you get to do whatever you want."

Something in his inflection, or maybe this whole week, sets me off and I can't hold it in. "Everyone else I know gets to have a life, Dad. What about me? When do I get to be normal? I'm not a child anymore."

He huffs at the questions, rubbing the bridge of his nose in frustration. "You can't simply decide whenever you feel like it to stay out all night and not tell anyone where you are."

"All night? It's nine the fuck o'clock."

"Language!"

"Sorry. But come on, it's not even that late. And we were in the dormitory of an all-girls *Catholic* school." I frown at him. "Am I not allowed to have any friends? Is that it?"

"That's not what I said." He crosses his arms tight to his chest. "Curfew is dinnertime on weeknights. You know that. If there's going to be an exception, your friends can come here and introduce themselves. Or your sister will be with you."

"Wait," Sloane objects darkly. "Why am I getting dragged into this?"

"This is so unfair. You can't keep me locked up in this house. I'm not your prisoner." I drop my glass in the sink, then stalk to the fridge to get the kitten milk. "Now if you'll excuse me, I need to feed Silver."

I storm up to my room and slam the door shut, then throw my backpack in the corner and turn my phone back on. Sloane, of course, has no respect for boundaries and comes barging in because she's the only one in this house with any right to privacy.

Ignoring her, I peek into the shoebox. The moment a sliver of light penetrates the darkness, Silver squeaks and shifts on the soft pink towel I'm using for her bed. Relief flutters through me, escaping in the form of a shaky breath.

"She still alive?" Sloane asks.

"Yes."

I close the box and set it down while I prepare the milk syringe and gather a few cotton balls from the plastic container on my desk.

"I know you're lying," she accuses.

"Why would I lie about that? She's alive. See for yourself."

"Not about that." My sister takes a combative stance against my bookshelf. Arms crossed and head cocked. "You weren't out with some new friend. Who was it?"

"Duke."

Her eyes all but pop out of her skull as her mouth falls open.

But I can't keep a straight face and crack immediately. "Jesus, relax. Of course it wasn't Duke. I just had to see your face."

Her shock turns to frustration. "I'm serious, Case. You know I'll find out. Don't make me CSI this shit."

"Calm down. Lawson and I—"

"*Lawson*? Are you fucking kidding me?"

"We took a drive through the country. Got ice cream. Nothing scandalous." Well, except for the stolen Porsche, but technically that happened before he picked me up.

"I thought you were smarter than this."

"Please. I can handle Lawson." I can't help but roll my eyes, which gets Sloane gritting her teeth.

"Seriously. Stay away from that guy," she orders, getting in my face. "You don't know him. Whatever he's said to you, I promise there's nothing good about his intentions. He's toxic and only ever looking for trouble."

Yeah? Maybe a little trouble is what I'm after, did she ever think of that? It's not like playing the good sister has spared me more than my share of misfortune.

Aloud, my tone takes on a defiant note. "Do you even know why you think that about him? Like, do you actually know anything about him? Ever had a real conversation with him? Because I have. And he was perfectly nice to me. In fact, he's the first person in a long time who let me feel like a human being and not a piece of porcelain."

Sloane sighs before lowering her voice. "Trust me. There are some things you don't understand—"

"Right, yeah. This again. I'm too stupid and naive, right? But you know what? I'm not convinced that's true—it feels like just a thing you and Dad and Fenn tell me to keep me in this bizarre emotional cage. Because God forbid I should wander outside your arbitrary boundaries to experience anything for myself."

She flinches. "It's not like that. You know it isn't. I'm looking out for you."

"Okay, well, do me a favor and don't. I can make my own decisions from now on." I clench my jaw. "Consider yourself relieved of duty."

"Fine." Sloane throws up her hands. "Have fun with that. Just don't say I didn't warn you."

"Yeah. Whatever. Bye."

I practically shove her out of my room and lock the door. Sloane's always felt this self-imposed compulsion to mother me, which for a while now has felt more like smothering.

Tonight, for maybe the first time, I can breathe. Lawson gave me that.

I settle on the bed and take Silver out to feed her. With her tiny, hairless body and no visible eyes or ears, she looks more like an alien creature from a sci-fi movie. And yet I'm already in love with her. According to Dad, I got my obsession for animals from my mom. Apparently, on one of their dates early in their relationship, Mom found a stray kitten on her way to the restaurant, and rather than ignore it, she scooped up the half-starved, mangy thing, tucked it in her purse, and kept the date. Dad finally suspected something when her purse kept meowing over dinner.

"You loved that cat," I say softly, talking out loud to Mom. "Dad said you cried for days after he ran away. I wish I'd gotten to meet him."

Silver makes a squeaking noise as she finishes eating. I stimulate her button to release her urine and stool, which is yellowy-green. Supposedly that means healthy. Afterward, I gently pinch her neck to check for dehydration and examine her body to make sure no inch of skin is blue or shriveled. Once I'm satisfied she looks okay, I tuck her back in her warm, cozy nest and close the box. She squeaks a few more times before going quiet.

God, I want her to survive. I know it's unlikely. Or at least, my head knows that. But my heart desperately wants Silver to live.

On my nightstand, my phone buzzes and I sigh when I see Fenn's name.

Obviously, I should ignore him. Or turn my phone off again until he's given up. Except if Sloane doesn't bother to give Fenn the all-clear, he'll show up at my window in the middle of the night demanding answers. Or worse, the front door. And tonight I'd just prefer some decent sleep.

I answer the call with a curt, "What do you want, Fenn?"

"Casey, what the fuck?" There's a short pause. "I wasn't expecting you to answer."

"Well, I'm here. What do you want?" I repeat.

"Sloane called me hours ago demanding to know what I'd done with you. Like I'd dumped your body in a ditch."

We're both quiet a moment while he considers his unfortunate choice of words.

"I've been all over town looking for you," he says, sounding frustrated.

"Yeah, I saw your messages. But I'm home now, so call off the dogs."

"That's it? You're not going to acknowledge how terrified we all were? Sloane had to be fully out of her mind to call asking me for help."

"I don't know what you want me to say. It was a lot of freaking out over nothing."

"We were worried about you." His voice becomes low. Husky. "*I* was worried."

"So now you feel like I owe you something?" I laugh sharply. "I'm supposed to do some penance or whatever because you were worried?"

"What? No," he mutters. "I'm just saying. You could have called somebody back. Shit. Your family was an inch from letting loose helicopters and search parties. After everything you've all been through—"

"Oh, okay, great. Tell me more about my family's personal traumas. In fact, if there's more on the subject you'd like to illuminate, I'm listening."

It's like he was born with his foot in his mouth.

"I'm sorry. That's not what… I'm just saying…" He trails off with a strangled expletive. "I was worried. That's all."

"This is your last reminder, Fenn—I'm not yours to worry about anymore. Leave me alone."

I end the call and throw my phone on the bed. Then I clench my fists and strain my neck, silently shouting into the open void of the ether until my jaw hurts and my whole body burns.

Why did it have to be him?

Any idiot could have wandered by the boathouse that night. Anyone could have slipped away from the dance to drink or get high. A couple sneaking off to get all hot and sweaty. Anyone else but Fenn.

My mind suddenly flashes with a thought that's taunted me since I learned the truth, the one that gets louder every time I hear from him now.

That I'd almost rather he never found me. That I'd just been left alone in that car, sinking for an eternity until the red glow dimmed. Because anything would be better than feeling this way. Love and hatred are bound so tight together inside me, I don't think I know the difference anymore.

My phone buzzes again. And while I know I shouldn't look at it—Fenn can only do more harm than good—I can't resist the impulse to pick it up.

Lawson: Good night, bad girl. Let's do it again sometime.

CHAPTER 25
FENN

"She hung up on me," I say aloud, though RJ is plastered to his computer screen.

"What'd you expect?"

I scowl at the back of his head. "I didn't ask to have your girlfriend drag me into this."

"Come on…" RJ spins in his desk chair to level me with a distinctly accusatory frown.

"What did I do?" I demand.

"I'm not judging, but…" He shrugs. "Don't tell me you weren't thinking this might be your chance to redeem yourself."

"What's that supposed to mean?"

"All I'm saying is, you can't act like you weren't at least a little excited about the idea of finding her in some kind of trouble and getting a second chance at being the hero."

"Dude. That's fucked up."

He turns back to his computer. "Maybe I'm wrong."

Whatever. Asshole. I get there's no shopping for sympathy from him where Sloane's involved, but it's more than a little manipulative to sound the alarms and get me all spun up only to tell me to piss off without an explanation. I guess I should be used to it by now.

Despite the false alarm, I'm left with a weird feeling I'd been speaking to an imposter. They sound like her. The same voice and inflection. But that person is someone else entirely. Our conversation puts an unsettled pit in my stomach. Whoever I spoke to just now wasn't Casey. It's all wrong and I have no idea what to do about it.

"It's fucked up, though, right?" I say while I wander our room with my phone in my hand, wrestling with the urge to call her back but knowing I'm supposed to be respecting her boundaries. "Casey doesn't disappear for hours and then tell everyone to get bent. That's not her."

"She's obviously going through something," he points out. "Gotta give it time."

It's not only tonight. I keep hearing about her getting in trouble at school, telling off chicks in the middle of class. It's like she's had a total personality makeover and everyone's walking around like they don't notice.

"I feel like I'm taking crazy pills," I say over my shoulder in his general direction. "There's obviously something up with her. I get she's still pissed at me, but it's not like we broke up and she decided to—"

I come up short when I notice RJ with an odd expression on his face. Sitting in his desk chair, he stares at his phone.

"What?"

He's reluctant to look at me.

"Dude, seriously. If it's about Casey, spit it out."

"Try not to do something stupid," he warns. "Sloane just texted me."

"Okay…?"

"Casey was out with Lawson."

The words hit me like they're in a different language. I half cough out a laugh because I know I didn't hear him right and there must be a wire loose in my head. Then the sober look on his face strikes me dead.

"Are you serious? Lawson?"

"Yes—"

I'm practically out the door before RJ can get out of his chair.

I storm down the hall to Lawson's room and throw open the door. The loud *crack* when it hits the wall echoes through the entire floor. Silas leaps off the sofa at the noise.

Lawson is on his bed with his laptop when I barge in. He's startled a moment before a sarcastic smile flashes across his face, and it snaps the last thread of self-control I might have had. I charge at him and rip the laptop out of his hands. It goes flying across the room to skid against the TV stand.

Gray eyes blazing with indignation, Lawson tries to hop off the bed, but I shove him back down.

"Casey? Are you out of your fucking mind? What'd you do to her?"

Silas launches toward us. "Hey, what the hell?"

"Fenn, chill," RJ says behind me.

I shrug his hand off my shoulder. "Answer me, Lawson, or I swear to God…"

"Much as I love a threat…" This time he pushes past me to walk over and pick up his laptop off the floor. "I was in the middle of something here."

RJ tries to grab me, but he's not fast enough. With an angry growl, I push Lawson up against the wall.

"Fenn…" He shoulders me out of the way. "I like you, but you put your hands on me one more time, we're going to find out who hits harder."

"I'm not fucking around. I know you were with her tonight."

"All right, enough," Silas commands. He and RJ pry us apart, standing between us. "Calm down a second and tell me what's going on."

"Shut up, Silas. You can fuck off too."

He flinches, offended. "What the hell did I do?"

"Seriously? I know you set me up, you shady bastard."

"What are you even talking about?"

"Fenn, come on." RJ tugs at me again. "Let's not do this tonight."

"No." I smack his hand away because tonight seems like a perfect time to ream out both these assholes. "You sent RJ to find Sloane and me that day because you wanted to break them up. You used me and you're a shit friend."

His face falls.

Yeah, that's what I thought. The mask is off. No one is buying the golden boy bullshit anymore.

"I swear I had no idea you were the one she was going out there to meet," Silas insists. "I never meant to screw you over."

"Whatever." He can sell it to someone else. Silas is the least of my concerns now. "I'm here about him," I snap, pointing my finger past him at Lawson. "You were out all night with Casey, and I want to know what the fuck you think you're up to."

He puts his hands up innocently. "She hopped in my car."

"You don't have a car."

"All right, she hopped in a car that I was driving."

"That doesn't make any sense."

Lawson backs away from the confrontation to grab a tumbler from the coffee table. It's filled to the brim with a dark amber liquid. He takes a swig before continuing with his defense.

"I was at St. Vincent's to pick up this other chick when Casey came prancing up to me to insist I give her a ride." He casually throws himself into an armchair with his robe hanging open over his bare chest, light-brown hair falling onto his forehead. "We went for a perfectly innocent drive. Talked about her bunny—"

I lunge again. "You asshole—"

"Her actual bunny," he interrupts, and I stop in my tracks. "I guess she rescued a rabbit the other day?" He shrugs. "I also thought she meant her pussy. It was very disappointing." He notes my thunderous expression and chuckles. "Sorry. Bad joke. Anyway, that's really it. She was pissed off at some girl at school and needed to clear her head. I took her for a drive, after which I delivered her in one entirely untouched piece." He meets my gaze. "Nothing happened."

"On your life."

"I wouldn't do that to a friend, Fenn."

Releasing a breath, I slump onto the arm of the sofa and rub my face. "No, I know. Of course not. I'm sorry, dude."

He hands me his drink, which I swallow in one burning gulp. It sticks hot and acrid in my gut.

"Uh…" He grins at me. "There's half a crushed Vicodin in there, so no driving. All right?"

Lawson's a fuckboy, but he isn't a liar. Not to his friends, anyway. The guy might be a walking red flag, but at least he's loyal, which is how I know he's telling the truth. Even if it does me no good to hear it. It kills me that Casey is turning to other people for support these days. I used to be the one she ran to when she was pissed off or needed to clear her head.

This is your last reminder, Fenn—I'm not yours to worry about anymore. Leave me alone.

Her cold words buzz around in my head. They hurt. But I also know there's no way I can possibly heed them. I *will* worry about her, and I *can't* leave her alone. I'll keep my distance, yes, but it'll take a hell of a lot more than Casey going on a joyride with Lawson to make me stop caring for her.

CHAPTER 26
CASEY

"YOU SET ME UP!"

The screechy accusation reverberates in the hallway the next morning. I lift my head from inside my locker to find Ainsley barreling toward me, proverbial guns blazing.

"Oh, hey." I give her a placid smile, then resume my attention on grabbing my history and math textbooks for first and second period. "You look nice today."

"You *bitch*," Ainsley spits out. "That was some sketchy shit you pulled yesterday."

I tuck my books under one arm and shut the locker. "I have no idea what you're talking about." I raise a brow. "Are you sure you're not the one who's been forgetting to take her meds?"

Her cheeks turn bright red. She's conspicuously alone, her sidekick Bree nowhere to be seen. I bet she's embarrassed about the way Lawson blew her off yesterday and doesn't want her friends being reminded of it.

"I don't know what game you're playing here, but Lawson Kent is—"

"Is what?" I interrupt. "A friend of mine? Yes, he is." My smile widens. "Are we more than friends? Sometimes."

"Bullshit. Maybe I buy the friendship part, but there's no way a guy like that would ever be with somebody like you." Ainsley gains some confidence, her tone hardening. "If he fucked you yesterday, it was out of pity. Throwing a bone to the crazy psycho. He was probably worried you'd commit suicide if he rejected you."

"Uh-huh. Keep telling yourself that." I eye her in amusement. "Is there anything else you want, Ainsley? Because I'd like to get to class."

She shoots me a furious look. "Just stay away from him. And stay away from me."

"I will gladly do the latter," I assure her.

Unfortunately, it's difficult to stick to that when I literally sit behind her and Bree in history class. And I'm almost disappointed when Ainsley ignores me the entire time. Now that I've beefed up my backbone, I'm enjoying cutting her down. Sadly, she spends all of class staring straight ahead with her shoulders rigid.

Since they're only two feet from me, I can't help but eavesdrop on their conversation. They're discussing the Snow Ball, which is being held at Ballard next month. Ainsley's bitching about how unfair it is that only Ballard students are eligible for Snow Queen.

"*So* unfair. You totally would've won," assures Bree, forever the suck-up.

"Doubt it," Ainsley says modestly, and I roll my eyes at her back. "It'll be a senior, obviously. Mila Whitlock. Or maybe Amy Reid. But Amy's boyfriend can't be king because he's at Sandover."

"Oh. My. God. Did I not tell you? He's not her boyfriend anymore," Bree gossips. "Gray says they broke up."

"No way. Silas Hazelton is on the market again?"

I can't stop a snort.

Spine stiff as a rod, Ainsley turns in her chair. "What?" she snaps.

"Nothing. It's just adorable, the high value you assign yourself. First Lawson, now Silas… You really think you have a shot with these guys, huh?"

Her face turns purple with anger, but before she can retort, Sister Katherine shushes us and orders everyone to focus on their assignments.

In second period, I slide into my seat next to Jazmine, who grills me for details about my escapade with Lawson. We chat until Sister Mary Alice marches by with her ruler and waves it around in a threatening manner. I swear this woman gets off on corporal punishment. She must have been a bloodthirsty prison guard in another life.

Later, after the lunch bell rings, I head to my locker to find my sister waiting for me. Sloane runs a hand through her long, dark hair and gives me a guarded look. After last night, we're still a bit cautious around each other. This morning at breakfast, she kept watching me like she was anticipating a sneak attack at any second.

"What is it?" I ask her.

"Dad's waiting for you outside."

My jaw falls open. "I'm sorry, what?"

"He tried texting you, but your phone's off—"

"Yeah, because I was in class," I interrupt irritably. "Why the hell is he here?"

"Hey, don't shoot the messenger." She backs away, shrugging. "All he said was he's waiting for you outside."

Crap.

It is never a good sign when a parent shows up at your school in the middle of the day. At least I know it's not an emergency, otherwise he would have included Sloane in whatever this is.

When I walk outside and see Dad's face, my suspicions grow exponentially. He's leaning against the passenger door of his black SUV, sporting his tweed blazer and a stern, no-nonsense expression that tells me he means business.

I reach the bottom of the steps and approach him. "What's this about?" I say in lieu of greeting.

He doesn't miss that. "Hello to you too, sweetheart." Opening the car door for me, he adds, "We have an appointment."

I'm half a second from spinning on my heel and running into the school when I realize it would serve no purpose. Dad would just call the Reverend Mother and she'd probably personally escort me back outside.

So as reluctant as I am, I slide into the passenger seat and buckle up.

He rounds the vehicle and gets behind the wheel, glancing over as he puts the SUV in drive. "Sorry to just show up at lunch, but this was the only slot she had open this week. Otherwise we would've had to wait two weeks."

I frown at him. "Who's *she*?"

"Dr. Anthony." Like a coward, he stares straight ahead, too afraid to meet my murderous eyes.

"Are you kidding me? This is beyond messed up, Dad. Would you *ever* do something like this to Sloane?"

"What do you mean?" He continues to avoid my gaze.

"You know exactly what I mean. If you and Sloane got into a fight, would you pull her out of school the next day and take her to a fucking psychiatrist?"

"Language, young lady."

I ignore the reprimand. "It's fine, Dad, you can avoid the question. We both know the answer is no. No, you wouldn't do that. Because Sloane is the strong one, right?" Bitterness burns a path up my throat. "She doesn't need a professional to poke around in her brain and try to solve why she would possibly get annoyed when her father loses his shit because she's a few hours late after school."

"This isn't just about last night, Casey. Your emotions are all over the place. Waking up crying from nightmares one day, angry and insolent the next. Dr. Anthony can help you regulate—"

"Stop," I order. "Just stop talking."

The betrayal I'm feeling is enough to make my heart race. My hands are literally shaking as I press them flat against my thighs. I take a breath.

"You and Sloane are unbelievable," I say flatly. "If I'm soft and show my feelings, there's something wrong with me. If I'm hard and try to control my emotions, there's something wrong with me." I exhale in a sharp gust. "Just let me be me."

He glances at me, sheer frustration darkening his face. "I'm trying to do that, sweetheart. But you're not being you. This isn't you. You don't get detention—"

"Sometimes I do," I interrupt. "Sometimes I get tired of being bullied and called a suicidal freak who drove into a lake—can you really blame me for that?"

"No, but…" He trails off, returning his gaze to the road ahead. "Let's see what Dr. Anthony says."

Dr. Anthony ushers me into her office thirty minutes later. Her practice is on the third floor of a brick building in Parsons, the second largest town within driving distance of Sandover. Calden, our nearest offering of civilization, does have a tiny medical practice and a vet clinic, but they're a bit behind the times when it comes to psychiatrists.

She towers over me as she gestures for me to sit. She's close to six feet tall, with the figure of a reed, no curves in sight. Her hair is cut short and streaked with gray. And though her face is angular, which ought to give her a severe vibe, she exudes warmth.

"It's good to see you," she tells me once we're settled on the two plush armchairs facing each other. She's not a *please lie on the sofa* kind of shrink. "How have you been?"

"You mean my father hasn't filled you in on my total mental breakdown?" I ask wryly.

Dr. Anthony's lips twitch in a faint smile. "Are you in the midst of one?" she counters.

"I didn't think so. But the way he and Sloane are going on about it, you'd think I need to be committed."

I lean back in the chair and draw my knees up to my chest, resting my socked feet on the edge of the chair. Dr. Anthony always asks you to remove your shoes in the reception area before coming into her office. I don't mind it. It's cozy.

"So, it's been about seven weeks since I saw you last," she says, watching me with those shrewd yet soft eyes. "Catch me up. Are you still being bullied at school?"

"Nope. They stopped once I started fighting back."

She nods. "I see."

"What?" I give a defiant look. "You don't approve? Shouldn't you be happy I don't care what they think about me anymore?"

She responds with a gentle smile. "It's not my job to approve or disapprove, Casey. It's not my place to judge. But, going by our previous sessions, you *did* used to care what they thought about you. What they said about you. You cared very much."

"Well, I don't anymore."

"I see." She reaches for the yellow legal pad from the table next to her chair and uncaps her pen. "What do you think changed?"

"I changed," I say simply.

Dr. Anthony watches me. Waiting for me to continue. It's one of her tactics—wait the other person out until they cave and spill their secrets. I watched a documentary on police interrogations once where one of the detectives interviewed said that silence was the greatest tool in his kit. People don't like stewing in silence. It's too awkward, and our instinct is to make it stop. Fill the silence. And the more someone talks, the more details they let slip.

Apparently I'm no different, because I keep talking. "I'm developing a thicker skin. The new and improved Casey. The strong one."

"I see."

"Could you please stop saying that?" I grumble. There's no condescension in her tone, only genuine understanding, but it still grates. "Look, you want me to catch you up? Here, let's catch you up. I still have the nightmares, but not as often. I still can't remember what happened at prom. Oh, but great news!" Sarcasm burns my tongue. "I found out who pulled me from the car that night. It was my best friend, Fenn, who, by the way, I started dating a few weeks ago." I laugh darkly. "Didn't work out, obviously."

Her eyes widen. "Well. That is a lot to process."

I hug my knees, ignoring the ripples of pain in my stomach. Every time I say Fenn's name out loud, it causes a visceral reaction. It physically hurts.

"Would it be helpful to discuss it in more detail?" she prompts. "How it felt to discover your friend was involved that night?"

"He wasn't 'involved.' He just showed up after the fact." Frustration tightens my throat and I swallow hard. I drop my legs and curl my fists on my knees. "You know what would be helpful, doc? If you could help me remember what fucking *happened* that night."

She doesn't even flinch at my language, but I apologize out of habit.

"Sorry, I shouldn't swear." I bring one hand up to rub my temple, feeling even more frustrated. Stuck. "Why can't I remember?"

"You suffered a head injury," she answers, her tone soft and rippling with empathy. "And you were drugged. Either of those factors alone could have impacted your memory. Together? I'm not at all surprised you're unable to recollect the events of that night." She sets her legal pad in her lap. "Have you been meditating? Last time we spoke, you mentioned you would try meditation again."

"I haven't. Every time I do it, my mind wanders. The only time I even got close to remembering anything was when I did the guided meditation with you," I admit. "That's when I remembered the voice."

"The voice saying you were going to be all right, that you were safe."

I nod, my heart speeding up again when I realize I can finally positively place that voice. "It was Fenn. He's the one who said it, while he was getting me out of the sinking car."

A chill suddenly runs through me, a lingering phantom sensation that washes over me sometimes. My body remembers how cold that water was. The sickening awareness of it rising up to my neck, minutes away from completely submerging me. Drowning me.

"We still have thirty minutes left in our session." Dr. Anthony searches my face. "Would you like to try another guided meditation?"

I swallow again. Then I nod.

CHAPTER 27
CASEY

On Friday night, a text from Jazmine sideswipes me into an anxiety spiral.

Jazmine: Ballard party at the lake. I'll pick you up.

My first instinct is to say no. I haven't been back there since prom night, and just seeing those words—*at the lake*—triggers a physical response in my body. Dry mouth and numb fingers. Dizziness and shortness of breath. Flickers and flashes of cold, wet darkness creeping up my legs grab hold of my throat and strangle me.

I should say no. Stay as far away as possible from that murderous body of water.

Then another voice tells me that's the fragile Casey talking. The wilting flower. The delicate princess of porcelain and air. What happened to disruption? What happened to taking back my autonomy and becoming unflinchingly, unforgivably present?

But there's more to it than that. Another motive that fills me with courage to face my Ballard demons. I won't give my father the satisfaction of telling him he was right, but...

He was right.

The session with Dr. Anthony was exactly what I needed. Not because I'm on the verge of a breakdown—but because I'm in desperate need of a breakthrough.

I *need* to remember. I can't keep living this way, plagued with this enormous black void where the truth of that night resides.

Still, the idea of going back without the proper support scares me a little. Jazmine is great, but we barely know each other. So I call Lucas for backup.

He picks up almost instantly. "Hey, what's up?"

"Will you come with me to a lake party at Ballard tonight?"

There's a short pause. "Are you serious?"

I laugh at his surprised tone. "I know, not what you expected to hear, right?"

"Nope." He laughs too, before going serious. "You sure that's a good idea? Can you handle it?"

"I think so, yes. Especially since I might have remembered something about prom."

I hear his intake of breath. "Holy shit. You did?"

"Sort of. I did a guided meditation with my shrink. Like hypnosis, but not quite. Basically just trying to unlock the memories."

"Oh right, didn't you try it before? Your doctor said she thinks the memories are still somewhere in your mind and you just need to bring them to the surface."

"Exactly."

"Okay, well, don't keep me in suspense," he grumbles. "What did you remember?"

I take a breath. "I can give you a ride."

"I don't understand."

"I remembered saying that to someone at prom."

It sounds so minor, but those six little words are huge. The first real shard of clarity I have about that night.

I still can't believe we managed to pry an actual nugget of memory out of my stubborn head. The last time we attempted it, it was like pulling teeth. This time it was far less difficult. Like a video game, where the first time you play it's excruciating to pass a level because you're muddling your way through so many unknowns, but after you've done it once and know the tricks, it becomes easier to pass. While Dr. Anthony coaxed me into a state of relaxation, I was transported back to prom almost instantly.

I'd always remembered the earlier parts of the evening—driving to Ballard with Sloane, watching the prom queen and king ceremony, dancing with my sister and her friends. After that, things get hazy. All I have are blurry shapes and random flashes.

Lots of bodies. Fancy dresses.

Spinning. Dancing.

My fingers around a cup.

Laughter.

My memory is like Swiss cheese, riddled with holes. I can't see what's happening during those holes, the images growing fuzzy and undecipherable before going totally black.

But this time, one of the holes was filled. I clearly heard my own voice saying, "I can give you a ride." And while I said it, I was looking at something pink. I vividly remember a flash of pink.

"I offered someone I ride, but I can't see their face," I tell Lucas. "And I remember seeing the color pink."

"Pink?" he echoes blankly. "Was it a dress? Hair color?"

"I don't know."

"Could it be a girl you were talking to?"

I suck in a breath. That hadn't occurred to me. For some reason I always assumed the person driving the car was a guy. But there's no reason why it *couldn't* have been a girl. The security footage only showed a shadowy figure in a hoodie running past the camera. The height and build suggested it was a guy, but I can't be totally sure.

"That's a possibility," I say out loud.

"Wait, this brings up another issue," Lucas says. "If *you* are the one offering the ride, doesn't that imply you were the one driving?"

"Fenn says he found me in the passenger side."

"You sure Fenn wasn't lying?"

I bite my lip. "I don't think he was."

"Okay, so that means whoever you offered to give a ride to ended up behind the wheel instead. Why?"

"I don't know." My phone dings in my ear. "Oh, hold on a sec. I'm getting a text."

Jazmine: Leaving soon. You down?

"That's Jaz. She's going to drive tonight. Are you coming or what?" I ask Lucas.

"I can't," he says in a sheepish tone. "I have a date."

"What!" I promptly forget all about my own drama. "Since when? Who is she?"

"This girl I met online. She's a gamer."

"That's it? Those are all the details I get?"

"For now," he replies, and I can almost see him rolling his eyes on the other end of the line. "Let's see how the date goes first. Then we'll know if there's anything else to tell."

"Fair."

"We'll be at the movies in Parsons so my phone will probably be off, but text me later to let me know how it goes at Ballard. Be safe?"

"I will," I promise.

We hang up, and I text Jaz saying I'm in. I have to do this. I can't keep hiding away in this house and jumping at my own shadow. I made a promise to myself. Okay, well, maybe it's more of a devil's bargain. But I've decided to embrace the bad bitch inside and go rogue. Because how long can someone live in total terror of everything around her before her personality withers and she forgets how to be a person?

After the accident and all the rumors, I thought I wanted to be alone, to keep everyone safely on the other side of thick, sturdy walls.

Now I realize those walls were my prison, not theirs.

Bad Girl Casey doesn't sit in her room sulking and feeling sorry for herself. She isn't scared of a lake or the whispers between the trees. I imagine if Lawson were sitting here right now, he'd smirk and cock his head. Goad me to throw on some thick black eyeliner and shock them all.

No more tears.

When Jaz texts to say she's on her way, I throw some clothes and makeup in a backpack because there's no way I can get out of this house looking like I'm headed to a party.

In the living room, Dad is crouched in front of a bookcase with board games piled around him on the rug.

"Want to grab your sister for some Scrabble?" He glances at me over his shoulder. "Or we've got Risk, Sorry…?"

"I'm going to take a pass on game night. Jaz invited me over to her dorm to study."

He sits back on his heels and his cheeks droop with disappointment. "It's Friday night. You'd rather be studying?"

"Just for a bit. Then we'll probably watch this awful reality show Jaz is obsessed with on her laptop. I'll probably spend the night, if that's okay."

"Are you sure?" he pushes. "We could play Pandemic. Or Monopoly."

"Sloane cheats."

"Everyone cheats at Monopoly." Sloane enters the living room and plops down on the couch to turn on the TV. "Anyway, I can't do game night either. RJ's coming by to watch a movie."

Dad stands up and grumbles under his breath. "Guess I'll make a cup of tea and read in the den."

"Sorry," I call after him. My phone buzzes in my hand and I give it a quick scan. "That's my ride. Gotta go."

Then I bolt for the door before either of them can think to stop me.

I practically take a diving header into the passenger seat of Jazmine's white hatchback, which she reads as her cue to gun it down the driveway.

"You rob the place on your way out?" she asks with a grin.

"No, but I nearly got hijacked into family bonding time."

"In that case, you're welcome."

I've never gotten undressed in a car going sixty miles an hour before, but I manage to change clothes with only a few bruises from knocking my elbows into everything. It's getting colder outside, so I opted for a pair of skinny jeans and a tight sweater. Jaz, meanwhile, chose to wear a short dress. It's black and made of ribbed sweater material. The top has long sleeves, but the bottom half barely covers her upper thighs.

"You're going to freeze to death," I inform her while doing my makeup in the visor's mirror.

"Sometimes you have to suffer in the pursuit of hotness," she says airily, driving the nearly pitch-black country road that circles the lake toward the Ballard campus.

"You do look hot," I concede, snapping my compact shut and reaching for my lip gloss.

I slather some on and hesitate before speaking again, then decide it's better to give her a heads-up than possibly blindside her.

"Hey, just so you know… I haven't been back to this lake since the accident," I confess. "I've been on campus. Like, inside the school itself. But not out here."

"Oh shit. I had no idea. Do you want to turn back?"

"No, it's fine."

I slide the elastic out of my ponytail and pull it around my wrist, then finger-comb my hair and let it fall loose past my shoulders. I haven't cut it since the summer, so it's longer than I usually wear it.

"Are you sure?"

"Positive. I just wanted you to know in case I freaked out or something. But honestly, I think I'm okay. Look—" I stick out my palms. "Rock steady."

She scrutinizes me for a moment as if gauging my truthfulness. "Okay. But if you need to leave, tell me. I'll get you out of there, no questions asked."

Her sincerity touches something inside me. It's been a long time since I've had a female friend I feel will actually have my back.

CHAPTER 28
CASEY

A FEW DOZEN CARS ARE PARKED ALONG THE NARROW DIRT ROAD leading to the lake. We pull up on the shoulder overgrown with tall weeds that bend into a green rug when I push open the passenger door.

"We're not going to the boathouse?" I say, unable to mask the relief in my voice.

"No, this is where my brother said to go," she answers, showing me her phone. "See? He dropped a pin."

Sure enough, the location marked on the map is on the southern edge of the lake. The boathouse is east and situated directly on campus. I think this part of the lake might be public property, in fact. Which makes me wonder if the Ballard party crowd had to relocate because the boathouse and surrounding area started being monitored more carefully after my accident.

Jaz reaches into the back seat and grabs a battery-powered lantern to light our way toward the sound of music. Through the trees, I glimpse tiny moving pinpricks of light, like fireflies in the blackness. Eventually the warm orange glow of a bonfire comes into view. The smell of smoke is thick and immediately imbeds into my hair and clothes until even my mouth tastes like flames.

When we step through the trees and I spot the dark stretch of water, I brace myself. Waiting. I thought being here might trigger something in me. Flashbacks or a panic attack. But nothing happens.

The relief is immense. Enough that I feel myself smiling and awkwardly bite my lip to conceal my excitement when we stroll up on the party. Music echoes through the trees and carries out over the expansive lake toward the small lights of faraway houses. Shadows dance all around us, figures cast in eerie fragments around the bonfire.

"Let's get a drink." Jaz nudges me toward a group of people standing around a keg.

My feet dig into the dirt, rooted to the spot for a moment. Getting here was one thing. Talking to people, being seen—that's another. There are ghosts everywhere. Faces from a life not so long ago and yet distant enough.

Jaz wasn't there the first time I returned to Ballard after the accident and those once-friendly faces had turned sour. How lonely it was feeling every room hush when I entered. The Living Dead Girl. How humiliating it was to hear the rumors start to swirl all around me, passed around by people I considered friends.

"You need me to carry you?" she jokes.

I let out a breath. "Nothing a few drinks can't fix, right?"

"That's the spirit."

It's not until we're too close to abort that I realize some of my old friends from cheerleading are among those around the keg. I stiffen, waiting for the onslaught. But when their gazes pass right over me and they continue talking amongst themselves, I realize they haven't even noticed me.

"Pour me one of those?" Jaz says to a cute guy with the spout in his hand.

"Sure thing." He smiles and grabs a red cup from the stack. "Have I seen you out here before?"

Her answering smile is coy. "You'd know if you had."

"I think you're right." He can't take his appreciate gaze off her bare legs.

I'm happy for Jaz. Really. Not here a whole two minutes and already she's found a flirt buddy. But their exchange draws the attention of my former squad, and when Gillian looks up from her cup and blinks, I know my short-lived anonymity is blown.

"Oh my God. Casey." She gawks at me like I've just walked up drenched and covered in mud.

The other girls turn in unison.

"I didn't even recognize you," Gillian blurts out.

"Wow, hey," Alex says. Her uneasy gaze quickly sweeps toward her friends. "How's it going?"

"How's it going?" I bark out a laugh, which gets Jaz's attention.

She questions me with a raised eyebrow while she sips her beer. I give a slight shake of the head to indicate I've got it covered.

Meanwhile, Alex's gaze wanders in a frantic attempt not to lock with mine. "Um, yeah. Been a while."

"And why's that, you think? Maybe because you told people I swallowed a bottle of pills and drove my car into the lake to abort my secret baby?"

Jaz spits her beer back into her cup. "Oh, shit."

"Casey, come on," Gillian interjects unhappily. "You know—"

"Seriously, Gillian? Spare me." I shake my head at her big saucer eyes. "Don't act like we're still best friends. Next time you write my name in a bathroom stall, at least try to disguise your handwriting."

Her cheeks turn redder than her hair.

Jaz clicks her tongue. "Man, not cool, Gillian."

"Okay, wait a second—"

"No, I have a better idea." I grab a beer from Jaz's cute friend and take a swig. "How about you all fuck off forever and I go back to enjoying myself?"

At that, I link my arm through Jazmine's, and we strut off on an adrenaline rush like I've never experienced before. It's exhilarating.

Once upon a time, they were my best friends. Gillian. Alex. Darcy. They were people I confided in. My ride or dies. Until it became more socially advantageous to turn on me. That's when they became my worst bullies, spreading horrible rumors about me in the aftermath of the accident when what I needed most was their support. I came back to school after the accident to realize I was an outcast. The butt of every joke.

"You've been waiting to do that for a while," Jaz teases as we pause around the bonfire.

"Like you wouldn't believe."

I suddenly feel liberated. From the embarrassment, from the fear of them. It's that feeling when you stare down your bullies and realize they can't have power over you anymore.

"Oh, there's Theo," Jaz says, waving at someone across the fire. She grabs my hand and starts dragging me away. "Come meet my brother."

Even if she hadn't prefaced it with that, I would've known instantly that Theo was her brother. The resemblance is uncanny, although he's a good foot and a half taller than Jaz.

He's wearing a T-shirt with the Ballard soccer logo on it, holding a beer in one hand and a cigarette in the other. Neither vice seems conducive to a successful sports career, but Jaz told me he's the star player of the soccer team.

Theo's expression fills with curiosity as he leans down to give me a hug, causing a cloud of cigarette smoke to burn my eyes.

"How come we've never met?" he demands, then glares at his sister as if she's to blame.

"Because we just became best friends," she tells him. "Which means you're not allowed to hit on her yet. Let me have this for a while, will you?"

I snort, while Theo feigns innocence.

"When have I ever hit on your friends, Jazzy?"

"You've macked on every single one since I was in the third grade, Theodore. I mean it. Hands off." She glances at me. "Trust me, you'll thank me for this later. He's way too slutty for you."

We chat with Theo for a while, until he wanders off when a cute junior catches his eye.

"Hey," I tell Jaz, who's been drinking her beer at a snail's pace. Since she's driving, she promised she won't have more than two drinks tonight, but I feel bad watching her nurse that one cup. "Are you sure you don't want to drink more? We could always leave your car here and Uber home."

"Nah, it's all good." She takes another teeny sip. "I wouldn't mind keeping a clearer head tonight, anyway. You know, just in case…"

I know she means in case I break down, and although I feel a pang of guilt, I'm also grateful to have a friend like her.

"*But*…if I'm not getting piss-drunk, I do require some other form of entertainment," she says with an impish smile. "Let's do a man sweep. Who do you think I should seduce tonight?"

I laugh, humoring her by peeking around the fire. I spot several promising candidates, but Jaz has other ideas.

"Hey, check it out." She nudges me. "Look who it is."

I turn to see none other than Bree from St. Vincent's, sitting on a log beside her boyfriend, Gray. She's wearing his letterman jacket with only her bare legs hanging out. She grips a red cup in both hands, giggling at something Gray said.

I keep forgetting those two are dating. Sloane thinks Gray is with Bree because she's extremely low effort and easily impressed, but I still think she's a weird choice for him. I was in nearly all of Gray's classes freshman and sophomore years, and he was always reasonably nice. Smart, funny. I can't say I've ever known him to be a bully himself, though he keeps questionable company. He's the best wide receiver on the Ballard football team, which comes with its own social baggage.

"Who's the dude?" Jaz asks.

"Gray Robson. He plays football."

"Nice."

She continues to admire Gray, who's probably one of the best-looking guys at this party with his brown hair, bright blue eyes, and boy-next-door face. His black Under Armour T-shirt shows off his broad chest and sculpted arms, and I don't miss the way Jaz homes in on those.

"You know what, I think you've inspired me." Something in her voice rings as a bad omen.

"I have?"

"Uh-huh," Jaz hums, taking a swig of her beer. "You stole Ainsley's guy the other day. I think I'll take Bree's."

A loud laugh pops out. "I shouldn't be encouraging this. It goes against my girl power philosophy."

"But?"

"But those two have been making my life miserable since school started." I shrug. "I don't have much sympathy for them."

The old Casey might have mustered up some compassion for Bree, who's so painfully dumb that sometimes I wonder if she understands half the malevolent shit Ainsley says. But ignorance is no excuse to silently stand by and watch your friend try to crush someone's self-esteem.

So when Bree wanders off to join a group of girls waving her over, I don't resist when Jaz says, "Introduce me?"

A moment later, we approach Gray.

His eyebrows shoot up when he notices me. "Casey?"

"Hey, Gray. How's it going?"

"Good." He surprises me by standing to hug me. We were never super close, but he's Ballard football and I used to be a cheerleader here, so I guess we've got history. "How've you been?"

"I've been great," I answer. "St. Vincent's is a blast so far. Your girlfriend's making me feel very welcome."

He gives me a wry look. "Is she now?"

"Oh yeah. She's so friendly, that Bree. Where did she run off to? I wanted to say hi." I glance over my shoulder, noticing Bree and her group appear to be leaving the party. "Is she leaving?"

"Yeah, they're doing some pub crawl thing in the city."

"Aww, so you've been abandoned?" I tug Jazmine closer to us. "This is my friend Jazmine, by the way."

"Nice to meet you," she drawls, sizing him up. "Casey says you play football?"

"I do, yeah. Are you a football fan?"

"No, but I can be." She grabs his hand and drags him toward the log. "Let's sit. I want to hear all about football."

Gray doesn't know what's hit him when she takes Bree's former seat beside him. Before he understands what's happening, Jaz has cast a seductive spell over the poor guy. I clock him taking a long look at her tits before sweeping his attention down her bare legs. Jaz leans into him, playfully touching his arm. Dude's a goner and he doesn't even realize it yet.

Deciding to give them some privacy, I wander around the fire, enjoying the heat against my cheeks. And then I spot him. Oliver Drummer.

Oliver is the quintessential It Guy. Quarterback. Gorgeous. Filthy rich and generally untouchable. Normally he's the type of guy I'd probably shy away from, but tonight I'm supposed to be fearless, right? So why not try on a persona who isn't the slightest bit intimidated by someone like that? Why not tell myself, if even just for tonight, that I'm the It Girl he's standing next to in all the yearbook photos? Stranger things happen in the forest all the time.

Beside the bonfire, Oliver looks deep in thought, staring into the flames. He's conspicuously solo, which might as well paint a giant target on his chest. I stroll up to the fire and stand next to him.

"You're thinking too hard," I say when he glances over to acknowledge me.

"What?"

"It's a party. You shouldn't look so serious." I lift a brow. "Something on your mind?"

"Oh." He smiles to himself, almost bashfully. "Yeah, just going over plays in my head. We've got a rivalry game next week."

"Is that why you're nursing that beer?"

"Want to know a secret?" Oliver leans in. "It's soda." He flashes a conspiratorial wink. "Don't tell anyone."

"Cross my heart," I promise. "Under one condition."

"Oh?" He licks his bottom lip, smiling. "How much is it gonna cost me?"

"Not much. Just tell me you dance."

He wraps one muscular arm around my waist and speaks against my hair. "Easy money."

Oliver walks me toward the other bodies that are dancing in lantern light and casting wild shadows among the trees. Here, the music is louder, and people move with their eyes closed and little space between them. Skin on skin. Sweat.

I don't think about how I look. I don't let self-consciousness seep into my good time. Instead, I watch myself reflected in Oliver's eyes. The way he appears almost mesmerized as we dance. Fascinated, even.

"Who are you?" he asks with a bewildered look.

"A figment of your imagination." I don't know why I say it, except I'm not ready for the truth to pierce the fantasy.

"You go to school around here, right? How have we never partied together?"

I only smile and continue moving to the beat that's almost supernatural the way it gets into my blood. The music is hypnotic, and I want to preserve this sense of mystery I've created around myself, even if I know it can only be a fleeting escape.

No sooner do I think it than Mila saunters up. The gorgeous brunette has been known to hook up with Oliver on occasion and was Sloane's best friend at Ballard, at least before she turned on both of us, just like the rest of them.

When she realizes who Oliver is dancing with, Mila cocks an

eyebrow at me like she's caught me shoplifting. "Well, well. You've got to be the last person I expected to see here."

"Answers at last." With a triumphant smile, Oliver stops dancing. "You know her?" he asks Mila.

She stares at him as if he's completely daft. "This is Sloane Tresscott's sister. Casey."

"No shit?" His mouth hangs open as he wonders how he hadn't recognized me. "Damn."

I dare say he looks almost impressed.

"Get me a drink?" Mila tells Oliver, who takes the hint and walks off with one last charming grin. Her expression turns dry when she aims it at me again. "Not trying to steal my guy, are you, Tresscott?"

There was a time I was intimidated by Mila. She was outgoing and energetic and sometimes vicious, the kind of person who could turn an entire lunchroom against you. And then she did it to me, and my fear of her seemed justified.

Standing here now, I almost can't remember what convinced me I was no match for her.

"Why not?" I retort. "You'd deserve it for the rumors you spread about me. No honor among thieves, right?"

I expect a biting comeback.

Instead, she deflates.

"Fuck. I should have apologized a long time ago." She winces to herself. "No, what I should have done is not be such a bitch in the first place. I'm sorry, Casey. For all of it."

"Save it for Sloane. She's the one you betrayed."

Mila sighs, casting her attention at the ground. "I would, if she'd talk to me."

"What do you expect? You know what she's like. She takes her grudges to the grave."

"How is she?" The sad hopefulness on her face is almost embarrassing. I get the impression she misses my sister. Must be a really humbling, crappy moment to realize maybe it wasn't worth it to blow up their friendship.

"She's great," I reply, because I'm not about to pretend that Sloane hasn't been thriving without Mila's company. "Lips perpetually glued to her new boyfriend, RJ."

"Yeah, I met him at the last soccer game." Her hopeful expression dissolves into one of visible envy. "He's hot as fuck."

"Who's hot as fuck?" Oliver demands, eyes narrowed as he returns with two cups of beer.

"You are," Mila says innocently, accepting one of the cups. "Who else would we be talking about?"

She winks at me when he's not looking, and I can't help a grudging grin in reply.

"Here." He hands me the other cup. "You were looking a little dehydrated, Tresscott."

"Thanks." I take a small sip, feeling Mila's curious gaze on me while I do.

Oliver holds out his hands, one toward me, the other at Mila. "Come on. Both of you. I've decided I need to make all the other dudes here jealous by dancing with the two hottest chicks at the party."

Laughing, Mila takes his hand and lets him yank her toward him. Then she gives me an expectant look. "Come on."

I snort at her. "As if."

She rolls her eyes. "We don't have to be friends, Casey. It's just a dance."

Reluctance still lingers inside me, but a glance toward the fire reveals Jazmine and Gray whispering to each other, Jaz practically in his lap. I can't see myself prying her from him anytime soon. And Oliver is a good dancer…

I slug back nearly half my drink and then plant my hand in Oliver's waiting palm. He curls it around mine, then draws me and Mila toward the throng of dancers.

CHAPTER 29
LAWSON

"GREEN FOR GIDDY, PURPLE FOR PASS THE FUCK OUT…"

It's my voice. I think? And someone responds, but it's like we're speaking underwater. I can't make sense of anything. There's no context.

With a groan, I open my eyes. Swallow my frustration, then a swig of bourbon. I give up. This remembering thing is goddamn hard.

Since my impromptu joyride with Casey, I've been trying to do her a solid by revisiting prom night, but it might be time to call it quits. Truth is, I'd ingested so many illegal substances at prom that even if I had a clear memory of that night, it would be impossible to trust its accuracy.

It's all a drug-induced jumble.

I remember nonsensical phrases that may or may not have been uttered by me.

I remember really shitty music.

I think I got my dick sucked at some point in the shadowy corridor outside the locker rooms, but that seems like faulty recollection on my brain's part because I also think the person doing the sucking was Silas? Which means it's bullshit, because one, there's no way in hell that ever happened, and two, when I do recall the blowjob in question, I remember running my fingers through long hair. Which would definitely rule out Silas and his buzz cut.

The only definitive memories I have, ones that can be verified by third parties, all take place *after* the excitement started. Searching the halls with Silas for a missing Casey. Sloane's wild, frantic eyes as she'd grabbed everyone by the collar one by one, demanding to know if we'd seen her sister.

"Hey, wanna shoot some pool?"

Fenn appears in my doorway, looking a little sheepish. Ever since he accused me of trying to defile his girl, he's been extra nice to me. I guess I appreciate it. I mean, my intentions aren't always the best, and yeah, I flirted with the girl—I flirt with every girl—but I didn't make a move on her.

I lift a brow. "There's a party at Ballard tonight. You're not going?"

"Wasn't planning on it."

"Well, I was. Just waiting on Silas to get back. His parents are in town for his sister's sports thing, so they took him to dinner."

The sound of Silas's name brings a dark cloud to Fenn's face. "Fuck Silas. Asshole set me up."

I shrug.

"Yeah, I wouldn't expect you to care."

Taking another swig of bourbon, I eye him over the rim of my glass. "He's wanted to bang Sloane for years. Saw an opportunity and took it."

Fenn snorts. "Of course you'd support that."

"I don't care either way. Your dirty little hookup with Sloane would've come out regardless, bro. You can't keep secrets from a girl like Casey. You would've had to come clean eventually."

His jaw tightens.

"Am I wrong?"

"You're not wrong," he grudgingly agrees. "But Silas is still a dick for what he did."

"Speaking of Silas and dicks," I say, slanting my head. "What are the chances he would ever blow me?"

"Zero," is the instant response. He stares at me. "Trying to seduce your roommate?"

"No. Just testing a theory," I say vaguely.

"Whatever. Get off your ass and let's play until you bounce. I need to get out of my own head for a while."

So we end up in the lounge, where our game becomes competitive from the get-go, rife with trash talk. Fenn's a good sport, though. He doesn't know how to hold a grudge, and that's a valuable trait people always underappreciate.

"What's the matter?" he taunts to distract me from realizing he's only a couple of shots away from winning the game. "Your date get grounded?"

"You know the worst part about you?" I return, sinking the last striped ball in the side pocket off a bank shot. Yeah, there's no way I'm letting him win. "I'm not allowed to make 'your mom' jokes when you say something like that."

"At least I know you can't sleep with her."

"This would be embarrassing if you were *trying* to let me win." I casually sink the eight ball that's teetering on the edge of the pocket to end the game. "What's our running tally now? Two games to zip? Let's wager a grand on the next one."

"How 'bout you just open a tab for me," Fenn says while he collects the balls to re-rack.

"I like where your head's at." It's my turn to break. I line up the shot and send two solids into opposite pockets. "Where's Remy tonight?"

"RJ? With the wife. Where else?"

"Your stepbrother sucks," comes Duke's snide voice.

We turn to find him striding into the lounge with a beer in hand. Nobody even tries to hide contraband from our housefather anymore. Mr. Swinney knows he has a better chance of reining in a herd of wild horses.

Duke throws himself into a leather armchair, swiveling it so he can see the pool table. "And he sucks at ruling the school."

I roll my eyes. "Jesus fuck. This again?"

"Dude, I think it's time to get a therapist," Fenn tells him. "Enough already."

"Everyone knows I'm right. They don't want to admit it, but they miss me. You know it's true."

Fenn shrugs. "Yeah? Maybe if you're nice to him, he'll give you the job back. Not like he ever wanted it."

"Fuck that. I'll get it back eventually." Duke lifts his beer to his lips and takes a long swig.

"I say you challenge the fucker to a rematch." Duke's lackey Carter twists around on the couch, throwing his unwanted two cents into the conversation.

As I chalk my cue, I give Carter a little smirk, which he pretends not to see. Carter's been deep in the closet since I've known him, only emerging now and then to get on his knees for me after swim practice. I like him a lot better when his mouth is otherwise occupied.

"He's too chickenshit to fight me twice," Duke says. "He knows the first time was a fluke."

"Keep telling yourself that," Fenn says before bending forward to send a striped ball into the corner pocket.

"Holy shit, we totally should've gone to Ballard tonight," someone blurts out. A couple of seniors are sprawled on the far couch, and one just shot up in a sitting position, jaw gaping as he stares at his phone.

"What is it?" His buddy leans in trying to see the screen.

"Check out this TikTok of the headmaster's little girl dirty dancing with some chick."

"Sloane?"

"Dude, no. Fuckin' Casey Tresscott—"

The cue in Fenn's hand hits the floor before the guy even finishes saying Casey's name. In a blur, Fenn is across the room and snatching the phone out of his hand.

"Yo, what the hell, man."

"Shut up," Fenn snaps.

As he watches the video, I lean my cue against the table and walk up to peek over his shoulder. From the phone, the tinny sound of music and incoherent shouting fills the room.

It's tough to make out exactly what's happening in the grainy video. I glimpse Casey's face and some guy all over her. Another girl's in the mix too.

I squint at the screen. "I think that's Mila?"

"And Oliver," Fenn growls.

A second later, he chucks the phone against the wall.

"Hey, asshole!" the senior objects.

"Come see me," I quickly appease the guy, because I can tell Fenn's in no state to deal with a confrontation right now. "I'll take care of you."

Fenn charges up to Duke with his hand out. "Keys. I need to borrow your ride."

"What's in it for me?"

"Not getting murdered," I offer with a grin.

Rolling his eyes, Duke stands up and digs into his pocket. He pulls out a set of keys, but rather than hand them to Fenn, he smirks. "I'm driving."

I snort softly. "Well, this'll be fun."

CHAPTER 30
FENN

THE PARTY'S IN FULL SWING WHEN WE STRIDE UP. AND WITHIN five seconds of our arrival, we draw attention. Chicks come over offering smiles and lingering hugs. Soccer team guys slap mine and Duke's shoulders, offering fist bumps. Old friends and acquaintances shout their hellos.

I ignore them all and scan the crowd for Casey. The video had shown her in the shadows, so I search the darkness where most of the dancing is going on. Dark figures grinding against each other, barely visible.

Duke pokes me in the arm. "She's over there."

I follow his gaze and my shoulders go ramrod stiff. She's still dancing with Oliver, though Mila is nowhere to be seen now. Casey's back is flush to his massive chest, her arms raised and moving to the beat of the pop song blasting out of someone's portable speakers. The bonfire provides enough heat that nobody's even wearing their coats, and a lot of the girls here are clad in skimpy tank tops. To my relief, Casey's in a long-sleeve sweater and jeans. But with the way she's rubbing her body all over Oliver, she might as well be naked.

My fingers curl into tight fists as I watch the most important person to me dance with another dude. As if sensing my presence,

Casey's head lifts and those blue eyes suddenly collide with mine. Then they ignite in a fire of anger and resentment.

Scowling at me, she spins around so her back is to me. She rests her hands on Oliver's broad shoulders and shakes her hips, and it takes all my willpower not to march over there and wrench her away from him.

"You good?" Lawson drawls.

"Do me a favor?" I say through gritted teeth.

He tips his head.

"Cut in."

Now he raises his eyebrows. "You sure about that?"

It infuriates me to no end that I'm sending Lawson in my stead to watch out for Casey, but the way her eyes blazed when they locked with mine, I know there's no chance in hell she'll let me anywhere near her without a massive fight. So I force myself to keep my distance.

"I need you as my proxy. Go over there and make sure she's not too fucked up."

"You're turning me into a babysitter?" He sighs. "Bro. I have an eight-ball all ready to go."

"Please. Just for a little bit. Go check on her."

If you'd told me I'd be sending Lawson Kent to put his filthy hands on the girl I'm obsessed with, I'd have laughed in your face. But here I am, standing there watching him saunter through the party. He draws the covetous gazes of girls and guys alike. With his tousled hair, his faded jeans and gray T-shirt, you'd never think he was heir to a billion-dollar empire. Most times he looks like a dude who just crawled home from some dive bar.

There's no worse feeling in the world than when Casey's face lights up at the sight of Lawson.

Motherfucker.

Maybe this was a mistake.

But then her joy fades, replaced by narrowed suspicion. He holds up his hands, and I know he's feeding her that careless "who me" bullshit he relies on when he's trying to convince someone he's not up to no good.

Another streak of jealousy heats my blood as Casey turns to speak to Oliver, who grins and says something in her ear before striding off. She and Lawson wander over to a log, where they sit down and start whispering to each other, while I watch in agony.

"You seriously sent Kent over there?" Duke chortles at me. "You crazy?"

I ignore him and walk on stiff legs toward the kegs. Some freshman there pours me a watered-down beer. I curl my fingers around the cup and stalk away, keeping a close eye on the fire while I study the crowd.

I spot the captain of Ballard's soccer team with a chick in his lap and a hand up her shirt. Nearby, I'm a bit startled to see Silas's ex with her friends, her face animated as she tells them a story that has everyone laughing. I always forget how pretty Amy is. She's got a girl-next-door vibe, like Casey, only she doesn't elicit any of the hot desire that Casey does. Still, when our eyes meet, I tip my cup at her, and Amy gives a tight smile before turning away.

I'm barely alone a whole minute before Mila sidles up to me wearing a short black skirt and a see-through top that reveals the black bra beneath it. Her dark hair is up in a ponytail, eyes twinkling as she flashes me a smile.

"Looking mighty lonely over here, Bishop."

"Nah. I'm doing just fine."

My gaze remains on Casey and Lawson. I almost crush the plastic cup when she laughs at something he says.

"Lawson usually likes them more experienced, no?" Mila furrows her brow, then lets out a laugh. "I guess he's running out of options. Plowed his way through everyone in a five-mile radius."

"You included?" I can't help but mock.

"Of course. Hooking up with Lawson Kent is practically a rite of passage." Making herself cozy, Mila links her arm through mine and rests her head on my shoulder. "Same goes for hooking up with Fenn Bishop."

I roll my eyes but don't ease out of her grasp. It's probably good I've got someone to lean against, literally, because I'm so tense, I'm afraid I'll keel right over.

Granted, Mila's probably not the one to lean on. She used to be a friend—and yeah, we did hook up once freshman year, before I got expelled from Ballard—but that was also before she decided to stab the Tresscotts in the back. From what Sloane says, Mila's the source of the rumor that turned Casey from a victim to an attention-seeking psycho.

The reminder triggers a jolt of anger, which has me easing away from her. "Why'd you do it?"

She frowns. "Do what?"

"Turn against Casey."

Her expression falters. She pulls my cup from my hand and takes a swig, her gaze briefly darting toward Casey. Then she speaks in a flat voice. "Because I'm a bitch."

"Really, that's your excuse?" A harsh laugh slips out. "Your girl Connie left a goddamn straitjacket in her locker."

"What do you want me to say, Fenn?" She sounds tired. Ashamed. "I did a shitty thing, all right? It was supposed to be a joke. We were all sitting around, and I was like, *how convenient* that she can't remember anything. She probably roofied herself for attention and accidentally drove into the lake."

"Doesn't sound like a joke to me," I say coldly.

"Didn't say it was a good one." She hands me back my beer. "And I didn't think my friends would run with the story. Turn it into a whole thing. I apologized to Casey tonight, if that matters."

"It doesn't."

"Christ, all you assholes and your grudges. I miss Gabe. He never took things personally."

I miss Gabe too.

If he were here right now, maybe I wouldn't be standing in the shadows with Mila Whitlock while Casey is fifteen feet away wishing I was dead. Maybe I would have the answers I need. But he's not here, and I can't sell out my best friend if I don't know for sure whether he's responsible for the accident. Especially when I owe him one.

We still haven't received a return message, and it's starting to frustrate me because I don't want to badger RJ every day about it. So far I've managed to sound more casual than desperate when I poke him about whether Gabe has made contact yet. But if we don't hear from him soon, I might have to do something drastic to talk to Gabe.

I wonder how hard it is to break into a military school. I feel like maybe I could pull it off? Or I could hire a mercenary team to extract him. That would be sick.

"Whatever. This is boring. I'm bored." With that, Mila flounces off in Oliver's direction.

I drink the rest of my beer and toss the cup on the ground, then hear a derisive snort from behind me. I turn to find yet another chick I've hooked up with.

"There's a trash bag like five feet away," Rae Minato tells me. Flipping her long black hair over her shoulder, she shoulders past me to pick up my discarded cup.

"Didn't see it," I say lightly.

She disposes of the cup and saunters back, all long limbs and sex appeal. I haven't seen her in ages, and I don't mind the view.

"You done checking me out?" she asks.

"Do you want me to be?"

Rolling her eyes, Rae stands beside me. Her distressed jeans are practically pasted onto her endless legs, a cropped blue Ballard sweatshirt hanging off one pale shoulder.

"Why are you alone right now, Fenn?"

I teasingly poke her arm. "I'm not alone, Rae. You're here."

Ignoring that, her impossibly dark eyes drift toward the fire, then narrow. "Who's the girl with Lawson? She keeps looking at us."

"Yeah?" My heart skips a beat. Casey's watching?

"Well, glaring more than looking."

Glaring, huh. That's a good sign. Means her feelings for me haven't been completely extinguished. You don't feel jealousy over someone you no longer care about.

"That's Sloane's sister," I tell Rae.

When a breeze pushes some hair onto her forehead, I beat her fingers to it, tucking the errant strands behind her ear.

Rae starts to laugh. "Yeah... I'm not interested."

"Why not? Didn't we have fun that night in sophomore year? It was at, ah, Molly whatever's place in Nantucket. Do you remember?"

"Martha's Vineyard, and I remember." Her tone has a bite to it. "Even if I wanted a repeat performance—which I don't—I'm not on board with you using me to make some other chick jealous. Your fuckboy antics get real old, Fenn."

With that, she sashays off.

Damn. The girl I remember from sophomore year was a lot sweeter. Granted, I deserved every harsh word. Not that I planned on hooking up with Rae or anything, but I *was* enjoying the murderous glares Casey was sending in our direction.

Running a hand through my hair, I make my way toward the fire. Mila and Oliver are now sitting with Casey and Lawson, and Gray Robson and some dark-haired girl I don't recognize. Casey's shoulders stiffen at my approach. Then she surprises me by flashing a little smirk.

"What? You strike out with that girl?" she asks mockingly. "You must be losing your touch."

Lawson chuckles. Traitor. When he notices my scowl, he shrugs as if to say, *what, I thought it was funny.*

Mila stares at Casey. "Damn, Tresscott. You're reminding me more and more of Sloane."

Yes, she is, and I don't like it. Because it's not who she is. Sloane is undeniably hot, but she's all hard edges. Some guys like the she-devil persona—God knows it turns my stepbrother on. But me, I don't want a combative relationship.

Relationship.

The fact that the word so casually penetrates my consciousness tells me how far gone I am for this girl. I never cared about relationships before. Never wanted one. Then I met Casey, and for the first time, I could actually see myself being someone's boyfriend.

Her boyfriend.

And I had to go and ruin it. Because that's what I do. I ruin things. Any time I'm presented with a decision that has two clear outcomes—right or wrong—I take the wrong path. Even when I think it's the right one, it still blows up in my face.

Shouts and screaming suddenly pierce the trees beneath the music. We all turn to realize it's the noise of people stripping down to run into the lake. I catch glimpses of bras and underwear. Boxers and tighty-whities. Some are going in naked, hands cupping their junk as they dash into the black water.

"That's what I'm talking about," Oliver says, hopping to his feet. He pulls Mila up with him and affects a pretty decent British accent. "Fancy a swim, luv?"

"Why, yes, I do." She's already tugging her shirt over her head, leaving her in a lacy black bra. "You coming, Casey?"

"No," I answer for Casey, my tone brooking no argument.

So of course, she gives me one.

Eyes gleaming, she gets up and starts undoing her jeans.

"No," I repeat. Low and gravelly. "Zip up those jeans, Case."

From his spot by the fire, Lawson laughs under his breath.

She ignores me, pushing the denim down her legs and kicking the jeans away. The sight of her bare legs summons a growl from the back of my throat. Okay, I'm pissed off. She's doing this on purpose and I'm not having it.

I take a step toward her just as she flings her sweater in my face. I shove it aside in time to see Oliver hoisting Casey over one shoulder. There's a blur of her white bra and panties before Oliver darts toward the sandy shore and carries a laughing, shrieking Casey into the water.

CHAPTER 31
CASEY

I'M DIZZY BUT LAUGHING WHEN I TUMBLE OFF OLIVER'S SHOULDERS. Water gets up my nose and I cough as my toes search for the soft, muddy bottom on the lake. For the first time all night, I experience a brief flicker of panic when the cold water surrounds me. But then I surface and hear the laughter and voices all around me, and I remember I'm safe.

Mila screams and splashes when Oliver lifts her over his head and throws her like a sack of potatoes into pure darkness. It briefly occurs to me I abandoned Jaz, but she looked quite cozy with Gray Robson before I sidestepped Fenn's grasp and dove into Oliver's arms.

Someone wades over with a bottle in hand, and the two dozen or so black silhouettes chest-high around me chant "Drink!" as some faceless person offers me a pour of tequila. I tilt my head back to accept. The sting is startling yet oddly refreshing. I'm not sure I taste it going down, but I feel it warm the pit of my stomach.

"Casey!"

My good mood fades at the sound of Fenn's voice. I ignore him, swimming toward Mila, who greets me with an impressed smirk. "Ooh. Somebody's in trouble."

We both watch the shore, where Fenn removes his shoes and hoodie before trudging into the water in jeans and a thin tee. "Casey, damn it. Answer me."

"She's over here." Mila rats me out and shoves me from behind.

I curse in protest when he reaches for me. "No. Go away, Fenn."

"Can't do that." Without warning or permission, he finds my hand and drags me behind him back toward dry land. He stops only to snatch up his shoes and sweatshirt with his free hand.

"Hey, she doesn't want to go with you." A dripping wet Oliver appears and plants a hand to Fenn's chest, blocking his path. But even I can tell Oliver's a little too unsteady and lopsided on his feet to put up much of a protest.

"Yeah, okay. How 'bout I leave her here, then, and you can explain to Sloane and her dad why you've spent the night pumping a minor full of alcohol."

Fenn pushes Oliver out of the way.

"Let go of me." I try yanking my hand free, but his grip is secure. "You have no right to do this."

"Maybe not. But you'll thank me in the morning."

Then he tosses me over his shoulder and my world is upside down and spinning sideways. That shot of tequila is less pleasant working its way back up my esophagus.

"Put me down, Fenn! I mean it."

"I know you do."

"Now! Put me down. Jazmine! Help!"

My friend comes barreling toward us, but rather than rescue me, I see a blur of black and hear a smacking noise as she slaps something in Fenn's palm.

"Hey! Blond caveman! If you're going to kidnap my friend, at least let her have her phone."

"I'm not kidnapping her," he mutters. "I'm taking her home."

"Put me down," I order again, batting one fist between his shoulder blades.

But he doesn't comply until he's marched us back to a shiny BMW parked along the dirt road.

He opens the passenger door and nods at me impatiently.

"I'm not getting in there."

"Let's go, Casey. You've had enough tonight."

"Where did you come up with this idea that you're allowed to show up out of nowhere and tell me what to do?"

"When every time you disappear, your sister calls to blame me for this bullshit."

"You're becoming just like her."

Fenn growls. "Get in."

This looks like Duke's car. Which is even more confusing, but I don't have the luxury of pondering that when a slight breeze pricks my skin, and a cold shiver reminds me I'm soaking wet in my underwear.

"Can you at least go back and grab my clothes?" I grumble.

"No."

Instead, he marches over with his hoodie and then roughly pulls it down over my head. It's too big, the hem falling past my knees, but it's soft and warm, and I can't help putting my arms through the sleeves to snuggle into the thick fabric.

"Can we go now?" Fenn gestures with the door open.

I could run back to the lake, but I don't have the energy to make him chase me. Besides, I have a feeling the tequila is going to make itself known sooner rather than later, so it's probably best not to have an audience when it spews out of me.

I get in, even if I'm not happy about it.

"Seat belt," he orders, then throws the door closed.

"Give me my phone."

"Only if you promise not to call 911 and tell them you've been kidnapped."

"You'd deserve that." I glower at him. "I just want to tell Jaz not to worry."

He passes the phone over, albeit reluctantly. With cold, shaky fingers, I type a message to Jaz, who texts back almost instantly.

Jazmine: You OK??
Me: Fine. Just pissed. He has some nerve.
Jazmine: Will you be mad at me if I point out how hot he looked when he was carrying you off?
Me: Yes.
Jazmine: Okay, I won't point it out then. Text when you're home so I know you made it back.
Me: You too!

Fenn doesn't look at me as we leave Ballard. He strangles the steering wheel and stares straight ahead, ignoring me until I start to fumble with the dash buttons.

"Stop it," he says. "What are you doing?"

"Looking for the butt heaters."

"Excuse me?"

"Duke's car has heated seats and I'm freezing. This is Duke's car, isn't it? And would it kill you to put some music on?"

Without a word, Fenn cranks up the heat and turns on the radio as well.

"I bet you're feeling pretty high on yourself now, right?" I finally locate the little knob with a picture of a seat and turn it all the way to the right. My seat warms almost instantly. "Swooping in to steal me away from a good time."

"That's what you call frolicking around naked in the woods?"

"Like you've never been skinny-dipping."

"I'm not an example you should imitate," he grumbles.

"That much we can agree on."

"You realize your pictures are all over social media now? Every perv from Ballard and Sandover will be gawking at you in your underwear."

"Which is practically the same thing as a bathing suit. So what?"

Am I thrilled at the idea? No, not really. And when the liquor's worn off, I might have a couple of regrets over tonight. Either way, it's a little late now.

And the last thing I'm going to do is give Fenn the satisfaction.

"Whatever you're trying to prove," he says gruffly, "trust me, it's not going to fix what's broken. It'll only get you further away from the solution."

I roll my eyes. "Whatever that means."

Fenn doesn't respond, and we don't find anything else to say to each other on the drive back to Sandover. It's dark and long, and I don't realize I've fallen asleep until Fenn opens my door and I wake up to realize we're in the senior dorm parking lot.

"Are you kidding me? Why are we here?" I demand in outrage. "Take me home."

He reaches over me to unlatch my seat belt. "Yeah, I don't think so. I'm not dumping you at your front door, dripping wet in your underwear and wearing my soccer team sweatshirt. I'm not trying to die tonight."

"Well, I'm not going in there," I say, crossing my arms in the front seat.

"Then we'll sit here till morning when everyone heads to breakfast and wonders why the headmaster's daughter is half naked in Duke's ride."

God, he's such an asshole.

A cocky smirk slants across his face. "Or I throw you over my shoulder again."

"I swear, I will punch you in the balls."

"Come on. It's warm upstairs, and I can give you some dry clothes. Don't be difficult."

I get out of the car, but only because I don't relish being cold and wet all night. "Don't tell me what to do."

Despite my protests, Fenn lifts me off my feet to cradle me in his arms.

"Could you just not?" I growl.

"You don't have any shoes," he says dismissively. "I'm not letting you cut your feet up on broken glass so you can blame me for that too."

Seriously. Such an asshole.

Thankfully, the halls are quiet when he brings me upstairs. Everyone's either asleep or out partying. Small miracles, I guess. The last thing I need is people talking about me and Fenn hooking up again. Because that is so over.

If only he'd get the message.

In his room, he turns on the light and locks the door, while I glance around warily and realize this is the first time I've been here.

RJ's side of the room is empty. He's still over at my place, which is both a relief and an irritating notion. RJ gets to hang out at my house past midnight when all my visitors have to leave by ten? Just another one of those double standards my dad loves so much.

On the other hand, if RJ were here right now, he'd be the first one to tell Sloane that I wasn't studying in Jaz's dorm, and I'd rather not deal with another lecture from my dad and sister.

Fenn throws me a T-shirt and a pair of sweatpants, then turns his back while I change. The clothing isn't exactly my size, but it's dry and warm.

"You look cute," he says, eyeing me with that adoring expression that used to make me nervous and excited in the best way and now only fills me with rage.

"No. You don't get to do that. You effectively kidnapped me. You understand that, right?"

"For your own good."

"So now what? I'm your prisoner?" I ask, pretending not to notice that he'd stripped out of his wet T-shirt. His abs ripple in the soft lightning of the room.

I wrench my gaze off his bare chest and kneel in front of the mini fridge, where I take an extra-long time to steal a bottle of water. By the time I stand up and uncap the bottle, Fenn has changed into dry clothes of his own.

"Why don't you tell me what the hell is going on with you lately?" He sits on the arm of the sofa, all self-righteous and proud of himself.

"Nothing's going on." And I'm getting real sick of answering that question. "Except that I'm trying to live my life, and no one wants to let me. It's like you're all terrified of me becoming my own person."

"That's not true." He rakes a hand through his hair, frustrated. "You've changed. All of a sudden you're picking fights, getting into trouble. Running around in the woods naked and drunk with people who less than a year ago stood in the halls laughing at you. Normally I'd be cheering that you've finally stopped caring what people think, but after everything, it feels like a cry for help."

I'm frustrated too now, speaking through clenched teeth. "I'm not drunk. I had two watered-down beers and the equivalent of one tequila shot. I feel fine. And I'm not asking for help. Least of all from you."

His reaction is slight but immediate, a flood of hurt filling his eyes before he averts them. For a moment I feel awful. I forget why I hate him. But the sympathy passes just as quickly.

"I've been there, okay?" His voice is pleading, eyes imploring. Those sincere blue eyes that are so easy to believe. "Hell, I probably still am. Or would be, if not for you. We get angry and sad and don't know where to aim it but at ourselves. We try to become someone else. Someone who isn't carrying around that pain."

I shake my head, a wave of exhaustion washing over me. I don't feel buzzed anymore. Just tired and dead sober.

"I know exactly who I'm mad at, Fenn. He's right in front of me."

"I get that."

"I don't think you do. And tonight only hurt your case. You realize that? Your jealous caveman stunt wasn't cool," I say flatly. "You fucking embarrassed me by running into the lake and dragging me away from the party. I know you view me as this innocent princess who's too pure to strip down to her underwear and go swimming, but I'm allowed to have fun and—"

"Christ! That's not why I ran into the lake!" he interrupts in aggravation.

"No? So you weren't jealous?" I challenge.

"No." He falters. "I mean, yes. I was. Ugh." He makes an agitated noise. "I was jealous when you started stripping, yes, but that's not why I went in after you. When he threw you into the water, I…"

Fenn trails off, his expression collapsing.

"You what?" My throat gets tight. Pulse fluttering weakly.

He stands and approaches me. I back away until my shoulders are against the wall and I'm trapped. He stops short when there's a foot of space between us.

"I panicked," he admits, his voice cracking slightly. "It was like… like suddenly I was transported back to prom, to that moment when I found you in the lake, and my heart just stopped. I don't even remember wading into the water tonight. All I remember is Oliver throwing you in, and you went under, and I…I was afraid."

His breath shudders out on a low wheeze.

I, on the other hand, can't seem to draw a deep enough breath. My lungs are burning, and my eyes start to sting.

"I'm sorry I embarrassed you," Fenn says, hanging his head shamefully. "It was irrational, but my brain was telling me you were in danger, that you might drown, and my first instinct was to rescue you."

"I don't need to be rescued." My words come out as a whisper.

He closes the distance, pushing a few damp strands of hair behind my ear. I don't realize until he does that I'm gripping his shirt in both fists.

"I'll be here to save you every time," he says softly. "Just like I was there that night."

I hate him for saying that. For thinking he's the center of everything wrong with me. And for being fucking right, because it's true—I can't go a day without chasing his name from my thoughts. I want him and can't stand him in equal measure, and my heart doesn't know how to reconcile that.

I blink back the moisture coating my lashes. "Why'd it have to be you?"

His answer is a kiss.

Fenn's warm hands grasp my face as he presses his lips to mine. Gently, but insistent. Every time we kiss, it's like a letter from a pen pal. One of those long conversations at the coffee shop when you close the place down. Staying up all night on the phone. Catching up on lost time. Picking up exactly where we left off no matter how much time and space has come between us.

I wrap my arms around his neck even as I know I'll hate myself for it later. Hate that all my anger, his betrayal, becomes superfluous when he touches me. How easily I'm won. Not because it's some trick or spell, but because he feels like home to me.

I let him kiss me because there's never a time I've stopped wanting him to, no matter how much I wish I could purge that desire from my heart. I kiss him back because kissing him is the closest thing I know to happiness.

Neither of us speak when he grasps my hips. Like we're both afraid to breathe too loudly and let this brief illusion evaporate and realize we're both still us and nothing's changed. I comb my fingers through his hair that's gotten a little longer since the last time I did this. It's still soft as I remember.

His hands find bare skin under my shirt. His shirt. Which feels like a blanket, and I'll probably take it home, where I'll throw it over a chair tomorrow and tell myself I'll wash and return it. But it'll just lie there for weeks while I close my eyes and remember the way he tastes on my tongue or how smooth his fingertips are when they skim my spine.

I swallow hard and bite my lip when he slides his hand under that shirt to grasp my breast. My knee falls to the side. The wall holds me up as he steps between my legs. I arch into his palm, and my tongue against his begs him to make me feel everything I'm too scared to admit I want.

Because he is everything I should run from.

"You're beautiful." Finally, he speaks. A reverent whisper.

Fenn pushes the shirt up my chest. He kisses the slight valley between my breasts before traveling a path to one nipple. He licks softly while I resist the shudder weakening through my limbs.

When he reaches between my thighs and his mouth meets mine again, I can only think of the times he was afraid to touch me. Afraid of moving too quickly. But we aren't those people anymore, kissing on a picnic blanket in the forest. He's a beautiful stranger and I'm the girl he left behind. A dream so fleeting, it practically never happened at all.

"I want to make you feel good," he says, breathing hard against my lips. "Will you let me?"

I should say no.

"Yes."

With a visible gulp, Fenn tentatively slips his hand inside my sweatpants. Applying pressure to the spot that banishes every small whisper warning me that when this fantasy wears off, we'll both go back to being ourselves and nothing fundamentally broken will have been repaired.

I grip his shoulders to hold myself upright, burying my face in his neck. Every short, shallow breath fills me with his scent while he massages me toward pure sensation. No thoughts but his skin. His heartbeat against my chest. His fingers teasing my clit.

Then his fingers are gone, and I'm ashamed of the desperate moan that's ripped from my throat.

"Don't worry. Not stopping," he says roughly, then walks me toward his bed. "Lie down."

I'm shaking like a leaf in the wind as I lower myself onto the mattress. Fenn peels my sweatpants off and tosses them away. A groan escapes his lips when his gaze focuses on my bare pussy.

"Fuck," he whispers and reaches out to rub his knuckles along my slit.

Pleasure shoots through me. I can't take my gaze off his face. The way his teeth are digging into his bottom lip. The way he sucks in a breath when he feels how wet I am.

"Has anyone ever made you come before?" The question is hoarse. Strangled.

"No," I say honestly.

I feel his fingers tremble against my heated flesh.

"Anyone ever gone down on you?"

"No."

So fucking pure.

I suddenly hear Lawson's mocking voice in my head, and for some reason it evokes a twinge of resentment. I'm not pure. Or at least, I don't want to be. I'm tired of being the fragile piece of china everyone is so afraid to break that they resist from touching altogether. Fenn resisted doing this for months, and the reminder emboldens me.

I spread my legs wider.

His choked expletive echoes in the room.

"Do something," I say.

An impish gleam lights his eyes, invoking memories of the Fenn I fell for. The guy who was always armed with a quip and a smile. The sight makes me soften, breathe easier, and I know he notices because his features soften too.

Then he licks his lips and brings them between my legs.

I jolt when he makes contact, gasping with pleasure. Oh my God. This is…

This is…

My brain short-circuits. I'm incapable of forming thoughts. I lose myself in the heat of his mouth against my aching core. My eyelids flutter closed and breathing becomes labored. I start rocking my hips, and Fenn moans, the sound vibrating like a cascade of notes across my body.

There's nothing tentative about his movements. My nails bite into his shoulders as he explores me with his mouth. Licking. Tasting. When he sucks gently on my clit, another shudder overtakes me. This time I give in to it, shaking on the bed while Fenn brings me closer and closer to the edge.

"That's it, Case," he whispers before slicking his tongue over my clit. Teasing. "Let yourself go."

So I do, welcoming the sweet oblivion of orgasm. The electricity firing across every nerve ending as pure bliss consumes my entire body.

But the peace is temporary. It begins to be subside even before he's placed a last delicate kiss to my sated flesh. Reality creeps in, forever determined to remind me there's no silence too permanent to make me forget what Fenn did.

When my eyes open, I push him away and scramble to sit up.

His brow furrows. "Are you okay?"

I swallow a few times. "That shouldn't have happened. I have to go."

Without looking at him, I find my underwear and his sweatpants, slipping them both on.

"You can't leave," he insists, but his voice is thick with unhappiness because he knows I'm already gone.

"I'll be fine." Eventually.

"At least let me drive you."

"I'll walk. It's not far," I remind him when he tries to object.

"You don't have shoes."

Shit. He's right. And there's no way I can fit into any of his and trudge ten minutes through the woods.

He gets to his feet, raking both hands through his hair. "Come on, I'll drive you."

Since I don't have much of a choice, I allow him to drop me off, sliding out of the car five minutes later with a muttered, "Thanks." My guard is back up, and not even the memory of how good he just made me feel can penetrate the shield around my heart.

"Good night," he says gruffly.

I close the door and hurry up the front path. Then stop in a comical skid when I realize I have no way to explain my appearance to Dad. I left the house in yoga pants and an oversized sweater. Spent the evening in a tight top and jeans. And returned home in a guy's shirt and sweatpants.

Fuck.

I start to panic, until I remember I told Dad I was spending the night at Jazmine's. That means he's already in bed. Probably took a sleeping pill too, which he's been prone to do lately. As long as the dogs don't go berserk, I should be able to creep in and upstairs without notice.

Luck is on my side. It's nearly two a.m. and both dogs are passed out cold. Bo cranks one eye open when I tiptoe past him. After he confirms it's me, he goes back to sleep. From her dog bed in the living room, Penny is snoring obliviously.

At the top of the stairs, I almost slam into RJ, both of us hissing in surprise.

We're like two burglars trying to rob the same house, only he got here first and is already escaping with the loot. I take in his rumpled hair and inside-out shirt, then lower my gaze to his fly, which is unzipped. Classy. I hope Sloane wasn't too busy banging her boyfriend that she forgot to feed my rabbit. When I texted her from the party earlier, pretending to be at Jaz's dorm, she promised she'd take care of Silver.

Rolling my eyes, I point to RJ's crotch.

He looks down, then shrugs. Completely unruffled as he zips up.

Then he gives me a wry smile, white teeth shining in the darkness, as he gestures at *my* outfit, instantly recognizing Fenn's clothes.

I offer a shrug of my own.

Sighing, RJ shakes his head and descends the first step. He pauses to glance over his shoulder. "Night," he mouths.

"Night," I mouth back, then slide into my bedroom and close the door behind me.

CHAPTER 32
SILAS

THIS BEEF WITH SLOANE HAS GONE ON LONG ENOUGH. WE'VE both been more than stubborn since our argument, but it appears her will is holding out longer than mine. Fine, then. I'll be the bigger person and make the first move toward reconciliation. I miss talking to her. I miss her sarcastic remarks and throaty laughter. If she needs an apology, I can make that sacrifice of pride. Because whatever she says in fits of anger, our friendship is ultimately more important than whatever rhetorical point either of us tried to make.

And honestly, without Amy in the picture constantly questioning our friendship, it'll be much easier to get back to normal.

Wednesday afternoon before swim practice, I toss my bag down on the bench in the locker room and pull out my phone.

Me: You win. I humbly apologize and throw myself at your mercy.
Me: Forgive me.
Me: Let's meet up and talk?

Sloane doesn't reply right away. Probably driving home from

school. But I know we'll be able to put this behind us once we have a real conversation.

With only a few minutes before Coach wants us warming up in the pool, I throw my phone back in my bag and get changed. Unfortunately, there's nothing I can do about locker assignments. RJ struts in with Lawson to the locker two down from mine.

It's become nearly intolerable sharing oxygen with him. The way RJ's practically claimed ownership over Sloane and the entirety of her social life makes me goddamn homicidal. Lately my best tack is simply avoiding eye contact so I don't get sucked into another self-righteous lecture about boundaries and loyalty from a guy who's been lying about who and what he is since the moment he got here. In a few short months, he's managed to turn everyone but Lawson against me. The fact that Sloane and Fenn can't see how he's manipulated them is beyond frustrating.

As I'm fitting my cap on, I can't help noticing RJ with his phone out. His thumbs tap across the screen seconds before my own phone buzzes on top of my bag.

Sloane: I'm not ready. I don't know if I'll ever be.

"Did you do this?" I growl at RJ.

He has the nerve to stare at me blankly. "Huh?"

"Don't fuck with me. Sloane. Just now."

He glances at Lawson for clarification, but my best friend merely shrugs. Swim goggles dangling from one hand, RJ gives me an irritated look. "Dude, I have no idea what you're babbling about."

"Then show me your phone."

He snorts. "Fuck off."

"If you did nothing wrong, then there's nothing to hide," I shoot back. "I saw you texting Sloane right before she refused to meet up with me. You told her to. Just admit it."

RJ stares at me. "I can't tell Sloane shit. And if you understood her at all, you'd get that."

Disbelief slams into me like a freight train. "Don't act like you know her better than I do, all right? I was in her life way before you got here."

"Come on, girls," Lawson mockingly interjects. "You're both pretty. Let's take it down a notch."

RJ and I are all but toe-to-toe on either side of the bench. Part of me wishes he'd throw a punch, so I could finally get him kicked off this team. Maybe kicked out of Sandover altogether.

"And it must burn you up," RJ tells me. Goading.

"What's that?"

"Finally knowing that all this time it wasn't Duke or her dad that kept Sloane from being with you. She's just not into you."

My hands tingle with the urge to break his face. "You'd like to think that, wouldn't you?"

"Okay then." Lawson once again attempts to defuse the situation. "Why don't we table this discussion for never?"

"And now," RJ continues, flashing a cheerless smile, "she doesn't rate you at all. How does it feel to be demoted from the friend zone?"

I shove him. Two hands to the chest. He comes back at me just as quickly, about to jump the bench, fists clenched, before Lawson throws himself between us and holds him back.

"Come on, man," RJ taunts. "You've been begging for this fight. I'm right here, asshole."

"Nice temper. You argue with Sloane like that too?"

"Watch your fucking mouth."

RJ makes a fool of himself having to be dragged away by Lawson in front of the entire team. I figured that'd be the end of it, but no such luck. RJ's need to be the chest-slamming gorilla in the room doesn't stop when we get in the pool.

After an initial warm-up, Coach Gibson blows his whistle and has us line up behind the starting platforms.

"Mason, Clark, RJ, Silas. On the blocks."

RJ intentionally puts himself in the lane next to mine. He proceeds to do that annoying compulsive habit where he slaps his thighs like he thinks he's Michael Fucking Phelps.

"Hey, remind me," he says over his shoulder, getting into a starting position. "What's Silas's record in the 400 free?"

"Uh…" Lawson eyes me cautiously. "Like a minute thirty-three?"

"Hey, Coach," RJ calls. He slides his goggles down over his eyes. "Get out your stopwatch."

"This isn't a race, Shaw," Coach barks back. "I want to see form. I want to see follow-through. Clean lines, smart breathing."

"You're dreaming," I tell RJ, staring straight ahead at the flat water and seeing only the lane ahead of me. "That record's getting me into Stanford."

"Then you better hope they're desperate for alternates."

When Coach's whistle blows, we're both off the blocks like our feet are on fire. I hit the water in a straight line. Every muscle is pulled into focus on a clean entrance and getting as much distance as possible powering through my dolphin kicks.

RJ is right beside me. Almost stroke for stroke when we breach the surface. We hit the wall for the first turn dead even and well ahead of the outside lanes.

The problem, though, with swimming a dead heat with the lane beside you is all the chop they churn up. White water is the enemy of speed. Ideally, you want to be the lone leader with nothing but clean water ahead of you. RJ apparently doesn't know this and thinks he can draft an advantage by hugging our lane line. I try squeezing every ounce of speed I can out of my kicks, grabbing the water with both hands and propelling my body as far as I can. Still, I can't seem to find an inch of distance between us.

After the second turn, I come up to a face full of water. I know he's intentionally splashing into my lane. Timing my breaths. Dirty fuck. But if he wants to cheat, he'll have to try a hell of a lot harder than that.

Turnabout is fair play, so I start hugging the lane line as well. I make a point of smacking it with my hand or kicking it with a foot to force a wobble that veers into his lane and obstructs his strokes. In a competition, this would obviously be illegal. Here, all's fair in love and war, right?

But I must get under his skin, because on the third turn he takes an extra dolphin kick past the resurface marker. A blatantly desperate move that proves he can't beat me in a fair fight. So I show him there's no honor among thieves. When I see him approaching the surface, I throw a leg out that connects square against his jaw. The result gives me almost a full hand of distance advantage. Then it's a dead sprint to the finish.

I can already feel the wall against my fingertips as I push with everything I have left. I don't even take breaths. I just keep my face in the water and kick as hard as I can.

Until I feel a sudden shove against my shoulder.

It's enough to throw me off my stroke, and I watch RJ's hands slam into the wall before mine.

"That was bullshit." Ripping my goggles and cap off, I jump over the lane line.

He gets right in my face, cheeks flushed and eyes blazing. "Don't start shit you can't finish."

Coach's whistle screams through the building. "Everyone out of the water. Now!"

We all haul ourselves out and stand behind the blocks. I notice Lawson watching me with a frown and resist the urge to give him the finger. Since when does Lawson disapprove of shit like this? He lives and breathes chaos.

"You two," Coach booms, pointing at RJ and me. "Push-ups. Go."

"Are you serious?" I charge over to Coach, incredulous. How is it not obvious RJ is the problem? "He was messing with me the whole time. I was defending myself."

"Yeah, I suppose I managed to kick myself in the face, right?" RJ throws himself in front of me like he's ready for another round.

"Learn to stay in your own lane."

Coach's whistle again screeches us to silence.

"Both of you shut the hell up," he barks. "I'm sick of your bickering."

"Coach, come on." I can't believe he's letting RJ off the hook on this.

"I don't know what's gotten into you two lately but keep it out of my pool." Then he shakes his head at me. "I expected better from you, Silas. Push-ups. Get on it."

"This is bullshit," I snap.

Fuck push-ups, and fuck RJ. I'm not taking the heat for a fight he started.

Coach shouts after me, but I ignore him as I head into the locker room.

CHAPTER 33
CASEY

IT STARTS IN MY TOES. A STINGING CHILL THAT QUICKLY CLAWS UP my legs. The fabric of my prom dress balloons around me as the car fills with black water and the dashboard lights flicker. The rearview mirror glows red, and I struggle against the strangling seat belt. Even before the rushing water reaches my lips, my chest is tight. I can't suck in a breath. Panic clenches my throat. Even my fingers are terrified as they flail helplessly to free me.

Then a *thump*. A *thud* against the door.

Fenn.

He's here. Fully submerged, floating outside the window that for now protects a small, rapidly decreasing pocket of air inside the car. I scream for him. Fumble with the latch, trying to push my way out. I manage to force the slightest movement that invites a violent rush of water that overtakes the interior. But I can't push my way free. The door's too heavy.

My eyes meet Fenn's in silent desperation to pull harder. *Get me out of here*.

Until I realize he's the one holding the door shut. Trapping me inside. Watching me fall deeper into the black. My limbs grow too cold to fight, and his vacant expression grows more distant.

Until finally the light leaves me and the water washes into my lungs.

I wake up coughing. I thrust upright with great, heaving, gagging gulps of air. Tangled and pinned by the sheets like I'm tied up in ropes. Heart pounding, I furiously thrash to untangle myself. I just need to be uncovered. Free. Space. I've never been claustrophobic, but even my room feels too small as I throw myself out of bed to tear open the window and look out at the deep forest behind the house. Miles of openness. The infinity of night.

My first instinct, once I've regained a semiregular heartbeat, is to reach for my phone. I find his name in my recent missed calls list and tap it without a real intention. It's reflex. One I should probably try harder to resist, but which I fall back on regardless.

"Casey?" Fenn answers after the first ring. His voice is hoarse, and my name comes out a little slurred. "Are you okay? What's wrong?"

"Why is that your first question?"

"At three a.m. I kinda just assumed."

"I'm fine. Sorry." I sit on the windowsill to listen to the noise the night makes in our yard. "Honestly, I don't think I expected you to answer."

"I'll always pick up for you."

Tears sting my eyes. It's unfair that I retreat to him when I need something. That I crave the comfort of his voice. The ways he understands me where others can't.

"Nightmares again?" he asks.

"You were in it."

"I'm afraid to ask."

"It wasn't good."

There's a pause. "Do you want me to come over?"

The offer makes me falter. For months when the nightmares came, Fenn stayed up with me on the phone, sometimes till break-fast the next morning, to talk me through it. We usually spoke about my mom, how her death triggered so many of my fears after the accident. The fixation on drowning. Somehow, he'd find a way to make me feel like happiness was possible.

But this is the first time he's asked if I want him to be here. Physically *here* with me.

And even when the better part of me still prefers to hate him, I find myself saying, "Yes. Can you?"

"I'll be there in ten."

Not long after, he tumbles in through the window, and we both wince when he lands on his knees with a *thud*. Freezing on the spot, I glance toward the door, but I don't hear the dogs out in the hall. Honestly, at this point, I really need to stop worrying about those two. Bo and Penny are sweet as pie, but they're terrible guard dogs.

"Sorry." His voice is hushed. "Lost my balance."

"It's okay," I whisper back.

We stand there for a moment, watching each other. It's three thirty in the morning and I'm in my pajamas: little pink shorts and a paper-thin T-shirt.

"You look cold," Fenn says, gaze darting to my chest before returning to my face. His lips twitch slightly.

I feel a blush form when I realize my nipples are hard and straining against my top. "I am." I kneel to gather the bedsheets I'd flung onto the floor. "Help me with these?"

Silently, we remake my bed, and I don't question myself too hard as I slide under the covers and lift one corner of the blanket for Fenn.

He hesitates for a few seconds, then removes his jacket and drapes it over the back of my desk chair. His shoes come off next, but he leaves his sweatpants and T-shirt on as he crawls in beside me. He starts to reach for me, then seems to second-guess himself, rolling onto his back instead.

We lie in the darkness, staring at the ceiling. Until finally he speaks.

"Do you want to tell me about it?"

"Not yet."

There's still too much adrenaline in my blood, the chemical flood that makes my skin hurt and my brain numb. Until the residual trauma wears off, I just want to be distracted, like watching a TV screen above the dentist's chair.

"I need a distraction." I roll onto my side and rest my head against my arm. "How's life? Anything cool happen lately?"

"Not cool, necessarily, but apparently RJ and Silas got into it at practice a couple days ago. Lawson had to break up some pushy-shovies in the locker room."

We speak in soft murmurs, both painfully aware of the late hour and the fact that Fenn will be murdered if he's caught in my bed.

"Oh, wow. Tensions in the region are escalating, then?"

"I don't know. Silas seems like he's imploding, and I think RJ's just lost his patience for Silas's total refusal to contain his attitude."

"And Silas thinks he's fighting over Sloane?" If so, it's a futile fight. I'm sure Sloane's told him in more ways than one that she's not into it. And my sister's generally not a person who changes her mind.

"I think it's more about principle at this point," Fenn says. "Well, jealousy. But in Silas's head, he's the injured party."

"Sounds like you've come down squarely on Team RJ."

He snorts a muffled laugh. "Silas is on my shit list for different reasons. Like I said, he's imploding."

I know the feeling. I haven't felt super on the ball lately either. Fighting with Sloane and my dad, on top of this thing with Fenn and the people at school. It's a lot, and I'm certain the recent stream of nightmares is related to that.

To make matters worse, having Fenn lying so close to me is absolute torture. His familiar scent, soap and citrus, wafts toward me, and I can't help from taking a deep inhale, needing to fill my senses with him. I watch the way his broad chest rises and falls with each breath. The way the long fingers of one hand play with the edge of the blanket.

It's not fair how much I still want him. How badly I'm craving his lips. My heart starts pounding again, not from the nightmare, but from need. Before I can stop myself, I scoot closer and rise on one elbow, peering down at him.

He bites his lip. "What?"

"I don't know. I…"

I kiss him, my hair falling like a curtain over our faces. Fenn threads his fingers through it and smooths the messy tresses away from my cheek. His mouth moves over mine in an infinitely sweet kiss.

"I missed you," he mumbles before sliding his tongue through my parted lips.

We can't stop kissing. I climb onto his body, and he wraps his arms around me, his hands caressing my back, my hips, my ass, as we kiss in the darkness. I feel the hard ridge of his erection trapped between us, and a shiver dances through me. As far as distractions go, this one is really, really good. Sometimes it's hard to believe that Fenn Bishop is attracted to me. Of the hundreds and hundreds of boys who attend Sandover and its neighboring prep schools, Fenn is hands down one of the best-looking. Drop-dead gorgeous. Which means he can have any girl he wants.

For some inexplicable reason, he wants *me*.

I bury my face in his neck and explore his flesh with my lips. We're both breathing heavily. And I'm about to combust from the heat. It's boiling hot beneath the covers, but I don't push them off us. Here in this warm cocoon, with our bodies wrapped up in each other, it's like a perfect secret between us, a shield that nothing can penetrate. No doubts. No anger or bitterness. It's just me and him, the way it used to be.

Fenn tries to protest when I kiss my way down his body. I didn't plan on it, but my lips are in control, coaxing me lower and lower, until I'm between his legs and my fingers are pulling on his waistband.

My mouth fills with moisture when his erection springs up.

He attempts another objection, his hand sliding in my hair to still me. "What are you doing?"

I shush him and wrap my fingers around his shaft. Then I lick a wet, teasing stripe from his base to his tip, and Fenn jerks on the bed. Before he can protest again, I take him in my mouth.

My pulse quickens, thudding in my ears as arousal builds inside me. I've never done this before. I didn't think I'd enjoy it this much.

A fragment of light irritates my closed eyelids. I raise my head to see Fenn lifted the blanket over his head so now we're both under it. His hazy, heavy-lidded eyes find mine in the shadows.

"Hi."

"Hi." A faint smile tickles the corners of my mouth.

"You're driving me crazy down there, you know that?"

"I know." Without breaking eye contact, I wrap my lips around him again.

The moan he chokes out is the most satisfying sound I've ever heard.

"You have no idea how many times I got myself off thinking about this," he says.

My heart thumps harder. I suck faster.

His hips move restlessly as he starts thrusting into my mouth, trying to go deeper. When he goes a bit too deep, I cough and release him, my eyes watering.

"Sorry," he says weakly.

"S'okay." I lick my lips and resume what I was doing, laying one hand on his thigh. His muscles quiver beneath my palm.

It doesn't take long before he mumbles, "Casey…I'm gonna come," and then slides out of my mouth and takes his dick in hand.

My throat goes dry and my pussy throbs as I watch him stroke himself to climax, spilling onto his stomach. I don't think I've seen anything hotter.

Satisfied with myself, I crawl back up his body. Cool, fresh air fills my nostrils when I emerge from our cocoon, and I suck in a deep breath. I reach for the box on the nightstand to grab a handful of tissues, which Fenn uses to clean up before he throws the wad in the wastebasket next to my desk in an impressive toss that meets its target. Then he curls his arm around me and captures my lips in a blistering kiss. His hand skims down my body and inside my panties. When he feels how wet I am, he opens his eyes and grins at me.

"That turned you on," he murmurs.

"Uh-huh." In fact, I'm wound so tight that it takes him less than a minute to bring me to orgasm with his fingers. I bite into his shoulder and rock into his hand as release washes over me in sweet ripples of pleasure.

Once my heart has settled in my chest, I straighten out my rumpled PJs. "Do you want to meet Silver?" I ask, feeling oddly shy. "I rescued her from a fox last week."

I see him smiling in the darkness. "Love to."

Gently, I set the shoebox on the bed and remove the lid. Inside, Silver is sound asleep in her snug nest, her tiny body burrowed in her towel.

Fenn sits up to take a peek, his features softening. "Damn. That's adorable."

Smiling, I rub my index finger over her grayish-brown fur. My gal is no longer blind, deaf, and furless. She's starting to look more like a rabbit and less like an alien.

"She opened her eyes a few days ago. And her ears have perked up." I bite my lip, worry gnawing at me. "She still seems so weak, though. I called this wildlife place the other day, and they said she shouldn't really be moving around until she's two and a half, three weeks old. But it seems like she hardly moves at all."

"How long do you plan on keeping her?"

"If she lives, I'll probably release her in a couple weeks. They usually leave the nest at three or four weeks. But I'll need to wean her first. I plan to do that soon."

"But if you release her, won't another fox just eat her up? She's so tiny." With considerable care, he strokes Silver's head.

"She might look small and helpless, but if she's healthy and can hop, she's meant to be out there on her own." I shrug. "The world is scary, but you can't avoid living in it."

"Are we talking about bunnies or humans?"

"Both."

I close the lid and place the box back on the nightstand. I scoot closer to Fenn, resting my head against his shoulder. He tucks the blanket around our lower bodies, and we sit there for a while. Silent. Pensive. It's four in the morning and the house is eerily quiet.

"You wouldn't let me out of the car."

He tenses. "What?"

"In my nightmare."

There's a long silence. Then, "Oh."

"I'm stuck in the seat, the water's getting higher, and when I see you, I'm relieved. Then I realize you've got me trapped and there's nothing I can do."

"Yeah, that's not great." His voice is strained. "But I understand. I think."

"I don't blame you for the accident."

"Right, but you do blame me."

I suppose we've never acknowledged it in those terms.

"And that's totally fine," he says. "Understandable. I'm not mad at it." He sighs, flustered. "You know what I mean."

"Everyone kept telling me that if I could remember more about that night, it would help. I could start to move on. Then I find out about you and…"

"It only made it worse."

Cataclysmically worse. The foundation of months of recovery

shattered by the most profound betrayal anyone could have inflicted on me.

"Because now I'm stuck. I can't forget and I can't move on." I hesitate. "I went back to my shrink the other day. She helped me remember something."

Fenn inhales sharply. "Are you serious? Why didn't you tell me?"

"Because I didn't want to. I'm tired of you being the first person I call whenever I need to talk."

Which is exactly what I did tonight.

I shake my head at myself. Clearly I haven't learned any lessons.

"Tell me what you remembered," he urges.

"I offered someone a ride, and they may have been wearing pink. Lucas thinks it could've been a girl."

His breath hitches again. "Fuck. Who could it be, though?" He pauses for a few beats. "I'm trying to think who was wearing pink that night, but it's all a huge blank. I didn't pay much attention to what anyone wore except for—what's her name? Hallie? The chick who showed up in that weird plastic wrap dress where you could see her tits and pussy. Headmaster Fournette made her leave and every dude there cried."

I snicker before going serious. "I don't remember what people were wearing either. Anyway. That's it. Sounds like I willingly got in the car with whoever it was, so that's something, I guess. I wasn't coerced as far as I know. But there's no way I would have willingly taken a Rohypnol cocktail, or whatever the doctors called it." I'm firm about this point. Nodding as if to punctuate it. "Even if I did choose to do drugs that night, I would've picked something a lot milder. Gillian and I had been talking about trying molly sometime, so if anything, that's probably what I would've done."

"Was Gillian at prom?"

"No. The sophomore cheerleaders were at a dance competition in Boston that weekend. I couldn't go because I bruised my ankle the week before and our coach didn't want to risk it. So I convinced Sloane to take me to the junior prom." I make a dejected noise. "I should've just gone to Boston and cheered my friends on."

He wraps his arm around my shoulder to draw me closer. When I hesitate, he mumbles, "Don't pull away from me. Let me have tonight."

He laces our fingers together, then brings our joined hands to his lips, brushing a kiss over my knuckles before pressing my hand against his chest. A stinging sensation pricks my closed eyelids. I feel his heart beating fast beneath my fingertips, a reminder that we're both alive. *I'm* alive, and largely because of him.

I let out a slow breath. "I'm trying to remember that."

"Remember what?"

"That I would have drowned if you hadn't rescued me. If I just keep focusing on that…" I blink and a teardrop slides down my cheek.

"Case?"

"Why did you lie?" I whisper in the darkness.

"I…" He curses under his breath.

"I want to forgive you, Fenn. Please help me do that. *Please*."

I'm hit with instant regret over raising my voice because the mistake causes a chain reaction of disastrous events. The dogs finally decide to be useful, mistaking my frustrated cry for one of distress. Loud, incessant barking breaks out through the house, Bo and Penny's footsteps crashing up the stairs as they barrel toward my room. My door is closed, so the dogs smash into it with a deafening *bang* that is certain to wake up the entire house.

"Shit," I hiss, my face paling. "Get up. You need to go."

He's two steps ahead of me. Hoodie on, shoes in his hands as he lunges toward the window.

"Casey?" Dad's muffled voice echoes from the hallway. "Casey!" He's getting closer. "What's wrong?"

As Fenn wrenches the window open, it occurs to me I forgot

to lock my door after I invited him over. My dad's hand now rattles the knob.

"Go," I plead.

Fenn throws his shoes out the window, then starts to heave himself over.

He doesn't make it in time. The bedroom door flies open, and a second later Dad's enraged voice blasts from the doorway.

"*Bishop! Get your ass back in here!*"

Shit.

CHAPTER 34
FENN

"So, how much trouble are you in?" Lawson asks over breakfast the next morning.

I was surprised to see him up and about before eleven a.m. on a Saturday, until he told me he'd never actually gone to bed. Apparently he'd pulled an all-nighter with some guys from Ballard and the eight-ball of coke I'd deprived him of last weekend. Equally surprising is the fact that he'd sat on a baggie of cocaine for an entire week without indulging.

Beside Lawson, Silas's head is bent as he shovels eggs into his mouth and texts with his free hand. Always on his phone these days, Mr. Popular. Must be on the hunt for new friends because Sloane wants nothing to do with him. Neither does RJ. Amy. Me. The tally's adding up for the dude.

RJ skipped breakfast, telling me to bring him back a muffin and coffee. He's in our room working on some hacking project. Building a script for who knows what reason. I gave up on trying to understand the shit he does in there.

"I imagine a lot," I answer, glumly moving my fork around my plate. I don't have much of an appetite. I should probably eat, though. Might as well get expelled on a full stomach.

Last night was…rough.

It was fucking rough.

The only silver lining is that Headmaster Tresscott didn't burst in when Casey had my dick in her mouth.

For a moment there, I genuinely thought he was going to lay a hand on me. He had the eyes of a feral animal whose territory you'd just stumbled upon. I wouldn't have been surprised if the dude's hands had turned into wolverine claws and he shredded me to pieces. Somehow, he'd managed to restrain himself, his jaw so tight, it looked like his face was about to crack in half.

His voice was deathly cold, eerie almost, as he ordered me to get out of Casey's bedroom and proceeded to march me downstairs. Meanwhile, Casey was hurrying after us, trying to plead my case, blurting out that it was *her* fault, *she'd* invited me over because of a nightmare, that I was only being a good friend.

It all fell on deaf ears. The headmaster threw open the front door and jabbed his finger in the air, commanding I get the fuck out.

"He seriously dropped an f-bomb?" Silas says, finally joining the conversation while I'm relating everything that went down.

"Yeah, he did." I don't spare Silas a glance, but I can't go as far as to ignore him altogether.

Lawson leans back in his chair, arms locked behind his head. "All right, what kind of damage are we talking about here? Pants undone?"

"Nope. Sweatpants. Firmly secured around my waist."

"Shirt?" Silas asks.

"I was fully dressed," I tell them. "Only thing I didn't have on was shoes. I threw those out the window."

Lawson snickers. "Nice." He purses his lips. "What about the bed? Sheets messed up? Covered in come?"

I wince. "Sheets and blanket sort of in disarray, but it didn't look like someone just got fucked on them."

"And did they?"

"Huh?"

"Did someone get fucked on them?" Lawson clarifies, expression flickering with humor.

"No," I say firmly. "Nothing happened." I pause. "Sort of."

"Nothing sort of happened?" Silas sounds amused.

"Exactly," I reply before biting into a piece of toast.

As I chew, a rush of dread once again fills my chest, ballooning up until it's all I feel. This isn't going to end well for me. Casey texted this morning assuring me she was working on her dad to go light on my punishment, but I'm not holding out hope. The man's always been relentlessly overprotective of his daughters. It's a known fact that if you mess around with them behind his back, you get expelled.

This past spring, I had to ask his permission to even maintain a friendship with Casey. Had to jump through hoops just to earn walking-the-dogs-away-from-the-security-cameras privileges. Maybe if I'd asked him ahead of time to take her on a date—an idea he would've shot down like a well-trained sniper—he might have shown me some grace. He allowed Sloane to date Duke, after all. And now RJ. But Sloane isn't Casey. In the headmaster's eyes, no Sandover delinquent is allowed to have any romantic notions about his precious baby girl.

So…yeah. I should probably start packing.

As if on cue, my phone lights up with a text from RJ.

RJ: Get back here. Now.

Shit. I assume one of Tresscott's minions is at my door with a summons to his office, but then RJ throws a curveball.

RJ: Got a message from Gabe.

Holy shit. *Finally.*

For a second, I'm relieved. Until I realize RJ wouldn't send out the 911 if it was good news. I grab the phone and type.

Me: What's it say?
RJ: Just get back here.

I scrape back my chair and pick up my half-empty tray. There's no way I'm finishing this meal now. My appetite went from nonexistent to never-coming-back.

"Gotta go," I say. "I want to shower and change before I face the music. I assume I'll be summoned any minute now."

"I'll pray for you," Lawson drawls.

Silas doesn't even look up from his phone. Ride or die, this one.

A dozen disastrous scenarios scramble through my mind as I leave the dining hall. What if Gabe confessed? Or he's pointed the finger at someone else? RJ's message was worse than cryptic, and it puts crazy ideas in my head. Like, is there a world in which Gabe throws me under the bus for the whole thing? Or what if he introduces a new suspect to the mix? A fleeting image of Silas in that car next to Casey flickers in my mind, but I dismiss it quickly. Silas was with Amy all night, and there's just no way. I'm sure.

Lawson maybe? No, I remember Silas saying the two of them had been searching for Casey together. And nobody mentioned noticing that Lawson, or Silas for that matter, were wet. If one of them were driving the car, at least the bottom half of their bodies would have been wet from wading back to shore.

Unless they changed before joining the search?

The speculation gets my pulse doing double-time. I'm quickly running up on full-blown panic. Everything between Casey and me hangs on what Gabe has to say.

I book it back to the dorm, where RJ is at his desk when I barge in.

"You better not be fucking with me," I blurt out.

He spins around in his chair. "Why would I do that?"

Because lately it seems like everyone's getting their kicks at my expense.

"No reason. Forget it. Lucas coming too?" I ask, surprised Gabe's brother hadn't beat me here.

"I haven't told him." RJ's voice is wary, which gives me pause.

"Why not? What'd Gabe say?"

He twists his lips, suddenly reluctant after making me sprint back here to get the words out of his mouth.

"Come on," I growl. "You're killing me. What was it?"

"He said, and I quote, '*Tell Fenn I know the truth.*'"

The words don't make sense in my head. It's like I woke up speaking a different language after a severe brain trauma. I try turning them over, backward and forward, but I still can't make sense of Gabe's message.

I was hoping for a clue. A hint about what happened at prom and whether he was the one in the car with Casey. And if so, *why*.

Instead, I get this. He knows the truth? About what? Prom, I assume. But what truth does Gabe think he knows?

My brain hurts. "That's it?"

"Yup."

"What the hell does that even mean?" I'm flabbergasted as I sink onto the leather sofa. I continue to run the message through my head, hoping to spark some insight. A frown mars my lips. "Did Lucas's original message to Gabe say anything about me? Show me what it was."

RJ hesitates.

I glare at him. "Seriously?"

"Sorry, it's a habit. Only reason I do well in this business is because I value my clients' privacy. Information dealing is lucrative, but only when you know how to keep your mouth shut."

"You can take that lucrative nonsense and shove it up your ass. I'm your stepbrother. What did his message say?"

Looking unhappy, RJ unlocks his phone and scrolls for a moment. Then he reads out loud.

"'Hey. I know you're probably furious and I don't blame you. Dad's an asshole. I've been working on Mom trying to get her on our side, but so far no luck. Just know I'm doing everything I can on my end to get you out of that place. Also need you to know—whatever Dad told you, I wasn't the one who got you sent away.'" RJ lifts his head from the screen. "Then he says I hope you're well, talk soon, yada yada."

I narrow my eyes. "The 'I wasn't the one' part is kind of sus, no?"

"A little. But it's not like he said 'it wasn't me, it was Fenn!'"

"True."

"I need to ask you something." RJ's chair creaks when he leans back and crosses his arms.

His uneasy expression raises even more suspicions. I curse when it dawns on me where he's going with this. "Are you asking if I'm the one who ratted him out to their dad about selling drugs?"

"You're saying you didn't?" RJ asks with a little too much surprise.

"Obviously," I snap, more than a little offended. "Gabe's my best friend. And his dad's a dick. Why would I want to get him in trouble?"

"Maybe you were trying to protect him and thought this was the only way to get him to stop dealing."

"Yeah, all right. So now I'm a shitty friend for *not* turning him in?"

RJ's nonchalance in the face of my rapidly imploding world is starting to get on my nerves. To him, this is all gossip. Practically television. But this has been the single most important and disruptive part of my life for the better part of a year. And somehow it's managed to get a lot worse in the last few minutes.

"I'm not passing judgment either way—"

"You sure?" I say coldly.

He frowns. "I'm trying to get to the truth."

A sharp laugh bursts out of me. Everyone around here has been lying about one thing or another for so long, I'm not sure we'd know what the truth looks like anymore. No one at this school is innocent, least of all the people in this room.

"What was Gabe's response to Lucas?" I ask.

"Honestly, nothing too exciting. He says he feels like he's in prison. Talks about some fight he got into. Asks Lucas not to put himself in the warpath for Gabe, says it's not worth it for Lucas to take the brunt of their dad's wrath while Gabe's away. Then he assures him he's fine, it's only another six months until he's eighteen and he can get the hell out of there."

My heart aches hearing that. Thing about Gabe is, he's a stupidly good guy. Always looking out for his kid brother. The only reason he dealt drugs in the first place was because of his father, not due to some delinquency on Gabe's part. I mean, the guy isn't perfect, obviously. He likes to raise hell every now and then, just like the rest of us. But he's not a naturally born criminal or some shit.

Mr. Ciprian was always close-fisted with cash, the kind of man who wanted his sons to earn their own way in the world. Growing up, any time I went over to their place in Greenwich, I'd hear lectures about the value of hard work and how Mark Ciprian was never going to feed his kids with silver spoons. I always felt so bad for Gabe and Lucas. Sure, work ethic is admirable, but you can't send your sons to the poshest prep school in the country and only give them an allowance of a hundred bucks a month. They'd get crucified.

"Did you forward Gabe's message to Lucas yet?" I say pensively.

"No, I wanted to talk to you first." RJ tips his head. "You still think Lucas might have insinuated to Gabe that you were responsible for his exile?"

"I don't know. But this whole thing feels shady to me." I shrug. "Let's test him. Forward the message to him now. If he didn't say anything to his dad or Gabe, then he's more likely to pass along Gabe's 'tell Fenn' message. But if he *did* somehow make Gabe think I did him dirty, he probably wouldn't relay the message, right?"

"Stands to reason." RJ unlocks his phone again to send Gabe's reply to Lucas.

Then we wait.

"Does he have read receipts on?" I demand, losing patience after about three seconds.

"No." RJ checks the screen. "But he's typing…"

I go on alert, sitting up straighter on the couch. A moment later, Lucas's response pops up.

"'Thanks. I owe you big, man,'" RJ recites.

We both stare at my phone on the coffee table. It remains silent. We know Lucas is by his phone because he literally just used it to text. And if he's got his phone in his hand, there is absolutely no reason why he would see those words—*Tell Fenn I know the truth*—and *not* pass them along to me.

"Maybe he assumes I'll do it," RJ starts, just as my phone buzzes and we both jump.

I snatch it up, relaxing when I glimpse Lucas's name.

"It's him," I say, hastily swiping to open the notification.

Lucas: Hey, heard back from my brother. Basically he's doing okay in there. Got into a fight with some skinhead, but he can hold his own.

I relate the response to my stepbrother, adding, "No mention of Gabe's message to me…"

RJ sighs unhappily. "Fuck."

But the phone chimes again.

Lucas: Also, I have no idea what this means, but at the end of his message he says: tell Fenn I know the truth.

There's a pause. Then a follow-up.

Lucas: Mean anything to you?

I relax fully. "Okay," I say with a relieved breath. "Maybe things aren't as shady as I thought. I've been tainted by Silas, I guess. Seeing enemies everywhere."

RJ snickers. "Hey, I could always tell that Silas was a secret prick. The nice ones usually are."

I text Lucas to say I have no idea what it means, but that I'll think on it. He responds with a thumbs-up.

"What now?" RJ rocks back and forth in his chair, leg crossed over his knee.

I run a hand through my hair, suddenly remembering there's a way more critical matter to be discussing. "Now I wait for my impending execution."

"Shit, I forgot about that."

"Me too." I lie down, resting my head on the arm of the couch. "We had a good run, though, didn't we? Enough brother bonding to last a lifetime."

RJ snorts. "More than enough." But his humor doesn't last. "He won't actually expel you, right? It's not like he caught you balls-deep inside her."

"Honestly, I don't know whether I'm annoyed by his timing, or forever indebted to it." I give RJ a wry look. "I was seconds from telling Casey the truth before he barged into her room."

"The truth?" he echoes, then understands. "Ohhh. Okay. Are you still planning to?"

After a second of indecision, I find myself nodding. "I have to. Especially now. Maybe if Gabe's message had provided even a shred of clarity, I might have—" I stop abruptly, realizing what I've done.

RJ hisses out a breath. "Motherfucker."

Goddamn it.

"You were covering for Gabe?" Incredulity drips from his voice.

I rest a forearm over my eyes, shielding them from his view. Then I realize there's no backpedaling here. No hiding from it. So I drop my arm and sit up.

"I'm almost certain Gabe was driving the car the night of Casey's accident," I say flatly.

RJ stares at me in silence. Like his brain is buffering. Then, "Oh."

"Yeah."

"And you kept it a secret all this time?"

I don't miss the note of accusation. Disapproval, even.

"I owe him," I say simply.

"He's your best friend, I get it. But to cover up something *this* huge? Seriously? How much loyalty do you actually owe the guy?"

"A lot." I rub both temples as all the stupid mistakes I've made over the years buzz around in my head like a swarm of hornets. "He gave me a get-out-of-jail-free card a couple years ago. I returned the favor on prom night."

"You gonna elaborate on that?" RJ grumbles when I don't continue.

Fuck. He can't leave it at that, can he? Always so curious, my stepbrother.

"Summer before junior year, Gabe and I were in the Hamptons. We crashed with Lawson at first, until his psycho dad kicked us out because we were partying too hard. So we went to stay at this chick Molly's place and the party continued. Our last night there, we find out Molly lives next door to some star player for the New York Yankees, and she says the guy has this ridiculous watch closet—"

"The fuck's a watch closet?"

"Exactly what it sounds like. Dude was obsessed with expensive watches and had an entire closet full of them. All displayed on shelves in their little fancy boxes. I thought it was hilarious and, well, like I said, I was beyond wasted that entire summer."

"Christ. You broke into the Yankee player's house?"

"Oh yeah. Long story short, after everyone went to bed, I got it in my fool head that it would be fun to break in and steal one of his precious watches. And somehow, I fucking managed to do it. This dude's security was nonexistent. Only one camera. Didn't even set his alarm before he went out. He and his lingerie model girlfriend were at a club in town, and I literally waltzed upstairs to their bedroom and had my pick of the watch closet. I chose the coolest-looking one and booked it out of there."

"Gabe wasn't with you?"

"Christ, no. Gabe's not an idiot. He tried to talk me out of it, but I did it anyway. Left after he went to sleep. Next morning was a shitshow. The Yankee finds his watch missing and calls the cops. We saw them pull up next door, and I ran to the beach and chucked the watch into the ocean. They questioned the neighbors, including us. I asked Gabe to cover for me, and he did it, no hesitation. Said I was with him all night, that I'd passed out cold and he was taking care of me, making sure I didn't vomit in my sleep and die or something. Obviously they didn't believe us at first, but that's when Gabe's dad stepped in. Mr. Ciprian used to be the Attorney General of the state, so he still had a lot of clout there."

"Gabe lied to his dad too?"

"Yup. Swore on the Bible—and the Ciprians are, like, super Catholic, so trust me, that meant something to Mark Ciprian. Gabe had my back, and his dad believed Gabe's story." I shake my head. "The Yankee was out for blood. If Mr. Ciprian hadn't covered for me, thanks to Gabe, I would have seen time. No question about it." Now I hang my head, the shame once again rising in my throat. "I barely knew Casey on prom night, man. She was basically a stranger. My loyalties weren't with her back then. They were with my best friend, who I owed big-time."

"But she's not a stranger anymore," RJ quietly reminds me.

"Well aware of that."

RJ has no idea how much it's hurt carrying this around. Thinking the worst of my best friend. Imagining him as the type of person who'd leave a girl for dead. He has no idea what it does to your own understanding of people, of yourself. I chose to protect Gabe over Casey, then tried to atone for it by protecting her after the fact. But it's not enough.

She deserves nothing less than the truth.

During our entire friendship, I've constantly been one careless syllable away from spilling my heart out. But then I would think about Gabe. He's my best friend and I'm half in love with her, but right now I've got neither and she's slipping further away. Every day Casey doesn't get answers from me, it's breaking her down a little more. Soon, she'll be in so many pieces, she might not find her way back together. Back to me.

Last night, she said she *wanted* to forgive me.

I just need to give her a reason.

The conversation is cut short by a knock on the door, bringing stricken expressions to both our faces.

RJ gets up to answer it, a second later glancing over his shoulder in relief. Not my execution orders, then. Tresscott is taking his sweet-ass time with this, intentionally prolonging my torture.

"Yo," someone says, and a pair of seniors trudge into our room.

The taller one, Xavier, nods hello at me before addressing my stepbrother. "Hey, so my two cousins are visiting from Manhattan this weekend. Was hoping to bring them to the fights tonight."

RJ stares at him. "So?"

"So, ah…"Xavier shifts his feet, shoving his hands in his pockets. "Can they come?"

"What the fuck do I care?"

From my perch on the sofa, I snicker under my breath. Poor Remington refuses to accept reality.

"They go to St. Michael's on the Upper West Side." Xavier continues as if RJ hadn't spoken. "You can vet them tonight if you want. Meet them before we go in."

"I don't want, and I won't be going."

Xavier's buddy, Tripp, looks confused. "You won't be going?"

"No. I'm busy."

I swallow another laugh. RJ's been making his obligatory weekly appearances at the fights since he took over leadership from Duke, but I guess he's done playing by the rules. I'm surprised it took him this long.

"So there's no fights?" Xavier presses. "But it's Saturday."

"You can fight. Or not. I don't care. How is this so hard to understand?"

The pair glance over at me for assistance. I respond with an amused shrug.

"I am busy tonight," RJ says slowly, overpronouncing each word as if speaking to a small child. "If they were being held tomorrow night, great. If they'd been held yesterday, great. But they are tonight, and I am busy."

"So we're doing them tomorrow night?" Xavier asks.

"Do them whenever you want!" he shouts before turning to implore me with his eyes. "Dude. Help."

I'm too busy laughing.

"This isn't some kind of test," he assures the guys. "I'm not interested in running shit. Tell your friends."

"So…tomorrow night?" Tripp asks.

"Get the fuck out," RJ pleads in frustration, physically shoving them out the door. He slams it shut and leans against it as if he's afraid they'll try to kick it open like the barbarians at the gate. "Why is this happening to me?"

I wipe away tears of laughter. "Did it to yourself, man."

A sharp knock rattles the door.

RJ's face goes red with frustration. "For fuck's sake! Go away!"

"Bishop," a different voice calls out.

Just like that, all humor fades.

This time, I'm the one to answer the door. I find myself staring at the smug smile of Asa, the headmaster's messenger boy.

I stifle a groan. "Let me guess. I've been summoned."

Asa ignores my sarcasm. "Headmaster Tresscott wants to see you in his office. Better hurry."

CHAPTER 35
FENN

IT'S QUIETER THAN A CHURCH IN HERE. I DON'T PASS A SINGLE person or hear a single voice on my way to Tresscott's office. The sound of my shoes squeaking against the polished floor of the wide corridor makes me wince. It's embarrassingly loud. Then my phone dings and it's even louder, like an explosion amidst the stillness.

I put it on silent, then check the message.

Casey: Meet me at our spot tonight? We have lots to talk about.

She's right. We do.

Me: Yeah, sounds good. And yes, we do.
Me: My phone's on silent now. I'm about to talk to your dad.

The desk in the reception area is empty. I walk past it toward the commanding mahogany door and give a quick rap.

"Come in," is the muffled reply.

I turn the knob and push the door open. Take one step onto the thick burgundy carpet before stopping in my tracks.

"Oh, fuck no," I mutter when my gaze connects with my father, who's sitting at Tresscott's desk. "No way. I'm not doing this."

I spin on my heel, prompting David to jump out of his chair. "Fennelly," he snaps. "Stop."

I don't want to stop. I want to sprint out of this building, steal someone's ride, and drive to another goddamn country. Canada. No, Mexico. Better weather.

Yet I also know running is pointless, so I resist the instinct and walk back into the office. I shut the door behind me and cross my arms tight to my chest.

Dad drags a hand through his blond hair. It's streaked with silver these days. I'm surprised his new wife hasn't coaxed him into coloring it. Or maybe Michelle thinks it's distinguished.

"Why are you here?" I ask when he doesn't speak.

That brings a spark of irritation to his eyes. "Edward Tresscott called me early this morning and told me he plans to suspend you."

My breath catches. A suspension? That's it?

I exhale in relief, wondering how on earth Casey managed to talk him out of expulsion.

"You look relieved," Dad says coolly.

I shrug. "I am. Figured it would be much worse. How long's the suspension?"

"Three days. You'll report here to Tresscott every morning and do your coursework in a neighboring office. He'll be keeping an eye on you throughout the day and checking your work after the last bell."

"Fine." I flick up an eyebrow. "May I go now?"

"No, you may not." He's visibly clenching his teeth. "Take a fucking seat, Fenn."

A laugh slides out. "Busting out the expletives, huh, Dad? Someone's having a temper tantrum."

"Sit down," he snaps.

I humor him, dropping my ass in one of the plush visitors' chairs.

Dad remains standing, his expression conveying a cloud of unhappiness. With a dash of disappointment thrown in there.

"Well? Let's hear it. The lecture." I lean back in the chair, unfazed. "It's always fun to listen to you pretend to give a shit. You've been doing it a lot lately, you realize that? I get it. Trying to impress Stepmommy. But you're wasting your breath."

He curses again, uncharacteristically pissed. It's jarring, considering his emotions have been in hibernation for so long. Maybe that's why I keep poking the bear. I'm tired of sleepy and disinterested. I'm itching for a fight.

And Dad doesn't disappoint.

"I've had enough of this," he spits out. "Enough of *you*."

"What else is new?"

"Stop. Just stop with this insolent, juvenile nonsense. You're eighteen years old." His face gets redder as he begins to pace, stopping every few seconds to level me with furious glares. "You're a goddamn adult, and you're climbing into girls' windows at four in the morning like some horny punk! And not just any girl! Edward Tresscott's youngest daughter! Have you lost your mind?"

I try to respond, but he cuts me off by slicing his hand through the air.

"I've put up with a lot of bullshit from you over the years. I've tolerated your smart mouth, turned a blind eye to the company you keep—"

"The company I keep?" I interrupt. "What's that supposed to mean?"

"Gabe Ciprian's a drug dealer! That Lawson boy's been in and out of rehab since he was thirteen!" Dad advances on me, scowling deeply. "And don't get me started on all the girls. All the parties. The condom wrappers strewn all over the fucking house. The booze. The fact that you've been expelled from every school you've attended, until I finally had to buy your way into this one. The one prep school nobody gets expelled from—and you nearly get kicked out of here too!"

He finishes with an angry huff, scrubbing a hand through his hair again.

"Am I allowed to respond now or are you still yelling?" I ask politely.

"I would love an explanation," Dad retorts. "*Love* one. Because I can't even imagine what you were thinking messing around with your headmaster's daughter."

"Casey's my friend." I shrug again. "She had a nightmare, and she called me because she was upset and needed to talk."

"And you couldn't talk to her over the phone?" He sounds frazzled. "You had to break into her house?"

"I didn't break in. She let me in."

"You were there at four in the morning, without her father's permission. She's seventeen years old."

"She's my friend," I repeat.

"Are you saying there is absolutely nothing physical going on between the two of you?"

I'm usually a pretty good liar—liar of omission, anyway—but I'm off my game this morning. And my split second of hesitation costs me.

"Goddamn it, Fenn! What the hell is wrong with you!" Dad shakes his head in reproach, practically oozing contempt. "Is this really who you want to be? An underachieving fuckup who drinks like a fish and thinks with his cock?"

"Sounds fun, actually."

He barks out an incredulous laugh. "You're not even taking this seriously, are you? I flew out here on an hour's notice to talk some sense into you—"

"I didn't ask you to come," I interject, my voice cold. "That's on you."

Dad stares at me for a moment. Then he sinks into the adjacent chair, burying his face in his hands. He sits there, in that oddly defeated position, for what feels like a full minute. I even consider sneaking out while he's not looking.

But then he lifts his head. "I'm ashamed of you."

Up until now, his criticism bounced off me like I was wearing a bulletproof vest.

This time, he does some damage. Direct hit. My chest clenches.

"I've given you leeway, Fenn. Tried to be patient. Understanding. Because I know how much you miss your mom."

I set my jaw.

"But you've gone too far—"

"Because I snuck into a friend's bedroom?" I demand in disbelief.

"Because you show no remorse for any goddamn thing you do, or any goddamn thing you say. You do whatever you want, whenever you want." He stands up, shoulders drooping. "I'm ashamed of you," he repeats.

"I don't care." I stand too, done with this entire bullshit conversation.

"You should care. Because I'm your father, and I'm the only family you have in this world, Fennelly."

Our gazes slowly connect again, and I flinch at what I see in his eyes. Condemnation. Disgust.

"Your mother would be ashamed of you."

My arm snaps out before I can stop it. It's a knee-jerk response, the instinct to defend myself from the wave of pain his words trigger.

There's a cracking sound as my fist connects with my father's jaw.

He rears back in shock. We're both shocked. My knuckles are tingling, and I stare down at my hand, blinking, confused. It's like that hand doesn't even belong to me.

I've never hit him before. He's never hit me. Hitting was never a part of our relationship.

Dad's chest heaves as he draws several deep breaths. He drags the side of his thumb over the spot where I'd struck him, then rotates his jaw.

"Dad. I'm…" *Sorry.* I want to tell him I'm sorry.

But he's already stalking past me. "Get your goddamn shit together," he says without turning around.

"Where are you going?" I call after him.

"Home." He still doesn't turn. I have to dart toward the doorway to be able to hear him. "I'm going home to my wife. And you will serve your suspension without complaint. I'll see you at Thanksgiving."

Then he's gone, and I almost keel over, my legs suddenly too flimsy to support my weight. I stumble over to a chair and collapse into it, mimicking Dad's defeated pose with my face buried in my hands, one of which still aches.

I punched my father in the jaw.

Christ.

Your mother would be ashamed of you.

As I sit there, hunched over, pulse weak, I can't stop from ruminating over everything he'd said. His words run on a loop until I'm unable to fight the conclusion that takes root in my mind.

He's right.

I *am* a fuckup.

Mom *would* be ashamed of me.

And I have no business letting a girl like Casey love me.

I groan into my palms. Goddamn it. What am I doing with this girl? I've known since the first time I had a real conversation with her that she's too good for me. She's the girl who rescues injured animals and keeps them in shoeboxes by her bed. She's the girl who forgives when she shouldn't and forgets when she ought to remember.

I should have just let it end. It was *over*, damn it. She dumped me. Rightfully so. But instead of letting it be, I pushed and poked and fought to get her back, and for what? So she can be with a fucked-up asshole who drinks too much and is best friends with a drug dealer who might have almost killed her?

She deserves better than that.

So much better.

CHAPTER 36
CASEY

"Thank you," I say from the doorway.

My father observes me over the rim of his teacup. He's in his study, drinking tea, an open book in front of him. It's the one I got him last Christmas, a historical account of the Hundred Years' War. He's been holed up in here all day reading.

"I know you wanted to expel him," I continue when Dad doesn't speak. "But I promise you, he didn't do anything wrong. Fenn's only sin was rushing over here when I needed him."

A muscle ticks in his jaw.

"Are you going to say anything?"

Dad sets his cup down. "What would you like me to say?"

"I don't know." I fidget with my sleeve. "Just something."

"All right. Here's something—if I ever find a boy in your room again in the middle of the night, he will be expelled if I have the power to expel him, and you will be homeschooled for your senior year. Understood?"

"Yes," I say tightly.

"And I expect you to keep the promise you made earlier," he adds, his eyes stern.

"I will."

During our hourlong talk this morning, in which I laid out my case for why Fenn shouldn't be punished too harshly for last night, one of my father's conditions was that I return to therapy. Weekly. I wasn't thrilled to agree, but I don't mind Dr. Anthony that much, and it seemed like a fair exchange to keep Fenn at Sandover.

He owes me, though. And I plan on settling that debt tonight—I won't accept anything less than the truth about prom.

"Sloane just put a lasagna in the oven," I tell him. "She said it'll be ready by seven."

Dad nods and reaches for his book. "I'll see you at dinner, then." Dismissed.

I wait until I've closed the door to roll my eyes. I get it. He's pissed that he caught Fenn in my bedroom. But come on, it wasn't *that* big a deal.

In the hall, I fish my phone out of the pocket of my zip-up sweatshirt.

Me: Hey, we still on for later? Dinner's at 7, so I'll be free around 9. Meet on the lake path?

Fenn is typing, but the dots keep appearing and disappearing for what seems like an eternity. I get bored of waiting and head upstairs. I want to shower and change before dinner.

My phone buzzes as I'm striding into my room.

Fenn: It kills me to say this, but you were right. It needs to be over. I'm not the guy for you, Casey. I'm sorry.

I stare at the message.

A second ticks by. Two. Three. Ten.

Still I keep staring. In the hopes that it will make sense soon. I even double-check it's actually written in English because my brain won't compute. My eyes see words like "over" and "sorry" but obviously my eyes are stupid and wrong. There's no way he's ending things with me.

Over text.

That's preposterous.

My pulse gets weaker, slowing to a crawl as I send back three words.

Me: Are you serious?

This time he answers straightaway.

Fenn: I am. I'm so sorry. You need to forget about me.

I exhale in slow, measured breaths. My pulse accelerates now. Faster and faster, until it's thundering angrily between my ears.

I cannot fucking believe this. This guy spent a month trying to bulldoze his way back into my life, begging my forgiveness on a daily basis. And until last night, I was standing my ground, maintaining my boundaries. But he steamrolled past those too. Last night when he held me in his arms, I was ready to forgive him, even without knowing the whole truth about prom. I'd reminded myself Fenn had saved my life, that I was alive because of him, and wasn't that the most important thing?

God. There must be something wrong with me. An inherent flaw in my programming that compels me to commit the same mistakes and be constantly amazed to find myself alone.

Or maybe's it's just Fenn.

Hiding in plain sight like a colorless, odorless poison.

Microdosing himself into my veins until my heart stops beating.

I can't believe I ever let him convince me he was my friend. I was so close to forgiving him, against my better judgment and every warning bell blaring in my head. But Fenn Bishop is impervious to all my natural defenses, slithering inside my brain to whisper just the right lies and empty promises.

I sink onto the edge of my bed, blinking rapidly to keep the tears at bay. Funny thing is, I thought this time he was ready to tell the truth, that after weeks of begging for the chance to come clean, he wouldn't screw it up this time. Only here I am again, the fool. Flat on my face.

The tears dry up as the pain surrounding my heart hardens into something darker, more hostile. Anger flares inside my skull, a deafening, howling storm of rage and resentment that intensifies each time I reread Fenn's messages.

I can't fucking stand it any longer.

Dropping my phone on the bed, I force myself to go take a shower. I crank the temperature to scalding and then stand under the spray, breathing in clouds of steam before tipping my face upward. I let the hot water soak me. Soothe me. Somehow, it works. I close my eyes, and the first peaceful thought I've had all day drifts in among the clutter.

The memory of speeding through the mountains with the windows down.

Eating ice cream in a random town.

Getting lost and forgetting who I am.

As the heat and steam loosen my tense muscles, I remember the last time I was happy. Not drunk-happy or revenge-happy or orgasm-happy. Just…happy.

After the shower, I throw on a pair of yoga pants, a striped sweater, and warm wool socks. I need to feed Silver before I'm called down for dinner, so I reach into my top desk drawer for the Ziploc bag of food I stashed there. Today we've officially graduated to alfalfa hay and plain pellets that are supposedly high in fiber. Silver still seems weak, though. I really wish she would move around more.

When I lift the lid of her shoebox and peek in, she's once again still.

"Wake up, kiddo," I say softly. "Alfalfa time."

I've been leaving her food in the corner of the box next to a shallow water dish. Usually when I prep her food, her eyes pop open and she makes the cutest squeaking noises. This evening, she remains silent.

"What's wrong?" I coo. "Come on, cutie pie, let's have some dinner."

Silver doesn't react. Ears don't even twitch.

It takes a little while longer before I realize what's wrong.

What's wrong is that Silver is dead.

I feel it happening almost in slow motion—I feel myself going numb. Shutting down. Just like Silver hadn't reacted to the sound of my voice, I don't react to the fact that she's gone. I stare at her motionless body. Then I replace the lid of the shoebox.

"Case! Dinner!"

At Sloane's shout, I exit my bedroom on autopilot, the box tucked under my arm. I go downstairs and enter the kitchen without a word, finding my sister in the process of removing her oven mitts. Steam rises from the lasagna pan cooling on the stove.

"Set the table?" Sloane says over her shoulder.

"Sure."

She turns, laughing when she spots the shoebox. "Silver's joining us for dinner?"

"She's dead," I answer.

"Oh shit."

"Oh, sweetheart." Dad's voice sounds from the doorway. He'd walked in just in time to overhear us. "I'm so sorry."

I shrug.

With a sigh, he walks over and gives my shoulder a reassuring squeeze. "I'll get the shovel."

"Don't bother." I ease out of his grasp and walk to the counter, opening the tall drawer that houses our trash can.

"Case?" he says uneasily.

"We always knew she was going to die. There's no point in a burial. Seems like a lot of effort for no reason."

There's silence in my wake as I drop the box in the garbage. I shut the drawer and turn around to find two confused faces.

"What?" I mutter.

"You always bury your strays." The groove in Sloane's forehead gets deeper. "You've been holding animal funerals since you were six years old."

"Yeah, well, I'm not six anymore. People grow up." I shrug again. "And things die."

Everything fucking dies.

CHAPTER 37
SLOANE

AT THE SEMIREGULAR MEETING OF THE TRESSCOTT & SHAW Detective Agency, these two intrepid sleuths have hit another dead end. As we sit on my back porch, RJ scratches the stubble dotting his chin and stares at the surface of the patio table like he's trying to decipher messages in the grain. The dogs run around like maniacs, chasing insects and the occasional squirrel darting across the yard.

"Can we send another message to Gabe?" I suggest. "Get his version of events from that night?"

"Even if Fenn was willing to put up another five grand, my contact's gone dark. Said it was too risky and he won't chance it again. So, short of sending a carrier pigeon or hiring an actress to pose as Gabe's mother..."

"So within the realm of realistic options...?"

"We've got nothing."

Awesome. Just great. For the first time in months, we have an actual lead. Fenn's confession that he was covering for Gabe. And yet we're still spinning our wheels.

I thought getting Fenn to admit what he knew would be the key that unlocked what happened at prom. But surprise! More questions. Like how Gabe Ciprian, of all people, would leave Casey trapped and stranded.

"What about the drugs?" RJ asks. "Gabe was definitely dealing?"

Bo charges up to him and drops a slobbery stick in his lap. Nudges him insistently with a slight growl until RJ chucks the stick back across the yard.

"Worst-kept secret at Sandover," I confirm. "Everyone knew where to go for their poison."

"I guess that tracks. No one ends up here by accident. Did Gabe ever go to Ballard?"

"Freshman year," I confirm. "But then he and Fenn got expelled for stealing booze from their housefather's liquor cabinet. After that, Gabe was sent to Sandover, and Fenn got shipped off to—fuck, what was it called? Some Swiss boarding school."

"Wait, really? I thought Fenn came here sophomore year."

"Yeah, like a month into the semester. He only lasted a few weeks in the Alps before they kicked him out. Honestly, I think he did it on purpose so he'd wind up here. He and Gabe were inseparable."

Bo returns with his stick and now Penny eagerly shoves her way up to RJ to encourage him to toss it.

"Where's Casey?" RJ grumbles. "Can't she distract these little dudes so they leave me alone?" Yet despite his complaining, he continues to throw the stick.

"She's in her room. Her rabbit died."

"Shit. That sucks."

I look over, troubled. "She didn't even bat an eyelash. Claimed she was prepared for it to die the moment she rescued it. But it was unnerving. Casey's not usually so stoic."

"Did she and Fenn get in another fight? Because he was looking pretty wrecked today too. Considering he avoided expulsion, he should've been riding high, but he spent the whole day sleeping." RJ looks as disturbed as I feel.

"Okay, that's weird. She didn't say anything about a fight, though."

Not that she would. These days Casey treats me like I'm the enemy. Meanwhile, I'm spending my Saturday night trying to *help* her, that ungrateful brat. I could be screwing my boyfriend right now, and instead, he and I are out here trying to piece together what happened the night Casey almost died.

"Has Lucas texted you back?" I ask.

Lucas is the closest connection we have to Gabe, since Fenn insists he never actually saw Gabe and Casey together at the prom.

"No, not yet."

I swallow my frustration. What I wouldn't give to assemble everyone in a room, Agatha Christie-style, and recite the evening step-by-step until the culprit is inevitably deduced. Agatha always made it look so easy.

"We don't have an alibi for Gabe while Casey was missing," I muse aloud. "He had access to drugs. And he had the opportunity to slip them to her."

"So, what's his motive? Why drug your sister and drive her out to the boathouse?"

"I mean, there's the obvious answer."

"You mean the nefarious sexual one."

"Yeah."

In the days that followed the accident, I was suspicious of everyone. Especially once it was confirmed Casey had been drugged. Knowing that fact, how could there *possibly* be an innocent motive for what happened that night? Someone we knew and trusted had tried to hurt her, and nearly succeeded in killing her.

Naturally, my fears turned toward the guys, but there wasn't one particular guy who stood out as a suspect. Until now.

"The tox report the hospital gave to the police had a bunch of stuff in it," RJ says. "From what I could find online, it's a cocktail similar to a roofie. A nice downer in the right doses. A mind-eraser if you want it to be."

A twinge of anger pulls at my insides. I remember how Casey was in tears at the hospital when the doctor told her they'd found drugs in her system. She got even more hysterical after he said they needed to do a rape kit since she couldn't remember what happened. They didn't find anything, though. No signs of sexual assault, or sexual activity of any kind, in fact. But that doesn't mean something didn't happen.

"Tons of people at prom were on something," I tell RJ. "I'm not sure what exactly, but whatever they took was the happy, touchy-feely sort of shit. Everyone dancing, smiling profusely. It was funny at first, then got annoying. But nobody else passed out or woke up in a lake. We don't know if it even came from the same stash."

"So Gabe can't tell us what he had, and Casey doesn't remember where she got it." He sighs, again at the mercy of the dogs to launch the stick for them. "And Fenn's clammed up again."

"Now you're starting to understand my life for the last six months. Dead-end central."

The vicious cycle of hope and despair. Chasing down clues with no conclusions. Doors slammed in my face.

"There is another suspect who fits the criteria," RJ suggests, his voice grim.

"Who?" I demand.

"Lawson. From everything I've gathered, no one can come up with his whereabouts for most of the dance. Couple that with his amateur pharmacist hobby, sexual adventures, and questionable morality…"

I bite my lip. "I can't argue any of that. But I also can't envision Lawson putting so much effort into getting laid. All he has to do is snap his fingers."

"Valid point." RJ's phone buzzes on the table. "Lucas," he says. "Let me see."

Lucas: Hey, sorry, I just saw this. I didn't stick around long that night. I didn't know anyone there.
Lucas: Think I saw Casey dancing with Mila and some guys at one point. Don't remember who.

Lucas: Can't remember seeing Gabe and Casey together at all. But yeah, Gabe was selling. That's his deal. I don't mess with it.

"Mila," RJ announces. "That's a lead."

Of course. Because somehow this had to become more complicated.

"About as useful as asking Gabe," I say flatly.

"Why?" He's almost offended at my lack of enthusiasm. "This has got to be more important than your feud, no?"

"This is the whole reason for the feud," I remind him. "If she were interested in being helpful, she wouldn't have been such a bitch after the accident."

"All right, fair. But some time's passed. Maybe she'll be more reasonable now."

It's cute he thinks that. Sweet, naive boy.

"You don't understand girl politics, babe. I can't ask her for a favor. It shows weakness. She would absolutely love having something I wanted and telling me to fuck off."

"This is stupid," he says. "You know that, right?"

That may be, but I didn't make the rules. These are ancient traditions forged from the earliest days of womankind.

"I'm telling you, Mila would rather shave her head than lift a finger to help me."

"Well, right now she's the only lead we have. Which means someone's got to ask her."

A tiny smile tugs on my lips. "There is *one* person she might find persuasive."

"That look makes me nervous," he accuses, leaning away. "I don't like that look, cupcake."

"How hard could it be? Spin a little game. Toss a little charm her way…"

"Flirt with her, you mean."

"Anything for the cause, right?"

RJ slouches in his seat, already dreading this plan. "You want to set a honey pot."

"You make such good honey," I answer with a sweet smile, batting my eyelashes.

"Don't do that." He winces. "It's creepy."

"Be a good sport, baby. Take one for the team."

"Jesus. All right." He groans. "If you'll lay off the sports metaphors." He stares at me, pondering the strategy. "Why do I feel like I'm the one who's walking into a trap?"

I push my chair closer to his and lift my legs onto his lap. RJ wastes no time planting a hand on my ankle, stroking it over my yoga pants.

"There will have to be some ground rules, of course."

He eyes me skeptically. "If I come right out and ask, she's gonna know something's up. She won't talk to me."

"Crash course in female psychology: We already know Mila has a little crush on you." I cock my head. "But what *really* excites her is the idea of taking something that belongs to me."

"So, if I have to be a little more convincing…" he says, like he's bracing to get kicked in the nuts. "What, like no hands? No below the neck?"

It makes me physically ill to entertain this idea, but what choice do we have? I remind myself there isn't anything I won't do for my baby sister. Especially when she's in the midst of a full-blown identity spiral.

"Just don't fuck her, okay?" I give him a light kick in the side, a silent reminder that I know these woods and every manner possible to hide a body on short notice. "I don't think I could control my gag reflex after that."

"Got it." He smiles impishly. "Don't do anything that would render me unfuckable in your eyes."

"See?" I move from my chair into his lap, looping my hands

around his neck. For being cooperative, he gets a kiss. "We're totally on the same page."

"You're adorable when you're jealous."

I don't deny it because I can already feel the jealousy creeping into me. I never thought I'd be concocting a scheme to dangle my boyfriend as bait for my mortal enemy. A few months ago I would've balked at the idea that I could trust anyone enough to set them loose on such a mission. And yet sitting here, I'm not sure there's anyone I trust more.

RJ made some mistakes in the beginning. I made a few of my own. But we got through it. Since then, he's devoted himself to the cause of finding out who hurt my sister, risking a lot to get us this far and doing all of it without complaint. There aren't many guys who would endure this journey. Especially for someone he barely knew when it all started.

Even if Mila is another dead end, I'll still be grateful he got us this far.

"So, when do we execute this honey trap?" he asks.

The dogs amble over and sprawl on the ground, now worn out and panting at his feet. I lean over to snatch my phone off the table, then take a moment to scroll through social media. As luck would have it, a solution quickly presents itself.

"There's a party at Ballard tonight." I grin at him. "No time like the present, right?"

CHAPTER 38
LAWSON

It's nine o'clock, and I'm comfortably cocooned in a swaddle of atmospheric soundscapes when Silas yanks one of my earbuds out. I open my eyes to find him looming over my bed.

"Let's go out," he tells me.

The meditative music becomes harsh and disorienting with only one half of the binaural arrangement in my left ear.

"Bro, pass. I'm still recovering from last night. Attempting to find peace and inner balance." I grab my earbud back from his rude fingers. "You're ruining my mindfulness."

"Whatever. It's Saturday night. I need a drink."

"You can drink here," I remind him. "I'll spare you a Xany if it'll get me out of any upright activities this evening."

I replace the earbud, but now Silas is banging around in his closet and stomping across our creaky wooden floors, disrupting my return to tranquility. What a waste of a Valium.

"Don't be a dick," he says.

I grin. "Well, that's uncalled for. I'm just minding my business over here."

He tosses me an impatient look over his shoulder. "I can't sit around this place another night trapped in this room or dodging glares from Fenn and RJ."

In his defense, Silas has endured an especially rough couple of weeks. He's managed to lose his girlfriend and make an enemy of almost everyone we know. I imagine he's feeling a tad sensitive.

"Pop some uppers and get dressed," he says. "It's the least you can do."

"Fine. But only because Scott is working tonight, and he's the one bartender in this hick town who makes a decent espresso."

"You're planning to drink espresso at the *bar*?"

"I told you, I'm in recovery mode. Can't remember the last time I got so trashed."

I drag myself out of bed and push hair out of my face. Fuckin' Silas. I just got out of the shower and put on my lazing clothes, and now he's making me work.

He watches as I ditch my sweatpants and trade them for a pair of faded jeans. "Who were you chilling with last night, anyway? You totally disappeared on me."

"Yeah, sorry. Didn't mean to ditch you."

Silas and I showed up at the party together yesterday, but he's not big on coke, so I went somewhere private to do my bump and wound up partying with a few guys from the Ballard swim team. Former teammates of Silas, in fact. But I keep that to myself. I know it's still a sensitive topic for the guy.

"You ready?" he says after I throw on a hoodie.

"Sure. Whatever. Take me to the espresso maker."

Except when we sidle up to the bar a short while later, I find out Scott apparently has strep throat. Jared is slinging drinks instead. The surly community college dropout always reeks of pickles and fresh animal carcasses, and he refuses to expand the scope of his beverage knowledge beyond the labels on the beer taps.

"If I gave you a hundred-dollar bill, do you think you could google 'espresso'?" I suggest to his vacant townie stare.

"He'll have a Johnnie Walker, straight up," Silas interjects with an accompanying elbow in my ribs. "I'll do a Guinness."

Jared shuffles off to do the bare minimum required of his chosen vocation.

"Could you try not to be a pain in the ass all night?" Silas grouses.

"Hey, I was peacefully minding my own business and not even remotely upsetting the townsfolk when I was so rudely kidnapped from my room."

"Since when are you such a homebody?"

Silas puts his back to the bar when his Guinness arrives, sipping it as he surveys the rather packed house. There's a twinkle of ill-intent in his searching gaze that, coupled with his god-awful choice of beer, already has me wary of the night's trajectory.

"Come on. Let's be social."

He nods toward a couple of girls sitting alone at a high top. They're new to these parts, judging by their startled rabbit expressions and nearly untouched glasses of rosé. They look a bit older too. College freshman, maybe.

"Yeah… I'm gonna sit this one out." I plant myself on a stool and cradle my drink. "The second Valium is kicking in, and I intend to become utterly useless in conversation any minute now."

"Fine," he grumbles in frustration.

Oh, the terrible betrayal.

Silas saunters over to the girls and is quickly invited to sit with them. Spending the last three years in a relationship means he hasn't had many opportunities to brush up on his game, but those All-American Boy good looks are all he needs.

Neither of the college girls are drop-dead gorgeous, though. They're cute, but average. There are far hotter chicks in this bar tonight, so I'm puzzled by his immediate interest until I spot a familiar face. Amy sits only a couple of tables away with some of her cheerleader friends, facing Silas and his new gal pals.

Interesting.

I'm not sure if he was intentionally trying to make her jealous, or just didn't want to look like a dateless loser, but either way, it's obvious he's aware of her presence. Those hazel eyes flick in Amy's direction, and I see the moment she notices Silas. Her freckled cheeks redden before she turns away, saying something to her friends.

I don't mind Amy. Never did, despite what Silas thinks. Sure, I taunted him about how vanilla his girlfriend was, but that's because, well, she's vanilla. What's wrong with stating the obvious? But I do like her. She's funny. Hates my guts, though, and I don't really blame her. I can be an asshole.

Tonight, I feel compelled to intervene. As I get up from my stool, I slug back the rest of my drink then mosey my way toward Silas and his new friends. I throw an arm over his shoulder and offer the girls a polite nod.

"Ladies, if you don't mind, I need to steal him back."

"Nah. Take a seat," Silas says, shrugging off my arm. "We're not leaving."

Well. I tried. But I'm trapped by his stubbornness and have no other choice but to join them.

"This is Zoey," he says, gesturing to the one on his right. Blonde. Pretty in a holiday family portrait sort of way, the one where they're all in the yard bursting out of a pile of leaves in matching outfits.

"I'm Kathryn, but you can call me Kat," the other says. This one has long, dark hair. Dark eyes. Face is a six but her body's edging on a nine, and I know exactly where this is headed.

"This is Lawson," Silas answers for me. "Forgive him, he was kicked in the head by a horse as a child."

We don't get through more than a few minutes of painful small talk before Silas finishes his beer and goes in for the kill.

"Kat, can I borrow you for a minute?"

Dude's got balls, I'll give him that. I glance over my shoulder to see Amy watching as Silas and Kat get up and wander toward the dart boards. A moment later, they slip away down the hall toward the restrooms. I'm about to look away when Amy notices me. Her light brown eyes darken to molten chocolate, narrowing at me as her mouth twists in an angry scowl.

Still hates my guts, apparently.

Zoey snorts. "Sort of obvious about it, huh?"

I turn back. "What's that?"

"Those two," she clarifies. "Not subtle."

"I'm sort of surprised at him, if I'm being honest."

Silas isn't the type to get a sneaky BJ in the ladies' room of a bar. Not under normal circumstances, anyway.

"Yeah, Kat came out tonight saying she wanted to be more adventurous. I didn't think it would work so well so fast."

"Crazy kids, huh?"

Zoey flashes an awkward smile. "Actually, I'm kind of glad you came over. It was going to be embarrassing sitting here by myself all night. I was third-wheeling it hard."

"Not all night," I assure her.

"Huh?"

"Three minutes. Tops."

She smothers a laugh by sipping her wine. "Oh. Right."

Even accounting for the ill-effects of Guinness dick, they aren't gone long. What's transpired is obvious enough on their faces, though, when Silas and Kathryn reemerge from the restrooms. Which wouldn't be a capital offense if only Silas could get his rocks off without making it everyone else's problem. Before they return to our table, he decides he must parade Kat past Amy's group.

"But I'd never done impromptu before," Zoey exclaims with a laugh, still unaware I haven't been following her tale about her recent debate club excursion to Oxford. "Lindsey is heaving up her breakfast in the airport restroom, while our coach is frantically trying to rescue her notes from the luggage before it spends the next eleven hours in the cargo hold all the way to London."

Silas inexplicably stops to engage Amy in a brief conversation I can only imagine is designed to inflict as much pain and humiliation as possible. Making Kat an unwitting accomplice. It lasts only a few seconds, but the moment Silas and Kat return to our table, Amy quickly abandons hers and walks out the front door. Immediately followed by her friends.

"That was shitty of you," I inform Silas as he sits down.

He lifts a brow. "What?"

"Amy didn't deserve that."

Kat nervously glances between us. "I don't understand what's happening."

"Don't let a guy pick you up in a bar," I tell her as I push back from the table. "We're all bastards."

Then I grab Silas and haul him up with me. He forgets sometimes I've got a couple of inches on him and a fair bit of muscle, so his protestations don't give me much pause as I drag him out of the bar and onto the sidewalk.

"What the fuck, Lawson?" He tugs his arm free of my hand and gives me a shove.

"What the fuck?" I echo. "Bro. It's one thing if you want to be an asshole to your friends. Bringing some poor girl into your twisted games is crossing the line."

"You're talking about Amy?" He lets out a sarcastic laugh. "That's incredible. The guy who's never had a single monogamous relationship is giving me a lecture on post-breakup etiquette."

"It's not just Amy. Your whole vibe is off. Something's up with you lately."

Incredulous, he scoffs at me. "You're one to talk."

"Under ordinary circumstances I might give you that, but I'm not the one who's managed to alienate every friend he's got in a matter of weeks."

"Seriously, Lawson? Look at yourself. You're a nihilistic, alcoholic drug addict who entertains himself by creating chaos and destruction everywhere he goes. You blew up a marriage because you were *bored*." He laughs again, cold and humorless. "So I had myself a rebound fuck in the bathroom. Big fucking deal. You're basically a professional screwup and you have no right to judge me."

"Listen, you're clearly in existential pain right now, so I'm going to overlook a few hurtful words in favor of the bigger picture. I'm trying to be your friend—"

He growls at me, a temper I've never seen from Silas erupting out of him like lava and ash. "You want to talk about friendship?" he shouts. "Remind me who was driving that night when Ballard's headmaster found his stolen car on the football field and wrapped around a goalpost?"

Silas shoves my chest, knocking me into the wall. Years of repressed anger finding its way to the surface.

"I got expelled for you! And when's the last time you've even said you're sorry?"

"I didn't ask you to cover for me," I interject irritably. "You're such a fucking martyr, thinking I owe you, but I didn't ask you to do anything. You took the blame all on your own, bro."

"I kept you out of jail or, God forbid, rehab. And what have you done since but keep drinking and swallowing more pills? I could have fucked Kat on the bar and made Amy watch. It still wouldn't be half as bad as half the shit you've done to people."

"Well, that's me, then, huh?" Looking into Silas's callous, rageful eyes, I don't even recognize him. "I'm an addict with daddy issues, so of course I'm a mess. What's your excuse?"

"Fuck you," he spits. "Clean yourself up before you try to analyze my life."

He storms off, and as I watch him go, I realize my hands are shaking. Even a full minute after Silas has disappeared into the darkness, my breathing is shallow and labored. Thankfully, I brought along a little helper and pop one in my mouth to take the edge off.

In seconds, the jitters subside.

And then a new distraction presents itself.

Casey: Hey, want to hang out?
Me: Impeccable timing, as always. Name the place.

CHAPTER 39
CASEY

SOMEHOW, OF ALL PEOPLE, LAWSON KENT HAS BECOME THE MOST reliable friend I've got. Jaz already had plans, and since I have no desire to hang out with Sloane and RJ and watch them eye-fuck each other all night, I find myself texting Lawson. He texts me back immediately, and we agree to meet at the old greenhouse in an hour, while I plot how I'm going to sneak out without alerting anyone.

Luckily, Dad never stays up late, even on weekends. And Sloane and RJ end up going out, after all. It's past eleven, which seems a bit late to start their night, but I'm not one to talk. I just arranged to meet somebody at midnight.

My shoulders tense when I hear Dad in the hallway. He pauses in front of my door, knocking quietly. "Case? You still up?"

"Yeah. Come in." I was lying on my side scrolling on my phone, but I sit when he pokes his head inside.

Concern flickers in his eyes. "How are you doing?"

"Fine."

He looks unconvinced. And sounds reluctant as he adds, "Do you want to talk about Silver—"

"No," I interrupt. "What else is there to say? She's dead. Are you going to bed now?"

Although it's clear he wants to push the issue, he finally nods. "Yes. I'm turning in. Try not to stay up too late on your phone. It's bad for your eyes."

"I won't. Good night."

"Good night, sweetheart."

Around eleven thirty, I start to hear soft snoring wafting from the end of the hall. Fifteen minutes after that, I get dressed, throw on a coat, and slip out my bedroom window.

It's a decent jog across campus, sticking to the perimeter and doing my best to avoid security cameras until I'm safely within the derelict zone—the area of Sandover's expansive campus that's sat abandoned and overgrown since long before Dad became headmaster.

I wade through tall grass by my cell phone's flashlight, following a map crudely marked on a Google Maps satellite image to find my way.

"Getting warmer," a voice suddenly calls from the darkness.

"Marco?"

"Polo."

I emerge from the grass, and the greenhouse comes into view. A black silhouette draped in ivy and fallen foliage. I scan the glass facade with my flashlight, searching for Lawson.

"This place is like eighty percent creepier than you made it sound," I say to what feels like empty night. "If you brought me out here to ax murder me, I'm not in the mood."

I've wandered this campus and its forests in the pitch-black countless times. Yet as I continue to approach the vacant, looming greenhouse full of broken panes and tricky shadows, I suddenly become hyperaware of every startling noise emanating from the surrounding trees.

"Lawson? Marco?"

"Polo."

I nearly jump out of my skin at Lawson's whispered reply. So close to my ear, I feel his breath against my face.

"Jesus." I spin around and find him smirking in the light. I give him a shove for good measure. "Jerk."

"Sorry," he says without regret. "I couldn't help myself."

"You're lucky I didn't take a swing at you."

"That would have been adorable."

"Oh, really. You don't know about my sick ninja skills?"

"Literally, sweetheart, I'd pay money."

"Uh-huh. You're lucky I'm a pacifist."

"Uh-huh," he mimics. "I really dodged a bullet there."

"You know, not to sound ungrateful for the company," I tell him, "but this place looks exactly like a murder lair. Maybe a few less chainsaws and pickaxes, but, yeah, definite dismemberment vibes."

"Don't worry, we're not going inside. The smell alone will ruin your night." Lawson chuckles. "This is where the hormonal meatheads come to make hamburger of each other."

"Really?" A thought suddenly occurs to me. "Wait, it's Saturday night. Isn't that when the fights usually take place? Are they already over?"

"No, got canceled." He sounds confused by his own explanation. "Weirdest fucking thing. We all got a mass text saying they're tomorrow instead."

"Can I look inside? I promise to hold my breath," I tease.

"Sure, but if you need to throw up, don't do it on me."

"Deal."

He takes my hand to guide me inside the greenhouse, which is mostly a hollow void. The place has been meticulously cleared of the debris and leftovers I would have expected to find. There are no empty pots and rotting shelves. No dried remains of once-flourishing flora. I sweep my flashlight over walls that are scrawled with graffiti. Toward the center of the floor are splatters and trails of what looks like dried blood.

Ugh, and he wasn't wrong about the smell. My nostrils fill with the pungent odor of sweat and blood, notes of decay and urine thrown into the mix. I try not to breathe through my nose as I continue to examine our surroundings.

"There's a lot of blood here."

He shrugs. "It can get…graphic."

We go back outside, where I gulp in the fresh air. The cool breeze rustles my open coat, bringing a slight chill.

I zip up the coat and glance at Lawson. "We're not sitting out here, are we? It's kind of cold."

"Nope. Follow me."

We make our way through the darkness, down a grassy path. At first the grass is well-trodden, as if many a shoe had passed over it. Then it grows tall again, the little trail becoming overgrown with foliage until finally we stop in front of a rusted iron gate. Less than twenty-five feet or so from the greenhouse is a smaller one, almost completely hidden by shrubbery and covered with browning strands of ivy.

Lawson pushes aside some vines and opens the door, entering ahead of me. "I stumbled onto this place last winter," he tells me. "I come here when I need to clear my head."

"And you need to clear your head tonight?"

"Yeah. Sort of."

I step inside and look around. The space can't be more than eight feet by eight feet, maybe a tiny bit bigger, and this room hasn't been cleared out. Racks against three of the walls contain old containers and the skeletons of potted rosebushes. There's a low cabinet that Lawson opens to remove a folded blanket, which he tosses on the ground for us to sit on. He also flicks on an electric lantern, and, best of all, a small space heater.

"This is cozy," I say, removing my jacket and making myself comfortable. Then I narrow my eyes. "Do you bring girls here to hook up?"

"No, why would I? I have a perfectly functional bed in my room."

"But you also have a roommate," I point out. "There's more privacy here."

He sits beside me, stretching his long legs out in front of him. "Privacy's overrated. I don't care if Silas watches."

The lewd implication brings heat to my cheeks. I always forgot how experienced he is. Even more so than Fenn. When it comes to hooking up, I suspect Lawson is more adventurous than all the boys at Sandover combined.

He takes a flask from his pocket and offers me a sip. I pass, because I'm not sure I could find my way out of here again otherwise.

"How are things with Fenn these days?" he asks curiously.

I answer with a sarcastic snort. "Excellent! I gave him a chance at redemption, and he ended things."

"Damn. That's gotta sting."

"Not anymore." In fact, on the walk over here, the storm subsided quite a bit. Now it's more of a low rumble in the distance, moving out to sea. "I gave him every opportunity to do the right thing. Try to salvage something between us. He made his choice." My tone flattens. "Fenn's dead to me now."

Lawson lies down on his side to prop his head on his bent arm. "I don't know that it's any consolation, but I've had a shit night up until now."

He's different tonight. A bit subdued. There's a distance in his eyes, as if he's partly here, but also elsewhere in his own mind.

"What happened?"

"Silas yelled at me." He says it first like a joke. A little pout. Then the mocking grin fades and the hurt is left unmasked. "We got into it before you texted."

"That doesn't sound good."

"Yeah… Apparently giving your best friend an impromptu intervention outside a bar is less than the ideal setting. And a sin worse than murder."

I lie down on my side too, using my jacket as a pillow. "Are you two going to be okay?"

His attention briefly drifts toward his fingers tracing patterns into the blanket. He tries to configure something of his usual flippant expression in the soft lines of his face, but it falters, never quite achieving the desired effect.

"Honestly, I don't know." He rolls onto his back, staring at the moon through the holes in the ceiling. "We've been through a lot together. But this time…" He folds his arms under his head. "He might be well and truly sick of my shit."

"Sounds like you're trying to look out for him. How can he be mad at that?"

"Well, when you've spent years as the proverbial black sheep, people tend to rely on that. Set their watches by it. And they don't take kindly to feeling judged by someone they credit with ruining their life."

"Wait. You've lost me. Silas thinks you ruined his life?"

Lawson releases a heavy breath, and in it, I hear the weight of this burden on his heart.

"It's a long story," he finally says.

"I've got time."

There's more hesitation.

"Oh, come on," I prod with a little shove. "Unburden yourself. Confession is good for the soul."

"Those nuns are starting to rot your brain, you know."

"We can stay here all night…"

He manages a slight smile. "Promises, promises."

Eventually, though, he gives in.

"I was at Ballard freshman year," he starts. I hadn't known that, but it makes sense in hindsight. "I got busted doing coke, and next thing I know, the housefather and Headmaster Fournette are tossing my room. They found enough pharmaceuticals in there to put down an elephant. I was promptly expelled. Then charged. Then pled down and got sentenced to in-patient rehabilitation, thanks to the best juvenile drug lawyer money can buy."

"I don't think it took," I say, biting back a smile.

Lawson manages a laugh. "Yeah, all I learned in rehab was how to better conceal my habits."

"The system works."

He hums in agreement. "Cut to sophomore year. I'm now another discarded youth remanded to Sandover to continue my penance. I have a swim meet at Ballard, which is the first time I see Silas again after months apart. So that night after our meet, everyone goes home, and the place is empty, for the most part. Silas and I sit outside behind the pool house with a thermos of Jameson I had stashed in my gym bag, and we have ourselves a little reunion toast."

Somewhere along the way, I've heard this story. Or a version of it. Now I'm realizing Sloane and Fenn and the rest of them never actually knew the truth.

"We're beyond smashed when I get the idea to go hunt for the headmaster's car. How we managed to find our way stumbling nearly blind across campus, I don't know. But there it is in the parking lot of the admin building." His voice changes. Becoming lower, more tired. "And for some inexplicable reason, Fournette left it unlocked. Keys right there in the cupholder. Fucking idiot. Silas tries to reason with me, begging me not to get in the car. Then he has no choice but to jump in the passenger seat when I rev the engine."

"So you were driving," I say. "But Silas…"

"The football field was wet," Lawson says by way of an explanation. "I spun out doing a bit of art landscaping and collided with the goalpost. We heard the sirens almost immediately."

"And he took the rap."

Lawson props himself up on both elbows. "I didn't ask him to do it. One of the officers asked who was driving, and Silas just blurted out it was him before I could even answer. He was being a good friend. We both knew where I was headed if the cops found out it was me behind the wheel. Silas, on the other hand, was squeaky clean."

"He got expelled and ended up here," I mutter, more to myself.

"No offense, but that makes a lot of sense now. I never understood how someone like him ended up at Sandover."

"Yep. His only crime was the great misfortune of befriending me."

"That's not true at all."

"I was there. I fucked his whole life."

Lawson tries to put on that nonchalant mask of his, but not very successfully. It doesn't do much at all to disguise the sincere sadness in his gray eyes. He's in pain—an emotion I'm not sure anyone in his circle thinks him capable of feeling. Lawson's got a reputation for being a good time boy. Perpetually on. His blood replaced with bourbon and Percocet.

Sometimes I think they forget he's a person.

"Listen to me," I say, waiting until he reluctantly meets my gaze. "You didn't ask him to lie to the police. Silas made a choice because protecting you was important to him. He can't turn around and hold you hostage for that. For guys like him, there are always going to be opportunities. He'll go to a good college, swim, maybe take a shot at the Olympics one day. But it's entirely up to him how everything turns out. You're not holding him back and his life isn't ruined. He's responsible for his latest meltdowns. Trying to make you the scapegoat doesn't change that."

"Nah. He was right about one thing," Lawson mumbles, sitting up. "I am a fuckup."

"Hey." I grab a fistful of his shirt and shake him a little. "You're not a fuckup. You've just exercised some poor judgment. And you can decide to change that any time you want. It's not a permanent state of being. Okay?"

His lips twitch. "If I say no, are you going to shake me again?"

I respond with a threatening glare. "Don't test me, Kent. You're not ready for this smoke."

He cracks a sincere smile, which gives me a greater sense of accomplishment than I've felt for a while.

"You probably shouldn't be so nice to me," he warns. "I'm sort of a bad influence."

"Well, I like being nice to you. And maybe I think I'm a good influence."

He chuckles. "I'll take that bet."

We fall silent for a moment. I watch the shadows cast by the lantern against the dirt-streaked glass panes. From the corner of my eye, I feel him watching me.

"I have a confession to make," I say, turning toward him. "I asked you to meet up because I was pissed at Fenn and wanted you to take my mind off him."

Lawson shrugs. "I know."

"What I'm saying is, though, I like hanging out with you, and I'm having a good time. So thank you."

"Come here." He scoots closer and throws an arm around my shoulders, giving me a reassuring squeeze. "You're a cool chick, Casey. And you deserve good things."

Lawson presses a kiss to the top of my head. When I look at him, I'm overwhelmed by some inexplicable sensation. A strange thought seems to emerge from the ether and strike us both unprepared. Lawson leans in. I tilt my chin up. And our lips meet.

CHAPTER 40
RJ

I MUST LOVE THIS GIRL. AFTER SLOANE HYPNOTIZES ME INTO agreeing to be her human fly trap, I sprint back to the dorm to change clothes for the party and grab my wallet. At this rate I can start skipping the gym with all the laps I've run across this campus lately.

When I get back to our room, Fenn is still in bed. Headphones on, lying on his back and staring at the ceiling. The guy's been in a perpetual state of existential crisis for the better part of the semester.

"You heading out?" He pulls one headphone off, watching me grab some fresh clothes out of my closet.

"Yes. Got a thing I have to do. I'll be back in a bit."

I strip out of my shirt and into a black tee Sloane says is her favorite. Figure that's good enough for a Ballard party. I'm not about to put too much thought into this and somehow wind up getting myself in trouble.

"Have fun, I guess."

"You okay, man?" I ask.

"Fine," is the terse reply. "Just had a shit day."

"You didn't even tell me how it went with the headmaster earlier," I prompt. "Other than to say it's only a suspension."

"That's all there was to it," he answers without meeting my eyes.

"Okay. And I assume you haven't told Casey about Gabe yet?" I put on a pair of jeans and then run a brush through my hair while Fenn continues to avert his gaze.

"You assume right."

I scrutinize him, wishing I could figure out what's so off about him, or that I currently had the time to give him my undivided attention. But I can't focus on Fenn's issues right now. I've got to get my head on right for this party if I'm going to get Sloane what she needs. I'll be damned if I come out of there empty-handed.

"All right, I'm bouncing. Night, bro."

"Night," he mumbles and rolls onto his side.

Sloane's waiting in her car for me downstairs. She smirks at my shirt when I hop in the passenger seat.

"I don't know how I feel about that," she says.

"Jealous?"

It's a cute look on her.

"Not even a little," she insists. "More betrayed, maybe? Don't spill anything on it."

"You might have to help me get the lipstick stains out."

"Watch it." She shoves my shoulder before pulling out of the gates and onto the road away from Sandover. "I sent you a picture of Mila to refresh your memory. Wouldn't want you spending all night flirting with the wrong chick."

"That's why you're the brains of the operation."

In theory, this might look like a choice assignment. Permission to hit on a hot girl with no repercussions. Except I haven't been the least bit enthusiastic since Sloane concocted this scheme. Not just because I know she isn't nearly as dispassionate about the idea as she'd like to pretend. Whether or not I get information out of Mila, this'll eat her up for a good while. But also, I'm entirely turned off by the idea of cozying up to someone who isn't Sloane. I don't know what's happened to me since we met, but it's like she's burnt my tongue and I can't taste anything else. Nothing gets me excited the way she does. Monogamy has gotten its talons into my flesh and it's holding on tight.

When we get to Ballard, Sloane pulls up to what looks like a dorm under renovation. There's scaffolding around the facade and building materials scattered around the lawn. Tarps hang over windows on the second floor, and I spot piles of shingles stacked on the roof.

"This used to be the girls' scholarship dorm," she explains. "There was always a bedbug outbreak or rats chewing through the wiring. I think a bat infestation in the attic finally created enough complaints from parents they had to condemn it and move everyone into the regular dorms."

"Fucking rich people," I mutter to myself.

"I'm going to wait out here," Sloane says. She turns in her seat to run her fingers through my hair, messing it up after I'd tried to tame it into shape. "I like it better that way."

"Should we have a code? Some kind of signal if things go south?"

She gives a slightly violent smile. "If you're still in there after two hours, I'm pulling a fire alarm."

"Fair."

She brushes a speck of lint off my shoulder and gives me a little smack on the cheek for good measure. "Go get 'em, tiger."

My dick twitches. "Okay, yeah. I think I like that."

"Behave yourself and you'll get a BJ for a job well done."

I throw open the car door. "Done deal."

It's mostly dark inside, oddly vacant when I first enter. Everywhere I look, there's evidence of construction underway. Doors off their hinges. Old drywall in crumpled heaps. Upstairs, however, music rattles sawdust through the floorboards and the weak glow of lantern light suggests the party starts on the second floor.

I follow the stench of weed past a pair of feet in the air, belonging to the chick doing a keg stand while a circle of guys hold the spout to her lips. They chant as beer trickles down her chin. Beyond them is a hotly contested game of beer pong. Beyond that, a table lined with flip cup participants. One team is already stripped down to their underwear, the girl in the Sponge Bob thong probably regretting several life choices.

Suddenly a small, localized quake rumbles down the hall, accompanied by a deep, guttural roar. The noise, drawing closer, becomes angry barking. A line of guys in Ballard body paint—and not a stitch more—gallop past me like a pack of angry mutts.

"Ballard Bulldogs rule," a coy voice whispers at my ear.

I look over my shoulder to realize Mila's saved me the trouble of sniffing her out. Last time I saw her, she was in her cheerleader uniform, which is always a solid choice of hot-girl outfit but no match for how good she looks tonight. She's paired a white crop top with a gray body-con skirt that reaches her ankles, and something about the long skirt/tiny top combo really works for her. Also doesn't hurt that I can see her nipples through her shirt.

"Was that one of those spontaneous demonstrations of school spirit I keep hearing about?" I ask, not bothering to hide the fact that I'm checking her out.

"Varsity initiation," she says, licking her lips like I'm the one who's unknowingly wandered into her web. "Well, one of the rituals, anyway."

"I'll never get the appeal."

"That's funny coming from a jock."

I wink at her. "You take that back. I won't have you besmirch my good name with such slander."

Mila pops a hand on her hip and glances around. "Speaking of slander… Where's the wife?"

"Sloane?" I offer a bored shrug. "Home, I guess. I'm flying solo tonight."

Her liquid-amber eyes narrow, skeptical. "No, I don't think so. Sloane hates sharing her toys."

"All right, so I wasn't technically invited." She's a tad sharper than I gave her credit for, so I change tack. "I came looking for my stepbrother. You know Fenn?"

"You could say that." She doesn't care to elaborate, but her smirk hints at a history I don't have time to explore. "Something wrong?"

"No, he's just in a mood lately, and I'm trying to keep him out of trouble."

"Aww." She makes a playfully pouting face. "That's so sweet. You're adorable."

"Hey, I know this guy!" Oliver Drummer saunters over to us and clamps a paw down on my shoulder, jostling me like I owe him money.

I try to remember if I've recently made his life more difficult somehow, but come up empty.

"RJ, right?" he prompts. "From that soccer game."

"Oh, yeah. Right."

Oliver's the Big Man at Ballard. Their Duke without the rap sheet. Smart enough not to get caught, I guess.

"You're a long way from home," he remarks.

Mila interjects for me. "He's looking for Fenn. Who may or may not be on a bender."

Oliver frowns. "Can't say I've seen him. But you should grab a drink and stay awhile. See how the other half lives."

I don't know if he means outside the barbed wire fences of Juvie Prep, or if it's a jab at my finances (or lack thereof), but I give him a nod either way because this self-important dipshit isn't my problem tonight.

"That's a great idea." Mila takes my arm, though her aim is unmistakably in Oliver's direction. "I'll show you where they're hiding the good stuff."

She spares him a challenging glare as she drags me off. Interesting.

Seems I'm not the only one with ulterior motives tonight. That should make my job a little easier.

Farther down the hall and deeper into the shadowy crevices of the party beyond the common room, each of the suites is like a tiny, contained universe of adolescent exploration and experimentation. Bumps of coke in 202, and two dudes wrestling in body paint for a chanting audience in 204. In nearly every corner, I glimpse couples in a tangle of lips and hands.

Mila brings me to a room where liquor bottles and red cups sit on a forgotten wooden desk.

"What do you like?" she asks.

"Whatever you're drinking."

She pours two shots of tequila and hands one to me. We cheers before tossing them back. She gives each of us a refill, this time sipping hers rather than shooting.

"Why are you really here?" she demands. No more good cop.

I pretend to ponder my response while sipping my own drink. Letting her believe her powers of persuasion are dragging it out of me.

"The truth?" I finally say.

"Yes."

"I've been stuck in this godforsaken town for months with the same ugly faces, and I just needed a change of scenery. I don't usually hang around one place this long."

Her gaze is reluctant but appeased with that answer. "Yeah, I guess it's kind of a sausage fest over there, huh?"

"Yup. And I'm also tired of listening to Fenn go on about his old roommate."

"Gabe," she confirms. "I know him."

I can't look too eager, but this is my in. "Oh, right. I think Fenn mentioned something about you guys. You were hooking up with him, yeah?"

Her body language changes instantly, becoming guarded and

closed off. She stands a little straighter as if prepared to bolt for the exit.

"Seriously?" Mila laughs at me. "I don't even know you."

Shit. I pushed too hard. Now I've got a limited window to salvage this.

"We can fix that," I say, winking again.

I swallow the rest of my tequila and pour another shot. When I offer the bottle, she pauses a moment. Appraising me. Whatever she sees, it overrides her better judgment. Or maybe Sloane was right—the opportunity to play with Sloane's toys is simply too tempting to ignore.

Mila holds her cup out and accepts another pour. "All right," she agrees, still wary but up to the challenge. "Come with me."

Again she takes my hand, drawing me even farther into the belly of this capitalist expression of rebellion. On the third floor, there is a distinctly different atmosphere. Colored lights paint the walls and wander the ceiling like a dizzy kaleidoscope. The common room is architecturally identical to the one below, but not yet touched by the renovations. Here, bodies pulse in a sort of chaotic unison to the beat of heavy trance music. The air drips with sweat and is so thick, it seeps into my clothes. Mila perks right up.

I'm afraid I might have to dance until she drags me through the crowd to a small leather love seat in the corner. She pushes me into it and helps herself to sitting across my lap with her legs draped over mine and her back against the cushioned arm.

"Comfy?" she asks, sipping her drink.

It's a bit loud in here for a conversation, but if this is what it takes to put her in a more talkative mood, fine. I'm adaptable.

I offer a wry grin. "You're not shy, are you?"

She shrugs. "I don't think you like shy girls. You want someone who will yank you around by the collar now and then."

Am I so transparent?

"Is that what you're into?" I drape my arm over her thighs. "You strike me as a biter. What's that called?"

Mila pulls her bottom lip between her teeth. "An oral fixation."

I keep my gaze on her mouth. Making it obvious too. "Yeah, that's it."

Her pleased smile tells me I've brought this mission back from the brink and she's in the pocket. Now I just need to steer us back to Gabe before I choke down too much more of this shitty tequila.

"You know, Sloane would kill you if she saw you like this."

I lick the corner of my mouth, still fixated on hers. "Good thing she isn't here."

"You're not worried she'll find out?" Mila idly plays with my shirt between her fingers. "Nothing stays secret in the private school group chat."

"We're not married, and it's my senior year. I intend to enjoy myself."

"I like that." Her hand explores my chest, fingertips sliding over one pec, grazing my nipple on their way toward my collarbone. "Self-determination is sexy."

"What about you?" I ask, gauging how far I can push my luck. "What do you want? Right in this moment."

She licks her lips, sliding her hand up behind my neck and into my hair. When she leans forward for a kiss, I let it happen. It's not a bad kiss. Even gets my heart pounding faster. Our tongues meet and the tequila tastes much better on her tongue than it did out of the bottle. But if there was any doubt I can only get hard for Sloane, this settles it. As Fenn would say, I'm learning what the opposite of a boner feels like.

When she tugs my lip with her teeth, I let out a quiet groan, but mostly because I'm hoping she doesn't draw blood. Otherwise it'd be me and my right hand for the foreseeable future when Sloane got a look at me.

We make small talk between gratuitous touching, until we finish our drinks and I decide to test the waters again.

"Should I be worried about Oliver storming in and kicking my ass for making out with you?" I ask with a chuckle.

"Nah. We have an open sort of thing."

"All right, good. And what about Gabe? Is he gonna break out of prison and hunt me down? Didn't you go to prom with the guy?"

"It wasn't like we were *together* together." She absently trails her fingers along my bare arm. "But, sure. We ended up hanging out all night."

"Really? You were with him the whole time? Wasn't he a dealer?"

"So?"

"So don't dealers have to duck out like every five seconds to move their product?"

Her lips curve in a smug smile. "Not when they're with me." Mila laughs to herself. "He was selling at the beginning, but then he and I started feeling each other, you know? So business was closed for the rest of the night. We actually ended up leaving together and going back to my room."

"How long was that?"

She chokes on another laugh. "Like, how long did he last?"

God, no. "I mean, was it a full-on sleepover? Because that sure sounds like a *together* together activity." I mimic her earlier phrasing.

"Well, he stayed till five in the morning, but you know, it was whatever. I drove him back to Sandover while the sun was still rising." She blinks. "I just realized that's the last time I saw him. Huh. Weird."

Yeah, weird.

I want to ask her if she's somehow managed to hear from Gabe since then, but she doesn't give me the chance. Her mouth is closing in on mine, and she kisses me again before I can voice the question. I close my eyes and remind myself that kissing a hot girl isn't the worst job in the world.

And wait for the opportune moment to take my leave and claim my reward from Sloane.

CHAPTER 41
CASEY

SLOANE SLEEPS IN AND SKIPS BREAKFAST, SO IT'S ONLY DAD AND ME at the table on Sunday morning. Quietly eating the eggs I'd overcooked and the bacon I'd nearly burned to a crisp because I've been unable to focus on anything since the second I woke up.

I went to bed last night with excitement still thrumming in my fingertips. I had a secret only one person in the universe knew about.

I woke up with an emotional hangover, the secret now a tight knot in the pit of my stomach.

Fortunately, Dad mistakes my mood for grief. He thinks I'm upset about Silver. I'm not. She was going to die anyway. Yes, I enjoyed taking care of her, but it's about time I stopped getting overly attached to every critter that crosses my path. I need to learn to grow a thick skin. Harden my heart. Otherwise I'm going to keep drowning every time something bad happens. Every time I lose someone.

"I'm taking the dogs out," I say once we're cleaning up after breakfast. "I think we'll walk to the lake."

"Don't let Bo swim," Dad warns. "I know he doesn't mind the cold water, but it's almost winter now and it'll take him forever to air-dry."

"I'll do my best," I promise, but Bo has a mind of his own when it comes to that lake.

Thirty minutes later, Penny and Bo drag me through the forest, traveling their well-worn paths to sniff at their favorite trees and coax squirrels to scurry out from under shrubs. Now that I'm alone again, I fall victim to the myriad conflicting thoughts swarming my mind like bees.

Last night was…

God, I wish I could say it was awful.

It wasn't. It was really great. And when it was happening, I never paused a moment to consider how I might feel later, only that it felt right at the time.

Now it's later. Now the consequences begin to creep in, and I feel sick. Because no matter how I break it down, I can't help this feeling I've done something wrong.

Betrayed Fenn.

Which is stupid, I chide myself, smacking down the thought as quickly as it emerges. We're not dating. He broke us up.

Yet the feeling persists. Lawson's his friend. The rules of civil society tell us that those boundaries are sacred. Crossing them so egregiously makes a clear statement: I hope this hurts.

But I never set out for revenge.

Despite everything, and against my better judgment, I still love Fenn. It's easier said than done to separate what he did, the lying, from all the ways he helped put me back together after the accident. The months he was my only friend. My best friend. He saw me in a way no one else could.

Now I know it was because he'd been there. He was the blurry figure on the other side of the glass while water rushed up my legs. He was the one carrying me out of the lake and laying my limp body on the ground with my lips turning blue and blood dripping from my forehead. He knew how close I'd been to dying, and how far I've come since.

"I wish you were here," I say out loud to my mother. "You would talk me through this if you were here. Or at least I hope you would."

I bite my lip. "I like to think you wouldn't judge or lecture me. That you'd just listen."

Ahead of me, Bo and Penny bark. I look up to see Fenn at the edge of the path, placating the excited traitors as they jump all over him and compete for attention.

Makes me wish I'd trained them to attack on command.

The nerves hit sideways. I'm half dizzy and ready to vomit. Like sudden onset heatstroke. Fenn approaches me, and I don't have the first clue how to talk to him anymore.

"Hi," he says tentatively, hands shoved in the center pocket of his gray hooded sweatshirt. His hair is messy, rumpled on the left side, as if he'd just rolled out of bed. "Your dad told me where you'd be."

I snort. "I'm surprised he didn't lead you on a wild goose chase."

"Honestly, me too. Although he did make it clear he's still not my biggest fan." Fenn shrugs. "He caved after I told him I wanted to find you to apologize."

Derision tickles my throat and comes out as a harsh laugh. "Well, I'm sorry you wasted your time." I whistle for Bo and Penny, but they're defiantly zipping around like a couple of caffeinated kids and couldn't care less that I need to make a quick escape. "I don't think we have anything left to say to each other."

"I shouldn't have ended it over text," he says. Gruff and remorseful. "I sat in my room all day and night yesterday, mentally ripping myself a new one." He shakes his head in disgust. Self-directed reproach. "Every time I'm given the choice between right and wrong, I always choose wrong. I'm a goddamn mess."

"Whatever, Fenn."

"Please," he insists, moving with me when I try to walk away. "I came to apologize for being so callous."

"I don't care. It's always *something* with you." I stop. A lump of despair lodges in my throat. "I don't want your apology for your crappy breakup text. I'm done with your apologies."

"You know I'd do anything—" His voice cracks slightly, "—for things to have turned out different for us."

My anger blooms out of the despair like a flower opening after a rainstorm. The quickest cure for depression is the rage Fenn induces in me when he so carelessly proves he'll never understand what his lies of omission do to me.

"You'll do anything? Do you not realize what bullshit that is? It's been weeks and you still won't admit what happened at prom. Because you're selfish, Fenn. Covering your own ass even if it means hurting someone you claim to care about. So like I said, I don't want an apology."

Once again, he rushes to keep step with me while I round up the dogs and make it clear this is me walking away from him.

"Casey, stop."

"No. I'm not falling for your traps anymore. You say you want to make things right. You're ready to be honest. Then you dump me over text like an hour before we're supposed to meet up and talk. You're a coward. And I'm not going to be the butt of the joke anymore."

"You're not a joke," he insists.

"Honesty isn't that hard," I say bitterly. "Just grit your teeth and bear it. It's simple." And then I sort of black out, or at least that's the only explanation I can come up with for what happens next. My mouth goes on autopilot as if my brain decides I should sit this one out. "Like this: I hooked up with Lawson last night."

For several seconds, he stands there staring at me. Unblinking. He's an engine that won't turn over. A dead battery. Stalled out and clicking. Empty.

My pulse shrieks in my ears as I watch his face for any sense of recognition. As I wait for a reaction. For anything.

Then his synapses start firing. Without a word or even the slightest flinch, he turns on his heel and walks away.

Any righteous fury I'd felt in coming clean is immediately doused by the weight of Fenn's devastation.

I guess honesty isn't always the best policy.

CHAPTER 42
LAWSON

I FIND MYSELF INEXPLICABLY STONE-COLD SOBER TONIGHT. ALONE in my room. Warm in the glow of an early-career Keanu action flick on TV. For the first time in, shit, half a decade, I'm not in the mood for a chemical disruption. Even turned down the joint offered to me by the guys a few doors down, which is possibly the first time in my adolescent history I've passed on getting high.

It's a shocking turn of events I might've shared with my therapist if he hadn't fired me for getting a handjob from his niece.

Still, despite the day's unencumbered self-reflection, I'm feeling unsettled.

Even Keanu on a surfboard can't calm the seas inside my head.

RJ bursting through my door doesn't help either.

"You free tonight? I need a wingman," he announces. He's wearing black cargo pants and a black hoodie featuring the logo of some band I've never heard of.

"Did we dump Sloane and need to pick up chicks?" I spare him a glance before gazing back at the lo-fi beauty of Southern California in VHS-quality film grain.

"No, we did that yesterday," is RJ's inexplicable response. "The fights are tonight. Need you to go with me."

"Yeah, about that. Why the fuck did you reschedule them to Sunday? Dudes need a buffer day for the swelling in the eyes and jaw to go down."

"I didn't reschedule shit."

"Nuh-uh. Mass text from Carter said the king had spoken."

RJ rakes both hands through his hair, looking like he wants to yank it out from the roots. "All I said was that I had plans last night and—you know what, forget it. Doesn't matter. Fenn's AWOL and I'm not asking Silas, so you're it. Let's go."

I raise my eyebrows. "You gonna fight?"

"No, I'm going to abdicate."

"What the hell does that—"

"Let's go, Lawson," he growls.

Then he exits and leaves the door presumptuously ajar, completely assured in his confidence that I'll join him.

And despite my firm plan to not leave this room tonight, I find myself following him across campus like the perfect Pavlovian specimen.

I'm not quite sure what the fuck just happened.

"You seem weird," he informs me while we trudge through the overgrown grass beyond the alleged limits of where students are permitted to traverse.

The groundskeepers don't bother to maintain the lawns out here, hoping that will serve as a deterrent, but it doesn't even slow us down as we head for the perimeter of the surrounding forest. It's an especially dark night thanks to the cloud cover that hides the moon and makes the occasional divot or protruding tree root especially hazardous. Even the animals and insects seem reluctant to emerge tonight.

For some reason, that feels like a bad omen.

"I seem weird," I echo.

"You haven't said a word since we left. It's not like you."

"Oh. Yeah, that was rhetorical."

Truthfully, I'm languishing in a kind of mental limbo. Struggling with strange new emotions I can't make sense of, which seem to intensify each time I allow my thoughts to drift and the memory of last night to surface.

I'm no doctor, but if I had to attempt an educated hypothesis, I'd posit that what I'm feeling is guilt.

Fenn's hardly owed my sympathies, but I'm not a complete bastard—what transpired last night was a clear betrayal to our years of friendship. The guilt is weighing heavy right now. And it's just one emotion among many.

In a way, Casey was my first. In that I was nearly, and somewhat regrettably, sober during the entire encounter.

Regrettable not because I didn't thoroughly enjoy myself. I did. But I'm not at all accustomed to suffering the aftermath of my actions with a clear head.

"So what now?" I question as the flashlights bouncing like fireflies through the trees begin to converge on our position.

"Now we find Duke."

When we arrive at the scene of the crime, I force myself not to look at the secret path that leads to the groundkeeper's greenhouse. The small, secret haven where I brought Casey last night and probably made one of the biggest mistakes of my life.

The main greenhouse is packed with bloodthirsty guys who spent the afternoon doing push-ups and pulling money out of the ATM. In the center of the room, two emotionally stunted upright primates rip their shirts off, flexing their muscles for the ravenous audience, as they prepare to do primal battle in lieu of finding literally any other way to deal with the perpetual trauma of high school.

RJ marks Duke as soon as we walk in and proceeds to shove his way through the crowd toward him. I'm caught in his wake and unable to free myself from becoming a third wheel to their conversation.

"Look who's come to slum it with the peasants," Duke remarks with a sarcastic grin that doesn't conceal his recent perpetual bitterness.

Lately, the dethroned ruler of the garbage heap has been acting like a divorcé watching his ex move in with her new boyfriend across the street.

"I came to deal," RJ retorts as an offer of truce. "At this point I'd pay you to take this shit off my hands."

"So you can't hack it, huh?" Duke's smile widens. "That crown is a little heavier than it looked, right?"

"I can't understand why anyone would want it," RJ groans back, utterly exasperated with the entire ordeal.

I swallow a laugh. Don't think I've ever met anyone who craves power or authority less than RJ.

"This school is fucked, Jessup. These people are insane. All I want is to be done with all of it."

"Say the word," Duke offers, "and I'll take the responsibility off your hands."

"I have conditions," RJ counters. "I'm not walking away just to let you revive your tyrannical reign."

Duke rolls his eyes. Already bored and yet dripping at the mouth to start swinging his dick around.

"First, as far as your 'rules' are concerned, there is a demilitarized zone between us."

Befuddled, Duke scoffs. "What the fuck does that mean?"

"It means, I'm exempt. From your bullshit rules and your taxes and whatever other crackpot, brain-wormed notions you come up with. From here on out, I'm a sovereign nation. Whatever transpires within my borders is none of your damn business."

"Fine. Whatever."

"Second, you leave Lucas alone too. Kid's not made of money."

"What are you, his mommy?"

I become distracted, or maybe it's more akin to panic, because I suddenly spot Fenn strolling inside. He lingers near the door for a minute, sweeping his gaze over the shouting crowd, but although he's no doubt clocked our position, he remains steadfastly standoffish.

Which only heightens my anxiety. Now I remember why I do my damnedest to avoid sobriety. Frankly, I can't recommend it.

Under ordinary inebriated circumstances, I might find my way to dismissing the whole thing out of mind. But Fenn's been such a sad sack lately, constantly in a state of crisis, that it feels like I've just shot Bambi's mother. And then fucked his girlfriend.

"With that out of the way," Duke says to RJ with a slap on the back, "now we can be friends."

"I wouldn't go that far," RJ says dryly. "Do we have a deal?"

"Deal." Duke sticks his hand out.

No sooner does RJ drop his guard to offer a handshake than Duke rears back and unleashes a left hook.

A loud exclamation erupts from the peanut gallery as the sophomore fight is abandoned for the hope of a real brawl to explode.

To his credit, RJ takes the sucker punch like a champ, though he's going to have a fat lip come morning.

"Cheap shot," he snaps at Duke.

"Sorry." Duke smirks cheerfully. "Had to make it official. Now we're square," he says, because he's the guy who has to have the last word. Always.

RJ adjusts his jaw, taking the parting shot as the price of doing business. "Better be."

"Come on." Duke throws his arm over RJ's shoulder. "We're basically family, right? You are screwing my ex."

"Is that what this is? Phase Two: Use me to get Sloane back?"

He laughs. "Dude, if you think she can get tricked into bed, you don't know her at all."

"Fair."

"Okay, listen up!" The master of ceremonies this evening takes the center of the circle where the previous bout has left a paltry smattering of blood and sweat. "From the junior class, Wynder and Hamill, step forward."

The next fighters emerge from their respective corners to face off. Money changes hands around them, bets moving in careful choreography.

"Let's go," RJ tells me. "I'm over this shit."

We've only taken two steps before a commotion stirs from somewhere deep in the scrum. Wariness crawls like ivy up my spine as I watch Fenn push his way to the middle of the room, taking the floor from the two fighters-in-waiting.

"I want next," he demands.

Just like that, my pulse quickens.

Shit.

The confused MC looks to RJ for a ruling, unaware of the recent transfer of power.

"What are you doing?" RJ calls out, frowning at Fenn. Like the rest of the room, he senses the moral fury with which Fenn has claimed the right of vengeance.

Fenn ignores his stepbrother. "Lawson," he hollers.

The greenhouse becomes deathly silent. Like a morgue.

His determined gaze locks with mine. "I'm calling you out."

The silence breaks, and the responding boisterous clamor through the crowd is both elated and perplexed. Me, I'm not at all confused by this turn of events. I know why I'm here and what I've got coming. It's plain on Fenn's severe face.

RJ turns to me for an explanation, but I ignore him to meet Fenn in the circle. My shoulders drop. I force myself to look him in the eye.

"I'm sorry," I say as Fenn pulls his shirt off and tosses it at the feet of the rabidly eager bystanders.

"Fuck you."

Fenn doesn't wait for a bell. He came prepared to pound me into oblivion, and so I let him. The first several blows are catharsis for both of us. I take the beating because it's the path of least resistance. Eye swelling. Mouth filling with blood. Call it penance. Call it self-pity.

I deserve this.

"Fight back, asshole." Eyes feral, Fenn grabs the front of my shirt and drops me to one knee with a right cross. "Hit me, damn it."

I'm almost numb, my nerve endings so brutalized, they hardly register the blows, only the violent ringing in my ears with each echoing *snap* of bone on bone. Eventually Fenn's rage—and frustration with my reluctance to trade with him—propels him to wrestle me into a headlock and clamp down until I'm forced to elbow him in the gut to free myself.

"That's it," he hisses. "Hit me back, you goddamn asshole."

He tackles me again, this time pinning me down with his knee between my shoulder blades, and my delayed sense of self-preservation kicks in, and we're both operating on reptile brain. I scramble to roll over, my fist snapping into his jaw before we both stumble to our feet. I hit him. And then I hit again. Because I'm angry too. Not with him, but at myself.

Because it's suddenly occurred to me that the one nice thing that's happened to me during this whole abysmal year is the only thing I wasn't supposed to enjoy.

We become angry, bloody animals in this circle. Inflicting pain and spitting malice. Until our arms grow heavy and the air is too thick to reach our lungs and we're choking on our own adrenaline.

I land a shot to his kidneys that doubles him over and forces Fenn to tangle up with me. In a red, blind flurry I elbow the side of his head until I lose my balance. He rams me into the ground. Fenn is able to get on top, sitting on my chest, his features taut with torment and hatred. He pulls back his fist as I stare up at him, knowing I'm about to wake up in the hospital or tossed in a ditch.

But the strike never comes.

Fenn, apparently realizing the limits of his own violence, stops himself.

"You're dead to me," he mutters, standing up. "You went too far this time, Lawson." I recognize my father in the way he gazes down at me with such contempt and disgust. "We're done here."

CHAPTER 43
FENN

My mouth tastes like metal and dirt. The throbbing at my temple flares across my face and settles into my swollen eyelid and aching jaw. I'm breathing shallow as I bend tree limbs and swat away spiderwebs, trudging through the dense forest. The pain is clarity. The clarity of purpose, but also consequence. All of this was inevitable. From the moment I set foot toward that boathouse. We were always going to end up here.

I don't know what time it is when I find myself under Casey's window. Late. I toss fallen pinecones and pebbles at the glass until she appears, yanking it open.

"Jesus, Fenn," she hisses. "What the hell are—" She stops abruptly. Aghast at the brutal image I make. "Are you okay? What happened to you?"

It sort of breaks my heart that she still musters any concern at all.

I hold up my phone. "Will you pick up when I call you? I don't want to shout at your window and wake the house."

"I don't think you should be—"

"I went to the lake because Gabe texted me during prom to meet him at the boathouse. That's what I was trying to tell you the other night before your dad interrupted us."

She blinks a couple of times. Then says, "Let me get my phone."

I call her number, and she picks up on the first ring, reappearing at the window. She's in those pink PJs that I love so much, her strawberry-blond hair pulled away from her pretty face in a low ponytail.

"Gabe was dealing that night, so we didn't really get a chance to hang out. He was ready to bounce by then, though. Suggested we get high in the boathouse. I was already wasted by that point, but I was like, sure, I'm down."

The words come out so quietly, I can barely hear them in my own head over the tinnitus ringing in my ears. I guess this is what disassociating feels like. I'm outside my body, a stream of consciousness emanating from somewhere deep in my psyche that I'm not entirely in control of.

"When I got there, Gabe was nowhere to be seen. Instead, I saw the back end of your car sticking out of the water. Red taillights. I jumped in to check if there was anyone in there and found you."

Casey watches me, riveted. Her mouth is slightly open. Eyes wide and terrified like they were that night.

"After I got the door open and was trying to get your seat belt off, I noticed a jacket caught on the parking brake. It was lying across the driver's side. Whoever was wearing it, they slipped out of it to escape." I briefly close my eyes. Well, eye. The other one is already swelling shut. "I saw the jacket and immediately knew who it belonged to. It was Gabe's."

Her face goes pale. I can almost read the images forcing their way forward. The flashbacks that startle her awake screaming in the middle of the night. Her brain constantly dragging her back into that water. Now, I know she's seeing Gabe's face beside her in that car.

"So I took the jacket and pulled you out. Carried you to shore. Found your phone in your pocket and texted Sloane where to find you. Then I left and caught a ride back to Sandover. Hid the jacket as the only thing that could tie Gabe to the accident. And never told a soul until now."

More than anything, I wish I'd been a better person then. That I'd understood what my choices meant.

"I was protecting my best friend," I admit regretfully. "Gabe covered my ass with the cops a couple years ago, and I owed him. My loyalty was with him that night. I didn't know you then, and I'm sorry. I wish I had."

There's an urgency in her expression, like she wants to speak but her throat is sealed shut. I don't give her the chance.

"I came to say goodbye. I finally realize the gravity of what I did to you, Case. I broke you. Stole everything that was good from you. Drove you to Lawson. It's my fault, and I understand that. And I'm done bothering you, chasing you. No more begging for second chances. You were right. I need to grow up."

Casey wipes at her cheek. "I wasn't trying to hurt you."

"I know. I deserve it." I swallow the pain seizing my throat. "I really do love you."

"I know you do." Her voice is barely a whisper.

"That's why I have to walk away."

And that's what I do.

I walk away and I don't look back.

Back at the dorm, I call a car then go upstairs to grab a shirt. RJ's already in bed asleep and doesn't so much as roll over before I leave again.

Sitting on the curb outside in the parking lot, my resolve hardens. For months, I had every chance to do the right thing. To tell Casey what happened. To stop myself from getting tangled up in her life where I had no business intruding. But I was selfish. Delusional. Constantly finding the rationale to excuse every boundary I broke, while knowing full well I would ruin her. Irrevocably. Steal her faith in humanity and turn her into another jaded, bitter girl destroyed by her piece-of-shit boyfriend.

I suddenly think about my mother. How everything would have been different if she never got sick. How grateful I am she can't see what I've become.

About an hour later, a car pulls up. The driver is rightly skeptical of my appearance and no doubt reaching for the pistol beneath his seat when I stand up from the curb.

"Where to?" he asks, wary of the answer.

"Police station."

CHAPTER 44
FENN

I'VE LOST ALL SENSE OF TIME IN THIS TINY ROOM. THE PALE BEIGE walls have started creeping in on me, seeming to inch closer every time I blink. My eyes fall shut for a second. A minute. I don't know anymore. Each time my one good eyelid flies open, another jolt hits the muscles in my face like a taser. My blood buzzes. On a hard metal chair, I sit at a small matching table and listen to the occasional footsteps and muffled conversations on the other side of the door.

When it suddenly swings open, I'm nearly knocked out of my seat by the commotion it brings.

"Fenn, Jesus. Did they do this to you? What happened?"

My father barges in first, carrying two cups of coffee. He places one in front of me, his expression flickering with shock.

I'd nearly forgotten the fight.

"No, it's fine," I answer hoarsely, realizing by the dryness in my throat I must've dozed off a little longer than I thought. "Just something I had to take care of."

Dad pulls a chair up to sit beside me, scrutinizing my discolored face. "What does that mean?"

"Unless Fennelly intends to press charges for an assault," a second voice speaks up, "I'd advise he not say more in this room."

A man in a crisp, dark suit stands against the door with a briefcase. He nods at a camera in the corner near the ceiling.

"Right," I say, nodding back.

I don't need a crystal ball to tell me he's my lawyer. He looks and sounds like one. Introduces himself as John Richlin, of Richlin, Ellis and Oates. It's promising that his name is first on the letterhead.

"Tell me what's going on," my father urges, more agitated than I can remember seeing him in years. But not mad, strangely enough.

Even stranger is the notion that I just saw him a couple days ago. It feels like a century has passed since I slammed my fist into my father's jaw.

The memory causes a rush of guilt to bubble to the surface. I don't know how I'm even able to look him in the eye right now. For the last several years, David's been a shit father, an absent one. By all measures, he deserves to get clocked in the jaw. And yet I feel sick to my stomach remembering what I'd done.

"Son," he urges when I spend too long staring at my torn, swollen knuckles. "Whatever it is, I'm here to help. Talk to me."

When the cops first left me in this interrogation room, I started practicing this conversation, but I never did get to a satisfying version before I fell asleep.

"I turned myself in," I finally say.

"For what?" he interjects before I can explain.

"Have you given a written confession?" demands Richlin.

Dad raises his hand to quiet the lawyer. "I don't understand. Tell me what happened. Is someone hurt?"

"Do you remember that accident at prom last year? With the headmaster's daughter?"

Confused, he searches my face. "The car that drove into the lake."

Nodding, I proceed to talk them through it. Taking them back to that night, as I've relived it hundreds of times since then. I explain how I covered for Gabe. How I suspect he was the one who drugged

Casey and left her in her car to die. That instead of telling the truth, I lied for him and hid the evidence.

"I admitted to everything," I finish. "I gave the police Gabe's jacket."

Without a word, Richlin walks out of the room. There's more muffled conversation in the hallway outside.

"Christ, Fenn." Dad sighs. "What were you thinking?"

"At the time? I thought I'd talk to Gabe and find out what happened. Get his side of things and help him figure out how to make it right. But then his parents shipped him off to military school and he was gone. I kept telling myself, soon, soon I'd hear from him and we'd get it all sorted out. Only that never happened and suddenly all this time had gone by."

I look up at him. Embarrassed. Ashamed. Feeling lower than dirt and totally undeserving of anyone's forgiveness. Still...

"I'm sorry, Dad. I fucked up bad."

"Hey." He grips my hands. "Hey, it's okay. We're going to figure it out, all right? I'm here. I'm going to take care of this."

"Why?" I find myself mumbling.

"Why what?"

"Why would you even bother?" I press my lips together, trying to control the wild stinging in my eyes. "I've been such an asshole lately. Last time we saw each other, I fucking *hit* you."

"You did."

"So go ahead, then." I let out a tired breath. "Disown me. Leave me in here to rot. God knows I'd deserve it."

There's been a lot wrong between us for a long time. I told myself I didn't need him. Didn't want him in my life. First chance I got, I was getting the fuck out and never going back.

But when the cops handed me the phone, there was only one number to dial.

"Listen, I was the adult, all right?" Dad lightly squeezes my left hand, which isn't nearly as beat up as the right one. "It was on me to do better. To keep our family strong after your mom passed. I didn't do my job and our relationship suffered as a result." He takes a deep breath, leaning closer as his voice softens. "I was lost without her. Watching her slip away was the hardest thing I've ever done in my life. I never imagined what life would be when she was gone, and suddenly I barely knew how to get myself out of bed in the morning. I spent too long feeling sorry for myself, instead of remembering you were right there suffering too. You needed your father. That's on me, Fenn. That was my fault."

"I didn't help," I admit. Those first few months after she died were hell. But it only got worse as the years went on. "I didn't have to run wild the way I did."

"No." He smiles sadly. "But that's also on me. I should have set boundaries. Been there more. It was easier to focus on work and leave you to your own devices than risk the hard conversations."

"So what now?" I ask, exhausted and entirely out of my depth.

"We try to do better. Forgive each other. Be a little kinder. We're so fortunate to have an opportunity to be a family again. With Michelle and RJ. I know she wants to have a relationship with you. And I'm hoping he's willing to get to know me better. Maybe, we can give it a chance?"

I hesitate, wondering if any of it is even possible. Forming a new family unit. Michelle's a nice enough lady, questionable taste in men and timing aside. RJ seems to like her well enough, anyway. And as stepbrothers go, I lucked out. Definitely not the worst roommate I could have ended up with this year. Given the circumstances, I guess it's not a terrible deal.

"Yeah," I tell him. "I think I can do that."

I'm not about to start feeling sorry for myself. There's no version of the last year where I'm the victim. Still, I get a little choked up at the thought we might have finally turned a corner. That there's a possibility I might get my dad back.

A quiet knock sounds at the door before the lawyer reenters.

"Here's where we stand," Richlin announces succinctly. "They've charged him with tampering, leaving the scene, obstruction, and failure to report."

"Christ," my father hisses.

That many, huh?

"It's entirely possible the DA will tack on a few more," Richlin adds.

"So, what do we do?" Dad asks impatiently.

"For now, I've secured his release to your custody. He'll have to appear before a judge in the next few days. In the meantime, I'll talk to the DA about how we might cooperate in exchange for certain considerations."

"Meaning what?" Dad demands, now sounding more like the man I grew up watching pace in his office chewing out subordinates.

"Maybe we get the charges reduced, if not dismissed. There are a lot of variables. Not the least of which is what the Ciprian boy has to say. I'd rather not make promises until I have more information."

"Let's get out of here," I tell my father. "I just want to go."

I'm starving. Exhausted. Barely able to keep my head up. The bruises and hairline fractures throb with every breath as any remnants of adrenaline are fully burnt out of my blood.

Mostly, I want to get the hell away from here before the cops change their mind and decide to throw me in a cell until my hearing.

Dad has his driver drop me off at the dorm. He tries to insist I stay at the hotel in town with him for the next couple of days—I'm suspended from classes, after all—but I convince him I need my own bed and a change of clothes.

RJ wakes up when he hears me come in from a shower.

"Sorry," I say quietly, putting away my toiletries. "Go back to sleep."

He sits up. Groggy. "What's going on? You going somewhere?" He rubs his eyes. "And what the hell happened with Lawson last night?"

My spine stiffens at the sound of Lawson's name. "Just go to sleep. Way too early for this."

It's nearly sunrise now. But RJ apparently decides it's not worth trying to go back to sleep. "What happened last night? Where did you disappear to after the fight?"

"I went to see Casey. Told her the truth."

"Whoa. How'd she take it?"

I shrug, because how do I even begin to answer that? "I don't know. I just sort of left after that."

"Okay…"

"And I went to the cops. Confessed to all of it."

He flinches, rubbing his eyes again as he slides up to lean against his headboard. "Oh. Shit, Fenn."

There's nothing funny about it, yet I chuckle to myself anyway. What a difference a day makes.

"You told them about Gabe?" RJ presses, suddenly wide awake.

His urgency is a bit confusing. "Yeah. I had no choice. I had to do right by Casey."

And weirdly enough, it felt liberating. Walking into a *police* station, willingly, had evoked a sense of freedom in me. I've been doing the wrong thing for so long that it felt good to finally do something right.

It felt right to do right.

The thought brings another chuckle, which fades when I notice RJ's unhappy expression.

"What? You're pissed I sold Gabe out?"

"Not pissed, no." He shoves hair off his forehead. "But I wish you'd run it by me first. Sloane and I aren't sure anymore if Gabe was the one driving the car."

I freeze. "What do you mean?"

"We followed a lead the other night," he explains. "I wanted to tell you about it today, or I guess, yesterday—" He glances at the sunlight peeking in through the window blinds. "But you were gone all day and night. Didn't reappear until the fights."

I nod. "I got a ride into town after I talked to Casey. Couldn't stand to be on campus. I had to get out."

"Casey?" he says blankly. "When did you talk to Casey?"

"I went over to her place this morning. That's when she told me about her and Lawson—"

"What about her and Lawson?" RJ's jaw drops before I can even answer. He's not a stupid guy, my stepbrother. "Oh, for fuck's sake. He didn't."

"He did." Then I forcibly exorcise all thoughts of my former friend from my head. I have too much other shit to deal with, primarily this bomb RJ just dropped in my lap. "What was the Gabe lead? And why the hell couldn't you text it to me?"

"I never leave a digital paper trail, man. You know that."

"You and your goddamn hacker morality code. What did you find out?"

"Gabe was with Mila all night. They left prom and went back to her dorm. She dropped him off here on campus in the morning."

I suck in a breath. "Are you serious?"

"That's what Mila says."

"Then why did he ask me to meet him?" I say, suddenly feeling confused. "We were supposed to hang out. He would have texted me to say he was going off with Mila instead."

"I don't know. Who knows how reliable she is, anyway. And even if they *were* together, it doesn't eliminate him completely. Mila doesn't remember the exact time they left the dance. Gabe could have slipped out with Casey, crashed the car, then came back and left with Mila."

"Christ. This is a mess."

"What happened with the cops?" he asks grimly.

"Not much. I gave them my confession and then sat alone in an interrogation room for four hours. Dad came and picked me up. He's staying nearby. Have to go talk to the lawyer again in a few hours."

"Fuck. What kind of trouble are we talking about?"

"Dad seems convinced they can keep me from doing jail time. I'm less confident."

We both sit on that possibility for a while. RJ watches me but doesn't speak, as if he's unsure what to say in this situation. I don't mind the quiet, though. After all the talking I've done tonight, I'm grateful for the silence.

CHAPTER 45
CASEY

SLOANE FROWNS AT MY NEARLY UNTOUCHED PLATE AS WE CLEAR the table from breakfast. Dad had already left for campus while my sister and I were still in bed. On school days, he's out of the house by seven thirty and in his office by quarter to eight.

"You okay?" she asks. "You don't look so good."

I scrape pancakes into the trash to the utter devastation of Penny and Bo, who are watching me with big, distraught puppy-dog eyes.

"Fine."

Sloane starts rinsing as I load the dishwasher. The tedium is helpful, sort of.

"Just tired," I add when she won't take her scrutinizing gaze off the side of my face. "And not in the mood for school."

We don't say much on the drive to St. Vincent's, parting without a word in the lobby. I feel like I'm moving in slow motion as I force my legs to carry me to my locker. Not even the sight of Jaz's grinning face can boost my lagging spirits.

"Where the hell have you been?" she accuses when I approach. She plants her hands on her hips. "I've been texting you all weekend."

"I know. I'm sorry." I open my locker, weary fingers flipping through the stack of textbooks. "It's been…intense."

"Care to share?"

With a sigh, I turn toward her, calculus book in hand. "Rain check? It's a lot to tell."

"Fine." She jabs my book with her index finger. "Lunch. You. Me. Gossip. Lots of it."

I crack a genuine smile. "Care to share?" I mimic. "What were those mysterious Saturday night plans you wouldn't elaborate on?"

Jaz shuts her locker and links her arm through mine. "I went out with Gray," she confesses.

My eyes widen. "No."

"Yes." Her lips quirk in a reluctant smile. "He's a goddamn choir boy, Casey."

"Not really, considering he's cheating on his girlfriend."

"I mean literally. He was a literal choir boy until he was thirteen." She sighs loudly. "Why didn't you warn me he was a nice guy? I don't like the nice ones. They're too…nice."

I start to laugh. "One, nice isn't awful. And two, I repeat my last point—how nice can he be if he's cheating?"

"Do you blame him considering who he's dating?" Jaz counters with a snort.

"Kind of, yeah. Doesn't take much effort to dump someone before moving on to somebody new."

Just ask Fenn. Not about the "somebody new" part, but how easily he's able to break up with someone.

I really do love you.

That's why I have to walk away.

The memory of Fenn's late-night visit and subsequent confession has been eating at me all morning. I hadn't slept a wink. Can barely focus on anything else.

Stop, I wanted to shout after him.

Stop.

Don't go.

I love you too.

He thinks he drove me into Lawson's arms, and he's not wrong. He had. But one night with another guy doesn't erase my feelings for Fenn. It doesn't erase months of long conversations and the intimate exchange of words, secrets, fears. He knows me better than anyone in this world, even my own family.

I understand now why he lied about prom night. He was trying to protect his friend. I'm not condoning it, but it makes sense. He's known Gabe since they were little kids. Gabe has been there for Fenn his entire life. Was there for him after Fenn's mom died. Of course he was torn about betraying that bond.

"In Gray's defense," Jaz says, jolting me back to the present, "he wanted to break up with Bree. I told him not to."

"Why the hell not?" I demand.

"Because it's been a week, and this fool is ready to declare his undying love for me." She snorts. "I'm not ready to husband up. Although he does have a great dick."

I choke out a laugh.

When we enter the classroom, the room quiets, a typical occurrence these days. As we pass their desks, Bree chatters on obliviously, telling Ainsley about some new makeup brand she's trying out. Ainsley shoots me a tiny frown but says nothing.

Ever since I poached Lawson from her, she's gone almost completely dormant. Every now and then a snarky word or two will spurt out, but for the most part, she keeps her mouth shut. If there's one good thing that came out of all the craziness these past couple of months, it's that I conquered my bullies. I guess that's something.

Lucas is sitting on the front step when Sloane pulls into our driveway after school. He'd texted to let me know he was coming by, but I didn't expect him to already be waiting. At our approach, he stands up, and although he offers his dimpled smile, I don't miss the flicker of concern in his expression.

"Hey," I say, greeting him with a quick hug.

"Hey."

"Come in."

Sloane unlocks the door and walks inside ahead of us, while the dogs dash around our legs. "Will you let them out to pee?" she asks me over her shoulder.

"Yeah, sure."

Lucas and I go outside through the back door. "I came to check on you," he says when we have a seat on the back patio.

"What for?"

"Well, uh, you know," he says hesitantly. "The big fight…"

"I don't understand. What big fight?"

"Fenn and Lawson went at it last night."

Fuck. Of course they did. My brain suddenly catches up, and I feel ridiculous for not anticipating the fallout.

"One of the guys broke the rules and filmed it, just because it was so brutal. I saw the video before Duke made him delete it." Lucas grimaces, apparently recalling whatever did that to Fenn's face. "It was uncomfortable to watch, not gonna lie."

I gulp. "So everyone knows."

"Yes and no. I mean, everyone put two and two together that it was about a chick, but I don't think anyone knows that chick is you."

That's a relief, at least. I can't imagine how mortifying it would be if all of Sandover knew I hooked up with Lawson. And if it ever got back to my dad… I shudder just thinking about it.

"Can I ask…" Lucas trails off, hesitant.

"I'd rather you didn't."

"Fair enough." He leans away, hands up in surrender. "New topic then: Snow Ball."

I recoil. "Really?"

"Really. I think we should go."

"Interesting, because I think we should skip it."

"Aw, come on. You went back to Ballard already and didn't have a panic attack. So let's do it. We can't miss what is certain to be a disastrously embarrassing rite of teenage passage."

"Sure I can."

"Jeez, Tresscott." Lucas has this annoyingly persuasive smile, and he deploys it with total disregard for life or limb. "You're killing me. Don't make me do this alone."

"You know," I tell him when he grabs my hands like he might get down on his knees to beg. "You could simply refuse to take part in such archaic rituals. I thought dances weren't your thing."

"They're not," he grumbles. "But I did some research for a couple of Ballard freshmen and we're doing the exchange at the dance."

"Exchange? Research? Have you become a secret agent since we last spoke?"

Lucas snickers. "RJ's bringing me into the business."

"The business? Like, his information racket?"

"Yeah."

I remember a conversation I had with RJ a while ago, in which he admitted he's a whiz at digging up information about people. A master of uncovering secrets. He bragged it was his superpower.

"I didn't realize RJ had dragged you into all of that."

"It's fun," Lucas says, his dimples making another appearance. "And you wouldn't believe how well it pays. I'm delivering two flash drives and collecting five hundred apiece. That's a grand for a few hours of online digging."

"That does sound lucrative."

"It is. Anyway, even if I didn't have another reason to be there, I would still ask you to go," he says firmly.

"Is that so? Shouldn't you be asking your gamer girlfriend?"

"Ballard doesn't let public school kids attend the dances," he reminds me, a bit smug. "So I guess I'm stuck with you."

"I don't know." I continue to vacillate. "I'm not in the mood for a huge social thing this weekend, Lucas."

"You ready for some tough love?" he says when I still won't

commit. "You need to shake Fenn and Lawson out of your head. Cut those emotional strings and fly free."

"Oh, yeah? And a dance is going to help me do that, huh?"

"If we crash the party together, sure." He sounds confident in his proposal. "Embrace the chaos, Case."

I can't help but laugh at his determination to put me in a better mood. And I suppose it's worked. I *do* feel better. And if I'm going to brave another dance, going with Lucas probably has the best odds of a good time.

"Fine," I relent. "If I don't change my mind before then."

"You won't."

After he's gone, I go to my room and do homework until dinner. Sloane left for a run while I was with Lucas, returning just as Dad finishes frying the garlic shrimp.

"Gonna grab a quick shower," she says as she flies up the stairs.

I carry the flavored rice and veggie dish I'd prepared and set it on the table. Ten minutes later, the three of us sit down for dinner. While we eat, I notice Sloane sending numerous uneasy looks my way, but when I ask her what's up, she says it's nothing and then focuses intently on her garlic shrimp.

I know my sister, though, so the moment Dad disappears into his study to read and drink his tea, I pounce on her.

"What's wrong?" I demand as we clear the table.

"So, there's been a development," she says in a soft voice, glancing toward the hallway. "I didn't want to say it in front of Lucas earlier, and Dad was already home when I got back from my run."

"What happened?" I already know this isn't going to be good news, so I brace myself for her response.

"Fenn turned himself in at the police station. He told them what he did on prom night. Stealing evidence, covering for Gabe. Everything."

All the breath leaves my body, my lungs seizing. "Are you serious?"

"Yup. RJ texted me the basics after school. I just met up with him on the path during my run and he filled me in on the details. There aren't many," she admits. "All I know so far is that Fenn confessed, his lawyer is handling things, and his dad flew in too. RJ says we should probably expect the cops to show up here and question you again."

I feel my face going pale. "Shit. Dad's going to freak."

I imagine he'll be livid when he learns that he's been letting me spend time with the guy who pulled me out of the car and left me there unconscious. Yet I'm not as worried about that as I am about the trouble Fenn might face.

My hands are weak and shaky as I place our plates in the sink. "Do you think he'll go to jail? Was he charged?"

She gives a grim nod and tells me the charges.

I'm queasy now, my stomach churning. "What if I vouch for him with the police? Tell them I know for a fact he wasn't driving."

"I don't think that's the issue here," Sloane says. "They don't suspect him of causing the accident. But he removed evidence from a potential crime scene after the fact. That's big."

It is big.

It's huge.

And the idea of Fenn being locked up for what he did makes me physically ill. For the rest of the evening, I'm on the verge of throwing up. Despite my better judgment, I can't stop myself from texting Fenn.

Me: I heard what you did. Are you okay? Any updates?

He doesn't respond, and I have a feeling it's purposeful. I can almost see him pacing his dorm room, telling RJ that he refuses to drag me back into this mess. *It's already bad enough she'll probably be questioned again*, he's saying. *I can't dump all my problems on her too.*

I can *hear* his voice in my head saying that. Firm. Thick with fortitude, determined to keep me out of it.

I broke you.

His gruff, sad words float around in my head, bringing a lump to my throat. Fenn thinks he's protecting me by ignoring me. He thinks he broke me.

I think maybe we broke each other.

The horrible notion stays with me all night. My phone stays silent. Hours pass and I can't fall asleep. I lie there in the dark, plagued with a constant stream of thoughts and a perpetual stomachache that doesn't go away. This hollow sensation in my gut won't abate, this nagging unease and emptiness inside me.

I thought I could punish Fenn for what he did, but trying to cut him out of my life only succeeded in ruining both of us.

Eventually I drift off. I know I do because it's around two in the morning when the nightmare forces me back into consciousness. I wake up coughing, gasping for air.

Oddly enough, I wasn't drowning. The house was on fire. I couldn't see the flames, but I could smell the smoke. It was filling my bedroom, seeping into every corner, curling up the walls toward the ceiling. Within seconds, the entire room was a suffocating gray cloud. I made the mistake of inhaling, and the smoke burned a path into my lungs.

I acted fast. Once I realized I couldn't stay in this room, I grabbed the shoebox from the nightstand and raced to the door. I could feel Silver's body jostling around in the box with each hurried step, and her loud cries pierced the quiet night. She was alive.

But now I'm awake. The bedroom isn't full of smoke. And Silver is still dead.

A sob flies out of my mouth, ripped from deep in my soul.

Oh my God. What the hell is wrong with me?

Tears flood my eyes, a gust of agony blasting into me, making me curl over on the bed. I suck in deep, agonizing breaths as shame and horror burn my throat.

I threw her in the garbage.

I threw her body in the fucking *garbage*.

With loud, heartrending sobs, I crawl out of bed and stumble to my feet. I can't remember the last time I felt this kind of pain. Not even the aftermath of the accident, the loss of all my friends, had triggered such a response.

I throw my door open and burst into the hall, startling Penny. She starts barking, and I don't even try to quiet her. I run on bare feet toward my father's bedroom.

He's already awake when I stagger inside, sitting up and flicking on the lamp by his bed. He takes one look at my tear-soaked face, hears the ragged noises coming out of my mouth, and flings his blankets aside.

"Casey," he says with the kind of horrified concern that only makes me cry harder.

"Where did you take the garbage?" I choke out, still struggling to breathe. I feel dizzy, swaying on my feet.

Dad steadies me with a strong, firm hand. "What? What's happening, sweetheart?"

Penny is still barking up a storm in the doorway, which draws Sloane out of her bedroom, her sleepy voice filling the hall. "What's going on—"

"Where did you put the garbage bag with Silver's body?" I plead, staring at my dad with huge, tear-filled eyes. "Where is she? We have to bury her."

"Casey—"

"Please," I beg. I launch myself at him and press my face against his shirt. "Why did you let me do that to her? Why?"

"Casey—"

"*Why?*" I start to shake, shudder, crying like a baby in his arms. "I'm so ashamed. Why did you let me do that?"

"Casey, we buried her."

CHAPTER 46
CASEY

My sister's gentle voice snaps me to attention. I lift my head and seek out her gaze.

"W-what?" I stammer. Breathing through the tears, I look from Sloane to our dad. "You buried her?"

He nods to confirm the claim. "We did."

"When?"

"After you threw out the box. You went up to your room, and we took her out of the garbage and buried her."

"Why?"

Sloane comes over and wraps her arm around my waist. She's taller than me, so she's able to rest her chin perfectly on my shoulder. "Because we knew you'd regret it if she didn't have a proper burial."

Another wave of emotion washes over me, weakening my knees. I sag into my sister's embrace.

"You were right—people do grow up," Dad agrees, reminding me of what I'd said that day in the kitchen. "And things do die. But the one thing that can never die is your compassion, sweetheart. You can't change what's imbedded deep in your soul. You loved that rabbit, just like you've loved every other injured stray you've brought home."

"Where did you bury her?" My tears are drying, slowly leaking from the corners of my eyes.

"Your sister picked a nice shady spot on the property behind the far shed, in that fenced-off area where the dogs don't go."

My breaths begin to steady. I swallow, speaking through the lump in my throat. "Can you take me there?"

Dad looks startled. "Now?"

"No, we can wait till morning," I say in a shaky voice. "Just don't forget."

"I won't," he promises, then grasps my chin with his hand and tips my head up. He searches my face. "Are you okay?"

I manage a nod.

"Are you sure? Do you want me to fix you a cup of warm milk? Hot tea?"

"I'm good," I assure him, and I'm not lying. I feel like a massive load has been lifted off my chest. Picturing Silver's body in the trash had ripped something apart inside of me, but those torn pieces of my heart are slowly stitching their way back together. "Let's all go to bed now."

"That's a good idea," he says.

"I'll walk you to your room," Sloane says, taking my hand.

We say good night to our father and go to my room, but rather than leave me to sleep, Sloane follows me in and sits on the edge of my bed.

"We need to talk."

"It's late, Sloane. And I just got off an emotional roller coaster. Can we save it for tomorrow?"

"No, we can't. In fact, this is the perfect time to discuss it. When you're feeling raw and your defenses are down."

"That sounds ominous." Swallowing my annoyance, I crawl back under the covers and draw them up to my neck. "Fine. Talk. I won't be able to fall asleep right away, anyway."

"Look, I get that you've gone through some rough shit. I do. And you have every reason to be upset and discouraged and anything else you're feeling." She exhales, shaking her head at me. "But whatever this act is you're doing, it doesn't suit you. This whole bad-girl routine has to stop. It's not you."

"It's not an act. It's a reaction to finally being completely fed up with the way everyone treats me like some fragile little mouse." Resentment tightens my throat. "Especially you."

"So that's why you're skinny-dipping with Mila and getting detention? Because your family is smothering you? Well, I'm sorry you're burdened with people who care about you."

I feel tired again. Exhausted. Of course. Sloane's always got to be the martyr. It's hilarious that she comes in here saying we have to talk about me, but somehow makes it about her.

"I don't want to fight with you, Sloane." My eyes start to feel hot again. "I just want you to understand me."

"I'm trying."

She scoots to the head of the bed, fishing my hand out from under the covers. I let her, only because her fingers are so warm and I'm suddenly feeling cold. Empty.

"Talk to me, Case. Please. I'm listening."

My heart squeezes. We've always been close. We didn't have a choice, I guess. Mom was gone, and the two of us were left to navigate a world hostile to girls without someone to teach us how to survive. Dad has done his best, but he can't possibly understand what we've been through. What we will go through. Since we were little, I've turned to Sloane to help me figure these things out. For better or worse, she's been my role model. Maybe that's why we fight so much lately. She has a hard time looking at herself in the mirror.

"I screwed up," I confess. "I hooked up with Lawson."

Her eyes nearly leap out of her skull. She opens her mouth then snaps it shut again.

"And I told Fenn. So, of course, he didn't take it well. Showed up here last night covered in blood and bruises."

She drops her head, biting her tongue. Her enormous show of restraint doesn't go unnoticed.

"I managed to make a mess of the whole thing, and I don't know how to stop making things worse."

After more silence than I'm comfortable with, Sloane readjusts her position, sitting cross-legged so she can peer down at me. "In a perfect world, what do you want out of all this?"

"This, what?"

"Well, do you want to be with Lawson?" She looks like she's holding back bile just getting the words out. It's sort of painful to watch.

"No. I don't think so. It just sort of happened."

She winces, nodding before I'm tempted to traumatize her with the details. "What about Fenn?"

If imagining me with Lawson makes her physically ill, I suspect that entertaining the idea of Fenn remaining an active part of my life nearly kills her.

"He knows what he did hurt me, and he really has tried to make it right. He showed up here last night to come clean and finally admit what happened at prom. And now he's gone and turned himself in. Might go to jail for what he did. And I know I'm supposed to be angry at him for that night, blame him for leaving me there and not telling me it was him, but I also wouldn't be alive if he hadn't shown up. I would have drowned." My throat clamps shut. "Like Mom."

"I get it. I feel the same way. I want to hate him, but it's hard," she admits, albeit grudgingly.

"I don't hate him at all. I've tried to, and I just can't. I'm stuck," I confess. "I can't move on from him and I'm so completely misera-ble all the time. He screwed up and he's been paying for it. But I'm paying for it too."

Fenn's greatest fault was trying to be everything to everyone. Protecting me and his best friend, who happened to find each other on opposite ends of a situation Fenn was unlucky enough to stumble into. He tried to do the right thing the wrong way. It was a mistake, and he's admitted as much.

"He hurt me, but I hurt him too. And I knew what I was doing when I did."

Sloane goes silent for a moment.

"Okay," she finally says. "Let me give you the benefit of my experience. Holding a grudge will never bring you comfort. It's not going to heal whatever wound his betrayal created. I thought I could write RJ off, but all I did was drive myself crazy. At some point, if hating them is hurting you, you have to try forgiveness."

"I want to forgive him." I bite my lip. "But doesn't that make me weak?"

"No," she says, her voice emphatic. "Not if the apology is sincere. Showing grace to someone you believe deserves it takes serious guts. Even more courage to give them another chance."

My teeth dig deeper into my lower lip. "It still feels like a weakness to me. Why am I always so quick to forgive people? Like, how many chances did I give Gillian this spring before I finally realized she was a snake? And even now, I can pretend to hold a grudge against her, but I don't. I told her off at a party, did I tell you that?"

"No, you didn't."

"It felt good in the moment," I admit. "I felt righteous. And then the next day, I felt bad about it." I laugh at myself. "I can't even stay pissed at a girl who whispered behind my back when she was supposed to be my best friend. I wish I was stronger about that sort of stuff. Like you."

"You are strong," she insists.

"Sure," I scoff.

"Casey. Look at me."

I force myself to meet her eyes.

"You're as strong as I am, maybe even more so. And you don't need to be like me. We're different people. You seem to think that my version of strength is the only one. That you're supposed to be tough and thick-skinned, hold grudges, tell bitches off at parties…"

I snicker softly.

"I will fight my enemies to the death. That's *my* strength. But yours? You will kill your enemies with kindness."

"That sounds so pathetic," I grumble.

"It's not. It's pretty fucking admirable. Kindness is a strength. Compassion, like Dad said. Forgiveness. Your version of strength is patience and resilience. Stop shying away from it. I wish I had even half of your softness." She sounds embarrassed now. "I've been trying to be softer lately. Not sure it's working."

Her words give me pause. I've always viewed Sloane as impenetrable, this force of nature stronger than any storm. Someone who faces down the world and never flinches. But if I think about it, she *has* softened a little since meeting RJ. Become a little more tolerant of others. Less rigid. Yet no less formidable. I'd still pick her first in dodgeball over anyone.

"There's nothing wrong with being gentle." She throws her arm over my shoulder and brings me in to lay my head in her lap. "Or a little vulnerable sometimes. Doesn't mean you aren't strong. I don't know anyone else who could have endured the year you've had and still be standing. Never forget who you are."

"Okay. And who am I?" I ask with a smile.

"You're Casey fucking Tresscott, and you're goddamn incredible."

CHAPTER 47
FENN

"You'll see, this is going to work itself out," Dad insists as he unpacks the paper bag of breakfast sandwiches he picked up from a café in town on the way to Sandover.

I grab a coffee and take a seat on the sofa.

"I'm not letting them throw you in jail for saving a girl from drowning. That's nonsense."

"It's not the rescuing part they charged me with," I remind him.

Dad gives me an admonishing glance. Incredibly, he's not yet come around to having a grim sense of humor about the whole thing. And while I appreciate his attempts to reassure me, I'm less optimistic about my fate.

"If that police department had done their damn jobs last year, we wouldn't be in this position. I'm not about to let them string my son up because they still haven't caught the real criminal. For that matter, the security at Ballard failed abysmally. Drugs on campus. Students wandering off. There's enough culpability to go around. You're the least of their problems, Fenn."

Maybe it's the sheer number of charges I hadn't considered that has me spooked. Or the way the thoroughly embarrassed police chief snarled and glared at me over his shoulder as he stood at the end of the hall getting the brief from his intake officer after I announced why I'd dragged myself into their lobby.

"Egg or no egg?" Dad asks RJ as he reads the scribble on the sandwich wrappers.

"No egg. Thanks."

RJ grabs a sandwich and a coffee and keeps a cautious distance as he eats at his desk. I think he's still worried that if I end up behind bars, he'll get saddled with the guilt trip. Ultimately, it was his digging around that precipitated my sudden eruption of conscience.

I've tried to tell him he's in the clear, but I suppose when all the facts become known, he's worried David might not see things the same way. If I have any say in it, RJ has nothing to worry about.

"I don't think it's up to us," I tell Dad, who's getting himself all spun up again.

"We'll see," Dad says, accepting the challenge.

Much as my appetite has evaporated over the last few hours, I shove some food in me anyway. It helps settle the nerves. A little.

I'm slugging back the rest of my coffee when Dad's phone rings. He yanks it out of his pocket, muttering, "Finally." Then he barks, "What's the latest, John?"

He strides away, pacing with the phone to his ear and his eyes on the floor. He nods a lot, which doesn't feel like a terrible sign.

"Yeah?" His head snaps up. "You're certain?"

My father's attention falls on me, but I can't decipher his expression.

"All right. We'll circle back this evening, then." He pockets the phone, a strange smile on his face as he turns toward us. "That was the lawyer. You're off the hook."

RJ's chair creaks as he rocks forward. "Wait, what?"

"Seriously?" I nearly choke trying to swallow. "How?"

"They dropped the charges. John still isn't clear as to why. He hadn't even gotten the DA on the phone yet."

"So that's it?" RJ asks, echoing my own confusion. "Fenn's in the clear?"

"Appears so. John's going to see what else he can find out, but it looks like we got lucky this time. Clearly, they came to their senses and realized there was no benefit in demonizing a good Samaritan for their own failures."

Call me a pessimist, but I have a hard time believing the police woke up this morning deciding to be nice guys. In my experience, that's not their standard operating procedure. RJ and I exchange a look across the room. If this year has taught us anything, it's to wait for the other shoe that's undoubtedly about to drop.

Nothing is this easy.

"Okay, then." Dad shakes his head, looking pleased. "I'll head back to the hotel and check out." He pauses, giving me an uncertain smile. "Unless you'd like me to stick around a while? Make sure everything's settled?"

"Huh? No, get out of here. You're cramping our style," I say with a grin.

"Or you can come home for a few days. Get your mind off things. I can tell the headmaster there's a family matter. Both of you," he adds to RJ.

"It's fine," I insist. "I'm good here."

"Same," RJ pipes up. "Just don't make me go to class. I thought this waiting-for-the-lawyer-to-call vigil was going to last all day. I mentally prepared myself for it, therefore I shouldn't be forced to attend classes."

I waggle my eyebrows at my dad. "If RJ leaves now, he could make it for second period…"

"Fuck off," my stepbrother grouses, throwing his empty wrapper at me.

I catch it easily. "Hey, it's not my fault *you're* not suspended."

"Not something to brag about, Fennelly," Dad scolds, but his lips are twitching with humor. "All right. I'm heading out."

We aren't a hugging family—we've barely been a prolonged-period-in-the-same-room family for the last several years—but in the interest of reconciliation, I get up and give him an awkward one-armed hug.

"Thanks for coming," I say gruffly. "It means a lot."

"Of course." The hug is uncomfortable for both of us, out of practice as we are. Still, it's progress. "Anything you need, I'm always here. You too, RJ." Dad grabs his jacket and slips it on. "Okay, I'll get out of your hair. Anything you think of, give me a call. We'll see you on Thanksgiving." He stops at the door. "Oh, and I do expect both of you to join us for a family trip over the holidays. Michelle's not taking no for an answer."

I roll my eyes, because of course he'd use this ordeal as a bargaining chip on the dreaded Christmas vacation.

"Yeah, okay," I groan. "But this is blackmail, you know."

"Tell her to go easy on the mother-son pedicures," RJ interjects. "And we get our own room."

Satisfied, Dad nods. "Good. Talk soon."

There's a learning curve to this for all of us. We're a bunch of loners trying to figure out how to live with one another. How to make something new out of bits and pieces of our old lives. I have a feeling it's bound to get messy, but I guess it's past time we stop resisting the inevitable. We're a family now. Come hell or high water.

"So that's something." RJ carries his breakfast to the coffee table to sit beside me on the sofa. "What do you think happened?"

"No idea. Maybe it's like he said. They didn't want the negative attention?"

"Somehow I doubt it."

As if spinning our wheels manifested it, there's a soft knock on our door. RJ quickly hops up to answer it.

"Hey. Is Fenn here?"

Casey.

My heart stops at the sound of her voice.

I leap to my feet, peering over RJ's shoulder to find her giving me a tentative smile. She texted yesterday asking if I was okay and if there were any updates, so I guess Sloane relayed to her that I'd turned myself in. It took all my willpower not to call her, to turn to her for comfort and hear her say that everything was going to be all right.

I resisted that urge because it's time to stop dragging Casey Tresscott into all my messes. She doesn't deserve the turmoil, the uncertainties. I meant every word when I told her I had to walk away from her. I've already caused so much damage in her life, broken off pieces of her innocence one by one. I'd never be able to live with myself if I hurt her again.

And yet here she is on my doorstep, those blue eyes full of concern for me.

"Can we talk alone?" she asks.

RJ looks to me for an answer, noting my slight nod before he holds the door open to let her in. "No sweat."

A second later he's gone, silently shutting the door behind him.

I'm suddenly terrified to be in a room with her. Embarrassed for what I've done to her and still feeling my own fresh wounds. Overwhelmed by the history between us, yet also the sense we've become strangers, two people who've forgotten how to talk to each other.

She smooths out the front of her purple sweatshirt, the oversized one she likes to pair with black leggings. It's one of my favorite outfits. Cute and unassuming and so perfectly Casey.

"You probably don't want to see me, I know, but this felt like something I had to say in person."

"Why aren't you at school?"

She shrugs. "The answer to that is related to what I came here to say."

"Okay," I say awkwardly.

I sit on the edge of my bed and nod to invite her over. Seems rude somehow to have a heart-to-heart over a half-eaten sausage-and-egg sandwich.

"I just got back from the police station."

My gaze flies to hers. "What? Why?"

"The lead detective who worked my case—Carillo? He's the one with the forehead mole and the terrible haircut?"

I snicker. "Yeah. I know who you mean."

"He called early this morning and asked us to come into the station. Me and my dad. So we drove out there and sat down with Carillo and the police chief—can't remember his name. They asked me a bunch of questions about you and Gabe and prom night."

"Yeah. I figured that would happen. What did you tell them?"

"Exactly what I told them last time. We went over what I remember—and what I don't remember. I told them about the flash of memory I had about offering someone a ride and how they may have been wearing pink, but they sort of brushed it off."

Anger tightens my chest. Would it kill these assholes to take this case seriously? A girl almost died, for fuck's sake.

Casey sees my frustration and nods. "Trust me, I know. They're basically useless. Anyway, they listed all the charges against you and said they wanted to discuss the next steps with us."

My shoulders snap straight. It suddenly occurs to me I know where this is going.

"I told them that as far as I'm concerned, you risked your own safety to rescue me that night," Casey continues, confirming my suspicions. "Whatever else you did or didn't do, it doesn't matter. You had nothing to do with the drugs or driving the car into the lake. You couldn't be sure what the jacket meant—all you had was a theory. I said that you made a mistake, but you're not a criminal. And that they'd never get me to testify against you."

"Damn it, Casey."

I can't sit still and launch myself off the bed, raking both hands through my hair.

"I was ready to accept responsibility for what I did," I tell her. Frustrated. "You don't need to protect me."

"Do you remember what you said to me the night after the party last month? After you carted me away like a caveman?" She cocks her head. "You said you'll be here to save me every time. Well, that's a two-way street, Fenn. I protected you, just like you've always tried to do for me."

I drop down on the bed beside her. "You shouldn't have done that."

"Agree to disagree," she says with the slightest hint of a smile. "So, I take it they already delivered the news? That they're dropping all charges?"

"Yeah, the lawyer called right before you got here. I'm in the clear."

She nods, pleased. "Perfect. Okay. Now that that's out of the way, which would you like to hear first—the good news or the bad news?"

"Huh?"

"Good or bad? Pick."

"Good," I answer on instinct, because I've received enough bad news this year to last a lifetime.

"The good news is, my dad recognizes that you saved my life and has agreed to let us keep seeing each other. As in, actual dating. Not just friendship."

My heart stops dead in my chest.

"What?" I don't understand what she's saying to me.

She ignores my stunned expression. "The bad news is, we're relegated to walks with the dogs for a month and maaaybe the occasional dinner invitation. With Dad present, of course. After that, movie nights might be on the table. Oh! More good news: We can go to the Snow Ball together. Quickly followed by bad news: Lucas, Sloane, and RJ have to come with us, and we're not allowed to slow dance." Casey grins. "But what he doesn't know can't hurt him."

I'm dazed. Just staring at her, unable to comprehend what is happening.

"Casey," I finally say.

"Uh-huh?"

I swallow the lump that rises in my throat. "We said goodbye."

"No, *you* said goodbye. And I'm rejecting it. I want to be with you, Fenn." She licks her lips, then presses them together. Unsure. "Do you want to be with me?"

The lump gets larger, choking me. I clear my throat. "Why are you so determined to keep giving me more chances?"

"Because you're worth it."

I start to laugh, utterly amazed by this girl. I swear, I don't know what to make of her.

"But if we do this," she continues, "I need you to let go of this idea you have about how I'm supposed to be. Sweet, innocent Casey, who needs your constant coddling. I don't need that, Fenn. You didn't know me well before the accident. Yes, I can be sweet, but I also lash out when I'm mad. I can be inexperienced, but also want to go skinny-dipping. I might wake up from nightmares sometimes or cry over an injured animal, but I'm not weak."

"I know that," I say thickly.

"I'm not the same person I was back in the spring," she admits. "I feel like parts of me have changed. I feel stronger. And I can't go forward with you unless I know you can accept me for exactly who I am, not who you want me to be."

"Casey, you're one of the strongest people I know. Hands down," I assure her, smiling faintly. "And I will be by your side when you hand those bitchy girls at school their asses or when you want to go skinny-dipping or do something wild and crazy. I'll be by your side no matter what. Ride or die. So, yes, of course I accept you for who you are." I stare at her. "What I don't get is how you're able to accept *me*? I screwed us up."

"Look. You lied," she says frankly. "That hurt me. But I also understand that you found yourself in an impossible predicament and made a split-second decision that turned out to be a mistake. You've owned up to it. That's the best I can ask."

"If I'd been a better person, I wouldn't have waited so long," I point out.

"Either way, I forgive you."

Those three little words affect me in a way I didn't expect. It feels like coming up for air. I've spent months clawing for the surface, never getting any closer to the light, and then suddenly, sky.

My voice shakes as I say, "You don't know how much that means to me."

"I do," she says softly. "Because I need to ask your forgiveness too. I was so angry, I didn't care if you got hurt. That wasn't fair either. I'm sorry, Fenn. About Lawson and all of it. I wish I could make it better, but I know nothing I say changes what's already done."

The reminder is like a punch to the gut. I didn't realize until she'd dropped that bomb how deep she could cut me. How dangerous she could be. Even when she wasn't trying. Even though I deserved it.

"You don't belong to me," I say through the gravel in my voice. "I have no right to tell you what to do or who to be with."

As much as I'd love to feel sorry for myself, it's Lawson who owed me something. He's the one who should have stopped it. If he gave a damn at all about our friendship. Clearly I expected too much from him.

"That's the thing," Casey says, sliding her hand into mine. "This time I'm the one asking for a second chance." She laces our fingers. "Maybe we're doomed. Maybe we'll screw it up again. But I'm sick of pretending I don't want to be with you. That my heart isn't breaking every time we walk away from each other again."

"Casey…" I trail off, unable to find the words.

"Do you still have the same feelings for me?" she asks so hopefully, I nearly fall apart.

"You know I do. But I don't want to be the reason you settle for less than total happiness."

She squeezes my hand and there's a strange kind of sparkle in her expression. "You want me to be happy?"

"More than anything."

"Then let's forgive each other, Fenn. Let's put prom night behind us and start fresh. Or, rather, go back to how it was before all the secrets and lies came out." She strokes my knuckles with her fingertips. "Take me to the Snow Ball this weekend."

Fuck me. I was ready to do it, to accept my fate. I said goodbye and left her to live a life free of all the ways I'd messed her up.

But damned if I can say no to her. This girl has a power over me that is absolute. I'm nothing if not completely at her mercy.

"Okay."

A brilliant smile fills her face. "Okay? You'll be my date?"

"Of course." I bring her hand up to press my lips against it. "I'll be your date."

CHAPTER 48
CASEY

THE THEME IS WINTER THREW UP ON ANTARCTICA AND THEN Antarctica threw up on *Frozen*. I've seen enough papier-mâché penguins to last a lifetime, and I'm not quite sure who thought it was a good idea to recycle the sets from the Christmas play and stick cardboard cutouts of Elsa and Anna in the sleigh instead of Santa. For a school that receives millions of dollars in yearly donations, you'd think they'd hire some expensive designer to decorate the dances. Although I do applaud whoever hung up the hundreds upon hundreds of silver-glitter-frenched paper snowflakes dangling from the ceiling. That's dedication.

"This is why people drop acid," Fenn leans in to tell me, his gaze focused on the undulating glittery snowflakes above our heads.

We enter the gym to the chorus of some old indie-rock track I never remember the name of. My mom used to play it in the car when we were little. Reminds me of taking the long way home from the grocery store or sitting in the driveway to let the song finish. I don't even know if they're real memories or my imagination filling in the gaps of stories Sloane used to tell me about her. But they feel real when I hear the melody, and it makes me smile.

"You look amazing." It's the third time he's complimented my dress, smiling at its short flouncy skirt.

A few days ago, Sloane and I went shopping in Parsons, and this cute silver number called out to me the moment I saw it. Silver in honor of my beloved Silver, whose tiny gravestone I left a bouquet of yellow mums on this week.

"You don't have to keep saying that," I say shyly.

"Yes, I do."

He's not too shabby either. Tall and broad, showing everyone else how a suit's supposed to be worn. I can't stop running my hands down the soft, crisp length of his lapels. It's oddly hypnotizing.

"We can leave anytime if you're uncomfortable," he whispers into my ear as he rests his hands on my hips, dancing close to me.

"No, I'm having a great time," I assure him. "Kind of feels like we time traveled here, you know? Got a do-over."

He smiles and pulls me tighter against his chest, his fingertips gently drawing circles against the small of my back. "I know what you mean. I wasn't sure I'd ever come back to one of these things. Definitely wouldn't have guessed we'd be here together."

"I've been thinking about it…" I start.

"Yeah?" Fenn looks down to meet my eyes.

"Where we went wrong the first time."

"All right…"

He's understandably wary. We did make each other a promise that if we were going to do second chances, it meant leaving the past behind. No throwing our mistakes in each other's faces every time we have an argument. We now operate in a strict guilt-free zone.

"We have to agree to trust each other with the truth."

His shoulders relax on a relieved exhale. "That sounds reasonable."

"Like, I'd rather someone be honest with me than try to spare my feelings, you know?"

"Same."

"There's a kind of manipulation in withholding information. I don't like feeling controlled. And I'd never want to make you feel that way either."

Fenn kisses the top of my head. "I can make that deal. You have my word—I'm never going to let you down again."

"You're allowed to screw up sometimes," I remind him with a playful yank on his lapels. "Let's just try not to make the same mistakes twice."

His eyes wander over my shoulder. "Off-topic... How long you think before Sloane is off surveillance duty?"

I follow his gaze when he spins us around to see Sloane and RJ conspicuously monitoring us through the crowd.

"She isn't subtle, is she?"

"As an air-raid siren."

I snicker, and we gradually shimmy our way farther from their prying eyes.

"She'll get there eventually," I tell him. "Sloane needs a little time to process the new normal and trust you again."

"I think you underestimate the pleasure she takes in despising me."

Yeah. Those two are a good distance from becoming friends again. As much as Sloane has preached forgiveness lately, she's not quite ready to trust Fenn yet, least of all with me. Still, it's enough that she's agreed not to give me grief about us getting back together.

"If it's any consolation, she's going away to college next year. Even Sloane can't have eyes everywhere at once."

He gives me a skeptical frown, which is sort of adorable. She puts the fear of death in his soul. I guess that's what big sisters are for.

"Speaking of trusting people again..."

His shoulders stiffen. Fenn knows exactly what I'm going to say before I even get the words out and rolls his eyes on a frustrated sigh.

"Sulk all you want," I tease.

"Let's not ruin a good night." His voice goes rough. Tired.

"I'm sorry, but you can't forgive me and still hold a grudge against Lawson."

"Counterpoint: Yes, I can."

"Fenn."

"I'm a multitasker."

He's a pain in the ass.

"What does it matter anymore? We're together. You're the one I want. Can't you let him off the hook?"

"It's not about jealousy," he insists.

"Then what?"

Fenn's voice grows more agitated. "He betrayed our friendship. I'd never have done that to him."

"Maybe not premeditatedly..."

For that, I get a chastising glare. "You didn't owe me any loyalty, Case. We weren't together. But Lawson *did* owe me that. So, no, I can't forgive him."

"It's not like he pursued me," I argue, while fighting an inward battle between guilt and frustration. "It just happened."

"Sorry, I don't believe that. Lawson's a conniving piece of shit. Everything he does is designed to inflict maximum damage. He can go to hell."

Fenn's demeanor takes a drastic dive, and it's clear we're not coming to any compromises about this tonight, so I let it go. No sense ruining the whole night over it. Better to let some time pass when cooler heads can prevail and the wound isn't as fresh.

We take a break from dancing, and Fenn goes to grab us a couple of drinks while I dart off to use the restroom. As I reach the double doors, Gray Robson intercepts me, flashing an awkward smile. He looks like a movie star with his black suit and handsome clean-shaven face.

"Casey. Hey."

"Hi." I offer a quick smile.

"I, ah…" He slides his hands into his trouser pockets. "Have you spoken to Jaz lately?"

Damn it. Jaz told me this week that Gray's been pushing her about dating officially and she's not on board. I sort of regret introducing those two. Especially now, when I can feel Bree's murderous gaze boring into me and Gray. She's standing at the punch table with Ainsley, and while she might not be the brightest bulb in the bunch, even Bree knows when her boyfriend's up to something shady.

"I talk to her every day at school," I say before edging toward the exit. "Sorry, can we do this later? I need to hit the ladies' room."

His low, frustrated voice stops me. "Could you just tell her to call me? Please?"

My response lacks any sympathy. "Go dance with your girlfriend, Gray," I tell him, then duck out the doors.

I'm halfway down the hall when I hear footsteps behind me. For fuck's sake. I spin, expecting to find that Gray had followed me.

But it's not Gray.

I freeze on the spot.

"Hey," Lawson says.

My heartbeat accelerates like a race car as he slowly approaches me. Like Fenn, he can pull off a suit like nobody's business. And I'm startled to notice he'd cut his hair, the light-brown strands no longer around his shoulders, but curling under his ears.

We haven't spoken since the night in the greenhouse. I hadn't known what to say to him, and clearly he returned that sentiment because he hadn't reached out either.

"Hey," I answer softly. "I…um… how've you been?"

"Been great," he drawls, then offers a cheeky smile. "Am I ever anything but?"

I see right through the cavalier response. "You're a terrible liar, Lawson."

A thoughtful gleam enters his gray eyes. "Not usually, no. Only around you, Casey."

I don't know why, but my pulse quickens at that. "I've tried talking to Fenn on your behalf," I start.

"Of course you have." He laughs under his breath. "But don't. He has every right to despise me." Lawson moves closer, his voice lowering. "I only came out here to check on you. I never even messaged you after that night to see if you were okay. That was wrong."

"I was okay," I promise him. "Still am."

A soft, sad smile touches his lips. "All right. Good." Now he steps away from me. "That's all I wanted." Another backward step. "I'm glad everything worked out for you two. Truly."

"Thanks," I murmur.

"Take care of Bishop. Someone's gotta look out for him now that I've been exiled."

Guilt pricks at my chest. "Lawson…"

"Joking, Tresscott. Just a joke." He starts to walk away, then stops again, turning to face me. I can't for the life of me decipher his expression. "Can I ask you something?"

I swallow. "Sure."

"You and me…" His cheeks hollow slightly, as if he's biting the inside of his mouth. "It was just a…random thing? There were no, uh, feelings in play, right?"

I hesitate. "No feelings in play," I confirm.

Lawson nods. "Yeah. Okay." Regret flashes across his face. "We could've been friends. I'm sorry I fucked that up."

Then he disappears through the double doors, which swing shut behind him.

He's right. We could have been friends. I forcibly push the sad notion out of my head and finally, blessedly, make use of the ladies' room.

When I come out a minute later, I bump into Lucas, who's exiting the men's room directly across from the ladies'.

"Fancy meeting you here." Those dimples pop out.

"Fancy," I agree.

Laughing, we converge in the center of the hall. Technically, Lucas came to the dance with us, driving to Ballard with Fenn and RJ, while I drove over with Sloane, but I've barely seen him since we got here.

"How was your mission?" I tease. "Did you make your drop?"

Lucas snorts. "Stop making it sound so…illegal."

I tip my head in challenge. "Isn't it, though?"

"All the information I gathered for these dudes was readily available on the internet." He blinks innocently. "No hacking involved whatsoever."

"Uh-huh. Suuuure." I reach out and tug his lapel in accusation. "I can't believe I'm friends with a criminal."

"Casey, sweetie, you're friends with many criminals," Lucas answers with a laugh.

I can't help but join in. He has a point. All the guys at Sandover have committed one infraction or another.

"I guess if I had to pick favorites of all the criminals I know, you'd be in the top three," I say generously. I reach out to fix his boutonniere, which is a bit crooked.

"Thanks," he says.

"This is cute," I tell him, touching the boutonniere. My fingertips sweep over the soft petals of the rose, a shade of hot pink that—

"I can give you a ride."

My fingers freeze. I stare at the pink rose, my throat going arid as a rush of déjà vu washes over me.

"Are you sure you don't mind?"

"Of course not. I'm ready to go anyway. I'm starting to get a headache, I don't know why. I've been staying hydrated."

"Okay, cool. I'll be quick," Lucas promises. "I just need to drop this off for Gabe and then we can head home."

Horror slices into me, rendering me speechless for a moment.

"Casey?" Lucas says in concern. "You okay?"

I edge away from him. Breathing hard, I press my back against the cool metal lockers that practically sizzle on contact with my suddenly flushed skin.

"It was you," I say.

More memories surface, playing through my jumbled mind.

"Casey, wake up! What the hell did you take!"

His dark eyes flicker uneasily. "What are you talking about?"

"It was you," I repeat. "You're the one who drove us into the lake."

CHAPTER 49
CASEY

EVEN IF I DIDN'T HAVE A CLEAR MENTAL IMAGE OF LUCAS SLIDING behind the wheel of the car, of me buckling my seat belt in the passenger seat, the panic that fills his eyes is enough of a confirmation.

"It was you," I say for the third time.

Those three words dominate my vocabulary now, as my brain struggles to make sense of why Lucas would do this.

It was him, though. He was wearing this exact suit, with that same rose pinned to his lapel. Well, not the *same* rose. The one from prom night died months ago. But the color. I remember the hot pink color. And I remember reaching out to straighten the boutonniere because it was crooked, same way I'd done now.

I remember feeling like my temples were going to explode, and so when Lucas said he had to run an errand for his brother, I offered to give him a ride.

I remember walking to the parking lot and unlocking the car, feeling my head get foggier and heavier.

"I told you my head hurt," I mumble, my breaths coming out shallow. "It hurt too much to drive."

Beads of sweat dot Lucas's forehead. He doesn't speak. He stares at me as if he'd seen a ghost. Still as a statue.

"You took the keys from me. You said we'd quickly go to the boathouse and then you'd drive us home." My temples begin to throb, just as they had that night. "I don't know why you lost control of the car. I…" I struggle to piece it together. "The drug you gave me had kicked in by then—"

"I didn't drug you," Lucas blurts out, his face paling. "Jesus, Casey! You think I drugged you?"

"You drugged me," I say absently, barely registering his denial. "That's why you offered to drive—"

"No, I drove because you weren't feeling up to it," he protests.

"—and then somehow you lost control and we wound up in the lake. And you left me in the car and ran away."

"No," Lucas moans. "That's not how it happened."

My ears ring. I suddenly feel a burst of pain blooming in my forehead, the result of my head smacking against the dashboard. Phantom pain flares across my chest, from the diagonal bruise left by the seat belt that kept me trapped as the water rose around my legs and my dress turned to liquid.

I can barely feel my lips when I speak. "Then how did it happen?"

"I thought you were dead."

His confession, laced with misery and bone-deep shame, echoes in the hallway. It triggers a rush of fury, white-hot and raw, vibrating in my fingertips.

"What happened in that car, Lucas?"

"It started even before the car," he says with a strangled groan. He starts to pace, to move erratically. Eyes darting as if he might run away or charge me at any moment. "Gabe was dealing at the dance, but Mila was all over him and he wanted to go home with her. Hook up, whatever. He was supposed to meet Fenn, but his phone died, so he told me to tell Fenn his plans changed. He gave me his stash and asked me to take it to the boathouse. He used to hide his shit under a broken floorboard out there whenever he came to Ballard."

Lucas stops pacing, pausing right in front of me. Every instinct tells me to get away from him while I can, but I want to know what else he can tell me about prom. And I'm terrified at what might happen if I leave and he chases me.

"I borrowed his jacket, was all ready to go. I couldn't find Fenn, so I was typing out a message telling him not to meet Gabe, but I never sent it because you interrupted me and then I forgot. You asked where I was going and said it was too far to walk to the boathouse and offered me a ride. You said you wanted to leave anyway because your head hurt."

"Because you drugged me," I spit out.

"I didn't." His face crinkles with anguish. Fists balled. "Swear to God, I didn't, Casey. Whatever you took, or were given, it happened before you and I ever got in that car together. By the time we started driving, you were already fucked up. Barely walking. Couldn't keep your eyes open. I honestly thought you had a migraine at first. You kept covering your eyes like the light was hurting them. I put you in the front seat just to keep you from collapsing in the parking lot, and the whole way to the boathouse, I was trying to keep you awake."

He slams both fists into his forehead, visibly anxious. "I suddenly had a bad feeling you were suffering from more than a migraine. I even wondered if maybe you'd gotten a concussion at the dance somehow. I kept reaching over to tap your cheek, telling you not to go to sleep. It was too dark outside. I lost the path and the car skidded, and suddenly there was water coming up over the windshield."

Lucas sinks to the floor, huddled against the lockers.

"There was blood coming down your forehead. Water was pouring in the car. You weren't moving. I tried to feel for a pulse, but there was nothing," he says, holding his knees to his chest. "Not even a flutter, Case. I thought you were dead."

I inch away from him in shock.

"And I panicked hard. My dad would literally murder me if I got arrested for crashing a car with a drugged-out dead girl at prom. And they'd say I roofied you or something. I mean, what the fuck was I supposed to do?" He makes a choking noise. "The water was coming so fast. And you were already gone. I thought you were, anyway. I checked for a pulse over and over, I swear. I never would've left you if I knew you were alive."

He spares a desperate glance at me, tinged with sorrow. I stand plastered against the opposite wall of lockers, chest tight, breathing shallow. I'm glued in place now. Unable to move if I wanted to, thanks to the phantom sensation of the water climbing up my legs.

"My jacket got caught on the seat belt and wouldn't budge, so I just took it off. I grabbed Gabe's bag and got the hell out of there. Ran as fast as I could all the way to the main road and grabbed an Uber outside the Ballard gates. When I got back to the dorm at Sandover, the housefather caught me coming out of the stairwell. I was soaking wet and looking guilty as shit. He made me open the bag—and what can I say at that point? I told him the drugs belonged to Gabe."

Lucas bites hard on his bottom lip. He looks like he's about to cry.

"I wasn't going down for that shit. No fucking way. But I knew Gabe would be furious with me, so I begged Dad not to tell him I was the one who ratted him out. I don't know what he told him. Gabe was gone, and I was here. And you... I thought you were dead."

"The red lights," I whisper.

He looks up. "Huh?"

"Do you ever see the red lights?"

"What are you talking about?"

"I see them. Every night. Because you left me there."

He scrambles to his feet and rushes at me. "I know. Fuck, I know." Lucas puts his hands against the locker on either side of my face. "I'm so sorry, Casey. I messed up so bad. I panicked, I admit that. But I never wanted you to get hurt. The crash was an accident—"

"You left me to die, Lucas." I shove him off.

"I thought you were already dead," he insists. "You know me, Casey. You *know* I'd never hurt you."

"But you did. And then you kept it a secret all these months! You let me torture myself obsessing over what happened that night. You even pretended to be helpful when I told you what I remembered! 'Maybe it was a girl,'" I mimic, scoffing at him.

He grabs my arm before I can scurry off, keeping me in place. "I'm sorry. Please. Don't go. I need you to believe me."

"Let me go," I say softly.

"You forgave Fenn," he says, pleading at me. Squeezing my arm too tight. "That means you can forgive me too."

"Let go of my arm—"

I barely get the last word out before he's suddenly snatched away from me.

My heart is pounding as I watch RJ and Fenn restrain Lucas by his shoulders. Sloane rushes past them to wrap a protective arm around me.

Lucas doesn't fight them. His entire body seems to sag, muscles giving out as he nearly collapses. RJ yanks him back up, but not violently. I don't know how much they heard of the conversation, but I get the sense they understand that Lucas isn't a danger to anyone.

Sadness grips my heart as our gazes lock.

"I'm sorry, Case," he whispers.

"I know," I say.

Because I can see his remorse, his shame, practically clawing its way out of his skin. His dazed eyes unable to focus as he sways on his feet.

He did a terrible thing to me. There's no denying that. But I think I believe him when he says he wouldn't have left if he thought I was alive.

Still, that doesn't stop me from nodding when my sister says she's calling the police. It isn't until she tells me the cops are on their way that I release a breath and peel my fingernails from the red, punctured skin of my palm.

CHAPTER 50
SILAS

LOOKING AT HER NOW, I DON'T KNOW HOW I PUT UP WITH AMY FOR so long. She's always been so insecure. Paranoid to a fault. Even tonight, weeks since we broke up, she still can't resist the way her eyes wander in my direction. Sparing glances over her shoulder when she thinks I'm not looking. It's so obvious. She believes she's got the upper hand by avoiding me all night, but it's not punishment when I know she's obsessed with me noticing she's ignoring me. It's so high school, I want to gag.

"Are we ever going to come to one of these things where Casey doesn't set off a manhunt?" I say to Lawson, who's standing beside me next to the empty photo booth.

Moments ago, it was like déjà vu all over again. A sudden frantic sprint to figure out where Sloane's perpetually misplaced little sister wandered off to. Turns out it was the same as last year. Except this time, it ended with Lucas being escorted out of the building by two plainclothes officers.

"I didn't have Lucas pegged as the type," I remark. "Doesn't get much more cold-blooded than leaving a girl trapped in a sinking car."

Lawson barely grunts a response. He's still nursing the bruises from his bro-down with Fenn the other night. Looks worse than that time he got cornered by the older brother of that chick he took to the Bahamas and left at the airport because he got drunk and wandered his way onto someone else's private jet.

"What do you think happens to him now?" I ask.

Lawson shrugs as he hits his flask again.

I grin. "Are you still sulking?"

Since the fight with Fenn, the little clique with RJ and Sloane won't give him the time of day anymore. I don't see the problem, frankly. Screw them all. I'm tired of them and their grudges, taking fights to heart and abandoning friends left and right. Look at me and Lawson—we fought outside the bar, exchanged some harsh words, and then put it behind us. Sloane and her crew really ought to follow that lead. And if they can't, well, then who needs 'em.

But Lawson is like the dog abandoned on the side of the road, looking longingly at the bumper as it drives away.

"Fuck them," I advise. "Who gives a shit?"

"At this rate," he murmurs at the rim of the flask, "I don't think any one of them would piss on me if I were on fire."

"So then get over it and move on. What's the point being all depressed over people who don't matter?"

Lawson shrugs again and tilts the flask back. "They were my friends."

Whatever. He's bumming me out. If I stick around much longer, I might throw myself off the roof.

I notice Mila and Oliver at a table with some Ballard people, and stalk off, tired of Lawson's sulking. Skirting the dance floor, I wander over in their direction. Mila's the first one to catch my eye and jerk her head to call me over.

She greets me with a smirk. "Silas."

"Mila," I mimic.

She's looking good. I'm surprised the faculty chaperones let her walk in here with that neckline. Her tits are practically spilling out of her tight red dress. I forgot how hot Mila is when she's trying. Though from here, it seems like she isn't getting the attention from Oliver that she'd prefer. She's staring at the side of his face while he talks to his buddies.

"I don't know what you did to Amy," she says with a vicious grin, "but I think it was an improvement."

"If you say so." I help myself to a seat beside her. "That's been over a long time."

Oliver laughs to himself. "Dude, she hates your guts. I'd keep an eye on your drink. Wouldn't put it past her to slip you some poison."

"If it'd make this dance over sooner, I might like it."

They all laugh, but I'm only half kidding. It's like every year I forget how unbearably lame these things are. And predictably disappointing.

"I definitely wore the wrong shoes," Mila says. She throws her feet in my lap with a sad pout. "Get these things off me. Please. Find a plastic butter knife and start sawing at my ankles."

I grin at her. "I cannot in good conscience let you walk around this gym barefoot."

"Unless you want to get ringworm." Oliver makes a gagging face.

Christ, I'd give anything to be enrolled at Ballard again. Just get the hell out of fuckup school. I think that place has managed to rub off on me, dragging me down to its level. I don't how I'll survive another semester without dropping IQ points.

Mila suddenly gets a weird look on her face. I follow her gaze toward RJ and Sloane, who just sauntered back inside to grab her purse and his jacket from a table.

"God, not you too," I say at the expression of longing.

"Shut up." She kicks me in the stomach. "You don't have any room to talk."

"Still pining over the one that got away?" Oliver dodges when she swings her arm to smack his shoulder. "He's coming this way. Hurry up and flash your tits at him."

Sloane's storm-gray eyes look right through me as she and RJ pass our table. Then her gaze flits toward Mila, her full lips turning up at the corners.

"He's a good kisser, huh?" she mocks, pulling RJ by the hand behind her.

Mila turns away, absolutely fuming as she moves her legs from my lap. If daggers could fly out of her eyeballs, Sloane would be a goner.

Oliver is grinning like an idiot. "What was that about?"

"Bitch," she hisses.

Like a dog with a bone, Oliver doesn't let up. "What, you kissed RJ? When the hell did that happen?"

Mila rolls her eyes, bitterly gnawing on the inside of her cheek. "He was at that dorm party last week, remember? Spent the whole night hitting on me. Then we made out a little."

Ballard's quarterback snorts a laugh. "Oh, shit. That's hilarious. Where the hell was I?"

"Last week?" I pipe up, confused. "They were together then." And as I recall from swim practice, RJ was quite insistent about the unbreakable nature of their relationship.

"And apparently she set the whole thing up," Mila says through clenched teeth.

"Why?" Oliver asks with a blank look.

"To make me look stupid. Because Sloane's a shitty person."

"Seriously?" I don't mean to laugh at her, but it's sort of sad. "Don't you ever get tired of coveting everything Sloane has?"

Mila flips me the bird. "Aren't you tired of coveting Sloane?"

"Dude." Oliver cracks up. "Burn!"

He's such a child.

"On that note, I think it's time for another drink," I announce, standing up.

Mila kicks my shin. "Get me one too."

"Get it yourself."

She twists her lips at the challenge and slowly rises to her feet. "You know, I might kinda like this new Silas."

"Good for you."

Oliver becomes distracted by something his running back says and absently taps Mila's arm to ask her to bring him back a drink too. Together, Mila and I go to the refreshment tables and grab a couple of bottles of sparkling water. It's hotter than hell in here and starting to smell like a dumpster full of broken perfume and cologne bottles baking in an alley behind a fast-food restaurant.

"So, what is it about Sloane's toys that makes you so damn jealous?" I tease Mila.

"It must be fascinating to be so delusional," she bites back. "What's it like inside your head?"

"How far did it get?" I try to smother a smirk, but I can't stop imagining how ridiculous Mila looked thinking she had a shot with RJ. "Just the tip, or…?"

"Fuck off." She meanders away from the table toward the alcove that leads to the locker rooms. Goading me to follow her. "You know you're, like, completely obsessed with them."

I admire her ass beneath the stretchy red material of her dress. "I'm not the one getting caught up in their weird role-playing kinks."

"You wish."

"If I wanted Sloane, I could have her. She's not worth the trouble."

Slowly, I back Mila into the darkened alcove, just out of sight of the crowded room. Mila narrows her eyes. Like a dare. Testing me.

"What about Amy?" she taunts. "She's also too much trouble?"

I press her back against the cold, painted cinder-block wall, my hands biting into her slender hips.

"I guess I bore easy."

"You bored now?"

"Not yet."

I cover her mouth with mine and pry her lips open with my tongue. Her body goes soft against me, kissing me back. Her fingernails lightly scratch across my scalp as her tongue teases mine.

I suppose some part of me always found Mila attractive. Despite what Amy thinks, I'd never paid much attention to anyone else while we were together. It never would have occurred to me then to wonder about my prospects with Mila Whitlock. Now, all bets are off.

When she lets out a quiet sigh, I open her legs with my knee and slip my hand under her dress. Skimming it toward the flushed skin on her inner thigh. Up to the warm, clenching place that makes her bite my bottom lip.

I dip beneath her panties and slide one finger inside her. My thumb finds the spot that makes her legs shake. She's so wet.

"Where did this Silas come from?" she says breathlessly against my mouth.

I don't respond. Grinding my hand against her core and making her breath catch in her throat.

Mila scrapes her teeth against the side of my neck. "Are you pretending I'm Sloane?"

"Does it matter?" I add another finger, thrusting it deeper inside her. "You're pretending I'm RJ. Or Duke. Or whoever else Sloane has that you can't."

Mila arches her back. Tugging at my shirt, my jacket. Urging me on.

Out of the corner of my eye, I notice Oliver pass by the entrance of the alcove. Even though he doesn't notice us, I make no attempt to remain undetected, not bothering to slow my movements. Mila, however, senses something's different and opens her eyes. Just past the corner where we're all but holding our breath, we hear Oliver asking if anyone's seen her.

Mila runs her tongue across her bottom lip. She begins fucking herself on my hand, hiking her knee up around my hip. Shoulders pressed into the wall.

It's the hottest thing I've ever seen. Fingering this chick while her date is twenty feet away, oblivious.

Not a total waste of a night, after all.

CHAPTER 51
LAWSON

I'M DONE. TIRED OF THE TERRIBLE MUSIC AND THE INCESSANT drone of voices. I feel like I'm trapped in a beehive. Everyone I even remotely like has already left, anyway. Or in Silas's case, disappeared entirely. I have no idea where he's run off to.

So I'm done. Ready to blow this Popsicle stand. As I shoulder my way through the throng of dancing, talking obstacles, I try not to think about everything that transpired tonight. Like the very public shunning courtesy of Fenn and Co. Or the tension-filled exchange with Casey in the hallway.

Or the fact that she'd hesitated.

I don't want to dwell on it, to wonder if it means something. Because of course it doesn't mean anything. I probably imagined it anyway.

No.

I can convince myself of a lot of things, but not that.

Casey hesitated when I'd asked if she had feelings.

"Watch it," someone scolds when I slam into them on my way out the door.

"Sorry," I drawl.

Both our eyes narrow in recognition as my gaze locks with Amy's.

"Whatever," she mutters under her breath.

"Amy," I say graciously. "You look nice."

She does. Her bronze-colored dress brings out the flecks of green around her light-brown irises. In the fluorescent lighting of the hall, her hair looks a bit reddish. She'd curled it into loose waves that fall over her shoulders. It looks good, makes you want to run your fingers—

I give a sharp intake of breath.

"Uh-huh, I'm sure," she says sarcastically, trying to move past me. "Have a good night, Lawson."

"Was it you?" I blurt out.

Amy stops walking, shooting me an irritated look. "Was what me?"

My mouth drops open as I stare at her freckled girl-next-door face. In a rare instance, I'm stunned stupid.

"All right, I, ah…" I pause to collect my composure and figure out how to best phrase this. "Don't take this the wrong way, but… did you blow me at prom?"

Dead silence.

Amy stares back at me, her own lips parting in surprise. But her eyes… She shutters them quickly, but I think I glimpse a flicker of panic before she does.

"Go fuck yourself, Lawson."

She tosses those long brown waves over her shoulder and marches back inside.

Guess I was mistaken.

I shrug off the crazy thoughts and text my usual car service to arrange for a driver. Not long after, I'm back at Sandover, wandering through the courtyard with a bottle of champagne in one hand and gin in the other because my room felt too suffocating.

In my aimlessness, I wind up at the soccer field, a great empty expanse surrounded by bleachers to fill with my ghosts. All their disappointed gazes cast upon my slumped shoulders. I stride to the center of the field and emerge into vast darkness. Open space. I tilt my head back and breathe in the stars, then find myself at odds with gravity and collapse onto the soft, prickly comfort of grass.

What the hell was I thinking, anyway? I had one job. Don't deflower my friend's estranged soulmate.

Worst thing is, I knew better. I had no business corrupting that, taking advantage of her sincerity. Because I could have stopped myself. There was a moment when we could have been friends. Except at any given moment, I'm incapable of not being a total disappointment.

Sloane hated me before. Now I'll be fortunate to escape an assassination attempt. Even Silas and his performative martyr complex of perpetual patience hasn't outlasted my worthlessness. I'm too tiresome even for Silas's pity.

A fucking joke.

And they're right. All of them. I waste every talent and advantage. A benefit to nothing and no one. I'm chaos and destruction, bored with my own existence and digging my fingers into the soil for something to hold me.

There's salt on my lips when I fish the phone out of my pocket. I swallow a mouthful of gin that stings my teeth and pull up a contact I rarely use.

"Lawson? Christ, what time is it?"

"Hey, Dad."

"What is it now?"

"No, I was just calling 'cause—"

"Are you drunk? I swear to God, Lawson. Is it so fucking hard to stay out of trouble? Go on, then. How much is it going to cost to bail you out this time, huh?"

"No, I'm not in—"

"You can't help yourself, can you? Take every opportunity you're given to be a constant fuckup."

"Yep. Okay, Dad. Thanks. I'm gonna go now."

The phone slips from my hand onto the grass. I leave it there, scavenging in my pocket instead for a tiny plastic baggy of pills I can't quite discern through the darkness. Maybe Valium. Or Vicodin. It's possible I had some codeine at one point, but I'm not even sure how long ago that was. At any rate, I'm certain the surgeon general would frown upon mixing these pills with booze.

Good thing he's not here.

I swallow and turn my gaze toward the stars, letting their gentle sweep across the sky draw my eyelids closed.

Goddamn redheads. Strawberry-blondes like poisoned apples.

Fuck.

I fucked it up good this time. And there's no coming back from it.

CHAPTER 52
CASEY

AFTER I'VE WASHED MY MAKEUP OFF, PUT MY HAIR IN A BUN, AND changed into my pajamas, I go to the kitchen to scrounge up something, instead finding Dad waiting for me at the counter.

"How about a cup of tea?" he offers.

"How about some ice cream?"

He smiles. "That'll work too."

I pull a tub of mint chocolate chip for him and black cherry for me, then grab two big spoons from the drawer.

"Sloane gave me the short version," he says as we both sit. "I do wish you girls had called me from the dance."

He's being especially diplomatic now. Despite the soft voice and gentle expression, I can tell Dad is fuming inside. Part of me still is too.

"If either of us had stopped long enough to take a breath, we definitely would have," I assure him.

Truth is, as much as Sloane held it together, we were both losing our minds. Stunned that Lucas could have done this. Devastated to finally know the truth. It's been a hell of a night. I'm still not sure I've fully grasped the situation, and I expect to wake up tomorrow and burst into stress tears.

"Most importantly," he says, digging his spoon into the tub. "How are you feeling?"

"Honestly? Not as relieved as I'd hoped I would be."

Dad doesn't respond. He does that thing that Dr. Anthony does when she waits for me to fill the silence. Enjoying his ice cream and giving me the space to collect my thoughts while I hunt for the chocolate chunks in my tub.

"This whole time, I thought the thing that's been the hardest was not knowing. That as soon as all the questions were answered, the weight would be lifted off my shoulders. But now I know the truth, and I don't think I feel any different."

"It's still a terrible betrayal. I'm not sure you should put too much pressure on yourself to feel any certain way right now."

"I'm just so shocked by Lucas," I admit. "I never even suspected it was him."

"I don't think anyone did."

I think about how tonight ended, with the cops showing up to arrest Lucas. They took statements from all of us, and the officer who interviewed me said Lucas was facing a lengthy list of charges. Leaving the scene of a crime, failure to report a crime. Possibly even attempted manslaughter.

That last one triggers a pang of doubt. I dig my spoon into the tub again. Then I falter. "He insisted he didn't drug me."

Dad studies me. "Do you believe him?"

After a beat, I nod. "Maybe it makes me naive or stupid or whatever, but I honestly can't see Lucas drugging anyone. His brother, maybe, but not him."

"Let's wait for the police to finish their investigation and see what they're able to turn up." Dad makes a derisive noise. "Not that I have much faith in their work."

"Me neither," I say wryly. "But hopefully they learn something useful after they question Lucas and Gabe."

Sorrow lodges in my throat as I remember the look on Lucas's face earlier. The guilt and horror over what he'd done. Despite the compassion I can't help but feel toward him, I also feel angry.

"I don't know how he was able to rationalize it all in his head. How he could look me in the eyes every day while lying to me. You're right. It's a terrible betrayal," I say around a mouthful of ice cream. Because it makes the whole thing easier to swallow. "That was another Ballard dance for the books, huh?"

Dad coughs into his spoon. "One might call that an understatement."

I laugh. "So, what time do the contractors show up to install the bars on my windows?"

He puts down his ice cream, sighing. "I know I've been tough on you this past year. A tad overprotective, perhaps."

"A tad?" I arch an eyebrow.

"It's a father's prerogative to worry about his girls. But you're not a little girl anymore. I recognize that. And I'm quite proud of how you handled yourself tonight."

"You mean I'm not under house arrest till I'm thirty?"

"Be patient with me. I'm old."

"Not that old."

"But I also know I have to stop coddling you so much," he admits reluctantly. "Whether I like it or not, you and Sloane are growing up. Can't stay my little babies forever."

"Ugh, Dad." He's embarrassing when he gets like this.

"I know. Still, I'm glad you're safe."

"Me too. All right. I think I'm off to bed." On a massive yawn, I drop my spoon in the sink and close the tub of ice cream. "I'm starting to crash pretty hard."

"Of course. You must be exhausted."

Dad reaches out for a hug and gives me a kiss on the forehead before I can escape.

"I love you. I'm always here for you. No matter what."

"Love you too, Dad."

We've been on a journey, the two of us. Figuring out our places, our boundaries with each other, after the past year had thrown our relationship out of sorts.

As far as dads go, I could have done much worse.

After I've showered and brushed my teeth, I walk back to my room to throw myself at my pillows and maybe sleep till senior year. Except when I open the door, Fenn's leaning against my desk. I quickly shut off my bedroom light and lock the door behind me.

"Are you crazy?" I whisper. "If my dad catches you, he's calling the SWAT team."

Fenn flashes a lopsided smile. "I wanted to check on you," he whispers back.

"A text would have sufficed."

"No." He approaches me to wrap his arms around my waist. "It wouldn't."

Then he kisses me. A sweet, brief kiss that ends before I've even kissed him back.

"But I'll go if you want me to," he murmurs.

"I didn't say that." Now that he's here, with his forehead pressed to mine and his chest warm against my body, I'm glad he came. "You can stay a little while. If you promise to be quiet."

Fenn presses one finger to his lips. Then presses those lips to mine.

Somehow, every time we kiss, I learn something new about him. Discover another way he makes me completely undone. As my fingers travel the breadth of his shoulders and comb through his hair, I notice for the first time how goose bumps emerge on the back of his neck when I rub my hand against the grain.

"I know I just saw you," he breathes against my mouth. "But I already missed you."

And in that moment, I find the relief that had been lacking, the sense of finality that's it over. The entire ordeal of the last year. I no longer have to be anxious wondering when the next blindside will come, constantly peering over my shoulder for more bad news. Afraid of being in my own skin. Scared to let myself love him.

Fenn walks us backward to my bed. We've never had a problem when our eyes are closed. When our bodies meet, there are no misunderstandings. I think it's when we see each other best. Honestly and completely.

He lies on his back against the pillows and draws me toward him, then drags my leg up over his hip. I feel him hard beneath my thigh. His breath catches slightly as I run my fingernails under his T-shirt and across his abdomen.

"I'm sorry tonight ended the way it did," he says.

"I'm not. We'll have other dances."

"Sure you wouldn't rather get a hotel room next time? Skip the formalities."

I shove his shoulder. "You're not that charming."

Fenn licks his lips, not hiding his smirk in the slightest. "I don't know. I think I might be."

He cradles the back of my head to bring my lips to his again. It's like he suddenly can't go even seconds without kissing me. Now that we've found a way back to each other, neither of us want to waste a second. So we lie there tangled together, becoming reacquainted with the ways we make the other breathe a little harder.

His mouth against my neck. His thumb gently skimming my nipples over my shirt. The way he grips the back of my thigh against his erection, and I know he's nearly crawling out of his skin to get closer to me.

"God, I want you." Then he rolls us over, pressing himself between my legs. His hand slips beneath my shirt.

Everything in me wants to give in to this moment. To have this with him. But I hesitate. Because a small but very loud part of me still regrets the chances we didn't have.

"Wait," I whisper.

He meets my eyes, pushing strands of hair from my face.

"I wasted my first time," I admit.

I don't regret being with Lawson. But I regret that it meant Fenn and I didn't have that moment.

"I want a do-over. And this time, I want it to be special. Not rushed. You know?"

Fenn eases away to lie on his back then brings me to rest my head against his chest. "I get it. Totally. I don't want to pressure you into something you're not ready for."

"I'm ready," I say, biting back a laugh. "Like, so ready. But I want it to be right. If that makes sense."

"I'm not going anywhere, Case. I love you, and I'll wait for you forever."

My heart expands in my chest, so full that it strains against my ribcage. Gripping his shirt in my fist, I lean up to kiss him.

"I love you," I tell him, watching the grin pull across his lips. "So much."

"We've got nothing but time," Fenn promises. "We'll wait." He kisses me again. "We'll wait for us."

EPILOGUE
FENN

TWO DAYS LATER

EVERYTHING ABOUT THESE OLD DORMS IS NOISY. THE FLOORBOARDS creak. Hinges squeal. Despite my best attempts, my entrance isn't subtle when I get back to our room just after sunrise. RJ rolls over in bed and scratches the crust from his eyes.

"Hey," he mumbles. "You just get in?"

"Yeah. Sorry I woke you. I was trying to be quiet."

I'm exhausted but too wired to sleep, so I spend the next couple of hours watching TV while RJ goes back to sleep. He gets up again around eight thirty, hits the bathroom, and returns to join me on the sofa, where he gives me a sidelong look.

"That's two nights in a row you've snuck over there. You know your luck won't last, right? Tresscott will catch on soon…"

"I needed to see her," I answer. "All this was a lot for her, you know? I like checking in to make sure she's still doing okay after everything that went down at the dance. I know she can handle it, but I want her to know I'm choosing her first. Making her my priority."

"Sure." He's serious for a moment, nodding. Then a goading smirk creases his cheeks. "And after you make sure she's okay…"

"No, it's not like that. We're going to take it slow. I still have a lot to do to prove myself to her."

"Good for you, man. Really."

There was a while there with RJ and me, when I thought our relationship might be unsalvageable. I'd done all this work to build a bond with him as brothers, only to have him see me through the filter of one of the worst days of my life. I worried I'd never get that trust back. But credit to him, RJ didn't give up on me. Even when I'm sure it would have been easier to appease Sloane and write me off, he had my back. I'll never forget that. And long as our misfit parents try to make this big happy family thing work, I'll always have his.

"Still can't believe Lucas was the one," RJ says glumly.

He was close with the kid, and I know this is eating at him. Not as much as it's eating at Casey, but RJ is definitely still shaken about it.

"What do you think that message from Gabe meant?" I ask suddenly. Now that I've got Lucas on the brain. "When he told Lucas to tell me he knows the truth?"

"Maybe he meant the truth about who was driving the car?"

"Maybe. But it felt more like an accusation, you know? Something related to me, personally."

"Yeah, it did. But honestly, I have no clue. And it doesn't look like Lucas is going to be filling us in any time soon."

"I hate mysteries." I heave a sigh, going thoughtful for a beat. "You know what I could go for?"

RJ glances over while flipping channels.

"Bloody Mary and pancakes."

He brightens. "Think they'll deliver?"

The door suddenly bursts open with a loud groan, so deafening the whole floor's got to be awake now.

A heavy bag *thuds* to ground.

Then a stunned silence follows as RJ and I turn to stare at the newcomer in the doorway.

I blink several times, needing to remind myself I haven't been drinking.

Gabe narrows those familiar dark eyes, scanning the room that used to be half his. He lingers over RJ's stuff before turning his attention to me.

A hint of a frown twists my best friend's mouth as he says, "What did I miss?"

**DON'T MISS ELLE KENNEDY'S NEW STEAMY AND
ADDICTIVE COLLEGE ROMANCE SERIES**

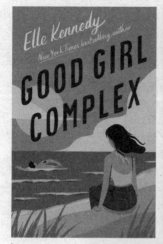

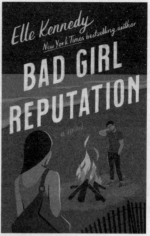

Available now from

PIATKUS

Do you love contemporary romance?

Want the chance to hear news about your favourite authors (and the chance to win free books)?

Kristen Ashley
Ashley Herring Blake
Meg Cabot
Olivia Dade
Rosie Danan
J. Daniels
Farah Heron
Talia Hibbert
Sarah Hogle
Helena Hunting
Abby Jimenez
Elle Kennedy
Christina Lauren
Alisha Rai
Sally Thorne
Lacie Waldon
Denise Williams
Meryl Wilsner
Samantha Young

Then visit the Piatkus website
www.yourswithlove.co.uk

And follow us on Facebook and Instagram
www.facebook.com/yourswithlovex | @yourswithlovex

PIATKUS